CALL OF THE WEST

Suddenly, in the tolling of the bells, Dylan heard sounds, dozens of sounds. He was hearing without hearing, with the dreaming ear. It was bedlam and sense, a cacophony and a harmony at once. Some of the sounds were voices, rough voices of men, snatches of bawdy *voyageur* songs. Some were shouts of men and women gambling. Some were the thump of hoofbeats and the roars of men fighting, some the pulsing of rivers, some the squawking of crows, some the moans of men and women in the act of love. Some of this bedlam fabric of sounds was ancient, some recent, some future. . . .

Standing there on the cathedral steps in the opulent midsummer sunlight, Dylan understood without understanding, and knew without knowing. He felt the blood and breath of his life.

He said softly and happily to Dru, "Let's go to the High Missouri."

Dru said, "It's time."

RIVERS
WEST

THE
HIGH MISSOURI

Win Blevins

BANTAM BOOKS
NEW YORK • TORONTO • LONDON • SYDNEY • AUCKLAND

THE HIGH MISSOURI
A Bantam Book / June 1994

ISBN 0-553-56511-7

Published simultaneously in the United States and Canada

Bantam Books are published by Bantam Books, a division of Bantam
Doubleday Dell Publishing Group, Inc. Its trademark, consisting of the
words "Bantam Books" and the portrayal of a rooster, is Registered in
U.S. Patent and Trademark Office and in other countries. Marca Reg-
istrada. Bantam Books, 1540 Broadway, New York, New York 10036.

PRINTED IN THE UNITED STATES OF AMERICA
RAD   0 9 8 7 6 5 4 3 2

This tale of a father and son is dedicated to the memory of my father, W. E. Blevins, Sr.

Aho, mitakuye oyasin

Acknowledgments

Thanks for help on this book to my longtime researcher, Ruth Valsing; to Montreal historian Kathryn Harvey; to Howard Rides-at-the-Door for help with the language and customs of his Piegan people; to Dorothy Holland for advice about the character Red Sky at Morning, and to Rose Fraser, Chris Guier, and Jacques Roux for some Canadian French.

This book is inspired by Joseph Campbell and his ideas. Its six parts are titled after the six parts of the hero's adventure in tribute to him.

What I want is to get what I write published, get enough to eat, stay out of jail, and get a little love.

—attributed to CARL SANDBURG

Part One
THE CALL

Chapter One

Dylan Elfed Davis Campbell looked at the lists of figures on the piece of paper. They squiggled. They dashed around like little black ants, racing here and there and everywhere. One thing they didn't do was sit still. The other was add up. If he had to look at them any longer, he would scream.

He told himself to take a deep breath.

If he did, he would choke—he was sure of that. Choke on air, on life itself. He clenched his fists and his teeth so hard he thought his entire body must be shaking.

Don't worry, he raged at himself, you can't die. You're already dead. Just past your twenty-second birthday in the first month of spring, you're dead. Call the embalmer.

It was Friday afternoon at the Bank of Montreal, and Dylan was proving that the amount in the cash drawers at the start of the day plus the amount deposited today added up to the amount of cash now in the cash drawers less the amount taken out in cash, or whatever the devil the formula was. He did this every day in the late afternoon. The figures never added up—they were too busy anting around. And when they didn't add up, he had to stay late, without pay, and make them do it.

"Mr. Campbell," called the nasal voice of the bastard MacDonald. They called him that jokingly, half with malice, because Dugald MacDonald was his rich father's son via a French mistress. Mr. MacDonald now said it in his snotty way, "Mr. Campbell, *will* you complete that post-ing, *please*?"

Naturally, he called across the entire bank from the door of his own office, so everyone would know the poor dumb Welshman was late again. One of Mr. MacDonald's office jokes was that the bloody Welsh were always bloody late, being by nature bloody poets and no men of business. Which irked Dylan, because he had as much Scots blood as Mr. MacDonald: half.

Dylan stood up. He gasped for breath. It came, and something changed—a door closed, or opened, or a breeze moved him as it moves the first leaves in a tree. It was as though he heard music inside his head, and the music was revelation. For a moment he was giddy.

Go, he ordered himself.

He stepped away from his desk, leaving the long columns of ants racing wherever they wanted. He crossed the room toward Mr. MacDonald, who stood there, transfixed, or stupefied—was the Welshman actually approaching the boss without the figures? Dylan enjoyed watching him stand there, dumbstruck.

Abruptly, Dylan stopped halfway to Mr. MacDonald. No need to get in his face, he thought, where his gross pores and long nasal hairs would be offensive. I may as well call across the whole bloody room, as he does.

He called, "Mr. MacDonald, take this job and stuff it up your arse."

Dylan could see everything as he would remember it from eternity, fixed in its tiny place, mouths open, eyes gaping, nostrils flared in astonishment. Everything was rigid, all eyes fixed immovably on ledgers they weren't seeing.

Mr. MacDonald just stood there. Struck speechless, Dylan thought with satisfaction.

Dylan had had no idea he was going to say that. Delicious. Sublime. Heavenly. He wanted to dance.

He stepped back to his desk, moving through a room fixed forever motionless, as behind a glass display case. He gathered his few things, put on his coat, and went out into the late afternoon of a wintry spring day in Montreal, 1820.

Let someone else catch the ants.

Oh Daddy Ni, ain't it grand?

In front of the great plate of glass bearing the distinguished firm's name, his bottom began to twitch. He wiggled it. His knees wobbled. He let them do it. His hands went akimbo. He danced a jig.

He knew immediately where, in his heart of hearts, he wanted to go. Not to his lodgings, and not to his father's house, no, somewhere else. But he didn't want to go there immediately. He wanted to walk, vigorously.

He hurried along the old wall of the city on Place Viger Station. He walked all the way to the hill called the Citadel. Montreal boasted that it was one of the oldest settlements in North America, founded by French in 1642. Though the English had taken over sixty years ago, the city was divided. The commercial and professional people were Britons and Scots, the working people French. It was built on the St. Lawrence River, at the confluence of great rivers that led into the heart of the continent. Yet the huge ships of the sea sailed all the way to these wharves and dispersed to the far corners of the earth.

He turned toward the river. It wasn't yet clear of ice. Soon the spring day when the rivers were clear, usually late in April, would become a key day in his life. He would be traveling the waterways as his predecessors had, using the powerful currents of the earth to carry him forth on God's mission.

He felt light, gay, *free*. He hummed a little tune, and then, feeling foolish, began to sing it.

> *"C'est le vent, c'est le vent frivolant,*
> *C'est le vent, c'est le vent frivolant."*

So went the chorus: "It's the wind, it's the frivolous wind." It was a song of the *voyageurs,* the canoemen, about the frivolous wind bringing a sad and unjust death to a white duck. He'd never known why he liked such a sentimental lamentation, and he didn't care. He was feeling absurd and wonderful.

He looked around and chuckled to himself. It was not a day to feel grand, not a bit of a fine spring day, but cold and drizzly, as Montreal often was, the light fading, the western clouds mottled gray and purple and mustard-color, like bruises. And a wind, a gusty wind. Only a romantic would call it frivolous. Today Dylan was a romantic.

He hurried around the seminary and rectory to the face of his one true home in Montreal, his soul's home, the church Notre Dame at Place d'Armes.

He passed out of the blustery day and into its haven, a passage that always seemed to him from one world to another, from the physical to the spiritual, from the mundane to the ethereal.

He stood at the back of the nave, taking it all in, the arcade where worshipers sat, above them the ceiling divided into conical sections by gilt moldings. In the center of the ceiling arched a circular painting of the Ascension itself, in heroic-sized figures. Beyond this end of the nave, the transept, its cruciform arms reaching north and south, and in its center, the area called the crossing, the region of the approach to the altar, where communicants crossed from the earthly to the heavenly and at the altar partook of wonder and mystery, the body and the blood of Jesus Christ.

Above the altar, like a canopy, was an open crown, supported by gilt pillars. Behind the crown, a full-sized statue of the Virgin Mary cut in white marble. On either side of the altar, paintings on scriptural subjects. For Dylan the center of all was the rich ornaments on the altar, whence came divine communion, the miracle of the divine service, the locus where ordinary life entered its spiritual dimension.

He slipped into a back pew and knelt.

Dylan had always been impatient of ordinary life. He didn't see the point of the business his father spent his life on—trading furs. It honored the temporal, not the eternal. He knew that business itself was a low undertaking. In the end, that was why he had quit his job today, not the affronts given by Mr. MacDonald. He could not bear the ignobility of commerce.

So he came here this afternoon to dedicate himself to

his heart's adventure, his soul's quest. Now he would give his life to the Church.

He let his eyes roam the great structure, the side chapels, the statuary, the ten stations of the Cross, the piers lifting to heaven. This was his home. It had always been his home.

Today, now, here, he began his great enterprise.

He felt given this enterprise personally, in a laying on of hands. His godfather was his father's best friend, Father Quesnel, a priest here. There lay a story. Auguste Quesnel had had great ambitions for God and the Church. In his heart burned an intense desire, a holy calling. He wanted to revive one of the greatest churchly traditions in Canada. He wanted to take the Gospel to the benighted of this vast continent, the Indians.

Starting two centuries ago, that had been the particular calling of the Jesuits of North America. They had walked boldly into the darkness, bearing the light. It had been a terrible responsibility, and many had paid with their mortal lives. But surely they had burnished their souls to a holy brightness, and had brought heathen souls to salvation.

About forty years ago Father Quesnel had been ready to enter the Jesuit order. He had gone to the city of Québec, there to prepare for the calling he had dedicated his life to, carrying the word of God to the Indians of Canada. When he got off the stage in Québec, he was greeted by his mentor-to-be with dire news. All Jesuits were former Jesuits, said the priest. The pope had abolished the order.

Abolished!

Not only was the order abolished, as it turned out, the missionary effort in Canada dwindled to nothing.

When Father Quesnel told the story in the Campbell parlor decades later, Dylan felt the devastation of that moment. To have a calling, a life, wiped out by the word of one man. Centuries of resentment of Jesuits all over the world had come to a head, said Quesnel, and the pope succumbed to pressure.

Father Quesnel attached himself to the single Catholic church in Montreal and spent his life administering the sacraments, counseling, preaching, doing the church's business—the ordinary tasks of any priest. He sometimes said he had discovered that such was the heart of the work of the clergy.

A decade ago, when the Canadian Church's missionary zeal was partly revived, and the St. Boniface mission founded on Red River, wherever in the interior that was, Father Quesnel said he was far too old to set out on a new venture.

So Dylan would pick up his godfather's torch. He wanted to be a priest; not a mundane servant of the people, but like the priest of St. Boniface, a torch bearer, a missionary to the Indians.

That was the biggest conflict he ever had with his father. Ian Hugh Campbell would not tolerate his youngest son's taking orders. Together, Campbell and Quesnel prevailed on the youngster to wait until the age of his majority, at least twenty-one, to make such a fateful decision. In the meantime he would learn banking.

Well, hadn't that come up fine? As shown by this afternoon's events. Dylan got restless on his knees, shifted his weight about. Now he was twenty-two. Now he was done with banking forever, with commerce forever. Now he would devote his life to his heart's desire.

He rose, slipped out of the pew and walked toward the altar. When he came to the crossing, he stopped in the light. On each end of the transept, north and south, light streamed in from the huge windows of stained glass. Doubtless the light outside, on this rainy day, was pale, gray, drab. But in this house of God it was transformed by the stained glass. Here it prismed into rich gold, royal blue, glowing rose, vivid scarlet, every glorious color.

Dylan walked to the center of the crossing and stood in that light, like a rainbow, a promise by God. He knelt, facing the altar. To him the crossing was a special place. Father Quesnel said that, literally, it meant where the east-west reach of the nave intersected the north-south line of the transept. But it also meant where the laity crossed to the place of the clergy, where the world crossed to seek spirit. Thus it was a region of miracle.

Dylan knelt in the center of the crossing and faced the

altar. He did not need to pray in words. His gesture was prayer, his being was prayer. He murmured a thanksgiving for his liberation, and promised his energy, his zeal, his love, his life to the mission task.

Tomorrow morning he would tell Father Quesnel his decision. It was wonderful. Now he would go to his father, who would rail against it.

Ian Hugh Campbell had lived among the dregs of the earth, the *voyageurs* and *coureurs de bois,* white men who penetrated the wilderness to trade for furs with the Indians. Campbell was fond of saying, "In the early days, the Frenchmen didn't convert the Indians. The Indians converted them."

Campbell made sure his son heard the stories. In the wilderness men took on Indian dress, manners, ways, he explained. They drank, stole, rampaged, raped, murdered—as Indians did. The ultimate signs of corruption: they took Indian wives, learned Indian languages, lived as Indians, mere beasts roaming the face of the earth, hunting, scavenging, rutting. Their very children were Indian. They permitted the light in their souls to be put out, and lived in darkness.

So Dylan Elfed Davis Campbell did not know how he would tell his ambition to his father now, to walk into this utter darkness.

The spot in the crossing where he knelt seemed momentarily to glow. He looked at his arms, trunk, legs. He thought the sun was striking him a little. He looked up at the stained-glass window in the south transept. Perhaps it was a little brighter. Perhaps the late afternoon sun was beaming at him through the drizzle. He thought of his father's cold rages. "If this is a miracle," he murmured, smiling, "I accept."

Chapter Two

D ylan hung up his coat, mopped his wet head, and looked at himself in a hall mirror.

No, lad, he said to himself in his father's voice, you'll not do. Again in his father's voice, You ought to wear a hat in this weather. A thousand similar thoughts murmured in the back of his head.

Dylan drew a deep breath. His father's house had a distinctive smell, not strong but sly, a smell covered by years of fastidious scrubbing and cleaning, one strangers might not even notice. It was the smell of illness. Ian Campbell had taken sick three years ago, which now seemed to Dylan the man's whole life. He'd taken a fever in the wilderness and come back to Montreal with his hands and knees all swollen, stiff, red, and arthritic. For a year he never left the house and was mostly bedridden. Rheumatism, said the doctor, a bad case. The treatment was rest, lifelong rest.

Ian Campbell settled down to resting, and rotting. To Dylan, the house had smelled like decay ever since.

It also smelled like fear. Like not saying what you mean, like smiling because you're supposed to, and feeling rivalrous with your father and keeping it quiet, and loneliness. Especially loneliness.

The house didn't change, except to get grayer and more worn. It was empty and lonely. Dylan was gone. Only his little sister—well, half sister—Amalie was still at home, and she was only waiting for the first proposal of marriage. Dylan thought she would take the very first, regardless.

Lonely. Because it was motherless. Two children by two mothers, both dead now, and Dylan remembered neither of them alive. His own mother, who was Welsh and insisted on his Welsh names, died a week after he was born. He couldn't even remember his father's last wife, Amalie's mother, a Frenchwoman. She died when he was three. Since no one in the family was permitted to mention her, Dylan didn't even know what she died of.

Two wives dead. As a schoolboy Dylan often imagined his father as some sort of evil wizard. He brushed women with his secret wand in their secret places, and they died of his touch.

He pushed his hair back. It was wet from the drizzle on this wintry day, and falling in his eyes. In the mirror he saw what his father called a likely enough twenty-two-year-old. His father often remarked that Dylan was good-looking, then followed with, "Why don't you make more of yourself, laddie?"

One more glance at his reflection. Aye, boyo, it's well you don't look as scared as you feel.

This house and this life were like seeds chewed to pulp. Perhaps once they'd provided taste and nourishment. Now he needed to spit them out.

Thus resolved, he stepped into the double door of the parlor. He tried softly, "Father?"

"Yes, Dylan," boomed the voice.

Dylan looked at the great chair by the French windows where Ian Hugh Campbell would be sitting, snuff-box nearby, snifter in his hand. The snuff would be cheap, and the snifter full of Burton's Ale instead of brandy. Dylan was well aware of his father's small pretensions: the house, struggling to be grand outside, much worn inside. The furniture, nicked and kept presentable only by much rubbing with oil. The housekeeper, whom his father could ill afford but couldn't let go. The closets of his father's clothes, mended and mended until to a sharp eye they resembled patchwork quilts. Since his illness, he wore only a dressing gown anyway.

There was nothing for Dylan here, nothing at all, and

never had been. Except Amalie, poor thing. But she was beautiful, and had beaux, and soon would be married and gone.

Dylan supposed his father's life would be over then. A harrumph. "*Yes,* Dylan."

He stepped near the great chair and looked at his father. Ian Campbell was sizable, imposing, with huge, menacing eyebrows, both eyes too wide open, like a bird's, and opaque, unreadable features. With his stocky body, big head, and no neck, he looked like an irascible owl. The man was forty-eight, but no longer full of piss and vinegar. Forty-eight, and his life was already over. Just empty motions for a few more years, empty gestures of acquisition, and empty ragings.

Step forth and disappoint your father, Dylan told himself ironically.

He stepped close enough to shake hands.

"Pour yourself a glass, lad."

Ian Campbell watched Dylan get a beer glass from the side table, pour his own drink, and then fill his father's brandy snifter up to the rim, all without looking into his father's face. Yes, beer glass—it seemed important to the lad to say, This is ale, not brandy. Not that the lad's palate cared. Or that he cared at all. His son didn't know what it meant to be well off, even to have riches within your grasp and see it all slip away. Because your body betrayed you.

Ian Campbell snorted. His body had betrayed him all his life, in fact, especially its appetites.

Something else the lad didn't know. What it meant to love your son and for your trouble get his contempt slung in your face.

Dylan lifted his beer glass in a salute and sipped, then set the glass on the little side table with his father's snifter and snuff.

"What's wrong now?" asked his father.

"Why should anything be wrong, Daddy Ni?"

Ian snorted at that language. When Dylan was small, Ian Campbell had revered the memory of his mother, and brought in the boy's maternal aunt, Meredith Davis, to take care of him and teach the boy a few words of the Welsh language and other things Welsh. Now the lad used these childhood indulgences to manipulate his father.

"You've been skulking out there in the hall, afraid to tell me something."

Ian regretted the words immediately. Maybe he was a little drunk. He often was these days. When he drank too much, he stated the truth of life with a matter-of-fact bitterness the young were not prepared for. He felt more and more bitter these days, and cynical. Since his illness, he never went down to the office of Campbell Trading Company, which now looked derelict. A man who had roamed the vast interior of Canada, he was housebound, almost bedridden.

If he could only get well! The doctor said he would have intermissions with his illness, but mustn't ever tire himself again. How could a man build an empire without exertion? He wanted to get well. His old partner, the Rat, was bringing Indian tar, a native remedy. Maybe it would help. He was only forty-eight!

"What happened, did you get discharged?"

Why did he speak so harshly to the lad? Since Dylan had moved out a month ago, he had asked his son that question on every visit. Dylan didn't know how it felt to try to give your son a better start in life than you had, and worry that you'd failed. You trekked the wilderness, paddled those bloody canoes upstream and down, endured hunger and freezing, looked red niggers in the eye and stared them down, and endangered your very soul—for what? So your son wouldn't have to. And now the sod didn't notice.

"Why do you say that, Father?"

"Claude MacDonald sent your trunk around a few minutes ago."

He handed Dylan a note, the envelope opened, the paper rumpled. So his father intercepted his mail and read it.

Dear Dylan,
        Uncle Dugald was just here in a frightful

temper—said you'd insulted him publicly and all
that. Whatever you did, old chap, you did it all
the way. He's livid.

He made me pack your things while he
watched, got a carter, and sent your trunk to your
father's place. Can't do aught about it, the family
owning the hotel, you know. The staff here is
warned not to admit you. Dreadfully sorry. I
guess you're stuck at your father's house for a
few days, at least.

But come round, please, I want to hear the
story of how you bearded the lion in his den!

Your friend,
Claude MacDonald

Annoyed, Dylan walked away from his father and
looked out the windows. Still gray, still drizzling, the light
fading, rainwater running down the glass, blurring his vision. Tomorrow is a new beginning, he reminded himself.

He wondered why his father was so bitter, so sure life
would turn to ashes in the mouth. Yes, two wives dead,
that was part of it, and his illness, and a sinking business,
all part of it. Even his housekeeper, Philomene, had disappointed him. For years Dylan hadn't known about their secret relationship. Then, suddenly one morning six weeks
ago, they were acting like rejected lovers. That was when
Dylan moved out.

It seemed clear that Philomene's love would be the
last in his father's life. Yet all that was not excuse enough
for bitterness, not to Dylan. If Ian Hugh Campbell wanted
to give up, why did he have to ruin his son's life?

His father didn't pursue the questions. He'd asked in
order to nettle, not to get an answer. Dylan tried to shock
him with the reply.

"No, Father, I've quit."

Campbell sniffed his disapproval.

Dylan wondered whether his father heard. "Don't you
believe me?"

"I believe you're a fool for moods, like your mother."
It was a theme of his growing up. To Ian Campbell, as to

Dugald MacDonald, the Scots were rough and ready and up to snuff. The Welsh were poetic, which meant moody, which meant weak, not up to the harsh business of life.

"*Hiraeth,*" muttered Ian Campbell, like grinding nuts in his teeth. Dylan knew his thought: Give me fine Scots, not melancholy Welshmen.

The pedal point of his childhood again. Whenever Dylan was sad, Ian said he suffered from *hiraeth,* like his Welsh mother.

It was Welsh for melancholy—according to his father, not just ordinary dejection, but a kind of world-despair that only a foolishly poetic people like the Welsh could be capable of. Dylan wondered why Ian Campbell had married Gwyneth, née Davis, if he despised the Welsh.

Dylan Elfed Davis Campbell was tired of telling his father what he was not, tired of denying afflictions he didn't have—bloody *hiraeth!*—and tired of asking his father for things. This would be the last bleeding time.

He turned away from the window. He looked at his father, squat, old, bitter, angry. He would approach his father for the last time, and his father would not refuse him.

He came back to the great chair, moved the ottoman his father never used, sat on it and looked up at this weak, tyrannical man.

"Father, I did quit the bank. I loathe it. I'm going to become a priest."

So. Ian Campbell knew better than that. It was not a priest Dylan wanted to be, it was a missionary. The boy had read too many books as a youth and got his imagination inflamed. Blackrobes bearing the torch of Christ to the benighted, indeed. The white men didn't raise the savages to civilization, no, Ian Campbell knew that firsthand, and it had cost him dear. It was the other way. The savages pulled the white men down to bestiality.

This was not the ambition of a grown man, thought Campbell. It was the fantasy of an adolescent.

"A missionary, you mean," he growled.

This had been Ian Campbell's fear for a decade. The father braved the wilderness, suffered privations of the body, temptations of the flesh, perhaps even put his soul in mortal danger, but for a prize worth having, by God, and a prize he could pass on to his issue. Respectability, so nicely symbolized by the exclusive Collège de Montreal, and a tidy bit of capital.

The son would throw it all away, would disdain the prize, instead would foul himself in the same wilderness, and for nothing. For an illusion. Throw away fortune, civilization, body, soul, all for nothing.

He repeated bitterly, "A missionary."

"Yes, Father." Dylan couldn't look his father in the eye.

He didn't restate his dislike of the bank, or his revulsion for the future his father kept hinting at, as accountant of Campbell Trading Company.

He didn't know what to say. He didn't understand why his father despised missionary work or loathed the interior. His father had never taken him among the Indians, even on a short trip. Instead he had disappeared for months at a time, once for more than a year, and come back with tales only of how vile it was.

"Juvenile," his father grunted.

Dylan hated his father.

The lad was too young even to know what he didn't know. His son knew nothing of the two country wives he had had, the women who gave him solace of the flesh during his long years as a widower. He knew nothing of the other lusts and vilenesses of Indian country. He knew nothing of the heartbreak out there. That one winter he, Ian Campbell, had stayed over, like a true *hivernant*, a winterer. His daughter by the Cree woman was ill with the coughing sickness, and he loved the daughter. He deprived himself and his two white children to stay with her, and in February she died.

All ten-year-old Dylan could say, when Campbell came home the next summer, was, "Daddy Ni, why did you miss Christmas? Daddy Ni, why did you miss Christmas?"

The boy adored Christmas, the singing of carols, and the time they all had as a family to be together over the holiday, most especially loved the way he would outfit himself like St. Nicholas and they would take presents to the children of widows of his employees. *Voyageurs* died in the wilderness, sometimes, and this was the Campbell family's acknowledgment. According to his aunt Meredith, the boy had sworn over and over that Daddy Ni would never fail to be home for Christmas, especially for the sake of the fatherless children. He cried furiously when Ian Campbell didn't appear, said the aunt. Ian Campbell knew he'd never quite won back the boy's trust.

But Ian Campbell was holding another child, a dark-skinned girl, day and night.

Fool. Fool who knew nothing.

Did "fool" mean Dylan? Or Ian Campbell? He snorted. Both, oh, yes, sod it, both.

Campbell repeated, "Juvenile."

Dylan strangled a retort. Carefully, in a measured way, he told himself it was a lie. Ian Campbell might say it was juvenile now. He wouldn't think so later, silently, in his heart of hearts. A priest was something Ian Campbell admired. He was proud of being a Catholic in a city where respectable people were Anglican when British, Presbyterian when Scottish. Ian Campbell would admire his son for keeping up the tradition of defiance.

"Daddy Ni," he began, "will you help me with Father Quesnel?" Now the old family friend, Dylan's godfather, would become the connection he needed. Once, Quesnel had been a frequent dinner companion, and their guest for the entire twelve days of Christmas. In those days it was a happier house, and the children had fun with his name—Père Le Chat Noir, they called him, Father Black Cat, for his feline features and black robe. "Speak to him for me. Or give me a letter to him."

Ian Campbell's owl eyes clicked sideways, toward Dylan, and clicked back. Stared straight ahead.

"Stupid," he muttered.

"Daddy Ni," Dylan whined.

His father stood up, fixed Dylan with an imperious eye. "You're a fool," he said. "What would the Church want with you?" He took his pince-nez off the little table by his chair and clamped them onto his nose. Set down his snuffbox. Lifted his snifter. Glared at Dylan through the glasses.

Dylan turned his back on Ian Campbell. He heard his father move to the buffet, pour himself beer. Dylan twisted his insides until he could hold them still.

"Daddy Ni," he began, "I need help getting started in the world."

His father, stalking with owllike awkwardness, moved back toward Dylan holding the snifter of porter. He put his owl-beak nose into his son's face. "You spit on my help," he said.

It was intended to provoke. But Dylan couldn't help himself. He felt the hot words rise through his gullet like vomit.

"You bloody hypocrite," rasped Dylan, "you—"

Ian Campbell flung the beer onto Dylan's neck and chin. It soaked his neck cloth and dribbled down his waistcoat.

"Bastard!" screamed Dylan, and grabbed for his father, and missed.

Dylan was surprised at Ian Campbell's agility, for a sick man. Campbell stepped back and picked up the small side table. Dylan felt transfixed by the sight, unable to move. Campbell hoisted the little table overhead. The snuffbox sailed into space. Campbell cocked the table and crashed it toward Dylan's head.

Their movements seemed retarded in time, as though for permanent memory. Dylan raised one arm. The table banged off that arm, but he didn't react. He simply looked at his father's face. They faced each other as enemies.

In this suspended time, Dylan shot his right fist slowly into the middle of that enemy's face. Mashed into the nose and pince-nez.

The pince-nez fell away. A thin cut marked the bridge of his father's nose. One drop of blood beaded up brightly on the cut, broke, and trickled down.

Dylan registered a glimpse of that owl eye, irate, stymied, confused, lost.

A scream palpable as bloody meat filled his throat, choking him.

Dylan brought it forth—a primal howl, raw, malignant, father-killing.

Chapter
Three

The dark figure in the garden waited. Dylan would come hurtling out the front door in a moment, he was sure of that. When the lad comes, this man said to himself, I will shadow him through the dark streets.

Through the French windows he took a last glance at Ian Campbell, his rival of more than twenty years. On one knee now, a hand to his cut nose, looking after the fleeing son.

The man in the garden, who was known as the Druid, had watched the Campbell family occasionally through these windows for twenty years. He had felt himself an outsider, shut away from hearth and home. He had wondered whether it was worth it, to give this up to go adventuring, to roam the world seeking the true face of the trickster life. Now he felt what else he had missed—the rivalries, the disappointments, the griefs, the bitterness native to families. And he felt compassion for Ian Campbell.

They always flee, thought the Druid. Don't you know that, Mr. Campbell? Because they must.

The front door slammed, and it was time to shadow Dylan Elfed Davis Campbell. After twenty years, this was the Druid's chance.

He stepped lightly behind Dylan, flitting from tree to tree, melting into shadows. First to the grocer, who was closed but sweeping up, and now where, laddo? Mr. Gleason's stable, perhaps? Dylan crossed the muddy street toward the back of the property. Yes, a good place on a night like this for a homeless boyo. The Druid himself and many another *voyageur* had slept on Mr. Gleason's hay.

A homeless boyo indeed. Well, the Druid believed the most precarious situations offered the greatest possibilities. Now to see if he could convince the lad.

He'd go into the loft and wait for his chance.

Dylan eased through the shadow toward the door. It was a wretched night, raining harder now, black as the souls of the godless, and no one was about. He was getting soaked making this careful and quiet approach to the barn. He was trying to be stealthy. With his mind shrieking at himself:

I have struck my father. I have struck my father.

His body shook, trying to slough off this impossibility. The fingers of the guilty fist trembled.

I have struck my father.

His soul shuddered.

He touched the edge of the big, wide-swinging barn door.

Cre-e-ak!

Holy Mary Mother of God, and I only touched it.

He waited for some irate proprietor or a watchman making rounds to holler out an alarm, or just to bash the head of the intruder.

Which he deserved. Shame raged in him.

No proprietor. No watchman.

Boldly he swung the big door a couple of feet. The hinges squalled like a stepped-on cat. If no one came, no one was around. Probably the rain killed the sound anyway.

Shame.

He went into the hay barn, with its smells of fodder, mold, manure, and the sweat and flesh of horses. The animal smells came from the front, where the horses were stabled. The rear of the barn was for storing hay. He knew it well enough—as a lad he'd often mucked out the stalls for a few pence. It would get him out of this nasty night. He closed the door behind him.

Pitiful accommodation, but welcome enough to unaccommodated man, he mused. The aggrieved old king, Lear, had to weather the storm on the heath, a terrible storm with howling winds—something about cataracts and volcanoes and oak-cleaving thunderbolts, as Dylan recalled. The old man called on the thunderbolts to singe his white head, and they did, and drove him mad.

If truth be told, he was an old man who wouldn't get out of the way and let the young live. So Dylan said to himself, anger sidling in on shame.

Now Dylan was unaccommodated—no family, no home, no lodgings, no job, no money, nothing.

Bloody hell, it was dark.

He groped forward until he felt one of the big supporting posts, and sat with his back against it. He looked around in the dark. He was not looking for avenging furies, he told himself.

He was starved. He took half a loaf of white bread out of his pocket, and an apple. He tore at them with his teeth, savaging them. In a minute or two all was gone. Not enough to eat. But then he had only a few bob left, mustn't waste it on luxuries like food and lodging, he thought sardonically.

Probably Claude would have sneaked him into the flat if he'd gone back and asked. But he'd be damned if he would. Ask the MacDonalds for aught, no more than ask Ian Campbell.

He'd make this place more congenial with a light. Since he couldn't afford a candle, he had bought a can with some oil from the grocer, and flint and tinder. He fished his handkerchief out of a pants pocket and mucked it around in the grease. Out of a coat pocket came a small box with his flint and tinder.

He struck sparks.

Came a voice from above, "Bloody idiot!"

Dylan shot the light high over his head.

A dark form dropped out of the loft above, like a giant bat, arms webbed.

Dylan lurched back against the post.

The bat figure lit on the dirt floor easily, as though floating to a perch. Leaned into Dylan's eyes. An old, leathery face, more or less human, a face that had seen many weathers. Grabbed the tinderbox and spat on it.

"Idiot," the creature repeated in the dark.

Dylan stammered, "I'd really like some light."

"Sit down and be still and close your eyes for a couple of minutes."

A hand guided Dylan down, his back against the post. The hand stayed on his arm, comforting.

"Can't you see the floor's covered with straw? Bloody good tinder to torch us all. Are your eyes closed?"

"Yes. Us all?"

"You and me and the horses. Naught else in here tonight, though there might have been, *engagés* and the like." The voice made a grunt that might have been a chuckle.

Engagés. The canoe men, the white men turned to beasts by the Indians, according to Dylan's father. Was this creature one of that riffraff?

"Eyes still closed?"

"Yes."

"Open them, sit still, and let yourself see."

He did. The barn was changed. Where there had been impenetrable blackness, there were now shapes, indistinct, yet ... He could make out two lines of posts, humps of hay, walls, even a handle that might go to a pitchfork leaning against a post.

"See now?" The shape next to him was obscure, featureless, deep in shadow. It might be human or demon.

"Yes, sort of."

"Still want light?"

"I think so."

"All right. Use your eyes, get that broom, and sweep a big circle clean, right down to the dirt."

Dylan didn't think he could do it—too dark.

He managed without difficulty.

"Now light your rag. I could see all you were doing from the loft. That's how it is when you let your eyes adjust to nature."

Dylan set the can in the center of the circle and used

his flint and tinder again. The creature blew hard on the sparks, and the handkerchief ignited. After a little more blowing, they had light. It made a queer pattern of flickering light and shadow on the old man's face.

The creature smiled. It sat on its haunches comfortably and looked up into Dylan's face.

Dylan squatted and studied the creature at eye level. All but the face was wrapped in a blanket—that's why his arms looked webbed. A knobby face, the surface hard and bumpy, as though cobbled, and of indeterminate age. Gray hair pulled straight back like an Indian's, braided and hanging nearly to his waist. The smile of a fellow who was amused, perhaps at his naiveté. The crinkles of a man who liked to laugh. One eye normal, rather an attractive green. The other eye the strangest color Dylan had ever seen—aquamarine, he supposed, but luminous, brightly beaming, as from a lighthouse at sea. Dramatic, eerie eyes, one ordinary, mundane, the other a beacon.

Dylan pushed back thoughts of the devil. Nursery-tale stuff.

"Would you like some real food, boyo? You tore up that bread and apple like paper."

"Yes, sir," said Dylan.

"Away with that sir, laddo, I'm not a bloody officer, just a working Welshman like yourself."

"Welshman?"

"Aye, laddo, like you."

"How do you know me?"

"I knew your mother right well enough, God rest her soul, Dylan Elfed Davis."

"Campbell," Dylan added automatically.

"Aye, Campbell, ill enough, but you don't have to admit it. Dylan Elfed Davis is a right good name by itself." The creature was grinning. "Davies, perhaps even better, more traditional Welsh."

Don't admit to the Campbell part—Dylan liked that idea, after today. Go stuff it, Father.

"And who are you, to know so much?"

The creature put out a paw to shake. Dylan took it. "Morgan Griffiths Morgan Bleddyn," he said, "of the

NorthWest Company, venturer to Rupert's Land. You may call me Dru."

He leapt up and scrambled up a post into the loft. At least he didn't fly. Dylan was relieved to see, when Morgan Bleddyn was gone into the dark recesses of the loft, that the post was studded with rods for climbing.

Morgan leapt out, flew on blanket wings like a bat again and landed next to Dylan, grinning. He really seemed to land featherlike, as though he had no weight.

He held something Dylan had never seen, wrapped in leather. He peeled back the leather to show . . . was it sausage?

"Pemmican, laddo. A man with true understanding is never afraid, a man with a woman is never without a fire, and a man with pemmican is never hungry." He cut a chunk off with his big belt knife and offered it to Dylan.

Dylan tasted. Good. Kind of like cold sausage. Sewn tight into a deerskin casing.

"Buffalo meat mixed with fat and berries," said Morgan. "Best winter food there is."

Buffalo meat. So Morgan Bleddyn, called Dru, was a beaver man. Well, said Dylan to himself, when you sleep in barns, you fall in with a low crowd. He looked up into Morgan's one eerily bright eye.

Dylan put out his hand for another chunk. The buffalo stuff was good. He'd heard his father's tales of *voyageurs* surviving on it for entire winters. Lies, no doubt, considering the source.

"Why are you called Dru?"

"Short for Druid," Morgan said. "They call me that because I'm Welsh. And other reasons."

"How did you know my mother?" he asked Morgan.

"Everyone knew your mam, laddo. She was a beauty."

"I've never met anyone who knew her . . . who could tell me anything about her."

"Is that right, laddo? Withholding of your birthright, that is. Has your father been raising a fine Welshman as a bloody Scot?"

"I'm Welsh and Scottish, half and half."

"Not from the look of 'ee, laddo. You've your mam's

eyes, truly, and her brow. More, you've got the Welsh-man's long head and dark hair. A thorough son of Cymru, I'd say."

"*Koom*-ree?" repeated Dylan phonetically.

"Aye. Our word in our own language for what the bleedin' Br-r-itons"—he exaggerated this word sardonical-ly—"call Wales. And our people are called the Cymry. That's thee and me, laddo." He paused and eyed Dylan. "Would you say you're more poet or merchant, laddo?"

Dylan didn't hesitate. "Poet." His father was the bloody merchant.

"Welsh, then, you see, not Scots."

Dylan shrugged. "Welsh, Scottish, British—what's it all come to, anyway?"

Morgan Bleddyn turned on Dylan his strange eye, like a blue lamp.

After a moment he said, "Well, laddo, long as it's yet winter, and we've got a fire, perhaps you'd hear a story of the ancient Cymry."

Dylan affected not to be too keen.

"Have you heard of Madog ap Owain Gwynedd, laddo?"

Dylan shook his head. The oily rag was burning low now. The lamp eye of the Druid creature seemed to shine a brighter blue still.

"Madog, son to the royal House of Gwynedd, is the true discover of this continent, boyo, whether you call it North America, like the white people do, or Turtle Island, as the red people do."

"Oh, there are wild tales that credit Norsemen and Irishmen and mystic monks as well," said Dylan in a lightly scoffing tone.

The storyteller recognized a challenge and took it with a glitter of aquamarine eye. Strange, how plain the other eye was. "All true, laddo, all true. All the old tales are true. None but tells us something of the human heart. The old tales of the Welsh, our bardic epics, are the stuff of the truth stone. You know the nursery stuff, the King

Arthur legends. I'll tell ye some of *The Book of Taliesin* one day. Know 'ee not that 'tales' rhymes with 'Wales'?

"For tonight, Madog. He's ours, for us Welsh of Turtle Island, our true forefather.

"He left Wales with thirteen ships in the Year of Our Lord 1170. He left fleeing the arguments of his father the king and his brothers. We Welsh are great and foolish arguers when we mischannel our gift for words. He came to these shores—not Iceland, like your mystic monks, or Greenland or Nova Scotia, like your Norsemen. No, to the shores of the Carolinas, laddo, no man knows just where. Some say otherwise, true, the American state of Alabama, perhaps even Mexico, but these are the corruptions the word is heir to. The Carolinas. And there he founded the first colony in the Americas and claimed the entire continent for the king. Not the upstart king of England, mind you, the king of Wales, his father. All this is ours by right, there is truth it is."

The Druid swept one hand wide. To Dylan its compass was not North America, just the close barn walls in a French-English city.

"He went back to Wales, did Madog, some twenty years later. He and his men had befriended the Indians—there was no thought of conquering them, a million people upon their own land! No, they befriended them, and lived among them and learned their language and their ways, and became leaders among them, and taught them ways of herding and farming and metalworking, and married them, and raised up children with two races in their veins, the breath of two ways in their nostrils.

"Madog came back to get more men. He left, and returned once more, ten years later—for more men.

"At that point, about the year 1200, he became one of the Triads, the Three Who Made a Total Disappearance from the Isle of Britain.

"Aye, laddo, he disappeared. Of course, there are those who scoff. The British, ever the subjugators, would rather see an Italian Colombo and an Englishman Raleigh, better those than a Celt. When it suits them, though, as when they want to lay claim to this vast land, they remember Madog, and his priority, and try to trump the French and Spanish with their sovereignty. Welsh sovereignty, there's a truth it is."

The Druid chuckled at the thought. "When I was your age, some rich Welshmen expatriates in London sent John Evans, said to be a good man of Y Cymry, to the New World to find the Welsh Indians. What he found we shall never know. Evans traveled in the interior, then went to New Orleans, and there he died.

"Yet even before we find the Welsh Indians, what a legacy, what a legacy Madog left. On not one continent, but two.

"First here on Turtle Island. He left signs everywhere. I have seen with my own eyes burial mounds such as the Celts made. I heard from a Methodist minister's own lips how his grandfather, a missionary, was saved. The good man was captured by Hurons and was about to be tortured at the stake when he cried out in his native Welsh tongue for God's mercy. And the elders of the tribe answered him in that language, called him friend, cut him free, and made him their honored guest for some months.

"Blue-eyed, red-haired, fair-skinned Indians—Turtle Island is alive with reports of them, among the red people and the white people. They were supposed to be the Mandans, but they are not, to my grief. But everyone has seen them or heard of them—the Snake Indians of the far western deserts report fighting them. The Aztecs knew of them. The Blackfoot say they once were great enemies. Somewhere, around some corner on this continent, we will find ourselves among them.

"And words, laddo, words everywhere, we Welshmen are word men. They say the Mandan words for 'valley,' 'hill,' and 'blue' are identical to the Welsh words for these enchantments, *cym, prydferth,* and *glas.* They say the words for one through ten in the Kutenai language are the same as the Welsh.

"It is like the smell of spring, laddo, or the signs of spirit—everywhere, in the air, the earth, the rain, manifest in the very feel of things, save to those who will not smell, breathe, feel. The strains of the Welsh Indians of Turtle Island are everywhere. One day I will find a small band of their descendants still speaking the Cymraeg, and I shall live with them forever."

"Remember, laddo, I said on two continents. For Madog brought back to Wales on his second journey the mixed-blood children of his men. He left them to marry among the Cymry. He married one lass to his nephew and a lad to his niece. Through them the blood of red men runs in the veins of the House of Gwynedd and the House of Tudor. Through them you and I are those creatures of legend, the Welsh Indians.

"As I hope you were raised to know, Welshmen are natural Indians anyway. Both are conquered peoples, both stepped on by the bloody Britons, not only then but now. Both are thought barbarous by the conquerors. Both are attuned to nature, which is why I am called the Druid. Both give high place to the poet, the singer of songs. Both are trying to keep their ancient and holy places and their ancient and holy ways. Both are, well, the way I put it, blood and breath mystics."

He fell silent for a moment, pondering. "It is as always that we lost this kingdom, there is truth it is. We men of Wales are visionaries, which is why we sing, write poetry, and hear songs in the empty air. We are adventurers. We are even soldiers, men of the bond of blood. But we are not conquerors, not empire builders. We leave that to the bloody British."

Dylan nearly quaked with fear. He felt drawn to this stranger, this countryman, this Druid. Yet the man held a terror for him, a terror he recognized, both old and familiar friend and malicious nemesis. He feared in this man what he feared most in himself. The man was mad. And it was a siren song madness, a call, a will-o'-the-wisp Dylan could not resist, and it would lead him to his doom.

Dylan wanted to pull back. He wanted sanity. Order. Predictability. Safety. He asked, "What will you do to find these Welsh Indians?"

The Druid smiled an easy and genial smile. "Why, I

will look my whole life through, and discover them everywhere and nowhere, and come to know on my deathbed
that what I sought was within me all along."

Dylan felt both relieved and obscurely disappointed.
There would be no mad quest after all.

"There is one particular place, by reputation most
wild, most beautiful, most strange, that I especially want
to search."

"Where?" asked Dylan breathlessly.

"The High Missouri," said the Druid.

"Where is it?" asked Dylan eagerly. "What is it?"

"Perhaps it is our blood's country, and our heart's
pastureland," answered Dru. "Would you care to hear a
song I've written called 'The High Missouri'?"

Dru set the stage. This, Dylan must recognize, was
the *canu penillion*, the ancient and honorable Welsh art
of the singing of verses, the singer accompanying himself
on the Welsh harp. They had no harp, of course, but then
they were only poor wayfarers, far from Cymru and too
late in the centuries, there is truth there is. Dylan would
have to imagine the harp, its harmonies gentle but pi-
quantly colored, and soft as the breeze. The language, of
course, would be Yr Hen Iaith, the Old Language of the
country. Dylan was to listen not with his ordinary ear, the
one that treated words like mere signposts pointing to objects in simpleton fashion, but with his dreaming ear, the
one attuned to mysteries, to the meanings within things.

The Druid assumed an erect sitting pose, his fingers
poised over emptiness, or on the strings of an imaginary
harp on his knee, and lifted his voice into the air.

Dylan couldn't understand a word. He had not quite
realized that the song would be in a foreign language. His
mother's tongue or not, it was alien to him. He could find
no knowledge in it, and felt impatient.

After a few stanzas, though, the song began to work
on him in subtle ways. Perhaps it was the strong and elaborate meter that propelled the words. Perhaps it was impressions from the sheer sounds of the words, sounds that
somehow meant rushing waters, winds among leaves, the

cries of strange, strange birds, the lonely calls of wolf dogs, the murmurings of grasses. Surely he heard something—or was this just his imagination?

He listened far into the music and the verses, and in his imagination traveled to the exotic world of the High Missouri, wherever that was, whatever it might be, a steppe, a plain, a mountain enlivened by a river. The name itself was all of the song he understood in the ordinary sense, the High Missouri, but it took on an allure for him, a romance beyond sense. And somehow, watching the Druid's plucking fingers, by the end of the song he could hear the music of the Welsh harp, an interplay of tones, soft, sensual, many-colored, whispering, whirling gently like mists, ever-moving and yet motionless at its heart. It was as though beyond the mists of a Welsh dawn, impossible but visible to the dreaming eye, stood radiant, still, and gleaming, a rainbow of sound.

The Druid's voice fell silent. He set down the harp he never held. The music evaporated into the emptiness of a musty barn.

Dylan felt no need to know, until some other time, the ordinary meanings of the magical words.

At Morgan's suggestion they slept in the loft. "The owner doesn't mind if we bed down," he said, "as long as we don't turn it into a hotel."

Dylan looked up at the floorboards of the loft. In the weak light of the rag candle, they looked rickety. "Is it safe, Mr. Bleddyn?" he asked, pronouncing the name Bleh-then, as the creature did.

"Call me Dru," said the man.

"Dru," Dylan corrected.

"Safe? Well, laddo, let's hope the likes of you," said the Druid, "can find a song of danger and adventure with the likes of me."

Four

Father Quesnel was not in at nine o'clock. Nor at ten o'clock. Nor at eleven o'clock.

The *marguillier*, a pockmarked fellow of officious manner, seemed to think Dylan was presumptuous to come back so often and ask. But he didn't say so. He wouldn't have given Dylan the courtesy of that many words, nor the kindness of saying when the good father would be in.

Dylan had a suspicion that his godfather was right behind that closed door, and the apprehension that he was in to everyone but Dylan Elfed Davis Campbell.

He thought of the abbreviation of his patronymic by Morgan Bleddyn. The way this Druid renamed him, left out his bloody father's Campbell, tickled Dylan. Where was Dru? he wondered. Would he ever see Morgan Bleddyn again? When Dylan woke this morning, the old boy had been gone. By the light of day, the world of romance was gone and a mundane world was in its place.

No sense sitting around where he wasn't welcome. Dylan closed the outer door on Pockmark Pompous and looked out on the day. The reason he didn't mind waiting for Father Quesnel was the weather. It was a gorgeous rendition of the first real day of spring, one of the vernal goddess's best efforts, he was sure, a miracle after yesterday's storms—balmy, with only a warm, gentle breeze, high, pillowy clouds, and sunlight flung prodigally between the clouds. The light made the dun-colored winter grass and the gray branches of the trees shine. The branches were barren—except for robins.

A grand day to be starting out on your life's adventure. Not the fanciful sort of adventure the Druid conjured up. Real adventure, witnessing for civilization in the midst of barbarism.

He was bored with wandering the streets, looking in the open doors of the coffeehouses where rich people ate when he had no money, feeling disheveled because he'd slept in his clothes. Maybe Claude would go to his father's house later and get his steamer trunk with all his worldly belongings. Dylan resolved he would never go there again.

He was hungry. He thought of the chunk of pemmican he'd breakfasted on. He looked at the warm sun. He decided to be hungry sitting down. There would be a bench by the site of the old church graveyard.

Would he ever see Bleddyn again? Being with the old man was entirely new and wonderful, a variety of enchantment. Perhaps this Druid was a wizard. Being with him was being in another world. It was like walking into a lake—the water was cold at first, but you kept walking until your eyes were underwater. It was frightening. Your reward was seeing a different world beneath the waters, perhaps a castle in shining, white marble, with mermaids singing and eels guarding the gate.

He shook himself. That dream world was child's stuff, and there was nothing to be gained from it. Except stories of his mother's native country.

He sat on the bench and yearned for more pemmican. Strange stuff, but good. Great, when you're hungry.

He looked around at the gravestones, many of them slightly tilted, the grounds a little unkempt. This cemetery had been full since before he was born. A melancholy sight.

Wasn't it fine? He had no home, no family, no place to live, no job. He was starting out in the world naked as a newborn babe.

Unaccommodated man.

He was newly afloat on the sea of the world, the sea of the world as it is, whether monstrous or beatific, as the Druid put it. He looked around at the end of all men represented all around him, slabs and monuments of stone marking their final resting places.

Full fathom five my father lies.

He did have his faith in God to assuage his fears about this naked launch. But even aside from that, he felt that all was well, the face of the earth to walk on was good. Even the darkness of wilderness was good, he felt sure, when walked in the right spirit. This was not a conscious thought but an unstated experience, probably the euphoric result of the sun on his skin, and the songs of the robins in his ears.

Came a voice,

"Let's talk of graves, of worms and epitaphs."

Dylan jumped.

The Druid clapped his shoulder cheerfully. He recited resonantly,

"Make dust our paper, and with rainy eyes
Write sorrow on the bosom of the earth."

"You scared me," Dylan said.

"Graveyards scare all of us," the Druid replied. "Old graveyards even more." Winking his one green eye and smiling, he sat down next to Dylan. He offered him a piece of pemmican. Dylan wondered if the aquamarine eye could blink, or if it always shone, like a lighthouse lamp.

Dylan took the pemmican and started chewing. "What was that drivel you were spouting as you came up?"

Dru turned the one eye baleful. "The bard of Avon, laddo. God created him British to balance a little all the poetry He gave to the Welsh, there is justice there is." His friend looked as much like the beaver hunters as Dylan feared—a *bandeau* of fur around the head, knee leggings, moccasins, and a *gâge d'amour* with a white clay pipe around the neck. A white man reduced to a barbarian, Ian Campbell would have said.

"How did you find me?"

Dru shrugged. "You said you were going to ask to become a priest this morning. I know Father Quesnel is your family's friend. Who else would you ask? Half an hour ago he went out the back door of the rectory, by the way."

Dylan scowled.

"He just came back in. You could probably see him now, for the good it will do you."

Dylan jumped up. "The good it will do me? I told you—"

"Go on with you, laddo, and do what 'ee must. When you're finished, meet me here. I have an idea. A grand idea."

After the bright spring sunshine outdoors, the room was dark, and it smelled of snuff. Father Quesnel often joked that snuff, fine snuff, was the final, irrefutable proof of God's fundamental goodness.

Father Quesnel sat behind his desk regarding his godson solemnly. He didn't offer his hand. He nodded toward the ladder-backed chair in front of the desk, and Dylan sat down. It was a hard, uncomfortable chair.

Until now Dylan had never been struck with the realization that Father Quesnel looked like his own father. Not in form or feature—his godfather was painfully thin and had features too large for his face—but in demeanor, in style. In owlishness. In superior attitude toward him, perhaps.

The young man fidgeted in the hard chair.

Father Quesnel regarded Dylan. The silence was getting oppressive.

Finally: "I have a note from Peche this morning."

"Peche" was his pet name for Ian Campbell. Dylan had never known why.

"Your father says you want to be a priest."

"Yes, Father."

Quesnel looked at Dylan. He scooted his chair forward and looked more. It seemed to Dylan that his face became more kindly.

"I'm your godfather, Dylan, and I think you would make an excellent priest. You're a young man of high ideals and a certain nobility of spirit. You'd be a credit to the seminary. I think you have a grand future before you, no matter how you serve man and God."

Dylan's heart sank. So I am to be turned down. *Why?* screeched through his mind. *Why?*

Father Quesnel opened a desk drawer, got something out, reached across the desk to Dylan. A piece of stationery. His father's script.

"Your father reports that you and he have quarreled. Quarreled seriously."

Quesnel looked at Dylan for confirmation. Dylan nodded.

"He's concerned about you. You're without a job, he says. Without money. Without clothes, even. He says all your belongings are there."

Father Quesnel looked hard at Dylan. Dylan kept his face unreadable.

"Are you and your father estranged, Dylan?"

Dylan hesitated, then nodded.

"I'm sorry to hear it. From your point of view, what's the problem?"

"He doesn't give a *damn* about me." Dylan meant his language to be harsh.

Father Quesnel cocked his head, looked quizzically at Dylan, arranged his wide, fluid mouth into a smile.

"He only cares about what I can do for him. Live respectably, unlike him. Get good connections for the family. Increase the family fortunes."

"Dylan." Said softly, sympathetically.

"He despises me."

"Dylan, your father loves you. You know that."

"He hit me over the head with a table."

"I'm sure he gets frustrated and angry. And I'm sure he loves you."

"I'll never go back to his house. Never."

"It's understandable to feel that way. Clinging to that resolution would only hurt both of you."

Dylan shrugged his shoulders.

Father Quesnel waited.

Dylan screwed the words together. He felt like he was prostrating himself. "Father, I want to become a priest. My ambition, my heart's desire, is to become a missionary. Will the order accept me as a seminarian?"

The words seemed to Dylan to ring in the air fatefully. He had a sense of abyss.

"Dylan, as I said, you would make an excellent priest, and I would welcome you to our seminary. There would be some questions to be answered. But we have talked about your yearning for mission work in the past, and you know that a priest must accept the duties the Church gives him."

Dylan interrupted, "My calling to the missions is unmistakable, Father." He touched his heart with a flat hand.

Quesnel considered and inclined his head sympathetically. "Yes. I understand. Admirable. You would help return the Canadian Church to its historic mission."

The priest waited, looking at Dylan. "My son, I ask you to mend your relations with your father and come back with your request."

"Impossible," Dylan burst out.

"Dylan, Dylan. There can be no question of accepting you for the priesthood under circumstances like these. Our seminarians need, among other things, the full support of their families. We avoid young men who come to us in a moment of disruption."

Dylan moaned. "Father, this calling has been in me from boyhood."

"Yes." Father Quesnel looked at Dylan thoughtfully. "I believe it has."

The priest rose. Dylan stood up as well. He repeated, "I believe it has. I believe you will be a missionary. And do good work for the Mother Church."

He offered Dylan his hand. "There will be questions to be answered, considerations, plans to be made. You can start upon this path as soon as you get right with your father."

Dylan felt hot tears well in his eyes as he shook Father Quesnel's hand. The young man jerked his hand back quickly and turned his head away. He hurried toward the door.

"Dylan," Father Quesnel called after him, "I hope to

see you back here tomorrow, and to present you to the ab-
bot."

Dylan didn't look back. *Impossible*, he screamed in
his mind.

He opened the door to the outside. The sun shafted
into the dark room and hit him in the eyes. He felt weak
in the knees. He staggered.

The Druid was standing there, smiling. He closed the
door behind Dylan with a final-sounding click.

"Come now, laddo," he said. "How about an adventure? A dalliance with life and death?"

They sang as they worked. Well, mostly Dru sang, and Dylan grunted. He told himself he didn't feel like singing—he'd just lost his lifelong dream, what he'd quit his job for, what he'd lost his family over. Why should he sing?

> *"Quand on part de chantier,*
> *Mes chers amis, tous le coeur gai,*
> *Pour aller voir tous nos parents,*
> *Mes chers amis, le coeur content."*
>
> *(chorus)*
> *"Envoyons de l'avant, nos gens!*
> *Envoyons de l'avant!*
> *Envoyons de l'avant, nos gens!*
> *Envoyons de l'avant!"*

It was a song of the French-Canadian boatmen, the *voyageurs* who went deep into the wilderness among the Indians. A song with a vigorous beat the canoe men used to time their paddling. It spoke of going home, so it added power to every stroke.

> *"Pour aller voir tous nos parents,*
> *Mes chers amis, le coeur content. . . .*
>
> *Envoyons de l'avant, nos gens!*
> *Envoyons de l'avant!"* . . .

"Let's go forward, fellows!" cried the chorus. "Let's go! You have to get wet to go to Canada."

> *"Ah! mais que ça soit tout mouillé*
> *Vous allez voir que ça va marcher!"*. . .

The men sing that they're eager to see their friends, to throw a party and laugh and sing.

> *"Dimanche au soir, à la veillée,*
> *Nous irons voir nos compagnées,"*. . .

> *"Et au milieu de la veillée*
> *Elles vont parler de leurs cavaliers."*. . .

The girls will talk about their other beaux until it's time to go home. Then they'll say to us, do you have other lovers? Do you?

> *"Elles vont nous dire, mais en partant*
> *As-tu fréquenté les amantes?"* . . .

Unspoken: They're thinking of dark lovers, of course, Indian girls. And we do have dark lovers, don't we?

> *"Envoyons de l'avant, nos gens!*
> *Envoyons de l'avant!"* . . .

A song to make the men work with a will: "Let's go home!"

Dylan and Dru were waist deep in the soft, wet, spring soil—shoveling. This was St. Anthony's at Coteau St. Louis, the new cemetery. Dru sang lustily and repeated the song over and over, apparently without getting bored with it. "You do this all day when you paddle, laddo," he'd said. On the hour he stopped and loaded his white clay pipe and had a smoke and a rest. He claimed this was the fixed custom of the canoe men.

I've lost everything, thought Dylan. Why am I digging a grave with the Druid?

Having no pipe, Dylan could not indulge. He didn't

want to smoke anyway—he wanted to quit digging these sodding graves, to sit on a pile of fresh dirt like the sexton and breathe the young breezes and . . . daydream about delicious female flesh. Yes, now that you're not going to be a priest, Dylan Elfed Davis Campbell, you can daydream of carnality.

The reality was, he needed the Halifax pound. The sexton, whose name Dylan kept forgetting, had offered them a pound to dig the graves, and the Druid had sweet-talked him up a few shillings. Life of a Montreal sexton in April, Dru said—digging graves for the corpses that have spent the winter in the dead house. But this sexton was a fat fellow, past digging graves, Dylan would have thought, and from the look of his nose, a tippler. He did nothing but lie about and produce one chocolate treat after another from his garments, look at them avariciously, and consume them bite by slow, savory bite.

I've lost everything.

Dru and the sexton also kept mentioning some "extra reward," and smiling at each other.

It was nasty labor, for a fact. Dylan's hands were blistered, some of the blisters had burst, and his hands were wet with blood and juice. His back ached right between the shoulder blades. And his lower back pained him. His calves hurt in the lower center. It irked him that a man as old as the Druid, at least as old as his father, could shovel for a couple of hours comfortably while he, young and presumably more fit, suffered from manual labor.

"Being used to it," said Dru, reading Dylan's thoughts. "I'm used to paddling all day—*Envoyons de l'avant, nos gens!*

"That's worse, paddling, because you can barely change the way you're sitting."

He looked Dylan merrily in the eye and lifted a shovel of dirt halfway. "Except when you go through rapids. Then you may sit in the river!" He made a mock motion to throw the dirt into Dylan's face and pitched it over his head onto the grass. Dust sifted on Dylan's head and neck. He climbed out of the grave and brushed off.

"Who's this grave for, Sexton?" asked Dylan. "You said twins."

"The Talon twins," said the sexton. "A sad case, both dead within ten days of birth. The mother is still languishing, they say." He added piously, "This world is a vale of tears."

"Ah, laddo," said the Druid, "you mustn't ask who a fresh grave is for." He threw his shovel onto the grass at Dylan's feet and, with bravado, lay down full length in the grave. "A man digging a grave should have sober thoughts of his own mortality—seen truly, it is always for him." Dru folded his hands across his chest and closed his eyes. He began to snore.

Suddenly he jumped up, mimicked the creaky movements of a skeleton, and grabbed Dylan by the ankle. He wailed, "I drag 'ee to thy end, Dylan Elfed Davies, thy woeful end." He tried to pull Dylan into the grave by one leg.

Dylan stood firm and glowered at him.

Dru let go and said in a relaxed way, "Better get in here, laddo, and lift your share of the load. Or whose shillings will ye eat on tonight?"

Dylan jumped into the grave and jammed his shovel into the soft dirt with his foot.

He hit something hard. He turned up the rock, but it wasn't a rock. A—

"Jawbone," said Dru. "The talking piece of a human being."

He reached for it. Laid it on an open palm. Studied it curiously.

Then the Druid gave a look of antic glee. He made his two hands into a mouth hinged at the wrists. The jawbone with its gapped teeth lay on the bottom hand. He made his hands flap.

"Quack-quack!" he said.

He danced around like a fool. "Who was buried here, Sir Sexton?" cried Dru. He flashed a wicked grin at Dylan and brought the flapping hands to his mouth. "I am Samuel de Champlain," he said in an orotund voice, "author of *The Travels of Sieur de Champlain* and governor of New France and in my person a highfalutin boiled shirt."

He waggled his ass and turned the flapping hands into

his face. "And tell us, Sieur de Champlain," he said to the hands, "of what consists the greatness of New France?"

He reversed the hands. "It's a place you can send Jesuits far, far into the interior. If the Indians don't eat 'em, the cold kills 'em. Or they confuse a New Testament with a compass and get lost. Either way, the world is rid of the dolts."

He talked to the hands. "And what should be our policy toward the benighted natives, Sieur de Champlain?"

The jawbone talked. "Why, we must save their souls by day," it pronounced, "and frig their wives by night."

Dru asked, "And what do we want with New France, anyway, Sieur de Champlain?"

The jawbone answered loudly: "What do you want with any virgin? Lust, me buckos, lust!" He thrust his pelvis suggestively, and laughed at his own act until he fell down.

"Let me see that," asked Dylan, his hand out.

Dru gave him the jawbone.

Dylan looked at it, turned it over, studied it. "This was a real person," he said softly.

"Aye, laddo."

"Spoke using this. Bit and chewed." He thought. "Kissed—here," pointing above the gapped front teeth.

"Doubly aye, laddo." He took the jawbone from Dylan and held it up. Mockingly, he quoted, "Alas, poor Yorick. I knew him, Horatio." He spoke quickly, seeming to snatch words out of the air. "Where be your gibes now? Your gambols? Your songs? Your flashes of merriment?"

He looked sideways at Dylan, saw puzzlement, and rolled his eyes. "The bard again, laddo."

He proceeded airily, a sprite now. "What if it was a fair maid died young? Kisses in vain. What if it was a great preacher, a Jonathan Edwards? Where are his perorations now? What if a diva of operas? Where her sweet arias? A father? Where his paternal advice? A son? A mother? A daughter? What difference now?"

He held the jawbone over his head and knelt in the dirt. "What if a man of power, who made lesser beings tremble with his commands?" He looked up at Dylan.

"Who is afraid of what may clack out of this fragment of bone now?"

He jumped up and threw the jawbone into the soft dirt. Slowly he spaded up a shovelful of dirt, looked Dylan in the eyes, and dumped the dirt on the bone.

Suddenly the Druid spoke in a new tone, soft, intimate. "Your mam was the last good woman. Do you know she's buried here?"

"My father would never talk about her," said Dylan.

"Do you want to see her grave?"

Dylan nodded somberly.

Dru hopped agilely out of the grave and reached a hand to Dylan. Dylan climbed out on his own.

"Hey!" exclaimed the sexton.

"We'll be back soon enough," said Dru, marching away. Dylan followed. "We mean to get paid." He didn't look back. He called over one shoulder, "And there's plenty of time before the angelus."

Dylan followed. Why am I wasting this day?

Why not? All is lost.

"You take after her, laddo." He looked Dylan in the eye. "She wanted you. She gave you life, and gave her life for you, and willingly. You are what she wanted above all things."

He sat down beside the gravestone. Carved on it was, GWYNETH DAVIS CAMPBELL, 1774–1798, REQUIESCAT IN PACE. Only those few bare and lonely words to tell him about his mother. Until now he hadn't even known how old she was when she died. His father had been too grieved, too angry at fate, too enraged to tell him even the essentials, or to bring him to St. Anthony's to see his mother's resting place.

"I have only this left of her," said Dylan. He slipped off the slender chain he always wore around his neck and handed Dru a gold ring with a stone. Dru fingered it. "A fire opal," Dylan said. "When she knew how sick she was, she asked that it be mine."

"It's beautiful, lad." He put it back in Dylan's hand. Dylan looked into the strange glow of its depths. "What was she like?" he asked.

"Comely, graceful, and full of verve. She had an effect on me like no other woman I ever met. I was a ruffian in those days, living it up. I would come around to her father's house and she would fix us tea and we would talk. That was all our courtship ever came to, a score of cups of tea."

He looked sideways at Dylan and smiled ruefully. "In those days I was not yet a *hivernant*, I didn't stay the winter in the wilds, but just went to the depot in spring and came back with the furs in fall.

"The winter of 'ninety-seven I spent here in town, like always, and I met her down at the river. They swept a spot for skating. My mates and I were skidding about on the ice on our boots and falling all over ourselves and acting the fool and having a grand time. Your mother and a few others were skating. Your mother skated alone, with great poise and very beautifully. Serene, something from another world. The way she skated—I imagined ballet would look like that." He chuckled. "She was a swan among ugly ducklings, there is a memory there is.

"My mates and I laughed about the silk stocking that thought she was better than the rest of us. I didn't know much about living, those days. Over thirty years old and had learned naught.

"Well, I couldn't admit to them that I was enchanted with her. So I begged off somehow and waited for her and approached her on the street. A right ragamuffin I must have looked, my clothes all patched and me looking like I slept in a barn, because I did, same as now. But your mother was a grand-hearted woman, an original, and she let me walk her home, and brought me inside and introduced me to her mother, God rest her soul, and fixed us a cup of tea.

"I discovered right off, that first afternoon, what moored me to her. To my mates I would say any old thing, and make a joke of it—certainly not admit to any elevated thoughts. But when I looked in Gwyneth Davis's eyes, I told the truth. Couldn't help myself. When she asked me what I wanted to do with my life, I spoke from the heart. Asked about my family, spoke from the heart. Asked about my feelings about things, spoke from the heart. Thus did she teach this pilgrim about himself.

"She wanted to know about Wales, and that was easier. She'd left the homeland as a schoolchild, never to go back. I told her the old stories, Owain Glendower, and Merddyn, whom you know as Merlin, and Arthur the King, and far older ones—the druid tales my granfer raised me on.

"Perhaps that was me hold on her. Certainly I wasn't much in myself, a good-for-nothing *voyageur*. But the old stories, they cast a spell.

"We saw each other regular that winter. She skated most days, and I walked her home and had tea. I was mad for her. Up to then I'd thought of little but adventuring." He looked up at Dylan. "Adventuring into the wilds, and into Indian girls. Your mam raised me from lust to love, a feeling a young man scoffs at. One he thinks he'll never have. Made me yearn to have a wife, a home, children. To find out what's next in life. That's what she wanted too, a home, children."

He looked up at Dylan. "You."

He chuckled, remembering. "I'd go away from her and wonder what was wrong with me. I thought I must be crazy. I'd find my mates and go to the taverns and the whores. Wake up in a barn, hung over, smelling of *putain*, and tell myself that was the life. That afternoon I'd be back at the river, looking for your mother. Looking with a yearning I've hardly ever felt since. And go home with her and drink tea instead of ale.

"Come spring, right about this time, I was supposed to go back to the depot. *Voyageur* me, braving the wilds. I thought maybe your mother wanted me to stay. I thought maybe there was a different kind of life for me here. She didn't say, except maybe with her eyes."

The Druid stared down at the ground now. "My other thought was, I'm kidding myself. A girl like your mam, above the rest of us, really, wouldn't consort with the likes of me. She wants a family—she's eager for children. She wants a proper home for them, respectability—she'll marry a merchant.

"Come April, I headed upstream in a canoe. She came to see me off—a merry scene, that always is. I told her I'd be back in the fall. I told her I loved her and ran like a coward for the boats. She said naught, save perhaps with her eyes.

"When I did come back, she was married to your father. Her mother told me, in a superior way—'Ian Campbell the fur trader,' she said haughtily. Not a *voyageur* like me with no prospects, but the owner of a fur company, even if it was a small one.

"Just before I left the next spring, she died."

For a moment he stared at the ground.

"I've always wondered, if I stayed in Montreal that summer, if my life would have been different. And hers."

He looked into Dylan's eyes. "I look at you," he said, "and think I might have been your father."

He studied Dylan. "You're a good laddo." He grinned. "I'd be proud to be your father. But I found something grand out there in the wilds too." A flash of something gleeful in his eyes. "They call it life."

What will I do? No matter what, I'll never go back to my father.

"To appreciate this treat," said the Druid confidentially, "you have to understand some things."

They were walking back to Notre Dame ahead of the sexton, who was snacking again, nibbling chocolate with a sensual pleasure that made Dylan feel like a Peeping Tom.

The Druid pointed up at the bell tower. "This sexton understands nothing," Dru went on. "He has no feeling for the bells. He rings them mechanically, as a monkey plays the barrel organ. If he's here another ten years, the bells will be all cracked and useless.

"The old sexton, my friend Gabriel, God rest his soul, he loved the bells. He cherished them, took care of them, loved them like children—he replaced the ropes so often the sodding priest complained about the cost.

"And he made music on them, there is a truth there

is. You should have heard him ring for a wedding, especially. He considered a wedding mankind's most glorious
event—he never married—and he made the bells merry
and full of sentiment, a great, sonorous rejoicing."

They stopped at the foot of the bell tower. "There are
only four bells, you say—there *are* just four, you'll see.
But for a special occasion Gabriel could make them sound
like a thousand. He had the magic."

Dru looked far away, reminiscing.

Why do I feel drawn to this old man? Danger, danger.

"He loved doing it. He'd dash from rope to rope
madly, heaving with his whole weight, riding the ropes
into the air, his eyes flashing fire, his lungs blowing like
bellows. Sometimes he would swing from one rope to another, to bring forth the next note more quickly. And he
sang as he made them ring—he sang at the top of his
voice, a majestic vocal music I know in my heart." Dru
smiled sideways at Dylan. "But I never knew with my
ears, because no one ever heard his singing above the tremendous clanging of the bells, not even him.

"That's what a man can do when he loves something."

Dru eyed Dylan with bemusement. "You know, that
Frenchman Blanchard thinks he bloody invented flight.
You know, the bugger that took his balloon up in Philadel-
phia with old George Washington watching? But
Blanchard didn't invent naught. Bell ringers invented
flight—you'll see.

"Anyway, Gabriel and I had a tradition, we did. Every year on St. David's day we rang the bells together.
Your father won't have kept you ignorant of St. David's
day?"

Dylan answered, "Our old housekeeper told me it's
the celebration of the patron saint of Wales. My father
never told me anything, even the date."

Dru regarded him. "Little enough to know," he said,
and continued. "A year or so after I lost your mother, I
quit drinking. It was going to be the death of me. But I
still wanted to get drunk on St. David's day. It was Gabriel
who came up with the idea of getting drunk on the bells
instead of brandy. He taught me to ring them with him.

Just on that one day. Laddo, did we make music? And did we get drunk? You'll see.

"All that's left of the old days is, when I'm in town, this oaf lets me ring the angelus on St. David's day. That's March first. When I'm late, like this year, I ring them on a day we pretend is St. David's. Like today."

It surprised Dylan—the bell tower was open to the weather on the sides near the top, and the inside roof was full of bird's nests. As a result, the four bells were streaked thick with white droppings. "The birds are jealous, you see," the Druid said with a wry smile. Where they weren't white, the bells were an antique, coppery green. They were mounted on huge beams, above and below each other in the tower, and varied from the size of a big package to the size of a carriage.

Dru showed him how they worked. When you pulled on the rope, which attached to a wheel where the bell was mounted on the beam, the bell swung toward the hanging clapper. "At that point the clapper makes a DONG!" said Dru. When you let go of the rope, the bell swung the other way—and thwacked the clapper, making another big noise. Dru raised one expressive eyebrow. "It makes an impression," he said dryly.

In the half-light the bells looked great and mysterious, humped beasts among mists. Dylan could see them only imperfectly. The bell tower let in only shafts of light, and it was nearly sunset, time for the evening angelus.

"They have names, ones I chose. Later Gabriel claimed it was ridiculous sentimentality. He was drunk when we did it, celebrating, but I think he liked the names too.

"You must get to know them." He grabbed a thick beam and hoisted himself up, then up onto the highest beam. "Come on," he cried to Dylan, "you can't make real music with a bell you've never touched."

Dylan looked down. How far was it to the bottom of the dusky shaft? His knees were queasy.

"It's the distance from life to death," called the Druid,

"and you'd be lucky to die in the service of the bells. Come on!"

Dylan climbed slowly. Soon he pulled up beside Dru, on the beam that supported the smallest bell.

"This is Gwyneth," Dru said, stroking the bell. GWYNEDD was painted on the bell in blue in an elegant hand. "Spelled the old Welsh way, you see." He brushed the letters with his fingertips. "Yes, after your sweet mam. She's a soprano, surprisingly delicate, as you'll hear, and utterly lovely."

Dylan touched the small bell with both hands. She was cold, spookily cold.

Dru slipped off the beam, hung from his hands and glided to the next beam, oblivious of the hundred-foot drop. Dylan descended more cautiously, and Dru grinned at him. "This is Mair, the alto, named after me granmer." Again the name was painted on the bell, this time in yellow.

He grabbed the beam, swung down and dropped. Now he kept going, dropped again to the biggest bell. He waited for Dylan to catch up in his cautious way.

"The big one here I named after Owain Glendower." OWAIN was red-lettered on the bell. "You'll be needing to learn more about Owain, laddo, the last true king of Wales. It is he, not Arthur the King, who waits on the isle of Avalon, one day to return and restore Wales to her glory."

He jumped up one beam like a cat. "The best for last." He pointed to the second-largest bell. "Dylan." Dylan clambered awkwardly up behind him. In that fancy script, just above the lip, was lettered DYLAN in green. "It's not every laddo that has a bell named after him, is it?" He looked Dylan in the eyes. "Yes, for you, the son I might have had."

He went on quickly, with a lightness that was not quite true. "He's a heroic tenor, and I do mean heroic—he peals mightily." Dru fixed his one good eye on Dylan. "He gives you something to live up to, laddo.

"Come." Dru leaned out and put both hands on the upper part of the Dylan bell. It didn't budge. "Let me show you—it's a thrill."

Dylan leaned his weight on the bell the same way. It still didn't budge. "He's heavy as a great stone, lad, and going nowhere. Now reach up and grab where the bell is mounted." Dylan could barely reach. He grabbed hard, thinking he was going to lose his foothold.

"Now wrap your legs around the bell, son. Go ahead—you must do this yourself."

Dylan had never been so scared. Half in panic, he jumped his feet off the beam and gripped the bell with his legs.

Dru reached beneath the bell and did something, Dylan couldn't see what.

DON-N-NG!

The great bell sounded its heroic tenor. It shuddered, and Dylan would have sworn it swung a little. He held on desperately. He could feel the bell vibrating in his fingers, in his thighs, in his forehead, in his chest, in his bones, in his teeth, in his soul.

They waited. They waited. The sound subsided very, very slowly, for long minutes. Dylan felt it vibrate through his body until the very end, and then perhaps a moment longer.

"Now may be you're ready," said the Druid.

Dru gave him a choice of bells to start. Dylan chose his own, the tenor named Dylan.

In the kind of ringing he knew, Dru explained, called change ringing, you rang certain memorized patterns, which did not repeat. Dylan would mostly ring the tenor Dylan bell, faster or slower as Dru would motion to him, but would sometimes have to ring another. So Dru would point to the ropes—painted blue for Gwynedd, yellow for Mair, green for Dylan, red for Owain—so Dylan would know which one to clang next. "It's a duet, laddo. The two of us will clang our spirits to the wide world.

"How do 'ee get a big bell like the Dylan started? You climb the rope a little first, to get your body weight all the way off the ground. The rope will start down, but very slowly, don't worry—just get a little higher. I'll help pull from below you to get it going."

When the bell really moved and you came down, said Dru, you took the chance to grab the rope still higher, and let its swing up carry you well off the ground. "That's the excitement, laddo, swooshing up. And back to the ground and back up. Watch me, laddo—do as I do." The old man looked at him queerly. "Mostly just *do*," he said. "Up you go."

He gave Dylan a leg up on the tenor bell.

Dylan did a couple of pull-ups and clung. He was afraid of the motion. Maybe the up and down would make him sick.

After some moments he realized that the rope was barely moving. He pulled up a little farther. Then Dru gave a big heave from the bottom.

The rope dropped. Far up in the half-light of the tower, the tenor bell named Dylan swayed a little.

And it began to happen. The rope pulled him up a couple of feet. Dru heaved and he sank. The rope lifted him, lightly, airily, beautifully. Dru heaved down.

DON-N-G!

Loud! The air shimmered with something quicksilver that was unseen but left ripples in its wake.

The bell took hold of him like magically powerful currents of air, and he surged into the twilight.

DON-N-G!

The bell dropped him—he fell, heart in mouth, toward the hard stone floor. The rope almost ripped through his hands, but he clutched it desperately. For a moment, just above the floor, he hung still in space. The Druid, close to his face, looked into his eyes with a wild grin. In that still moment came DON-N-G!

Up he went, catapulted. He was flying. As in his dreams, he was flying.

Now the sound in the tower was beginning to split his ears—a din, a clangor, a great proclamation, the song of the Dylan bell to the sensate world.

The Druid was setting the other bells to ringing, sailing up and down on the ropes.

The sounds rang now, everywhere, from every angle, like powerful sunlight off the myriad waves of water. Tones and overtones glanced off the stones of the tower, twirled in the crannies, pulsated from floor to roof. It was not merely ear-splitting, it was brain-splitting, soul-splitting.

The rhythm of the Dylan bell quickened. DONG-DONG!

A desperate drop! DONG-DONG!

An exhilarating sail upward! DONG-DONG!

He had the extraordinary sensation of freedom. He laughed out loud. Everything gone! Home, family, job, money, plans, calling, future—all demolished! Mind almost gone—he could barely think. He was swooping up and down in a bell tower with a mad Welshman, his world destroyed, and he felt dizzy, he felt wild, he felt free.

He cried or laughed, or both at once, into the din. And heard nothing but the clangor. Laughed again louder, uproariously, foolishly, madly. And soundlessly.

CLON-N-NG!

A new sound. The Owain bell, the bass of the quartet—Dru had gotten it going. CLON-N-NG!

The roar now was beyond imagination. Thought was impossible. Consciousness beyond hearing was impossible. Dylan was in a world of sound, his mind was sound, his soul was sound. To resist, he knew intuitively, was to die. He gave himself up to the sound—the valiant clang of his Dylan bell, the quicker chimes of the soprano Gwynedd and the alto Mair, the thunderous bass throb of the Owain. The rope lifted and dropped like a huge, vertical ocean wave pitching him up and down, and he could only surrender.

A touch on his shoulder. Dru. The old man swung his rope like a pendulum sideways and he rode up, grabbed another rope, glided smoothly onto it, and dropped out of sight ringing a new bell.

Coming back up, the Druid pointed to the rope of the Owain bell.

Strange—Dylan could feel Dru's lithe movements in his body, and he felt no fear—he was beyond fear, in a new world of possibility. He rocked his rope toward the red Owain rope, grabbed it with one hand, then both, and let go his feet, grasped the red rope firmly.

He swung sideways. Miracle.

He flew up. He lost himself sailing up toward the great bell, into the soul-splitting sound. He felt the sound in the rope, in his organs, in his skull, like when he'd whanged a tuning fork once and pressed the base to his head. This was magnified a thousand times.

Down he went, up, crazily, dizzyingly. Dru touched his shoulder and pointed again. All right—sideways, up, sideways to a new rope, down, up and to a new rope, down. He danced from rope to rope, he strutted, he pranced, he soared.

He was possessed utterly by ropes and soaring and the terrific sound and most of all by vibration. A mad spirit had his soul. He was like a leaf skittering above the trees in a hurricane. By giving in, he gained freedom, and could dance on the treetops.

He danced not through air but through the dimension of sound. And danced, and danced, as he sprang from rope to rope.

And heard. Heard not with his ears but his whole body—skull, chest, fingers, feet. With his heart, his liver, his gut, his balls. They tingled, they vibrated, they resonated to the great pulse as the heavens resonate to the music of the spheres.

Time ceased. Society ceased. Religion ceased. Thought itself ceased. His whole being had become a tuning fork, and he quivered, he became vibration.

He had no idea how time passed. Later, after one or two eternities, he saw the Druid lying on the stone floor, resting. Dylan realized he was nearly exhausted. His fingers wouldn't hold on much longer. On his next swoop down, he let go of the rope and dropped to the stone floor.

He lay still. The giant reverberations lifted him and dropped him like a stick borne by great waves. He lay still. He did not move, he did not think, he did not imagine, he did not feel emotion, he simply heard. Energy surged through him. And at last it began to ebb.

The great clangs subsided very slowly. DONG-DONG changed to a vigorous DONG, and kept that identity for a while. After a time you could tell it had faded a little—it was definite but no longer vigorous. Then the clangs spaced themselves further apart. The soprano and the alto, Gwynedd and Mair, became a tinkle, charming in the wind, and then fell silent. Dylan lost its manliness, or subsided to a more quiet manhood, and at last fell silent. Finally Owain was alone, an occasional soft, basso utterance, a calling of the end of time.

Then only soundless vibration, and then silence.

Time again flowed into Dylan. He had an extraordinarily vivid impression that he'd been dreaming, or having a vision. Yet he could feel the prickly grip of the rope in his hands, and feel that ferocious reverberation all through his body. No, he hadn't been dreaming. Yet he had.

He blinked. He stretched. He clutched and unclutched his tired fingers. He shrugged and squiggled.

He acknowledged that thoughts were in his mind again. He sensed that he would soon want to move, to walk upon the earth. He would even be hungry again. He might indulge in small sounds like human conversation.

But not yet. He was dizzy, exhausted, his head reeled, he was disoriented. The bells had held sway, and now nothing did, not even himself.

"Sit up, laddo."

The Druid's voice.

Dylan rolled onto his side. Put one palm flat. Pushed up. Sat.

The world tilted, then righted itself.

He looked at Dru. Dru's face—he saw now—was the face of a benevolent angel. Dylan smiled happily.

"Get to your knees."

Dylan did. He felt clear-headed now. His world was balanced. It was the stone beneath his knees, the earth beneath the stone, the support of all. He felt the warmth of Dru's hands on his shoulders. They were face-to-face, on their knees.

"Laddo, is your mind empty now? Like a cup with milk all spilled?"

"Aye, emptier than empty," said Dylan, chuckling.

"Everything?" pressed Dru. "Education, tradition, religion, civilization—everything?"

"Aye, more than everything," answered Dylan. He could still feel the stupendous vibration of the bells singing in his mind.

"In this state of emptiness will you consent to become a Welsh Indian?" His tone was both mocking and solemn.

"What . . . ?"

"Ask not, laddo. Surrender."

"Aye," said Dylan giddily, "I surrender."

"As a Welsh Indian you must undertake to seek the one true grail, life. Do you accept this quest?"

"Aye," said Dylan.

"Do you accept me as your guide?"

"Yes," said Dylan.

"Will you go adventuring with me into the vast wilds, or if the call comes, to the ends of the earth?"

Dylan looked the Druid in the eyes. "I will."

"Casting aside all obligations, all ties, all previous promises, all preconceptions, all beliefs, all old ways, will you seek the grail?"

Dylan straightened, looked solemnly at Dru. "Yes."

"As a sign that you are a new man," said Dru, "I strip you of your old name." His eyes were merry. "Sod Campbell." He took out his belt knife and laid it on Dylan's shoulder. "You will earn names aplenty, but first you will lose one. Now you must be known as Dylan Elfed Davies." He touched his knife to the other shoulder.

"Rise, Sir Dylan," he said stentoriously, "and go forth to adventure."

Dylan stood up unsteadily, stumbled forward, grabbed Dru and embraced him.

Dru hugged him back.

When they moved apart, Dylan asked, "Where next, my guide?"

"You, laddo," replied Dru, "are going into the wilds like a good Welsh Injun."

"The wilds."

"You are a Nor'Wester now."

Part Two

JUMPING-OFF PLACE

Six

D ylan couldn't believe himself. He was thigh deep
in the coldest water he'd ever imagined. It made
his knee bones ache.

He had his strength more or less into the cordelle, a
braided rope sixty feet long. He and Dru were dragging a
canoe gear and trade goods, and a full-sized human being
in the boat. They were cordelling up the stream because
the water was too swift and too rough for paddling.

Insane—when it's too tough to paddle, you wade.
Against the current, on a slippery bottom, with ice still lining the banks. Fall and you become an iceberg.

"Heave!" Dru shouted back at him over the roar of
water. Then something about "lose it."

Lose what, our lives? Dylan heaved mightily and re-
sentfully.

One foot slipped and he went down hard.

He inhaled water. Bloody hell! He snorted it out hard
and shook his head violently.

Now he was wet to his head. Not that he had any
clothes to get wet, not to speak of. Dylan went like the
others, in a cotton shirt, deerskin breechcloth, and moccasins. He was freezing now, and his nipples felt like
spikes.

He heard a kind of chanting from the boat, echoed
and fractured by the roar of water. Saga—the bastard Saga
was singing while he and Dru heaved their guts out. Dru
said Saga had to stay in the boat—you needed a steersman

to keep the bow off the bank. Well, next time Dylan Davies would bloody well get to ride while the others slaved.
Bloody well.

They were eating *sagamité*. Again. Dylan couldn't believe it. They'd had *sagamité* for every meal since they left Montreal. He'd lost track of the days, but it was more than a week—nearly two weeks, he guessed.

When Dru handed out the *sagamité* the first night, Dylan thought the old man was just muddling through because they'd had such a long day. Dylan fell asleep before they ate anyway, so he didn't taste it. Until an hour before dawn, when they had it again, cold. A taste like corn, sort of, texture like pudding. Tolerable. When Dru served it up that night, Dylan began to wonder, and decided Dru was testing him. He refused to complain until the sixth or seventh or whatever night, and then he complained bitterly.

Which made Saga laugh at him. That was the first time Saga had laughed or otherwise indicated he had human responses, like a sense of humor. Saga was tickled at his protest, Dru explained. Saga's name, the old man went on, was not what you might think, a word meaning a long, episodic, heroic tale. It was a short version of *sagamité*. Because he loved the stuff. "He thinks it's ambrosia," said Dru, "manna from heaven. He complains when we get to Montreal and he has to eat their cooking."

Dylan wasn't sure that Saga was tickled. He didn't think the half-breed was human enough to be tickled. He could smile angelically, maybe, but not be tickled.

Saga was beautiful, perfect, beyond the human, like a statue. He was of medium height, slender, supple as a teenager, though he was surely older than Dylan. He had black hair streaked with auburn, delicate-looking hands, and an exquisite face. He might have been an elf, or one of the six-winged angels called seraphim. Only his musculature, his eyes, and his complexion made him seem one of the earth. His muscles were hard and strong, as you could see when he lifted the heavy bundles. His eyes were restless, flitting everywhere constantly, never still. His skin was Indian-dark, and somehow that changed everything.

He could have been one of the seraphim, but he looked like a devil.

He had one more peculiarity. He didn't speak to Dylan. He talked to Dru past Dylan, around Dylan, over Dylan, and through Dylan, but he didn't talk to Dylan. And the Druid acted like he didn't notice.

It therefore annoyed Dylan that they always spoke French. Saga's French was excellent, said Dru, but his English was hit-and-miss. Fortunately, Dylan had spoken French *en famille* almost from infancy. The servants were all French-speaking. Saga's French, though, felt like a gesture of shutting Dylan out.

Dru explained *sagamité*. It was corn boiled to mush in lye water, usually served with chunks of salt pork, or small game or fish, thrown in. Since they didn't have any salt pork, and didn't have time to hunt or fish, Dru joked that Dylan Davies hadn't even earned the mocking term the real Nor'Westers gave the hirelings who paddled the big company canoes and lived on *sagamité—mangeurs de lard,* pork eaters.

Dylan wasn't a *mangeur de lard* anyway, said Dru. He was a Welsh Indian.

My arse, thought Dylan, saying nothing.

The Nor'West Company fed the canoe men east of the depot on *sagamité* almost exclusively. It was cheap because the Saulteur Indians around Lake Superior grew the corn and traded it willingly. It was easily available. It didn't spoil. It was nourishing enough to keep the men working sixteen hours a day. And the *voyageurs*, as Dru put it, were too heroic to complain.

Too dumb to complain, thought Dylan.

Dru was full of stories of the heroism of the Nor'Westers. They could paddle, cordelle, and portage sixteen hours a day, singing lustily all the while. They could make a canoe swim up a rapid like a fish. They could whip grizzly bears one-handed, take on their weight in wolverines, and satisfy a covey of Indian women without getting tired.

Sometimes Dru told epic stories about canoe races on the lakes. It seemed the Nor'West men loved to outpaddle the men of the Hudson's Bay Company. The Nor'Westers had bigger canoes with more weight per paddle, but that just made them more avid. They went to it with a fine, high will, and a penalty was supposed to await the first guide who lost a race to the Englishmen: His head would be the new prow ornament.

Dru spun one about a monumental race between several boats of each company on a big lake. The *voyageurs* paddled all day with one Nor'West outfit only slightly ahead. Then all that moonlit night without a rest—same result. Then all the next day without a rest. Still the Nor'West men in front. Toward evening, as they were making a final sprint for the depot, one Hudson Bay man got so exhausted, he passed out and fell into the lake. Two Nor'West canoes and two from his own company passed him by—they wanted to win. The last boat in the race, an undermanned Nor'West craft, took pity on the drowning man and picked him up.

The rivalry between the two companies was sharp in every way. Sharp and treacherous and sometimes bloody, Dru said. Men had killed each other, less from wanting more furs than from hatred.

It took Dylan some time to figure out why the men of the two companies despised each other. Hudson's Bay was a hoity-toity outfit, supposedly given all of the country draining into Hudson's Bay as a grant from the British king. Who had no right to grant it, according to the French. So they opposed this Honourable Company with their own outfits. Where it used its vast financial resources, they used their wit and pluck. Where it moved magisterially, they moved fast and first. Where it had legal rights, they were outlaws.

They loved it. They made close connections with the Indians, learned the languages and the ways, even married Indian women, had savage children. Meanwhile the British maintained their air of superiority, forbade their men to mingle unnecessarily with the savages, and proposed that the Indians should adopt white ways.

The French had one huge advantage. The British had to wait for instructions from London. Ships had to cross the Atlantic, and stockholders supreme in ignorance had to vote. The French, though, were on the scene. They were individual entrepreneurs, unorganized but bold. They knew the country, the forests, the streams, the Indians. They could do the right thing and beat the British to it. They pushed farther and farther into the wilderness. The best the bloody British could do was follow them a year or two later and build a fort nearby.

When England took over Canada, the competition only got hotter. Scots came to Montreal with their capital and their spirit and their daring, and organized the French outfits into the NorthWest Company to compete with HBC more sharply than ever. And whipped them, just as the French had when they were on their own.

Dru and Saga were Nor'West men. They laughed at the pretensions of the HBC fellows. Stuffed shirts. Copycats. Cowards. Ignoramuses. Prudes. And worse. Thieves and murderers, said Saga darkly. Pretending to speak to Dru, not Dylan.

So Dylan Davies would be a Nor'Wester as well as a Welsh Indian. And if he wanted to be a real Nor'Wester, to stay in the country known as the *pays sauvage*, the wild country, or the *pays d'en haut*, the high country, said Dru, he must learn to like *sagamité*, and maybe even Saga.

"Dylan Davies," Dru always called him now, to remind Dylan that when they signed him up with the North-West Company in Montreal, they'd left off his last name and changed the spelling of his middle one. To make it harder for his father to trace him, the Druid said. Besides, among the Welsh, *Davis* and *Davies* were all the same name.

Dylan liked his new name fine. But most days, after spending sixteen hours bending his back to the paddle, a miserable, quick meal of *sagamité*, a short sleep, and another miserable, quick meal of the stuff before dawn, he didn't like Morgan Griffiths Morgan Bleddyn much at all.

They sang tirelessly. They sang flying downstream, they sang laboring upstream, they sang in the rain and the sunshine, they sang when they were happy and when they were miserable. They sang when Dylan didn't feel like it.

Saga, who seldom talked, and never to Dylan, never got tired of singing.

Dylan thought the songs were strange. The lyrics of this original song, for instance, were delicate, refined, beautiful:

> *À la claire fontaine*
> *M'en allant promener,*
> *J'ai trouvé l'eau si belle*
> *Que je m'y suis baigné.*
> > *Il y a longtemps que je t'aime,*
> > *Jamais je ne t'oublierai.*

Even in English it was romantic:

> At the clear fountain
> As I strolled by,
> I saw the water was exquisite
> And dipped myself in it.
> > I've loved you so long—
> > I will never forget you.

Sometimes they sang it as beautiful and sentimental. Other times it came out bawdy. Dipping yourself did not mean bathing, and loving the lass "so long" meant not a state of the heart but a feat of the loins.

Lots of the songs had double entendres, and some of them were downright obscene. Dylan was glad Father Quesnel couldn't hear him singing them. And if Dylan didn't sing, Dru jokingly splashed icy water on him with the paddle. Then he apologized insincerely, and said that singing kept the stroke going strong, emphasizing "stroke" in a vulgar way.

When they weren't singing, they amused themselves by telling Dylan lascivious stories about Indian women. Dylan would do what every newcomer to the interior did at first, *oui,* they said, rut like a rabbit. The Indian girls were free until they married, and they did as they pleased. Behind any handy bush. Or without bothering with a bush. They did things white women wouldn't do, they surely would. It was all perfectly normal among them, not even needing discretion.

And the married women? Their husbands would lend them for a trifle, a few beads, perhaps. Not quite as pretty as the young maids, true, but more clever.

All the talk did what Dru surely intended—kept Dylan hot and bothered. So Dylan asked *le bon Dieu,* as Dru called Him all too casually, for strength of spirit. A man was not a beast. A man did not behave like a rabbit, or any other wild creature. The hallmark of a man was that he was civilized. He did not go naked. He did not sleep in holes in the ground. He did not eat his own young. He did not lie with his daughters, or his neighbor's wife, or any other female casually—did not rut. He sought God-given love to elevate his baser feelings, and in the absence of that feeling, he abstained from sex. He did these things because he had a soul, and knew it was holy.

All these things Dylan told himself—firmly.

And Dylan would go even further. He would allow his love only paternal and fraternal expression. For he meant to come back here one day as a missionary, and it would not be right to indulge himself carnally with a people he intended to save from carnal indulgence.

This abstinence would be difficult. Dru had told him that the Indians thought one of the funniest things about blackrobes was their celibacy. So they might think the celibacy of a vigorous unmarried young man who was not a priest still funnier, or perhaps repellent. Strength of spirit would be required.

Particular strength of spirit because, God help him, he wanted it. He didn't want to die without feeling what sex was like. He was imagining the feeling with every rhythmic stroke of the paddle. And then his mates would come up with another bawdy lyric about the thrust. . . .

The end of it all was that he knew he wanted to taste sex before he took the cloth. It was not a sin that would put him beyond God's love. He would confess it when he next saw a priest. But he would not permit himself that weakness here, not in front of the people whose souls he intended to save.

* * *

Despite the singing, the trip out was brutal. They had started ahead of the big freight canoes, the *canots de maître* the company sent to the great June rendezvous every year. It had been a warm winter, and the streams were mostly free of ice. Besides, Dru had dispatches to deliver along the way, one of them well off the route. Dylan didn't understand the Druid's place in the NorthWest Company, but it was unconventional. For instance, he and Saga often snowshoed to Montreal in the winter, when the rivers were frozen, and only the most experienced men, *les bons hommes,* could dare that. And Dru was bloody well mysterious about his dispatches.

Since Dylan was a novice, they made him the *milieu,* the paddler in the middle. That's where they always put the new men, Dru said. The *avant*—front paddler and guide—was Dru, and the *gouvernail*—steersman—was the damned half-breed. Up toward a thousand miles into the *pays d'en haut,* and Saga still hadn't spoken a word to Dylan.

Not that there had been time to talk. The canoe road had been mostly upstream. Often up rapids and waterfalls. Or down them, which was even more dangerous.

The canoes of the NorthWest Company that were headed for the bit interior depot, Fort William, the center of the company's operations on Lake Superior, went up the Ottawa River from Montreal, through a network of rivers and lakes to Georgian Bay, across the bay—Dylan's first look at what the French called the sweetwater seas—along the northern edge of Lake Huron, and across the entire northern shore of Superior to the depot.

You not only paddled the canoe against the current, you poled it. Sometimes you cordelled it (pulled it with a long rope). When things got really tough—because there were big rapids, or you had to cross a divide—you portaged.

Dru told Dylan these portages were easy, laughably easy, because the outfit bore almost no freight. They seemed unpleasant enough to Dylan. The three of them beached the canoe, unloaded the four bundles, or *pièces,* of goods they were taking along, and then loaded up Saga—two bundles packed on his hips and held in place by a tumpline across his forehead, 180 pounds of weight altogether. Saga just grunted and moved out—at a trot. Dru and Dylan put the canoe upright, not bottom up, on their shoulders and followed him. Then Dylan and Dru went back and hauled the other two *pièces,* one each to make it easy on a beginner like Dylan, said Dru.

It was done quickly but not easily, because Dru and Saga portaged at a pace full of fury, for reasons that were never explained. At the far end of the portage they'd get seated, Dru would mutter something about Dylan having it too easy, and push off.

They worked like brutes every day. They moved the canoe—paddling, poling, cordelling, portaging—from daylight to dusk. As they came into the longest days of the year, this meant sixteen hours a day. The only respite was a stop every hour for a pipe. And a little time at dawn and sunset, for the wretched *sagamité.*

If Dylan had come to the wilds for freedom, this seemed more like slavery.

"Where are we going?" he asked.

"After the grail," replied the Druid.

Dylan couldn't remember what grail he'd pledged to pursue.

Dylan staggered sideways. He lurched into a birch tree, and it propped him up before he could fall to the ground. He sank to his knees.

He had never felt so awful in his life. His legs were shaking. Not just quivering, actually shaking. He was grateful to be on his knees, so they couldn't clatter against each other.

His back ached. His neck was screaming at him. He eased his head back against the tumpline, but it followed him, and that made pain shoot up his neck at a new angle.

He cursed the two ninety-pound *pièces* strapped onto his back. He cursed portaging. He cursed the distance he'd come, slowly and painfully, across the path, the rocks, the duff, the muskeg of the portage. He cursed the stumbles, the rocks that hurt his feet, the mud that sucked at his moccasins, and most of all the steepness of the route—not only the climbs, which strained his legs mightily, but the parts that looked flat and were uphill, and especially the parts that were downhill and made his thighs labor to keep man and burden from rollicking down the trail.

If only he could fall and roll like a rock to the end of the portage.

He cursed the cache they'd raised, which made four extra *pièces* of ninety pounds each. He cursed the Nor'Westers who invented this so-called heroic tradition—to either make pork eaters into real men, *hommes du nord,* or break them. He saved his most bitter curses for those said to carry three of these *pièces,* 270 pounds, to show off. He profaned the tradition of running portages at a trot, fully loaded. He swore at the NorthWest Company. He blasphemed the Hudson's Bay Company, which made this tactic necessary. He cursed the Welsh Indians, if this was their lot, and the High Missouri, wherever it was. He cursed the fur trade itself.

Most particularly and bitterly he cursed his mentor, Morgan Griffiths Morgan Bleddyn, who claimed to think this test was good for him, and maybe even thought it was funny.

He wanted to fail it. He wanted to go home. He wanted to eat his favorite dessert, syallabub, instead of *sagamité*. He wanted Claude and their rooms. He wanted a book to read. He even wanted the bank, and Mr. MacDonald. He wanted his father.

No, goddamn it, as a matter of fact, his father was what he didn't want. He was Dylan Davies now, and proud of it.

He looked around. Time to do it. He got from his knees onto one foot, then the other, leaned his burden against the tree and pushed.

Nothing. He couldn't get the rest of the way up.

Dylan fought back tears. He would become a real Nor'Wester.

He centered his burden, the *pièces,* carefully on the tree. He squirmed his feet back under his bottom. He squeezed his thighs encouragingly with his hands.

Now. He groaned as he pushed—a ferocious moment of pushing.

Nothing.

Idea. He would inchworm his way up the tree—first his bottom, then the top of the *pièces*.

Bottom against tree—it worked. Felt like a corncob, but it worked. Now the top *pièce*. He arched far back. Got the right angle. Pushed.

Lost his balance. Pitched sideways. Toppled onto his face.

He couldn't breathe. He tried to suck and drew nothing. Desperate, he turned his face to the side, out of the damp muck of the leaves. Still nothing. He tried to draw in sweet air—wasn't there a sky full of air?—and got nothing.

Then, suddenly, his lungs heaved, and shuddered, and filled.

Tears came.

Lying in the muck, he wiped his face, and his hand came away bloody.

He bled and cried lava flows into the fetid and fecund turf.

Something touched his shoulder.

He wrenched his body to roll over and went nowhere. The *pièces* lay on him like boulders, crushing him.

He twisted his head sideways. Saga was poking him with a knife.

So Saga was heading back for his second trip already. Dylan told himself that the knife meant nothing, it was just one of Saga's standoffish ways. The half-breed didn't shake hands either. Or talk to him.

Dylan dry-heaved.

He wanted to die.

Dylan sobbed. He beat the earth with his fists.

Saga slipped the tumpline off Dylan's forehead. He rolled the *pièces* off onto the ground. He sat back on his haunches and watched Dylan.

What a strange Englishman, thought Saga. His people called all white people Frenchmen, but this was an En-

glishman. Not a bad fellow, really. Eager, good-spirited,
willing to learn. Then moody sometimes. And now self-
pitying.

Saga felt not quite right in the way he was treating
this stranger, not talking to him. But the stranger wouldn't
accept that he was a stranger. He wanted to be a comrade
from the start. He didn't know the distance that must lie
between a Métis, any Métis man, and an Englishman. He
didn't know about the longtime enmity. He assumed too
much.

And there was the matter of Dru's attitude toward this
Englishman. Saga remembered once standing in that gar-
den with Dru and looking through the windows at this
Dylan, this . . . Dru had acted foolish over him.

Saga did not feel foolish. Monsieur Dylan Davies
would have to earn his way, all of it. And if Saga's silence
bothered him, well, there was something for him to learn
in it.

For now, though, the Englishman needed a hand.

For long moments Dylan lay still. He refused to look
up at the half-breed. It seemed unbearable to accept a
kindness from a man who didn't even talk to you. Finally,
Dylan rolled onto his side and drew his legs to his chest.
Then he sat up. Looked Saga in the eyes.

Amused. The bastard's eyes looked amused.

Saga lit his little white clay pipe, puffed, and watched
Dylan. He didn't offer a smoke.

Dylan brushed himself off. He stood up. He had no
idea what he would do now. He'd failed.

He heard the scraping of canvas.

Saga stood there with the *pièces* in his arms and a
quizzical look on his face. No one lifted 180 pounds easily, but Saga had done it in a matter-of-fact way.

Dylan submitted to his fate. He turned his back to
Saga and accepted the weight of the bundle on his hips
and shoulders, the pull of the tumpline on his forehead.

Without a word he turned down the trail, ordering his
legs not to collapse, at least until he was out of sight of
Saga, who was sitting there, puffing his pipe contentedly.

Dylan thought, I'm going to die before I make half of the first trip. On my gravestone, a miserable wooden slab, they'll write with a burnt stick, "Not a true Nor'Wester."

Then Dylan realized. The bastard Saga still hadn't spoken to him.

Upstream, downstream, across lakes no one had ever heard of, every which way Dylan could imagine, off the regular canoe highway, for reasons Dylan didn't know. Twice they stopped near forts somewhere, Dylan had no idea where. He and Saga would stay in camp several miles from the fort while Dru went in to talk to someone. He never said who, or why, or what he told them. It was the bloody war with HBC, but that's all Dylan knew.

HBC had a prior claim on nearly everything, it seemed. Some king long dead had made things difficult for everyone by giving the company a grant of all the land which drained into Hudson's Bay, which the nabob couldn't even point to on a map. So the Nor'Westers were intruders, if the grant was valid.

Which according to the Nor'Westers, it wasn't. We French were in all this country before you bloody British heard of it, they claimed, and even beyond into Athabasca, so we have prior rights.

But, said the Hudson Bay men, you Nor'Westers are mere pedlars, chasers after money, while we British have a noble and imperial vision.

Bloody hell, said the Nor'Westers, we know the Indians, we understand them—hell, we *are* them. You want to make them into proper little lords and ladies.

And so it went. Each company resented the other, fought bitterly for the furs, competed with maniacal intensity. The HBC, though, didn't have the expertise of the Nor'Westers—the knowledge of the country, of the Indians, their languages and ways. Nor did they have the enterprise. So they always followed the Nor'West men into new country and set up a post a mile or so away. Imitators and leeches, the Nor'Westers called them.

Habitually, and gleefully, the outfits bribed Indians loyal to the other. When convenient, they stole from each other. Occasionally, they murdered. Sometimes they took each other's forts by force of arms. Once in a while, hypocritically, they got warrants and arrested each other for these various crimes.

So what messages was Dru delivering? He wouldn't tell. Just wartime intelligence, he murmured.

He got Dylan utterly lost. All Dylan knew was that they were somewhere in Rupert's Land, the vast area of fine fur country in the watershed of Hudson's Bay. He didn't know where within two hundred miles. All he really knew was that he wanted to stop paddling.

"Top o' the mornin' to ye."

It was the Druid, grinning at him and beaming at him with his lamp of an eye.

Then he saw what was wrong. It *was* morning, not night, and he was waking in the light, for a change. Dru had let them all sleep in.

It didn't mean much to Dylan. He was always exhausted. Always thirsty. Always hungry. He felt needy in ways he hadn't known he could need. And he was continually humiliated by his weakness on all the portages. Saga never mentioned it. He only smiled, mockingly. Dylan looked often at the scalp dangling from his sash, and wondered why on earth he kept it. It made the crown of his head itch.

"I said, 'Top o' the mornin' to ye,' " repeated Dru. A Welshman acting the Irishman. Dru had many faces, many roles, many guises, which he interchanged playfully. One of his games was keeping information to himself—any information, like where they were going, and where the High Missouri was.

"Bottom of the universe up yours," replied Dylan indifferently. Right now he didn't feel like playing.

Dru chuckled warmly and clapped Dylan on his blanketed shoulder.

"I've got a surprise for you," he said.

"I need a drink and a thousand harem girls to fan me and rub oil on my aching body," murmured Dylan. He could barely get the words out.

I must not think of women carnally.

Dru lit up. "Well, that might be possible. I do have high wine stashed upstream ten more miles. But first you have to get there and meet my family."

"Your *what*?"

"My family," Dru repeated. "At the village above. I'm your familiar spirit, but I'm Anastasie's mate."

Chapter
Seven

There was almost no current against them. Though Dylan barely dipped his paddle in the water, the couple of miles went quickly. He was thinking, You never know with Dru. As you never know he has a family until he drops it casually.

They pulled the canoe onto a beach near some wigwams. No people ran to greet them, but scores of dogs did.

Dru waved to someone—some women—and left Saga and Dylan to bring the loads. If Dru expressed eagerness to see his family, it was only in the spring of his step.

It was a birchbark wigwam on the edge of the Indian camp. Dru's people were apparently three women, who were moving around an outdoor fire, cooking.

Before Dru could offer any introductions, Dylan sagged to the ground, got out of the *pièce*, and collapsed full length on the earth. Dru grinned.

Women were present. Dylan felt a little self-conscious about his clothes. He had gotten used to shirt, breechcloth, and moccasins on the canoe road, with just Dru and Saga. But now, in a sort of society, they seemed silly.

The oldest woman handed Dylan a wooden bowl full of stew and a metal spoon. "I'm Anastasie," she said with a smile.

He liked her immediately. She was a handsome woman in her forties, striking in a plain, strong way. She was tall, taller than Dru or himself, with an athletic-looking body. She looked him in the eye with the confidence and directness of a man. Though she was light-skinned, gray-eyed, and had rusty hair streaked with gray, an Indian facial structure shone beneath the white-man features—strong bones, wide nose, and wide cheeks.

Dylan ate lying stretched out. It was some sort of meat and something they called wild rice in a thick, pungent gravy. Eating it felt like swigging a magic potion. He could feel relief flowing into his legs, making them tingle. Into his back, into the muscles of his neck, into his arms, even into his fingers.

Anastasie filled his bowl again, and Dru's and Saga's bowls.

Now the women sat on the ground and ate.

Dylan rested his cheek on the ground. He noticed how cool and delicious it felt.

He woke up a little. Hands, strong hands on his neck.

"You need to learn not to strain your head forward into the tumpline," said Dru. He was squatting near Dylan's head. Dylan didn't know what the hell he was talking about.

Weight on his ass. Hips—human being sitting on him. He turned his head and looked back. A glimpse of face.

One of the strong hands pushed his face back down.

Female human being, tickled at him.

"You haven't been introduced to my sister Marguerite," said Anastasie's voice.

"Sister in the Cree manner," put in Dru, "cousin in the white way."

Dylan crooked his head to look at her.

Marguerite pushed his head down again. "Lie still and enjoy," she said. Her hands moved under his shirt to the muscles between his neck and shoulders. They felt strong, understanding, altogether wonderful.

Down onto his back. Onto his side ribs.

Onto his ass.

"Whoa!" said Dylan, wriggling. The breechcloth left most of his ass bare.

Dru stayed him with a hand on the back. "Let her do it," he said. "It's her way, and it will help you."

Against his better judgment, Dylan tried to relax. Did relax—he was so tired, and it felt so sweet.

Marguerite turned around and sat backward on his ass. He was aware as she sat down that she was not slender. Her hands felt good on the backs of his thighs, the outside of his thighs—the inside of his bare thighs.

He squirmed.

Marguerite thumped her hips into him. "Be still," she ordered.

He lay there and got rubbed. And lay there. And turned over on command. And permitted the front of his thighs to be rubbed, and his arms, and his chest, even his nipples, and finally his forehead and the small areas around his eyeballs. There Marguerite's fingers found painful pockets of tension, and worked little miracles. So sweet.

Finally she lifted off him. Dru offered him a hand to sit up. Dylan could have sworn Marguerite looked at him lecherously. She handed him a cup.

"High wine," said Dru. "Drink it, and we'll have a smoke."

Dru loaned Dylan a pipe, a small white clay affair like the one the old man kept tucked through the pouch around his neck, what he called his *gâge d'amour*. Just kinnikinnick, he said, not proper tobacco like they would get in the *régales* at Fort William. That fort on Lake Superior, Dylan knew, was the center of the NorthWest Company's operations in the wilderness. Dru and Saga kept talking about the tobacco, the food, brandy, and other grandeurs available there.

They lit the pipes with embers from the fire and puffed silently for a while, and had nips of the high wine, a fancy word for trade alcohol mixed with creek water.

The women moved around doing small chores and then gathered close. Dylan had trouble keeping his eyes off Marguerite—her hands had made him feel all foolish. She kept smiling like she had a secret.

I must not think of Indian women carnally.

"Sarah," said Dru without getting up, "this is my

friend Dylan Elfed Davies, a pilgrim, Welsh Indian, and seeker of the grail. Dylan, this is Lady Sarah, Saga's wife." Out of some obscure need, Dylan stood. As he inclined his head to her, he nearly toppled over. Dru gave him a hand back to the ground. Lady Sarah looked nothing like a lady. She was short, plump, and bulldog-faced. Her habitual expression seemed to be a sensual smirk. She gave the introduction only the faintest acknowledgment.

"And these good people all together"—his arm embraced Anastasie, her cousin Marguerite, Saga, and Lady Sarah—"are my family *sauvage.*" One of the secrets, Dylan thought, you like to keep as long as you can.

"The women are more or less Cree. Children, far back, of French-Canadian fathers and women of the country. Now children simply of the country, half savages. Half may not be enough." He laughed at his little witticism.

"They travel with us sometimes, and live here sometimes, and sometimes at Fort William, usually with the Crees. Saga is a Red River breed." Dylan didn't dare ask what that was. "They are not Welsh Indians," Dru said.

"Where are the Welsh Indians?" Dylan asked once more. From what Dylan could gather, no one but Dru had even heard of them.

"I will say this much: the dreaming Celtic eye is here upon this continent. In these lands men breathe in vision with the very air."

Dylan interrupted. "What do you mean, 'the dreaming Celtic eye'?" Sometimes he got impatient with Dru's Celtic mysticism. He wanted to sleep.

Now Dru turned the lamp eye on him. It made Dylan nervous—he always felt ridiculously exposed by that eye. Tonight he had inebriation to reveal. The day's hard work had left him not a spiritual creature, not intellectual, not emotional, but physical alone, and half drunk.

"I'm sorry you do not know," the Druid said slowly. "They do not teach such things at the Collège de Montreal, do they? No, they teach that the universe is a clock, ingeniously devised by God, ticking away in perfect, natural order. Hah-hah!" He wagged a finger at Dylan. "The Druid has heard a thing or two."

Dru got serious. "Well, it won't wash, this mechanical world. For it has blood and breath in it, lad, and even spirit. The dreaming eye lets you see that."

He tapped out his pipe and refilled it. "No man can explain the dreaming eye, but every man can find it within himself. Let me tell you a story."

He raised his voice into a songlike narrative:

"A midwife of Llangwrog in Gwynedd, Meg of name, was shopping at the market in Caernarfon. A tall and handsome stranger approached her there. 'Come quickly,' said he, 'my wife is about to deliver a child.' The stranger put Meg up behind him on a splendid black stallion, and away they galloped, swift as the wind.

"Through a dark wood they rode, to the top of a ridge, and there it stood—a grand castle, handsome and glittering. In the castle in a beautiful chamber lay a lovely woman on a fine four-poster bed, near her time. And presently she brought forth a gorgeous boy child.

" 'Here,' said the handsome man, handing Meg a vial. 'Rub this ointment on the child's eyes, but make sure it doesn't touch your own.'

"Rubbing the ointment in, Meg blundered—she got a speck of it into her right eye. Instantly everything was different—the castle was a hovel, the bed a pile of rushes, and the lovely woman was only Myfawnwy, a poor woman of the town.

"Terrified, Meg let out a chilling scream and ran for her life—out of the hovel, over the ridge, through the dark wood. She never slowed down until she was home in Llangwrog.

"Months later she suddenly saw the man again, at the market. Boldly, she went up and asked him, 'How is Myfawnwy?'

" 'She is well,' he replied. 'Tell me, which eye are you seeing me with?'

" 'The right eye,' answered Meg.

"Without a word the man raised his walking stick and poked the eye out."

The Druid chuckled to himself, and studied Dylan.

Dylan thought the story was dumb.

*   *   *

"Your bed is laid in the trees," said Anastasie. "Marguerite will show you."

Marguerite took Dylan's hand to lead him through the darkness. The night was filled with moon shadows. Light and dark played on the new grass and on the shimmering leaves of the birches. All was elusive, mysterious, perhaps frightening.

Everyone else seemed to be sleeping in the wigwam, he thought—why am I alone exiled to the trees?

He was a little unsteady from the high wine, and needed Marguerite's hand. Her flesh felt pleasant. *I must not think of Indian women carnally.*

It was a low lean-to of canvas, nestled in a grove. Marguerite led him close, let go his hand, and lit the candle lantern hanging from a pole. The light shone warm and yellow on the interior of the lean-to. It struck him as picturesque—cool, white moonlight dancing on a world of darkness, and in the middle of it the warm, yellow light on his bed place.

His blankets were laid out. Beneath them were a buffalo robe and more blankets. Perhaps Marguerite's blankets.

She gave a chuckle, low and affectionate.

She put her arms on his waist and gave a playful tug.

Dylan lurched and stumbled. She pulled him and held him and swung him down before he knew it, flat on his back on the blankets.

She straddled him at the hips again, pinning him, and reached for the buttons on his shirt.

Dylan felt something take hold of him from inside. His hips lurched sideways—it didn't feel like he was doing it, the hips just took over. His arms pushed Marguerite the rest of the way off him.

"No," he said softly, "I can't." He meant it—he couldn't. It wasn't a choice. Holy Mary Mother of God, he said to himself, a twenty-two-year-old virgin. He didn't know whether the name of the virgin was spoken as an oath or in reverence.

Marguerite cocked her head, looking at him appraisingly. She seemed to decide to take it lightly. "Funny

Frenchman," she said, and pinched his cheek. Then she
was up and off into the darkness.

He turned and lay on his side and stared into the
moon shadows. A strange world, moon shadows, where
nothing was solid, all shapes were shifting, objects became
phantoms and phantoms objects. "Holy Mary Mother of
God," he murmured faintly.

He had a dream—or maybe it wasn't a dream—he
thought his eyes were open, and he was seeing a fantasy.
He was at the bottom of a lake in winter, when it was frozen, swimming around with a family of beavers. He could
breathe perfectly, and felt content enough, except that he
was cold—not painfully, terminally cold, just chill, sometimes miserably chill. The beavers could go into their
lodge, but for some reason he couldn't. Then he noticed
that they were going up out of the lake. He saw that the
ice had melted, and a world was half visible beyond the
surface. The beavers went into this world and built dams
and ate and played. For some reason, he couldn't go. He
might go, but he was afraid to. The world out there, he
knew, was brightly lit, and you could even feel the warmth
of the sun, like melted butter on your skin. Down here everything was tinted aquamarine, half lit, and half cold—
chill, chill, chill.

Chapter
Eight

Dylan was standing where, all his life, he had wanted to be. They called it simply the depot. It was the wilderness center of operations for the NorthWest Company. A thousand miles deep into the *pays sauvage*. Even a gray June day couldn't keep it from glistening, not in his eyes.

True, his fantasy had been different—he had dreamed of wearing a black robe. He had dreamed of coming as a savior, not an adventurer. Nevertheless, to be here was the fulfillment of a dream.

Though he wasn't wearing a black robe, he was handsomely decked out. Dru had helped him get outfitted at the company headquarters in Montreal, and today, for the first time, he was wearing his finest country clothing. Though it was also almost his only covering, it was fine—cap of knit wool against the cool evening, cloth shirt with pleats and drop shoulders, drop-front pants of a homespun wool called *étoffe du pays*—they had belled legs and were helped up by braces—moccasins made by Marguerite, and a splendid, colorful sash to give it that *je ne sais quois*.

He felt grand. He was sashaying out into the society of the NorthWest Company's depot, all the half-breed wives and children and *les sauvages,* and he was looking fine. Maybe he was only a *mangeur de lard* now, a fellow just out from the city, with no real time in the interior, no knowledge, and no ties, but he intended to fix himself today toward becoming a *hivernant,* the canoemen's term for a fellow who had passed a winter in this remote country, an initiate, an experienced man. Which would give him the right to strut.

The depot was no rude wilderness outpost. Forty-two buildings palisaded in a rectangle faced the loading docks near the mouth of the Kaministikwia River and a grand vista of Lake Superior.

Dylan had been busy in camp since they got in this noon, but Dru had told him all about the doings at the depot. Every June the city partners brought trade goods out from Montreal, and the partners who wintered in the *pays d'en haut* brought furs in from the most remote wilds. They did not just exchange goods. They sat and planned how to fling their empire even farther, to stay ahead of the bloody Hudson's Bay Company, which was Here Before Christ and thought it owned North America, and how to twist its tail in the bargain.

They always succeeded, said Dru, not because they had the best plans, but because they had the best men of the wilderness. While the nabobs of Hudson Bay studied maps and developed theories about trading for furs from a boardroom in London, the NorthWest Company's *hommes du nord*—men of the north—knew the land, knew the peoples, knew the ways, knew how to get the furs, knew how to live in wild country. It was an advantage no gentlemen could match.

Dylan had a start on becoming one of these wilderness savants, if only a start. Dru had worked with him on his shooting, though he didn't own a gun yet. His fire-making skills were coming up. His eyes had improved a lot—now he saw the still, silent animals they passed, and knew where other animals hid and where they lived. He had a start on reading sign of man and beast. What he didn't know—didn't have a clue about—were the Indians. An *homme du nord* knew Indians. From this point, the jumping-off place into the real interior, Dylan would begin to learn.

His heart was set on it, and for a special reason. He had come to the wilds to see Indians, get to know them, learn to help them. He had discovered that you couldn't know them without knowing the land they lived on. Their life was a kind of weave, and its threads were, as Dru put it, all the four-legged, winged, crawling, burrowing, swimming, and rooted creatures. The red man, unlike the white man, seemed to Dylan somehow *of* this congregation, intimately part of the weave.

Dru had been teaching him both to understand and appreciate. That was the advantage of being apprenticed to the Druid, the master of woodcraft.

The pleasure was how much Dylan loved the learning. The canoeing had become a kind of idyll for him, hardening the body, yes, and uplifting the spirit. Often, it was learning, seeing with Dru's eyes, listening with his ears. And often it was a sense of blessing, a subtle glory that came to him, especially on the long evenings as they approached the summer solstice. The sun, arcing far to the north, shed a kind of splendor through the long twilight. The water glowed gold, and the air turned a lilac-tinged silver, pearly, liquid, crystalline.

Yes, he was a civilized man, Dylan said to himself as he pushed the canoe gently through evenings like this, and proudly so. Somehow he was a civilized man who belonged here. He felt that, breathed it. And he would show the *hommes du nord* that he belonged.

Now Dylan had an appointment with Duncan Campbell Stewart, one of the wintering partners. He didn't know exactly what the appointment was about—Dru had arranged it. He did know that through it he might get a job that would make him a *hivernant.* Dru warned Dylan that Duncan Campbell Stewart was a man of many prejudices and peculiarities. A Campbell like my father, thought Dylan. He shook the thought off. Campbell was no longer a clan, really, nothing but a name, and not any longer Dylan's name. He wondered what the fellow's peculiarities were.

Dylan walked through the main gate of the depot, between buildings, and into the large quadrangle faced by the main buildings. The big building across the way, he'd been instructed, was the Great Hall. Here, said Dru, the partners lived and dined in absurd luxury.

Dylan entered the Great Hall. A bust scowled at him

from atop a pedestal. Simon McTavish, the first head of the NorthWest Company, said the identifying tablet. Dylan recognized Lord Nelson in a huge portrait, and a painting of the Battle of Trafalgar. Having little feeling for such painting or sculpture, he passed on and knocked at the door on the left. A low, hard-edged voice bade him come in.

Duncan Campbell Stewart stood to an immense height, perhaps an entire foot taller than Dylan. "Welcome, Mr. Davies," he said. He pointed to a chair on the other side of the small Queen Anne writing desk. The room was sumptuously appointed: bed, couch, writing desk, chairs of a luxury that would befit even the elder Mr. MacDonald, and silver candelabra.

This wintering partner, on the other hand, was skeletally slender. He had great, shelving brows, and eyes so deeply recessed as to be invisible. His craggy face made Dylan conscious of bone beneath flesh—he might have been looking at a fleshless skull.

Stewart gave him a dry, lifeless handshake, his fingers like withered stalks, and Dylan sat.

"Now, according to the word Mr. Bleddyn sends, you're looking to become a *hivernant*. He says you're a graduate of the Collège de Montreal, so I'm sure you read and write and figure well."

"Yes, sir. I signed on as a *voyageur* with Mr. Bleddyn, and I want further employment. I am determined not to go back with the *mangeurs de lard.*"

Stewart swiveled the seat of his chair halfway from Dylan, smiled thinly—a skull's smile—and stared at a far wall. Odd to think of this sepulchral figure as a Campbell clansman. Not that his father's side mattered anyway. "Are you? I wonder. I wonder what it is you want in the *pays sauvage.*"

Dylan had no idea how to answer him.

Duncan Campbell Stewart felt curious about this young man. They had no idea, none of the young ones did. "Tell me about yourself."

"My father is a ... merchant, but peddling bores

me." Dylan stopped, and Stewart saw his embarrassment. *Pedlar* was the Hudson's Bay Company insult for a Nor'Wester.

Stewart looked from underneath his brows at Davies. He knew his shadowed eyes made others uncomfortable. "Are you an idealist, then?"

Davies hesitated, then spoke. Stewart was a sophisticated man who would understand. "My first thought was for the priesthood, sir. In the last century the Jesuits were active among these Indians. I wanted . . . I wanted to get that program started again, to be a missionary to this country, to save the souls of these Indians."

God help us, thought Stewart. He said only, "An idealist indeed." He regarded Davies for a long moment. "Do you know what an idealist is, young Mr. Davies?"

"No, sir." Stewart saw that like other youths, Davies hated to be played with this way.

"An architect who designs buildings without water closets. In other words, a man who sees with his dreams instead of his eyes. That can be dangerous in this country *sauvage,* Mr. Davies."

Davies nodded. Polite, anyway, and Stewart meant to take advantage.

"I, too, came here an idealist." He swiveled back toward Davies. "I am a graduate of the University of Edinburgh, Mr. Davies, and of All Souls College, Oxford." Davies looked surprised. He must have thought Oxford was closed to Highlander barbarians.

"My great model was Adam Smith. Have you heard of the late Professor Smith, Mr. Davies?" Stewart raised the dark, craggy eyebrows.

Dylan told himself there was nothing to be intimidated about. "No."

Stewart spoke deliberately. "He taught that trade is the great ameliorating influence of civilized man. Good not only for the economy of men, but for their souls." Stewart gave a short, hacking, humorless laugh, like the grate of chisel on marble. "Naive, Mr. Davies. Naive." Dylan pictured Stewart cutting that word into the marble of Professor Smith's tombstone.

Stewart stared into space. Dylan wondered what

scenes he was seeing, remembering, vast murals of dark, recollected pictures of life in the *pays sauvage*. Scenes that would account for his sepulchral manner. "Professor Smith saw with his dreams. But he was never here to see . . . *actual* Indians, was he?"

Dylan didn't know what to say.

Stewart turned his head, and his darkened eyes to Dylan and spoke gently, in a tone that imitated kindness. "Mr. Davies, I find your company engaging. Will you come in to dinner with me?"

Dru had told him about the extravagant dinners at the Great Hall. Dylan could hardly refuse. Surely Dru and the family wouldn't mind. "With pleasure, Mr. Stewart," he lied.

It was an immense dining room, seating up to two hundred people formally, according to Stewart. He and Dylan were ushered to seats at a table running perpendicular to the head table. Only Montreal partners sat at the head table, said Stewart, "their innocence protected against intimacy with the likes of us wintering partners, who have rubbed shoulders too familiarly with savages." The pecking order was something like Montreal partners, wintering partners, factors, clerks, and guides.

Dylan thought he would hardly be able to hear for the hubbub. The men were in high spirits. They met here only briefly once a year, and celebrated when they had the chance. And these diners, Stewart pointed out, were not the engagés—hired men—out from Montreal or the *hommes du nord* from the remote country. These lived in tents outside the palisades and ate their *sagamité* there, that and pemmican, said Stewart. The diners here were the brains and the power of the NorthWest Company.

The diners fell quiet when the man at the center of the head table, whose name Dylan never did get, stood to propose a toast with the fine West Indian rum before them. "To the Mother of all saints," he intoned. "Hear, hear" rang all around the huge room. The man to that fellow's right then stood and offered, "Up the king." More cries of assent. The man to the left of the fellow proposed, "To the

fur trade in all its branches." And so went the last two
toasts, alternating right and left, "To *voyageurs,* wives, and
children," and "To absent partners." Rousing cheers all
around.

Then, swiftly, the food was served. A filet of lake
trout first, with peas and butter from the fort's farm. Delicious, Dylan thought. Next an entire goose per man, with
a thick gravy and wild rice. Dylan ate only half, because
it seemed too rich. Last a piece of buffalo hump almost the
size of a man's upper arm, with potatoes and parsnips. He
thought he was much too full to do more than sample the
hump, but it was the best meat he'd ever tasted. He stuffed
himself unpleasantly full. Then they brought several des-
serts, mince pie, boiled spotted dick, blancmange, and
pastries, which Dylan didn't even look at. He did take a
cup of tea. All the others ate like trenchermen, and Dylan
wondered how they managed. The only exception he could
see was Stewart, who hardly bothered to eat, but took on
liquor mightily.

A prodigious amount of food altogether, introduced,
washed down, and followed by a more prodigious amount
of spirit. After the rum to start, a bottle of wine per man
with each course, and brandy after. Dylan had not imagined human beings could drink so much. The din grew to
a roar, like the sound of a ravenous pack of beasts, Dylan
thought. He was glad when Stewart suggested they repair
to his rooms. And pleased when he noticed that Stewart,
like himself, walked with the delicate care of the man conscious of inebriation.

Stewart lit one candle, put it well away from them,
and settled into one of his high, straight-backed chairs. He
was the sort of man who would prefer a hard chair to a
comfortable one. He waved Dylan vaguely in the direction
of an opposite chair. He lolled his head back and gave a
loose, easy chuckle. His body was partly lit by the flickering candle, his face in darkness.

"I dare say you've heard a few tales of this wilderness," said Stewart. "And its Indians, oh yes, more than a
few. I'm not interested in the ways in which these . . . fa-

bles are petty lies—stuff of escaping murderous tribesmen, slaying grizzly bears, defeating seven-foot warriors in mortal combat, sighting monsters, all that sort of thing. I'm concerned with the ways in which they mince oh so scrupulously around the truth."

Drunkenly, wildly, Stewart jerked his head forward and at Dylan.

Jarred, Dylan suddenly wondered if he could have seen the man's eyes when his head was back. He had the most uncomfortable feeling about those eyes, a fancy that they were lightless, mere black holes. He still couldn't see them in the wavering candlelight.

"You, however, come to the wilderness to bear the truth and let it shine forth. The truth you uncover in the good, black book." He repeated, "*Black* book," and snorted. "You ask me for a job to send you deep, deep into the heart of darkness that you may illuminate it with your beacon of truth. Foolishly, you do not fear for your soul." He cast a look like a shaft at Dylan.

Now Stewart spoke softly and gently. "You do not understand the nature of darkness." He regarded Dylan sympathetically. "No, you surely do not understand darkness, and what it will do to men.

"I was like you, young Mr. Davies. I brought here an idealist's mind. Once." He lost a moment to memory, or simply to silence. "Oxford by God University, yes, All Souls College."

Stewart brought his mind back to the present. "I wonder if you wish to know." He pondered, then felt himself speak in a tumbling rush. "I shall tell you anyway. I shall give you the last chance to save your soul. You will know the truth, and it will set you free."

The hard, snorting laugh again. "But you do not know what free can mean." Stewart looked into his past—yes, yes, in the name of all devils, it did mesmerize him. He forced himself back to the present. "Free to become . . . what?

"I'm told you know the Cree a little, Mr. Davies. They are hardly Indians. And Mr. Bleddyn's people are half white in their ways, of course. So you know nothing of *Indians*.

"The job I might have for you is at Fort Augustus, near the foot of the Rocky Mountains. To get there you must travel as far from here, Mr. Davies, as you have come from Montreal. And spiritually farther, much, much farther.

"There you find real Indians, young man, not these half-creatures of the eastern and middle wilderness. The Piegans." He chuckled low. "When the Jesuits first came among these half-creature Crees, they too were real Indians, Mr. Davies. And do you know what the Jesuit missionaries felt, so far back there in the seventeenth century, when they looked upon this new, unredeemed continent of the spirit? I commend to you a book named *Relations,* their own account of their insights. It's in our library here, which is surprisingly good. They felt, Mr. Davies, that they were looking into a wilderness of the human spirit. And they saw there the ultimate horror—the human soul untouched by God."

Stewart felt himself shiver. He looked at his hands. He felt his lips move toward rictus. Then he picked up the thought: "It terrified some of those worthy priests, Mr. Davies. It caused crises of faith. It even cost holy men their faith, and their souls.

"They came to light the darkness, and the darkness extinguished their light.

"Lord, I believe," Stewart intoned mockingly, mocking himself especially. "Oh, help thou mine unbelief."

The candle was dimming, and they were sitting in near darkness. Stewart rose, got the candle, lit another one from it and set both candlesticks on the floor on either side of his chair. Dylan was struggling to stay awake. It was very late, and he had difficulty following Stewart's words. Yet he was intrigued by the man's manner. His face was full of . . . Dylan didn't know what.

"Can your idealist's mind imagine what real Indians such as the Piegans are like, Mr. Davies? No, not yet. I must tell you." His voice was still gentle, but tinged with ironic, bitter acceptance.

"I began to know what they are when I saw the

women butchering buffalo. The Piegans are mass slaughterers of buffalo, of course—that's how we get our vast quantities of pemmican; they trade it to us. Their most successful method is to create an open-ended vee from brush, ending upon a cliff. Then they drive the brutes into the vee pell-mell, and they fall over the cliff to their deaths."

Dylan disregarded this account of the Piegans—Stewart was simply describing someone as yet untouched by God's grace. His own interest was not in the story, but the storyteller, Stewart himself, his soul half revealed by the strange face and the soft, uncanny voice.

"One senses that their favorite device, though, is to stampede the creatures into rivers at flood stage. They drive them relentlessly, one after the other, and buffalo are like sheep—they panic and run where the others run. I have seen them, Mr. Davies, so thick in the river that they walked on each other's backs. All being swept downstream, the ones on the bottom merely drowning first. By the end of the day, a man could have walked five miles downriver on buffalo carcasses and scarce have gotten his feet wet.

"They do not even butcher them all. They kill for the love of killing.

"It was one afternoon when I really watched them skinning and butchering that I began to understand. The women do all such work, and do it with relish. I saw scores of them among the carcasses at the bottom of the buffalo jump, up to their elbows in blood and up to their knees in viscera. For a moment I was repulsed, and felt sorry for them. Then I realized that they were exhilarated. Woman after woman would cut off a slice of the liver, dip it in the bile, and eat it, raw. Many would drink the blood, and it ran down their faces and necks and bosoms. Some cut open the stomachs of the great beasts and drank, unaltered, the stomach contents.

"Even that was not the heart of the matter. The truth was, they enjoyed it, relished, gloried in the gore.

"So I was less surprised, later, when I saw the women torture captives.

"Yes, Mr. Davies, women. Nurturers, yea, those who

suckle the children. When warriors of other tribes are captured, or sometimes white men, the women, not the men, become their tormentors. They torture the poor wretches slowly, with unimaginable patience, savoring each infliction of pain. I have seen them stick a dozen long splinters into a man's skin, and light them and watch them burn the flesh. I have seen them flay a human being, bit by bit. I have seen them cut off a man's eyelids, sever a man's penis and stuff it in his mouth. Even I, Mr. Davies, who am the blackest of the black, quail at giving you further details.

"Unto death, of course. But the point is, death can be delayed for days, to augment the savage entertainment." Stewart was silent for a moment, perhaps looking into dark shadows. "I could tell you more."

He regarded Dylan with his lightless eyes. "And what about us, Mr. Davies? Does it matter how one treats such creatures?" Stewart seemed to look down at his hands, then jerked his head up toward Dylan. "But I see I'm a poor storyteller—I've lost your attention. And a poor host—I failed to notice that you're falling asleep." He stood and carried a candle to an alcove.

"You will stay here, of course. It's much too late for you to return to Mr. Bleddyn's camp, and ruffians are about this time of night. I insist. You may use this cot."

Drowsily, Dylan followed toward the cot. He knew he'd fall asleep the moment his head hit the pillow.

"Perhaps you'd like to fold your clothes over that chair," Stewart offered.

Dylan shook his head. He didn't care, he would sleep in them.

Before he laid his head down, though, he wanted to see Stewart's eyes—Dylan felt that he hadn't seen them clearly in all these hours. He peered up toward the tall man. Now Dylan was far below the great shelves of eyebrows, and the candle cast light into the deep recesses.

Strange, very strange. The eyes didn't seem to catch the light, as eyes always do. They were dark, flat, opaque, without life. Empty.

Dylan felt the need to say something, he didn't know what. He must show he'd been paying attention. He stretched out on the cot and closed his eyes. Appeasingly, he asked, "What you discovered, then, is that Indians are beasts, animals without souls, and beyond redemption?"

"No, young Mr. Davies," said Stewart mildly. "They're human. Entirely human."

"Then what is the point?" asked Dylan querulously. As consciousness dimmed, he felt a little annoyed.

"That you discover their darkness in your own heart. But perhaps you must find that out for yourself."

Chapter Nine

"**Y**ou want something to eat?" Dru wore a knowing smile. But what could he know about the phantasmagorical journey Duncan Campbell Stewart had put him through? Dylan wondered.

Were Indians really like that? Did the *women* torture captives? Probably Stewart was mad.

"You want something to eat?" Dru repeated. He was pointing at the inevitable *sagamité*. Maybe the knowing smile was about the way Dylan walked. Every step made loud crackles, like a popping fire, in his head. He would never drink so much again.

"I ate," he said curtly. Talking turned the popping into a roar.

He actually had eaten. Stewart had coffee and hot rolls brought to the rooms, and Dylan took coffee and one bite of buttered bread. As they breakfasted, Stewart had been impeccably polite and remotely formal, as though last night's revelations had never taken place.

Maybe they hadn't. Maybe his own disordered imagination, previously inflamed by Ian Campbell, had run wild.

Stewart had asked Dylan to come back in a couple of days about the job. His manner announced clearly that Dylan was not to inquire further right now. Dylan wasn't up to asking about anything anyway.

"Where is everybody?" he asked now.

"Wait a little," said Dru with a secret smile.

Wait? How about, Lie down by the wigwam and be still until the head stops roaring?

*   *   *

When he stirred, he had half memories. A rotund French Canadian moved into and out of his mind, a merry, agile fellow he'd shaken hands with. Or was it a dream?

"Did you introduce me to someone?" he asked Dru.

"A trader, Louis Rémy."

"Plump?"

Dru nodded. "Well-girded, a raconteur, a scalawag, and master of two wives. Or is it two among each tribe?"

Dylan wasn't sure what the joke was. Did white men really take two wives? He wasn't sure of anything. He shook his head, and regretted it.

"Come look," said Dru.

Dylan sat down next to Dru in front of the fire. The Druid handed him a horn of gunpowder, a small horn of primer, a shooting pouch, and a rifle cover sewn from a piece of blanket. In the pouch were a bar of lead, a mold for making balls, a handful of flints, and some patches. Last, Dru handed Dylan the rifle itself.

"A J. Henry Northwest gun," explained Dru.

Dylan dared not hope. It was a proper rifle, not a musket or a fowling piece, oiled and polished until both the wood and the brass glowed. He tested the lock. It had a good, firm action. He saw that the sighting style was a blade in front and no rear sight. For a side plate it had an undulating serpent cast in brass. Surely a fine weapon.

"If you go to buffalo country for Stewart," Dru said, "you'll need better than an old fusil." The gun he'd been letting Dylan practice with, the model the company traded to the Indians.

Dylan looked eagerly into Dru's one eye. "It's yours," Dru said with a smile. "My *au revoir* gift to you."

"*Au revoir?*"

"Saga and I have a trip to make to Athabasca now. I suspect you'll be going to Fort Augustus. Unless you choose to go back to your family. You've already had a fine adventure."

"I'll never go back to my father," muttered Dylan. He felt a pang of loneliness. He hadn't thought . . .

"You'll need a good rifle to shoot buffalo, then.

That's what they do at Fort Augustus in the autumn. Make pemmican."

Make pemmican. Right, as Stewart said. Dylan wondered if they really did it by drowning them en masse. "The job isn't promised," he said.

"I believe the decision is yours," said Dru.

"Before, I thought you said *we* make pemmican at Fort Augustus."

The Druid smiled enigmatically. "Saga and I will be along," he said. "We have to go to Athabasca first."

Why don't we go to the High Missouri instead? thought Dylan. The grand, untouched country? Looking for the Welsh Indians?

Instead of asking, Dylan pretended indifference. He hefted the Henry rifle and held the sight on a slender birch fifty yards away. He wondered if he could become an excellent shot. He checked to see if the ramrod was straight and moved easily. The rifle was in good condition.

So that's why Dru sent him to Stewart. The Druid didn't want him around on the trip to Athabasca, wherever that was.

"I have a motto I'd like to inscribe on the powder horn for you. Would you like that?"

Dylan hesitated.

"The rifle and accoutrements are yours whether you stay in the *pays d'en haut* or not."

"I'd like that," said Dylan.

"I'll do it." The Druid thought a moment. "Dylan," he said in a tone of significance, "I rang the bells and you heard them and came here. Now you and you alone must decide whether to stay."

"Why did you ring those bells?"

Dru smiled and shrugged. "It's my blood and breath mysticism, laddo."

"Let's try the rifle," said Dru.

Dylan lolled his head about, then shook it no. "I don't think my head will stand loud noises yet," he answered.

Dru smiled teasingly. Dylan hung the pouch over his

right shoulder to feel the fit of it on his flank. It seemed good.

"Why did Louis give it to you?" Dylan asked.

"He didn't give it, he traded it," answered Dru.

"What did you trade him?"

Dru looked Dylan in the eye. "Marguerite," said the Druid. "As a second wife." He grinned. "Got a good price for her too."

Marguerite? The girl of his own fantasies?

Dylan sat on the hilltop and watched them load the canoes in the mouth of the river, this Rémy Dylan had met but not met, and his crew and family. The family apparently included two teenage boys, a younger girl, a first wife—real wife—and Marguerite.

Dylan was amused at himself. He felt jealousy and shame, yet he had committed sins with Marguerite only in his mind.

He felt betrayed. By Dru. Irrational but true.

How could they treat women this way—buy and sell them?

Rémy beamed a broad smile toward everyone. It looked lascivious, loathsome.

"There was no way around it," Dru said, sitting down. "Her husband died."

The glance Dylan threw him looked like contempt. Why was the laddo so hot?

"It's the only way for her," Dru explained gently. "There's no life for a woman without a family. Not in these parts."

Dylan ignored him.

Dru let it sit awhile.

"It's customary, you know," said Dru. "A man of position has more than one wife. It's expected, if you can afford it."

Dylan seemed to keep himself from quivering with anger by an act of will.

Oh, well, thought Dru, the laddo is conventional sometimes. He went down to the water to say good-bye.

Dylan dreamed.

Restlessly, helplessly, hopelessly, tossing and turning, he dreamed. His mind transported to him lurid images of every kind imaginable. Rémy and Marguerite, yes, and himself and Marguerite, and the three of them in acts either repugnant or impossible, yes. But worse than this. Creatures half man, half beast, mobs of them, fornicating foully in obscene positions, performing obscene acts, eating dung, pissing on creatures who until their degradation were human beings, and worse.

At the library of his Collège de Montreal, Dylan had seen engravings of paintings of the New World by a Dutch painter named Hieronymus Bosch. The librarian said they were based on the tales sailors brought back shortly after Columbus discovered the new continent and its peoples. They were full of horrific man-beasts and devils, hideous creatures, monstrously deformed and distorted, engaged in bizarre and grotesque practices. At the time Dylan and the librarian chuckled about Bosch's absurd misrepresentation of the New World.

Now, in his dream, he remembered the Bosch paintings and saw that his dreams were their progeny. That was no comfort, for his dreams were also like the tales he'd heard of the doings of Indians, the tales Stewart brought him, the tales that now might be all too true. Maybe Bosch's images of the New World were not an absurdity, maybe they were the real *pays sauvage*, and he was trapped in a nightmare both sleeping and waking, walking through a dreamscape of horror both day and night.

He slipped from the strange double reality of dream—dreaming while knowing it's a dream—back into the pure singularity of the dream illusion.

He was fornicating lasciviously with an Indian woman, a striking-looking creature. She had four white stripes on her face, two scars slashing from the outside corner of each eye to her earlobes, like giant cat's whiskers, and two thin streaks of white hair diverging back from her widow's peak. She had a wickedly sensual face and a voluptuous body. As they made the beast with two backs, they rolled over and over on hot coals of hell, and the skin of each was blistered and suppurating and pocked with deeply burned craters.

Yet even more painful than the horrible burns was what he felt as he rolled over and over fornicating—the agony of spirit, the utter absence of love, the unreachable, inviolate darkness of soul.

"Anastasie dit il est temps de donner à manger les Christiens au lions." Anastasie says it's time to feed the Christians to the lions. Which was the way Anastasie announced every meal.

It took Dylan a moment to register that the voice was speaking French in the inimitable accent of the Indians. And he didn't recognize the voice. He pulled his blankets over his eyes. He was afraid he'd wake to a reality even more appalling than his dream.

A hand shook his shoulder.

Dylan opened his eyes and looked into the face.

He choked back bile.

It was the face of Fornicating Woman in the dream. It even had one of the four white stripes. A thin pink-white scar ran in a straight line from the corner of her right eye to the right earlobe.

It was a sensual face, a face that spoke of strong weathers—desire, anger, hatred, temper, passion.

"Tu t'appelle comment?" Dylan asked hesitantly. What's your name?

She seemed amused at his hesitation. She was a woman who would demand boldness, and give it.

"Fore," she said with a beguiling smile. For a gut-squeezing moment he thought she was going to say Fore-nicating Woman. But she only smiled that smile.

The temptations of the flesh rose in Dylan. Fore stood up and started walking away from his lean-to, the site of his fantasies of Marguerite, and now of Fornicating

Woman. He watched the undulating hips of Fore, and his body stirred.

"*Allons,*" she called back. Let's go. Then in clumsy and almost indecipherable English, "Tahm to feed the Chrees-tee-ons to thee lah-ohns." Her laughter made a brittle, tinkling, discordant music in the air.

"Fore can teach you snares," said Dru, eyeing Dylan across the fire.

"Whose idea is that?"

Dru chuckled. Saga, Lady Sarah, Anastasie— everyone smiled over their bowls of stew.

"*Ma ideé,*" Fore put in saucily. My idea. She gave Dylan a so-what look.

"It's a good idea," said Dru, "if you intend to stay in the *pays d'en haut.*"

"Maybe," said Dylan.

Dru ate a little, chewed, spoke casually. "With or without a woman?"

"Without," Dylan said with some heat. He thought he heard Fore snort, but he didn't look toward her. She was eating near Saga.

"Hard to do," Dru said mildly.

"You'll die," Saga said sardonically.

Dylan jerked his head toward Saga. It was the first time the half-breed had ever spoken to him. Dylan would remember those first words.

"Women's work," said Anastasie, mediating. She gave Saga a mind-your-manners look.

"Actually," said Dru in a reasonable tone, "you can live in the *pays d'en haut* without a woman. It's just hard." He flashed a grin at everyone. "The jackasses of Hudson's Bay do it, which shows how smart it is." That got a little laugh.

"We need women. Gather the wild rice. Find the onions, Jerusalem artichokes, mushrooms, and berries. Dig the roots. Make the clothes. Build the wigwams. Cook. Other such." He smiled. "Keep your blankets warm."

"I can take care of myself," Dylan said. He felt like this immoral talk was making his testicles ascend.

Dru shrugged. "If you stay almost entirely in the fort. But that would be robbing yourself of what you came to experience, the *pays sauvage,* and the people *sauvage.*" Dru didn't look at anyone—was he hinting at experiencing Fore?

The Druid resettled himself on his haunches. "You know Sage and I make a trip to Montreal lots of winters. We take expresses, for a good price.

"We go by snowshoe. Who makes the snowshoes?" He paused significantly. "Anastasie and Lady Sarah do. Who makes the pemmican we take? Women. Who makes the *sagamité*? Women." He spread his arms eloquently.

Dylan was consciously not looking at Fore. Why? he asked himself. I just met her. He said to Dru, "I can learn."

"Then learn," said Dru. "Learn how to make snares and set them. Fore will teach you this afternoon."

Dylan didn't want to go anywhere with Fore alone. To him she was still Fornicating Woman of his dream, and it made him feel eerie. "She's so young." She was probably his age.

"She learned from her grandmother, who taught me. Already she's better than either of us."

Dru got up. Motioned Fore up. Jerked his head at Dylan. "So let's go."

Fore spoke in French, teasingly throwing it all at him fast. He couldn't learn it at this speed, but could merely be impressed by her expertise. He might have been tickled, might have been offended, but in fact she just gave him the willies.

From time to time the Druid would add something, a bit of lore that let Dylan see into the ways of the rabbit better. Or the raccoon, or the marmot. There were so damned many of them. So many habits and habitats to learn, so much . . . And all of this traditional knowledge, Fore said, would be different in winter.

"Now we trap a marmot," she said. "You see." She smiled provocatively, and gave her head a follow-me jerk.

*   *   *

"Why are you acting spooky?" asked the Druid as they walked.

Dylan looked at him sidelong.

"Don't worry," said Dru, "English is still too much for her."

Dylan trod the path thoughtfully. Should he tell Dru? He felt shaky. "How do you spell her name?"

Dru shrugged. "Her language isn't written. You can spell it the way you want. F-o-u-r, F-o-r, F-o-r-e, whatever. I think she's named for her grandmother, and I don't know what tribe the grandmother was from, so I can't even say what language her name is. Just Fore."

Dru was just warming up. "Now, you could associate it with something. Like forelock, but she doesn't have one. Or forest, which makes her mystical and mysterious. Forthright, which she is, about whatever she wants. Even forward. Forethought—there's none of that in her, nor forlorn.

"Knowing you, it makes you think of foreskin. If you forge your tool in her hot oven, you can abandon hope of forgiveness. But maybe fornication will be your good fortune. It's better than your prudery."

They took a few steps in blessed silence.

Dylan changed the subject. "Where'd she get that scar, do you know?"

Dru bobbed his head. "She did it herself. Took a piece of obsidian—sharp as a woman's wit, that stuff—and . . ." He made a quick cutting motion across his own cheek.

"Why?"

Dru shrugged. "Passion, rage, self-dislike." He thought for a couple of steps. "The young man she wanted chose another. A woman more pliable." Dru chuckled. "When she lost him, she . . ." The cutting motion again.

"A year later, last summer, her rival died in childbirth. The young man came hanging about again. Her sister would have been glad to get rid of her. Fore wouldn't even speak to him."

"Her sister?"

"Her older sister, much older, is the sits-beside-him wife of the Crane. Fore is the third wife, the youngest.

That's their way, to marry the husbands of their sisters. She's unruly, ungovernable, and will never be content without being a sits-beside-him wife." Dru shrugged. "Her sister would like to get her another husband."

"What ways," Dylan muttered.

"Your disgust will not serve you here. Nor your sense of superiority."

Dylan jerked his head to look at the Druid.

Dru put a kindly hand on Dylan's shoulder. "So why are you acting so spooky?"

Dylan struggled with himself to speak. "I had a nightmare last night. A whole goddamn bagpipe regiment of nightmares." He smiled sardonically. "Thousands of human demons in hell, fornicating wildly."

"I used to dream about sex a lot," said Dru with a warm smile. "Still do occasionally."

"I saw her in the dream," snapped Dylan, nodding forward at Fore. "She was the one I was . . . In my dream her name was Fornicating Woman."

"Perfect," said Dru. "*For*nicating Woman."

Dylan kept his tone serious. It still gave him the willies. "She even had that scar," he said. "In fact, twin scars on both sides, and matching streaks of white in her hair."

Dru shrugged. "So you've seen Fore around and you have imagination."

Dylan insisted, "I'm just human, trying to become spiritual."

"No," said the Druid mildly, "I don't think so. I think you're a spiritual being trying to become human." He grinned. "Would you like to become a pagan Piegan?" "Piegan" and "pagan" he pronounced the same way.

That afternoon, Dylan learned that his fingers were too clumsy to braid strips of bark of the red willow, that he couldn't figure out where to set a snare, that he couldn't set it ingeniously enough, that he couldn't catch small game, and generally that left alone in the *pays d'en haut,* he would starve.

So he'd never make a pagan Piegan.

* * *

"Anastasie," Dylan said, "what's a sits-beside-him wife?"

They were in the wigwam after supper. She smiled a friendly, sisterly smile at him. He loved Anastasie's broad, strong, plain face. He was beginning to think everyone here but her had secret designs on him.

She was making him two more pairs of moccasins from deer hide. Plain moccasins in the puckered-toe style, no beadwork, no quillwork, no nothing, she had commented teasingly.

"I too-too make you deerskin shirt. One only. That's all time. Anastasie not your mother." His cotton clothes tore up fast in the wilderness—he'd be naked if he didn't get more clothes somehow.

He would also need mukluks from thick moose hide or buffalo hide for the winter, she said, but she didn't have time to make them now. Maybe he could trade some woman something for them, if he ever earned anything. Or maybe he would get a wife, at his age, instead of begging from his "Indun" older sister. A-a-ch. That's the way Anastasie talked.

Now she took a needle out of her mouth and stuck it in the hide so she could converse. She drew around his feet on the hide. Her awl, needles, and sinew lay nearby. The Frenchmen tried to trade her Frenchman thread, she had said—she called all whites Frenchmen—but it was weak stuff compared to sinew. Your moccasins would fall apart with Frenchman thread, she said scornfully.

"Most *Induns*," she said with a roll of the eyes, "understand good you have two or three wives, many as can afford." She liked to say "Indun" with a little fillip because she thought it was funny that the Frenchmen would call all the people of Turtle Island by one name when they were so various. The whites, on the other hand, according to her, were all the same.

"Morgan tells that you Frenchmen too-too had many wives before you got this civilization. Now you come here and want us be too-too foolish like you. Lots of times women, their men be killed, so how would they live if they couldn't be second wife, or third? Must die too-too, starve?

"Older man, his wife die, he take younger woman, make children. Woman can not do when she older.

"So. Man who can afford, have several wives. Then he must be good hunter and trapper, bring in lots and lots meat, feed his big family. Lots of skins for clothing, too-too, all such. Not many men can do."

Dylan began, "But—"

"Yah," Anastasie interrupted. "I know your mind. Dirty mind. You make fuss why have ...?" Boldly she made a circle with the thumb and forefinger of one hand and slid the forefinger of the other hand in and out. She shrugged helplessly. "Frenchmen. Peoples grown up, they do such, yah. Is good. All two-leggeds, four-leggeds, wingeds do that. Is right. If I die, you think Morgan not do that more? Hah. He call it in English 'twat,' in French *'chatte,'* is good either way."

Dylan was scandalized.

She'd finished drawing. She pushed him off the skin and began to cut. Dylan saw that she had real scissors.

"You Frenchmen half crazy. You make things good. Rifle, needles, pot, beads, such like too-too. But you understand nothing." She pronounced it *know-think.* "What you think good, hah? Civilization, that good. Make you smarter dan us savage." She picked up her awl and began to jab holes through the skin with a vigor that scared Dylan. "You speak two language—I speak four. You no know where is small animal. I feed family on dem. You got pretty weave cloth"—she held up his worn shirt—"I got skins of deers, last longer. You got compass but get lost. I go here Moose Factory back, no trouble, just my eyes." She tapped her temple.

"You go on plains, die from thirst widdout I show you water holes. You not watch deer, moose, buffalo, know how dey do. People of Turtle Island, we watch. You starve, we eat.

"Morgan say you got good, black book." She was the only person who called Dru by his given name. An assertion of rights, or an intimacy. "Blackrobe come here some-times. I stuff ears with mud. Frenchmen only peoples I know kill dere own kind. People of Turtle Island not do that."

Dylan had had about all he could take. This attack on civilization and the Bible—it was too much. Civilization, which had built the great cathedrals, created art and music and literature, discovered the secrets of the stars . . .

Whoa, he told himself. She has no light to see by. That's why she doesn't see.

"Sits-beside-him wife," he prompted her.

"Why you want know?"

"Dru said Fore isn't a sits-beside-him wife, she's the third wife."

"Yah, but she like you, think maybe she be your wife."

"I'm not interested."

"She know how make interested." Anastasie smiled and did the circled thumb and forefinger trick again.

"Sits-beside-him wife," he said.

"Yah, I not forget. So. One wife always first wife, first mother. When two wifes, second maybe little sister, help first wife, do what first wife say. Same any number. First wife say we cook this, we cook that, you set snares, you gather wild rice, all such. First wife have first place, sits beside him. In wigwam by fire only wife sits next to man. S'all."

"Is there never jealousy?"

" 'Course jealousy. 'Course all bad things. Wives people, good and bad like people. Try live better. This way all women get be mother."

Dylan thought about it for a long moment. It was ugly in the sight of God. But he cared for his friends too much to say so.

"Anastasie, do you and Dru have children?"

She shook her head no. "Long time, two husbands, I have only one child. Died at birth. I maybe cannot again." She didn't raise her eyes to his. From his oblique angle he thought he saw grief flick across her face.

"Does Dru have children?"

"Could be. Has been in every village on Turtle Island. Never he knew of any children. Didn't stay long enough to know." Now she raised her eyes to him. "Except you."

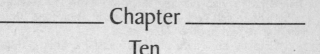

D ylan went stumbling toward him. Dru was working on Dylan's powder horn with a scribe. Saga was eating *sagamité* again. Dylan glared at Dru. "I talk to you," he snapped.

Dru looked at Dylan, at Saga, back at Dylan wonderingly.

Dylan walked away from the fire into the evening shadows. He didn't know what the hell he felt. He was dust in a whirlwind. Whatever it was, there was outrage in it. And confusion.

You run away from home and . . .

When Dru came up, Dylan blurted, "Are you my father?"

Dru looked into his eyes softly, not knowing what to answer.

"Are you my father?" The words were getting sharp.

Dru felt his eyes flutter nervously across the distance to Saga, and back to Dylan.

"Anastasie says you're my father."

"She believes it," Dru said sadly.

"You aren't?"

"No, I don't think so," he said.

"Whaddya mean you don't *think* so?"

Dru stepped farther away from the fire, found a bright spot in the last glow of the twilight, sat, and patted the ground next to him for Dylan to sit. When Dylan did, the

Druid spoke gently. "I might have been your father. I might. Nearly was. The last time I saw your mam, she gave me . . . more than one of those cups of tea." He looked past Dylan into the shadows, across his own years to his young self and a young woman. There one life was cast down, and another taken up.

"I loved her," Dru said. He paused a while. "Regrets are insights that come too late.

"I don't know what that act, on a blanket in a grove on a spring afternoon next to a picnic basket . . . I don't know what it was for her. For me, it was committed in a kind of fury, a wave of self-dislike that came crashing down on us both. She was the first woman I ever made love to that I loved." He met Dylan's eyes and held them. "I'm sorry to say that it came out as anger. I couldn't bear those feelings in me, and I lashed them into her.

"She held me tenderly after, and when I raised my face, I saw hers was wet with tears.

"I know now they were tears of good-bye. She couldn't give me what I couldn't give myself. I don't know what you call it.

"I didn't like myself well enough to do right by me or her or us. Stupid youth I was, and already thirty, too far along in years to be so . . . whatever. Callow.

"I told myself, lying like a scoundrel, that I'd got what I wanted, I conquered. The next day I waved back at her from a canoe, all sashed up fancy as a *voyageur*, and set out for this country. Conquer some more up here, I told myself. And again when I get back to Montreal, and everywhere in between. Lusty laddo, I told myself, Tommy Twat, Charles de Chatte." He smiled wryly and shook his head. "The lies, the lies.

"When I got back to town, as I said before, she was married to your father. He was hell for respectable, which is not quite the same as self-respect, but close enough for city folks. She wouldn't see me, of course, and soon it was time for her confinement. And your father got wind of me nosing about and came and told me to make meself scarce. Quite properly.

"I done that. Probably was glad your mam had relieved me of the responsibility of acting like a man.

"Next I heard, she was dead." He flashed the aquamarine eye at Dylan. "I can't tell you how awful that was. Just like meself, I stayed drunk for a week. Thought most gravely about throwing meself in the river. Which I deserved." He held Dylan's eyes. "What pulled me out of it was you, laddo. The thought that you were alive. The thought that you might be my son, and you were alive. That pierced through everything and touched me. That was the beginning of something for me . . . don't know what.

"Burning curious I was, so I went to the church to have a look at the date of your christening. Might possibly have been me as was your father, probably not. She married Ian Campbell about a month after I went strutting upriver. You might have come along three weeks late, more likely a bit early.

"But I needed to think you were mine. Never let on about it, just believed it meself. Kept my tongue about it for a long time. Would check on you now and then, quiet inquiries, watch you in the schoolyard, suchlike. Looked through the windows of your house sometimes. Got into the habit, winters, of coming back to Montreal, mainly to see you. Thought you looked like me, more so then than now.

"Then I got hooked up with Anastasie, and no children came, for whatever reason. Bothered me, it did. She'd had one before, and now didn't make any more. Her brother yelled at me about it once, and I told a whopper. I said I had a son, Dylan as was called Campbell but was truly Bleddyn. Yes, I did."

Dru looked long at Dylan. "And the story spread, got all around, got hard to put a stop to. Lots of folks believed it, and I never denied it.

"Until last summer. I wanted to bring you out here. As I have done." He let this sit. "Told Anastasie you aren't mine. Just wanted to set things right."

He chuckled without humor. "She doesn't believe me. Thinks I'm trying to make it less important than it is, you being here. No one else believes it either. Not Saga, for sure. Though I've told him.

"It's lovely, laddo. Tell a lie, and you have to live with it."

*   *   *

Dru regarded Dylan gravely. Dylan wanted to reach out and touch him.

"I'm sorry," he said. "I wanted you to be mine. I did. You saved my life."

Dylan put a hand on Dru's arm. "Thank you," he said. "I wish you were my father, not Ian Campbell. Thank you."

Dru smiled at him. "I it is what needs to thank you." He covered Dylan's hand with his own. "You saved me first, just a kid as you were. Then you changed me. You helped me grow up. I wanted to be good enough to be your da."

His eyes twinkled. "So there you are, father of the grown-up Morgan Griffiths Morgan Bleddyn, itinerant and druid, who otherwise would still be a callow youth."

They went down to the river for a smoke. A smoke seemed a good reason for Dru to go anywhere.

Dylan blurted it out. "Are you Saga's father?"

"No, laddo, grown when I met him."

"Do I need to be careful of Saga?"

Dru chuckled. "He would like that, but no, you don't need to. He's very jealous of you, thinking you are my blood."

Dru looked at the powder horn in his hand. He began to cut it with the scribe again. Looking down, he said, "I suppose he thinks you'll get whatever I couldn't give him."

"I can trust him, then?"

"Completely. He would never allow my son to come to harm. Which frustrates him."

As Dylan thought. The bastard wasn't trustworthy. "Why?"

"He's all lusty for Fore. Has been since last year this time."

Dylan waited for an explanation. Dru was scribing away.

"Every July we have a grand ball to celebrate. Big affair, partners out from Montreal, wintering partners, *voy-*

ageurs, hommes du nord, Indians, Métis, everybody.
Dancing—good orchestra, flutes and fifes, fiddles, bagpipes. Lots to drink. Wild dances—reels from Scotland,
jigs from Québec, Indian steps. Celebrate our one time a
year together.

"Let's just say that on the night of the dance, many
a virgin at sundown isn't a virgin at sunup. And every Indian lady has her husband's forgiveness in advance for
whatever she does on that night.

"Last year what Fore did was Saga.

"But she's uninterested in him," Dru went on, "completely uninterested."

Not so completely, thought Dylan.

Dru looked at him directly. "She's interested in you."

Dylan shrugged. Why did these people have this bent
for rutting? At that moment the warmth in his loins told
him why. "Why would she want me?"

"Most Indian women do. Want a white-man husband.
The little reason is, to them white men are rich in beads
and cloth and hatchets, bells, needles, all such foofaraw.
Seems like a wonderful power to them. The big reason is,
white men are important in every tribe, the source of lots
of good things for the people. White man equals big man.

"Here," said Dru, handing him the powder horn.

The inscription was fancy, in cursive lettering, the
capital letters elaborately cross-hatched and curlicued. It
said,

> *I, POWDER, with my Brother BALL,*
> *Hero-like, do CONQUER all.*

"What does it mean?" asked Dylan.
"It means we'd better practice shooting."

"Young Mr. Davies."

It was Duncan Campbell Stewart, long and tall and
wearing a skull's smile.

Dylan blew the smoke away from the muzzle of his
fine J. Henry gun before he said good afternoon. He won-

dered whether Stewart had seen him shooting at and missing the wood chips set on a stump.

"Is he a marksman, Morgan ap Bleddyn?"

"Not yet, Duncan." It was a kind answer, considering.

"Why do you call him that?" Dylan said bluntly to Stewart. He was tired of old men keeping secrets from him.

"It's an old joke between us, lad," said Dru.

"It means Morgan son of Bleddyn," answered Stewart with a smile. "Expressed in the Welsh way."

"Bleddyn being me da," said Dru.

"Do you know it means 'wolf'? Though I'd say he's more coyote, the shapeshifter."

"Whichever suits me fancy at the time," said Dru, playing.

"He's a man of many names," said Stewart to Dylan.

"Why do people call him the Druid?" Dylan asked.

Stewart nodded gravely. "Because he is a master woodsman, so skilled he surely conjures the help of the forest gods, or is a druid himself."

"What is it that you do superlatively well, Mr. Stewart?"

"My privilege to ask questions first," said Stewart. "The prerogative of age."

Dylan nodded.

"You have not given me a response about the position I hold for you, young Mr. Davies."

"I'm not ready yet," said Dylan, adding teasingly, "to sell my soul to the devil."

"Ah, you've already done that, Mr. Davies. Unless I'm much mistaken. I have another question."

Dylan nodded again.

"Why did you change your name when you came to the *pays d'en haut?*"

Dylan looked sharply at Dru. "You can't really walk away from anything, laddo," said Dru.

"No need to be ashamed, young Mr. Davies. Many men here have fled their identities, for many reasons. In your case, however, it's curious. To give up a fine Highland clan name for a common Welsh appellation. My Campbell ancestors might be offended."

"I'm not a criminal, Mr. Stewart, so the why concerns none but me."

"Well enough, young Mr. . . . Davies. Would you like me to send word to your good father of your safety?"

Again Dylan looked sharply at Dru. He felt snared. He answered with forced equanimity. "It's kind of you to offer, but no, thank you. Now show us your marksmanship." He offered the gun.

Stewart raised his left hand as though to push the rifle away, and for the first time Dylan noticed a slender case in the hand, such as might hold a flute.

"Perhaps with other weapons, young Mr. Davies."

"He's a knife man," said Dru. "Like a bloody Scot, enamored of steel."

Stewart held the case forth and opened it. On a satin lining, knives, glistening like silver.

"You throw them, young Mr. Davies," said Stewart. "I'll confess I'm proud of them. Sheffield, of course, and custom-made. Let me show you."

From the lid of the case he took one of two leather holsters and strapped it on—behind his right shoulder. Then the other. He lifted the knives gingerly and slipped them into the holsters, their hilts coming just above the top of the shoulder. Then he squared himself toward a birch tree ten paces away. He seemed, perhaps, to take a deep breath, or in some way to relax his posture, and his countenance became trancelike.

The arms moved so fast, Dylan was not sure which moved first, right or left.

Whick! Whick! went the knives, like the sound of a whip cutting the air.

The knives were in the center of the birch tree at chest height.

Dylan had to rehearse it to himself. Stewart cocked the elbow, grasped the hilt behind his back, and threw straight forward from that odd position.

Dylan walked over close to the birch, Stewart following. One knife had penetrated a couple of inches. The other was tight against it, half an inch higher. It stuck clear through the tree, making a long split in the fibers.

Stewart jerked the knives out hard and handed them

to Dylan. They were light and flat, like big letter openers,
the hilts with only slender handles of ivory, smooth as polished marble. The edges were sharp enough to make his
knees weak. Something in the feel of them stirred his
blood. He grinned foolishly up at Stewart.

"Will you try them?" asked Stewart.

Dylan demurred, but Stewart insisted.

"Don't pass it up, laddo," said Dru.

Stewart showed him how to stand seven paces from
the target, how to take a single stride with the opposite
foot, how to release at a certain point and follow through.
Dylan missed repeatedly, or hit the tree with the hilt, or hit
it sideways and watched the knife clatter off into the
weeds. Even missing, he liked the motion of his arm, the
thrust of his upper body, the logic of the flow of force into
the knife. Most of all, he liked the feel of the knives in his
hands.

After six or eight throws, he stuck one. And then another. And another. They were thrown softly but accurately.

"They fit your hands nicely," said Stewart, "and I
think you have a touch."

Stewart took the knives and threw them with extraordinary vigor. *Thunk! Thunk!* He walked forward, wrested
them out of the tree, held them delicately, almost like fon-
dling something. Then he thrust them to Dylan hilts first.

"They're yours," he said.

"No, no," said Dylan foolishly.

"Please, young Mr. Davies, permit me. It will gratify
me very particularly."

Dylan looked at Dru, uncertain, looked at Stewart.

"I am retiring from this . . . savage land. I have carried these weapons . . . because this place requires a man
to . . ." Something moved in his shadowed eyes. "I'm
leaving behind that way of life, forever I'm sure. I want to
make a gesture."

Dru was looking at Stewart ruefully. Dylan wondered
why. They had so many secrets, these old men.

"You are my clansman. I judge you to be an idealist,
like my former self. I wish to give the knives to you . . .
symbolically. What they mean, you must discover." He put

them into Dylan's hands, and the case, and held Dylan's hands on them with his own.

Stewart looked down at Dylan with his gray, shadowy eyes in their cavernous sockets. "This is your responsibility. Learn to throw the knives accurately and with great force. That is their nature, and it yearns to be fulfilled. Learn to kill with them. Learn to hunt. Learn even to hunt deer."

Something shifted in the Scot's eyes, dark, obscure.

"However, I urge you not to let them drink human blood. They thirst for all blood, indiscriminately. You are different. What you must do ... that's your duty to discover."

He gazed at Dylan with enigmatic urgency.

Then, in a hearty way, Stewart said, "I must walk about and see some gentlemen. You practice your throwing technique."

Leaving, he turned back to them. "Young Mr. Davies, the ball is tonight and I leave before noon tomorrow. I shall expect an answer from you in the morning, early."

Chapter

Eleven

A nastasie and Lady Sarah were in front of the wigwam. From the distance, where Dylan was walking up from the river, it looked strange. Anastasie appeared to be in a trance, slowly, slowly twirling in front of Lady Sarah. Then Dylan saw that Anastasie was wearing a satin gown, floor length, very dressy. And Lady Sarah was holding a large hand mirror mounted on wood, with a handle, so Anastasie could study her own appearance. She was turning her body slowly, and twisting her head to look, like a young girl going to her first dance and whirled on the wind of enchantment.

"I forgot," Dru had said last night. "I promised her I'd take her to the grand ball this year. Wait till you see her all got-up."

No question Anastasie was going, and on the wings of romance. Lady Sarah took the mirror and inspected her bulldog face. Yes, it was a show. Anastasie had even painted her head. The part in the center of her head was vermilion, and green and yellow lines waved across her forehead. The effect was barbarous but striking.

The annual fling of the NorthWest Company, they'd said, and the grandest of times. He didn't know if he was invited. No one ever told him anything around here.

"You're going," said Dru, in a tone that hinted, If I have to go, you do too. "We're all going." Seemed grumpy about it.

Now Dru said, "Get dressed. You're borrowing my outfit, the one laid out there." He nodded his head at clothes on a boulder behind Anastasie, still transfixed by her own image. It was a black frock coat with long tails, dove-gray waistcoat, and scarlet neck cloth. "Anastasie loves it," Dru said, "and keeps it for me. Too sodding dandyish. If you wear it, she won't make *me*."

"Oh, Dylan," gushed Anastasie, "we'll have so much fun. The dinner is . . ." She rolled her eyes.

Dylan held the jacket up and looked at it. Yes, grand, something to strut in. He didn't mind playing the swell. And his knives would look great on the back of the jacket. Even if they were mostly empty menace.

Suddenly Fore was planted in front of him with cocked hips. She gave him a roll of eye and a flirtatious smile.

Dru said, "Mr. Stewart is escorting her."

Dylan looked from Dru to Fore and back to Dru. "But—"

"Laddo, the lady wants to dance, especially with Mr. Stewart. It's an honor for her."

"Monsieur Stewart, *comme il est beau*," said Fore mischievously. *"Est-ce que vous voulez marcher avec moi à la Grande Salle?"* Will you walk me to the Great Hall? She tucked her hand into Dylan's elbow, ready to march.

Dylan didn't know what to say. Yes, he supposed he would deliver this provocative woman to the rooms of the man who would make a whore of her.

That did not unnerve him so much as the way she had painted her face. Two white lines from each eye to earlobe, and two echoing white lines slanting back from her widow's peak.

Fornicating Woman.

Dylan was half drunk. It was a solution to his anxiety. He kept looking across to Fore during dinner and seeing his dream of the Bosch figures, himself and Fornicating Woman rutting on the coals of hell, in terrible agony. The awful thing was, it appealed to him and heated his blood.

Perhaps Fore knew his dilemma and enjoyed it. She seemed conscious of his glance, and was smiling with extra vivacity with Mr. Stewart. Dylan wondered if she was speaking English. Clearly she understood enough to have overheard him telling Dru about the dream and how Fornicating Woman was painted. He also wondered if she had played Fornicating Woman with Mr. Stewart in his rooms in place of a drink before dinner.

It was Stewart she wanted, she and Dru had hinted. Not Dylan, nor even Saga again, but Stewart. Thank God, he told himself.

A wicked celebration, this ball, that led men and women into the suites and cabins and bushes and under the canoes, and sent back mournful cries of love. Dylan would be no part of it. He would ease his nerves with wine.

The drinking was legendary, said Dru, averaging as much as ten bottles of wine per man. Dylan didn't believe that for a moment. He would keep his drinking moderate. Just enough to ease his nerves when he looked at Fore.

The diners were gala—the partners in short clothes and swords, the clerks in sober dark suits, a few guides like Dru and Saga in the colorful *voyageur* style. Most men were making a display of polished weapons. Mr. Stewart carried a sword. Dylan couldn't name the type, but maybe it was a centuries-old sword within his clan. For some reason, Dru carried only a knife, and Saga only his quirt. As usual, Dru was pledged not to drink.

The native women attired themselves in Louis XV gowns and other country copies of European fashions, and sometimes jewelry worthy of a courtesan. They wore this garb with decorum that would have suited a duchess. It made Dylan feel he was not in the *pays sauvage* but a fantasy country, a place created by an artiste of fey imagination.

The dinner was lavish. They ate with silver and drank from crystal. The napery was Irish linen. Three courses had come so far—baked whitefish with mushrooms, venison roast with boiled potatoes, smoked hams with corn pudding, and white bread—light, fluffy, delicate, with butter from the fort's farm, a particular treat.

Dylan, Anastasie, and Lady Sarah ate moderately. He noticed that Dru and Saga acted like they were storing up for the winter. Dylan was sure they wouldn't be able to dance. Saga was also imbibing like an Indian. Dylan wondered if he was a binge drinker, as many Indians were reported to be. He wondered if the bastard was even half trustworthy.

It didn't matter—not tonight. His black mood of the last few days was evaporating. He didn't have to sin, and he wouldn't. He was a free agent, he could remember the light and live by it. He could stay here. He could go deeper into the wilderness. He could go back to civilization and stay there. He could return here as a missionary. A free agent.

He'd asked Dru what he should do at the banquet. "When among wolves," Dru answered, "howl."

Howl he would. Tonight he was in the *pays d'en haut,* he was celebrating, he was eating and drinking handsomely but moderately, and he intended to dance—to cavort, frolic, gambol, to spin his body through the air and feel rapturous.

Dylan was thrilled. Anastasie and Lady Sarah stuck to the traditional steps of their people, but Fore danced like a peasant white woman—vigorously, athletically, yet with an insinuating élan all her own.

Most of the native women danced in the Ojibway and Cree manner, bobbing up and down sedately in one place, sometimes leaving the ground with both feet. A few Indian and mixed-blood women did the jig step, sometimes comically so, but most of them kept to their dignified bob.

It was the white men who were riotous. They set their feet to following the jig, a demonic dance of fast-running triplets that took you over, wore you out, and left you spinning. The orchestra gave it a driving rhythm, fiddles, fifes, flutes, and underneath these nimble skirmishers, the babble and drone of the bagpipes. Dylan gave himself up to the dance. It was exhilarating.

Not that he danced every dance. He sat out some of the reels and the naughty French songs, and occasionally the band would let the dancers cool off while they sang out a tender Scottish ballad. Dru muttered about wanting a Welsh harp, but no need for that. Dylan thought these highland jigs could not be beat.

Fore never sat down. Mr. Stewart took the first dance, Saga the second, Dylan the third, Mr. Stewart cut in, she came back to Dylan, Saga cut in, she came back, and so on and so on. Dylan danced with Anastasie and Lady Sarah of the bulldog face as well, in their manner, without touching. Fore was more fun.

He was beginning to get hot—both sweaty hot and lustful hot. It was the way Fore looked at him while they danced—not that she didn't look at every man that way. It was impertinent, brazen, blistering with sensuality. What did she want? Whom did she want? Dylan supposed she and Mr. Stewart would go back to his rooms and dally once more.

When Saga cut in again, Dylan decided to ignore Lady Sarah and Anastasie standing by the wall. He would take a break in the cool air of the long, north country evening. He loved the long mother-of-pearl twilight. Maybe he would go down and see the other dance of this gala evening, the one of the common *voyageurs,* the one held down at the *cantine salope.* From in front of the Great Hall he could hear a solitary fiddle crying out a maudlin tune across the meadow.

It was another world down here. These were rough Frenchies, paddlers out from Montreal or seasoned men of the north country, illiterate, uncouth, and carnal. They were having their blowout after one six-week season of hard paddling, and before another. They danced like animals, some of them agile as cats, others lumbering as bears, all strong, robust, and vigorous. They were drunk. So were the women, Indian and mixed-blood women in their deerskin dresses. Perhaps it was the wine in Dylan that made them look barbarously wonderful.

Someone struck up a second fiddle in raucous harmonies with the first. Someone else banged something metal like a drum.

A Frenchy hollered something indecipherable, and most of the dancers stopped dancing and ... They were mock-paddling. Yes, pretending to be in a canoe, yes, going up a rapid, getting knocked around by the waves, yelling in excitement, paddling more fiercely.

The canoe flipped! Down went all the *voyageurs* and their dark ladies, knees knocking, heads thumping the ground, feet waving. Dylan saw hands groping bosoms and bottoms and crotches of both sexes, and heard claps of lascivious laughter. One fellow cried that poor Pierre had drowned, and Pierre acted out a mock expiration, arms akimbo. Up came the paddlers to get back into the dance. One couple scurried hand in hand into the lavender twilight and the lake-wet fog.

Cantine salope, whores' saloon, they called it. No wonder. Not that it was so much different in the Great Hall. There the bribes were bigger, the manners less direct, the licentiousness the same. The smell here was different. Instead of perfume, there was raw sweat, pungent and spicy, at once noxious and bracing, the aroma of the beast.

At least the devil made his lure enticing.

The wine in Dylan wanted to dance. Or was it the devil? God help me, he thought, I don't care. His legs started moving without him.

A hand took his.

Fore. Fornicating Woman, her face and hair slashed with four white stripes, slashes of Bosch. Fore without Mr. Stewart.

Their bodies joined in the dance.

He didn't know how he had gotten here. They were singing and laughing raucously, he knew that, and they started canoeing again, and naturally fell and linked legs and arms and lips and other parts.

I'm in an orgy.

He accidentally fell between the legs of Fore, perfectly crotched.

Be still, Dylan Davies! he ordered himself, but it made no difference. He was beyond caring. He felt like his body was crawling on her.

She didn't move seductively. She nicked up swiftly and sucked on his earlobe. He felt it in his cod.

Then she squirmed like a fish and slipped away. Ev-

eryone was up, and Fore gave him a hand up and they
were dancing again, and she held something to her mouth.
One of his knives. He felt the holsters and the left one was
empty. The blade gleamed luridly against her white teeth
in the last ebb of the light. She slid a small pink tongue
out and licked the length of the knife, drawing it gently
sideways, never stopping the dance, never hesitating or
missing a beat. Then she slipped the knife back into his
holster and ran her tongue along his jugular vein.

He danced. She danced. She spoke not at all, French
or English, as though wordlessness was a pact between
them, a bond, or a spell. He knew the spell not with his
mind, as something acquired, like learning, or civilization
itself, but in his bones, as he had known the vibrating of
the Dylan bell when he touched his forehead to it, in his
bones, in the core of his being. The spell was like a river's
strong current. They were swimming in it, living in it, and
the river was coursing strong, throbbing strong, the flow of
his own blood.

Dylan and Fore, Fornicating Woman, left the dancers
wordlessly, in the thrall of their pact. Standing against the
rough timbers of the *cantine salope,* in silent concert,
Dylan committed his first carnal act. Fully clothed, they
joined, copulated, mated, rutted, fornicated. She touched
him but would not let him touch her with his hands—not
her face, not breasts, not hips, nothing. She used her lips,
her tongue, and her hands variously and creatively. When
at last she mounted him—it was the only place she let him
touch her—he was finished immediately, but she kept on
fiercely and in an urgent rhythm that made it all happen
again without pause.

He was pushed helplessly against the wall, weak,
pulled wherever she wanted, wherever the dark and word-
less currents of her throbbing animal nature took them. He
was bobbing along at sea, hanging onto something, he
couldn't say what, rising and falling with the swells, lost,
hopeless, rising and falling, falling and rising, world without horizon, world without hope, amen.

*   *   *

When she had sapped the juices from him again, Fore took his hand—now the touch of her mere hand was electric—and led him back among the dancers. He thought he would stumble, but he danced. If he stopped dancing, he would die.

It was mad. Even now that he had frigged Fore, frigged her wantonly, drunkenly, lewdly, his thirst for her was not slaked. He wanted her more, again and again. He would frig her until he dropped. Then, terribly, he would want her all the more, with desperate urgency. All this he knew absolutely, and was helpless before it.

Two Frenchies fell to fighting right under the dancers' feet. When Dylan paused, Fore urged him with her body to keep dancing.

Brawling, they were. One woman pleaded with them to stop, another cackled them on. Dylan wondered which one they were both wanting to frig. One man, smaller and wearing a pigtail, squiggled to his feet. He jumped onto the other's barrel chest with both feet. Whoof! went Barrel.

Dylan and Fore kept dancing.

Pigtail stepped off and jumped high to stomp again. This time Barrel got a bear arm up and grabbed Pigtail by one ankle. Rolled and twisted at once.

A screech of agony from Pigtail, almost in tune with a scratching fiddle. His body whumped the earth.

They danced.

Sounds of scuffles, half-mute cries.

When Dylan turned toward the fighters, Barrel was kicking Pigtail in the face. Barrel flung his huge body, all his weight, full length onto Pigtail, the embrace of a dark beast assailant. The smaller man lay utterly still for a moment. Barrel put his mouth to Pigtail's cheek.

Pigtail screamed.

When Barrel raised his face, leering, his mouth was red with blood, and he spat something out. Pigtail's ear was a scarlet quarter moon.

Fore whirled Dylan away from the sight. She slid close to him, flicked her pelvis briefly against him, pulled back, smiled. His Fornicating Woman, lewdly happy.

A tap on his shoulder.
Saga. And Mr. Stewart.

"My dance, I believe," said Mr. Stewart.

Fore hesitated, looked into Dylan's eyes, brushed her crotch against him briefly, and turned into Mr. Stewart's arms.

"Of course," she chimed, the first English words Dylan had heard her say.

He felt the separation like a baby thrust from the womb into the cold night air. He stood there for a moment, stupefied at the emptiness of his arms, the cold against his chest and belly.

Before the couple moved off, by the light of the fire, Dylan could see Mr. Stewart's cod big in his pants.

"And my turn next," said Saga, his eyes on Dylan, his words to Stewart. After the muteness of the spell, Dylan was mystified by all these words.

"I have a gift for her," said Saga. Mr. Stewart danced away with Fore, but Saga continued to speak as though to him. He was drunk, slurring his words.

Dylan's eyes, by arcane forces of the blood, were held on Fore. She was smiling and chatting toward Mr. Stewart's face high above her own. She was social, out from under the sway of the spell that held her to Dylan. Mr. Stewart appeared to be looking not at her but out into the darkness at whatever he always saw in such places. Since the sun was finally down, Dylan could see little of Fore's upturned face but her eyes and teeth flashing gaily, and the slashes of white paint on her face and hair, her escutcheon.

"I have a gift for her," Saga repeated loudly, insistently. "Not to be given up against a wall."

Dylan looked at him. Grinning knowingly, lewdly, Saga held up his quirt. "This," he said. Dylan looked him in the eyes, aware that Saga was at last talking to him. "She can use it as chastity belt like the Cheyennes," he said, cocking his crotch and sliding the quirt through it. "Or she can ask me to use it as a goad." He panted, thrust his hips vulgarly forward, over and over, and whipped imaginary haunches with the quirt. "Beg me."

Dylan hit him. Before either of them knew it. Heel of hand hard to nose.

Saga sat down hard. Dylan stood there stunned.

Saga rubbed his nose. Came away with blood on his hand. Stood up slowly, warily, staggering a little, and smiling slyly, crookedly.

He ran at Dylan head down, butted his chest. Dylan went sprawling. So did Saga, too drunk for balance.

They both worked their way onto their feet, cagey, looking at the other, ready.

Dylan charged Saga. The half-breed stepped aside with surprising grace, grabbed Dylan's left arm, slung him into the crowd.

Everyone had stopped and was watching now, cheering, jeering, guffawing, yelling, hurrahing. This was one of the gentlemen against one of their own. Fore was studying Dylan intently, mesmerized.

The fighters approached each other, watching, ready. Saga jumped and kicked Dylan in the chest with both feet. They both went down, but Saga was up instantly. He stomped Dylan in the belly.

Hurt, hurt. Dylan blinked the world back into existence. The hurt was worse, but his brain was working. If Saga stomped him again now, he would be dead. Though his soul was dead, he didn't want to die. He wanted to fight. And frig. And drink blood.

Want stirred him. His gut hurt—he was sure something was broken. He rolled to his knees, holding his breath against the pain. Straightened from his knees. Saw Saga holding the quirt, leering down. Knew he was going to die.

He would die fiercely, beastlike. He would revel in what he was, and die. He struggled to his feet.

Slash. On his light shirt. It stung but was tolerable.

Slash. On his legs, not too bad.

Slash. On his face. Terrible. He touched his mangled skin and brought away a handful of blood.

Slash. The other side of his face. He was stunned, paralyzed, helpless.

Slash. His neck, an awful pain, and the sensation of choking. He was done for now.

Came a voice, Mr. Stewart's voice. "The knife, lad."

Dylan didn't know what it meant. He wasn't skilled enough yet to make an effective throw. Or did the voice mean a throw?

Slash. One of Dylan's nipples exploded in pain.

He staggered backward, away. He had to get farther away, seven paces, to throw a knife.

Saga let him go, perhaps drawing out the kill. Darted in. Slash! Between the thighs, perhaps intended for the balls. Saga darted back out.

The foes looked at each other, Saga mockingly, crouched low, Dylan standing upright, helpless.

Dylan straightened himself for the gesture. He thought through the motion, imagined it vividly. In imagination it was elegant, beautiful, perfect. He would make his quixotic gesture with good form.

He reached his right arm back slowly over his shoulder, grasped the hilt with his fingers.

At that moment Saga charged.

It was all wrong.

The distance was too short.

Saga's head was where his chest should be.

Dylan threw, threw with abandon, threw merely to make the motion he imagined. As he let it go, he knew it was a bad throw.

THOCK!

The sound made Dylan shudder. The crowd babbled agitatedly.

Saga stood still for a moment, poised, stopped in his charge. He crumpled up and rolled to the ground.

His left eye was all blood.

The knife gleamed in the eye socket, silver rampant on a field of crimson.

No, now Dylan saw the knife lying on the ground.

Mr. Stewart stepped forward and picked it up. He rolled Saga onto his back and wiped at the blood with a white linen handkerchief.

Dylan knelt beside them. "The gash is against the shelf of bone above the eye," said Mr. Stewart. He wiped it away again so Dylan could see. The blood welled, fresh, alive, animal.

Mr. Stewart handed Dylan the knife. "The custom," he said mildly, "is to use the tip, not the hilt."

Dylan held the knife. Blood streaked it, hilt and blade, human blood, the sign of all his broken vows.

"I'll take him to Mr. Bleddyn's camp," said Stewart.

Good. Dylan didn't care. His world was rage.

He stood up, looking for Fore. She met his eyes. He held out his hand. She stepped forward and took it.

He led her into the darkness, his cod thrust against his pants, thirsting for blood.

Chapter
Twelve

Dylan came back to camp after dawn besotted with high wine, with sex, with iniquity.

"He's going to be all right," said Dru softly, as though in a convalescent's room. "He's sleeping." Dru inclined his head toward Saga's lodge. "It swelled up ghastly," Dru went on, "but Anastasie poulticed it, the swelling is down, and the eye looks safe."

He handed Dylan a bowl and spoon by way of invitation. Dylan didn't even look to see if it was stew or *sagamité*. He didn't intend to eat for days.

Dru murmured again, "He'll be all right." He paused. "You were out of bounds throwing that knife."

"Bastard was going to kill me."

"No, he wasn't. Used to, he would have. If he got drunk and you took his woman. You know about Indians and drink."

Dru repeated the lecture about Indian drinking philosophy: Whatever you do when you're drunk, it's the rum, not you, and you're not responsible. Dylan didn't give a sod about that.

"I told you Saga's not like that anymore. Though he did get a hair carried away. You're going to have nice scars on your face."

"Bastard woulda killed me."

"I told you," Dru said more sharply, "you can trust him."

Dylan turned his mind back to his mission. "I want to

go to Athabasca with you." The precious mission they were still being so secretive about.

"No," said Dru mildly. "That needs to be one for Saga and me, just the two." He looked Dylan in the eye. "Your job is to look into yourself and find your decision. And tell Mr. Stewart."

"Frig Mr. Stewart."

"More like his lady friend, the tale has it."

Dylan said nothing. Actually, he knew what his decision about Mr. Stewart's offer was. He'd known last night, when he first thought that Saga might be really hurt, and he imagined he could go to the wild and remote Athabasca country with Dru. It gave him a thrill of joy. In a night of debauchery and rage and guilt, a genuine thrill of joy.

The wilderness was in his nature. An evil nature, perhaps, but his.

He wanted to try. "How about the High Missouri, then? How about the truly wild lands and the truly wild Indians? I want to be a Piegan pagan."

The Druid shook his head. "It's not time yet," he said softly. "There's a time.

"By the way," Dru went on, "have you seen the shape of the scars you're going to have?" He offered Dylan Anastasie's hand mirror.

Dylan took it and looked. He had a bright red welt and a slender scab from his left eye to his earlobe. Another from his right eye to that earlobe. He barked a hideous, imitation laugh. The marks of Fornicating Woman.

Fort William
Lake Superior
26 July 1820

Father Auguste Quesnel
Notre Dame Place d'Armes
Montreal, Canada

Dear Father Quesnel:
    I write you on a momentous occasion.

He took a deep breath. He could hear Stewart rustling papers in the background, but he did not want to look at the man. He wanted to concentrate on the task at hand. He wanted to write without smudging the paper Stewart had kindly given him. And he wanted to calm the beating of his heart.

> You may not know that I have joined into the fur trade. I go under a new name. Perhaps this adventure will seem to you precipitously undertaken and foolish. Yet it has been my fondest wish, since a mere child, to walk this country, ride its rivers, breathe its air. Yes, I wish the circumstances of my coming here had been different. Yet it seems not ill to arrive at the place dreamed of by an unexpected path.

> As of today I begin a contracted term of four years as clerk of the NorthWest Company, thanks to the consideration of the bearer of this letter, Duncan Campbell Stewart. My station is to be Fort Augustus, on the Saskatchewan River well nigh to the Rocky Mountains themselves, and the center of trade with Indians known as Piegans and Crees. If they have a reputation as Indians most savage and barbarous, I can say only that I welcome the severest challenge. My task at first will be keeping records of the trade with these Indians, and later executing the trading itself, which I am assured requires the utmost in tactics and will.

> As yet I have no idea what my undertaking might be at the end of the four years. I will say that I yet harbor some hope of one day venturing to this place in a sacred cause. In fact, I say more: Even now, under the flag of commerce, I hope to hold high a light in this darkness.

> Those last words may seem prideful. True, I have discovered, during my venture, that I have the failings of any man, and more. True, I cannot hope to bear any light through my own power. My commitment, therefore, is to seek constantly

through Holy Mary Mother of God the strength of the Divine.

I write to ask several kindnesses: Would you please relay my good wishes to my sister? (Tell Amalie I picture her as a bride already, and a mother before my return.) Would you tell my father that I am well? I half wish to write him, but my soul is divided in its feelings. I hope that one day I will wish to see him again, and he to see me.

Last and most important, Father Quesnel, would you pray for my soul? I cannot but tell you that it is fearfully assailed, and the outcome is in doubt. I promise that I shall remember every day the good words you taught me against occasions like the present.

He thought a moment. Should he sign the letter with his old name or new one? If he signed the old, that would keep up the deception. And signing the new would be a declaration.

I remember you and your counsels gratefully.

yr obdnt servant,
Dylan Davies

He had tried three or four letters, and then decided he had to tell her in person. On the way here he prepared perhaps eight speeches, attempts at eloquent explanation. All night long, after every bout of fornicating, he'd tried to get one out, but the words never came, or even began to come. It seemed hopeless.

Here in the half light of dawn he got the first three or four words out. "Fore, I . . . must go . . ." He stopped, helpless before his ineptitude and his iniquity.

She looked into his face and saw his heart.

"Must go," he mumbled. "To Fort Augustus."

She looked him in the eyes, into his soul, and he saw

something shift in her eyes. Understanding of his baseness, he supposed.

She made a disgusted face. Then she sprang up, grabbed her clothes, and started walking away perfectly naked. She spun on one heel, came back, and spat on his belly.

It served him right to be unable to pray.

He slid from the rock onto his knees on the moist, fertile earth. He formed words in his mind asking Holy Mary, Mother of God, to intercede for him with her Son, to help Dylan Davies the lost to soften his heart, to remove the scales from his eyes and let him dwell in the light once more.

He tried to murmur the words, but he couldn't even get them out—he felt so self-conscious, so stupid. His own black deeds knotted his tongue.

He had been kneeling there, it seemed like an hour. He could not pray. He rose, helpless, and looked wildly around the glade. He was a thousand miles from civilization, and truly alone for the first time in his life.

He could bear the thought that he had abandoned God. He was a wayward mortal.

But what if God had abandoned him?

Part Three

THE BELLY OF
THE WHALE

Chapter
Thirteen

I t was the music, really, that made it so . . . alien.
His mind whirled a little, and he commanded it to stop.
The music, yes, the infernal wailing-chanting, quavering high in the scale, sliding melismatically downward
and softer, sailing high again, bursting up, then arcing
down, like the howl of a wolf. But more grating, by far,
than a wolf's cry, because it was human. To Dylan's ears
it was not graced with the human.

Dylan kept telling himself that if not for the music,
surely, this ritual, this whatever-it-was of the North Piegan
Indians, would not seem so . . . He would be able to bear
it. Which he wasn't sure he could.

He looked sideways at the man who brought him
here, Bleu, the fort interpreter, and got a stern look for his
trouble. There would be times, Bleu had told him, when
they could take a break from this ceremony, and Bleu
would let him know. Obviously not now.

The dark and the bonfire didn't help. The dancing
figures, firelight flickering off their red bodies, looked like
devils. Dylan looked at his other companion, the Balmat,
for help. The Balmat was a lively young blacksmith.
Dylan thought he might become a friend. He watched the
dancing with an expression of pleasant curiosity.

The drums were almost worse than the singing. The
violent metrical thump made Dylan flinch sometimes, but
that wasn't what drove him crazy, it was the relentlessness
of the beat, the feeling of timelessness, the sense that it
drove on forever, it never stopped. Even when the drums

were silent, the beat would thump at you in your brain, in your blood.

It was tied somehow to the corporeal, the bodily, the carnal, the physical without soul.

He shuddered.

It was a scalp dance, Bleu had explained. Dylan had expected to feel repulsed by dancing over human scalps, but this was far worse than he expected, not something merely bloodthirsty and bestial, but a macabre celebration of . . . He didn't know what.

He told himself that his job was to learn the language of these Piegans, and their customs. It was not only a task the factor at Fort Augustus assigned him, but also his pledge to Dru. He didn't know if he could stand it.

Bleu explained the parts of the dance casually, sometimes wittily. Nobody knew what the fort interpreter's real name was, if he even had a baptismal name, but his common name was Sacré Bleu, a joke of a name. His English approached gibberish, and even his French was larded with Indian words. He was plenty peculiar himself. He liked to brag that he had as many bloodlines as a stray bitch had studs—Piegan, Cree, Ojibway, Assiniboine, French, English, Scottish (he didn't claim Welsh), spic, and nigger—as he called them—and the darkest strain of each. He was of indeterminate age, but Dylan was inclined to think he was close to sixty. Swarthy and thick, he had the gnarled physique of a troll. Sometimes he seemed simply hearty and vulgar, but sometimes his eye looked sinister. And certainly he knew the sins of the flesh, intimately.

The Balmat seemed tickled by Bleu.

Dylan cringed at the thought that this was what a lifetime in the *pays d'en haut* made you.

Bleu had explained the ceremony in his cryptic and sardonic way. The dance leader was a woman called a berdache, and there were five parts. First she danced around waving the scalps. Improbably, this was called the courtship dance. Then she paired off males and females of all ages, and they danced. In part three, the round dance, men chose female partners and they danced. In part four women did the choosing.

The screeching and the barbaric drumming reached a

peak of intensity and stopped. There was quiet for a moment.

"What next?" whispered Dylan.

"The climax," said Bleu in French, "the dance of the buffalo mating."

Dylan couldn't stand it. "Let's go!" he snapped.

Dylan felt relieved the moment they got out of the circle. The night air was crisp and cold. The horses were staked beyond the cottonwoods. They would have a head-clearing ride for two or three miles to Fort Augustus. Dylan had the sense that Bleu and the Balmat were amused by him.

They were strange, these young Englishmen the company sent out, each more naive than the last. Bleu ran short of patience with them. They knew nothing of life, and you could tell them nothing. He was supposed to teach this one about the Piegans. *Bien sûr,* he explained the dance, at least what of it the kid was willing to hear. The lad's morals—or what the innocent thought were morals—plugged up his ears.

The man known as Bleu to the Englishmen and Frenchmen, and known to a dozen tribes by a dozen names, and to a dozen wives as much man, didn't understand it. They asked to know but the information made their brains boil. How can you learn when your brain is boiling?

Bleu had thought of telling this Englishman, the young Monsieur Davies, a little of what berdache meant. After all, Rain-in-Her-Hair, the leader of the dance, was not a woman, not exactly, or not what Monsieur Davies thought was a woman. After all, Bleu thought wickedly, she had a cod and a pair of balls. Berdache, the French Canadians called such people, *ake'skassi,* the Piegans called them, every tribe had its own name. Men-women, born men, living as women. People who had the medicine of man and woman in one body. . . . It was hard to explain.

The Englishman could see that a deer wasn't an elk and a porcupine wasn't a beaver, even if they looked a little alike. Why couldn't he see that the English were one

thing and the French another and the nigger and spic and
Indun yet others? Why did he have to be horrified by the
differences?

Because that's the way your Englishman was.

No, Mr. Stewart, it is not the country that is godless.
It is the natives.

Dylan was watching the women butcher their autumn
buffalo kill. Like carrion birds they flew in among the carcasses with their knives and axes, hacking and pecking at
the steaming flesh. The prairie itself became an abattoir,
and in a few minutes its floor was so wet with blood the
ground sucked at your moccasins.

The great bodies were ripped open, the skins huge,
dripping red flags, the guts strewn on the ground, blood
gouting everywhere. The women, their arms and legs and
dresses and even their faces and hair soaked in crimson, cut
pieces of raw liver and sucked them into their mouths. They
drank the rank bile, even drank the stomach contents. From
all this rose the steam and stench of corporeality, of blood
and gut and kidney and heart and testicle and womb, spilled
on the ground, laid open in its foulness. Dylan thought it
showed what man would be without a soul.

Dylan thought the plains, seen right, had a certain
stark beauty. Even the plants that grew upon them, the willows, the cottonwoods, the berry bushes, and the vast car-
pet of thick grass, had a dry-land loveliness. Even the
buffalo was majestic, only partly undone by its stupidity.
No, the godlessness showed in the human beings who
thrived upon the buffalo, the Indians.

He could admire their ingenuity in making everything
they needed from the great brute. Meat, of course, and every kind of clothing from the hide. Also the war shield,
from the thick skin of the neck. The hides also made blankets. With the hair removed, a cover for the lodge. The
sinew became string, the stomach a pot, and the bladder a
watertight bag. The bones were used for scraping tools, the
hoofs for glue, the horns for drinking cups. The long chin
hairs were braided into rope. There was more. Even the
dung was used—as fuel for fires in a woodless country.

And every part of the buffalo could become a totem, a medicine object, worn on the head, around the neck, tied to one arm, hidden in the medicine bag, a mad, barbaric emblem of what they mistook for divine.

The attitude of the Piegans toward this beast was bizarre and perverted, a combination of worship and blood lust. They followed the buffalo, they let the buffalo determine their movements and season, they danced to it, they dreamed of it, they made medicine of it and for it. In short, they worshiped it. Surely it said everything about a people that the object of their devotion was a dumb, dirty beast full of flies and maggots, of foul and grossly corporeal body, offering food for the body but none for the soul.

It was the buffalo the white men came for as well. The Piegans didn't trap beaver. The trade here was essentially pemmican, made by cutting the meat into long strips, drying it on racks high above small fires, pounding it into powder and tiny fibers, mixing lots of fat and some dried berries with it, stuffing it into the sacks that kept it dry, so it would last all winter and longer.

Dylan might be able to trade for the pemmican. Having seen the butchering, he didn't think he could eat it again.

Today they would appear on the plain in front of the fort to trade. Quite a show, it would be, said Mad Jack. "You must learn to barter with Indians, me boy. That's your job, to learn to pamper them, humor them, indulge them, praise them, outwit them, and let them have some of what they want for lots of what you want." Mad Jack cackled. Sometimes he seemed as bedlam as the Indians. They were children, he said, transparent, guileless, susceptible to flattery, impulsive in their desires. Yet they could be cunning, devious, vengeful, murderous. You had to go among them, trade, and come back with your scalp and a handsome profit for the NorthWest Company.

Mad Jack said, "Follow my lead and keep your mouth shut."

Fine, thought Dylan.

Dylan had his questions about Mad Jack O'Malley. In

a firm run by Scots, he was an Irishman who had risen high enough to command a post. Fort Augustus was important, the center of the trade of the North Piegans and the Cree and all the other Indians of the Saskatchewan River. Yet even in his high position he was intemperate, immoderate, and inclement. Quick to wrath, indignation, and vexation, full of rage and fury, and intermittently drunk, very drunk indeed. His very manner of speech told his disposition: He stood too close to a man, his body tensed for a fight, fists clenched, voice raised, and talked with animation, spittle flying. The Indians were said to be afraid of him. They dealt peaceably with Mad Jack because they feared he was truly crazy.

Bleu said maybe he was.

Though he claimed to speak more languages than he had fingers and toes, Bleu's English and French were poor, except for words for the vulgar bodily functions. He didn't answer certain questions, and Dylan could never tell why. Either he didn't understand, or he thought the question was dumb, or . . . You couldn't tell. He had a way of responding with stock words and phrases that made no sense:

Will Horn of the Bull compare our prices to what the HBC will give him? "Thank you," Bleu would say.

Why don't the Piegans do more trapping? "Just as you say."

Are women just property to Indians, like horses? "Chin up, there's a good fellow."

Do the Indians believe in more than one god? "Tallyho."

"Tallyho" was his favorite. Dylan had no idea where he'd gotten it. It was funny to think of anyone riding to hounds in this godforsaken place. What Bleu meant by it was mysterious as . . . Everything was obscure here.

First Mad Jack told Bleu and Dylan to check the security of the fort. This meant walking around and looking at the fortifications, arms, and guards. Mad Jack told Dylan privately that he asked Bleu to do this because he knew Bleu told the Indians the fort's so-called secrets, and Mad Jack wanted them to know how high the cost of rushing the fort would be. This was in case the damned HBCers got the Piegans hot enough on rum and inflammatory talk to take a notion.

The exterior wall was a palisade as tall as three men, the logs squared where they butted up against each other and sunk four feet into the ground. Below the top ran a gallery, all the way around, to give the guards protection and an ideal angle for shooting. At the corners were blockhouses, and in these bastions sat three-pound cannons. In one room, stout and well-locked, were plenty of Nor'West rifles and muskets, plus a powder magazine. Altogether it was a fortification that made Dylan sleep easier, two thousand miles from civilization.

Since today was trading day, guards were posted. The Piegans had come in yesterday afternoon, pitched their lodges near the river on the side away from the HBC post, Edmonton House, which sat insolently within sight of the NWC fort. Last night Mad Jack and Dylan got the trading room ready.

"When will they come?" Dylan asked Bleu.

"Thank you," said the scoundrel, eyes wandering off.

"How long will it take?"

Now Bleu favored him with a skeptical glance. "Tallyho," he said.

They walked outside the fort to meet the chiefs. The farther they walked, said Mad Jack, the greater the compliment to the visitors. As soon as the guards reported the Indians on the way, Mad Jack, Bleu, and Dylan hurried out toward them. When the chiefs saw the traders coming, they stood contentedly and waited.

Clearly they were dressed for a great occasion. They wore their most ornately quilled or beaded shirts, breechclouts, leggings, and moccasins. Several wore buffalo robes painted with huge sun signs, which Dylan admitted had a strong, primitive beauty. Their hair was elaborately combed into bizarre shapes and held in place with bear grease and feathers. Necklaces of tooth, claw, and shell abounded. Most faces were painted gaudily, and some men wore paint instead of shirts.

They stood in line, and the traders passed down the line to shake hands with each chief. Bleu told Dylan softly that they stood in the order of their coups, from most to least. You could tell the coups, he said, by looking at the feathers on the staffs they carried. When Dylan asked why some coups brought the greatest honor and others the least, Bleu answered, "Just as you say."

Finished with handshaking, Mad Jack led them back to the head of the line, produced his medicine pipe, lit it, and offered it to the four directions and to the sun. When the grand chief had taken three puffs—it must be exactly three, whispered Bleu—he got out his own pipe, lit it, presented it ceremoniously to the powers, and invited Mad Jack to smoke. Then the pipe was passed to all the chiefs, and to Dylan and Bleu.

On orders, Dylan kept a scrupulously straight face while he puffed. He felt self-conscious as a choir boy with his first solo.

After Mad Jack gave the chiefs a little tobacco, he presented them with some rum. This was the real stuff, about fifty proof. As the trading went on and the Indians got drunker, Bleu had said, the liquor would get more and more diluted. Since their craving for rum was said to be prodigious, and this drink was powerful, Dylan was surprised to see the head chief dip his fingers into the cup and shake a few drops onto the ground and a few more into the sky.

On the way back to the fort Mad Jack muttered that these Piegans seemed in no hurry to get drunk, so the trading would be hard. It's hell, he said merrily to Dylan, not to be able to take advantage of an ignorant bugger whenever you feel like it.

The trading was an education. Mad Jack let the Indians into the fort only a few at a time, the head men first. The interior of the fort was in separate rectangles—the lodgings of the fort officers, including Dylan, the lodgings of the blacksmith and other artisans, the smithy and carpentry shop, an area for horses, a common area, and the trading rooms, where goods were stored and traded.

After the Indians got into the room, there was more ceremony. The chiefs claimed they loved the Nor'Westers like brothers, even like their own children. They promised to stay away from the HBC men, who were not worthy to be called men anyway. They explained through Bleu that they had done as well as they could for their good friends, but not as well as they meant to do, and they would do better next time.

In overblown and absurd language Mad Jack returned their compliments, their love, and their good intentions.

The Piegans seldom had many beaver plews, or pelts, to trade, just a few they got from other Indians. Now, after the summer season, they had none. They brought a few wolf pelts, and the summer skins of ermine, otters, and other small animals. They did their best to trade things the white men didn't much want—dried berries, herbs, roots, and the like. Then out came their dried buffalo tongues, which were prized moderately. Next to last came bags of pemmican sewn shut for preservation, quite a few of these. They were holding back, Jack said, and would bring more later, when they were more desperate for drink. And finally what they were most proud of, buffalo robes, skillfully and lovingly tanned, some even painted. It was the best hide you got in this miserable country, said Jack, but it was no cash crop compared to beaver. If it wasn't for pemmican, the Nor'West men wouldn't be in this country.

For these items the Indians wanted rum, tobacco, rum, hatchets, rum, knives and axes, rum, guns, rum, powder and lead, rum, blankets and cloth, rum, beads and vermilion and other trinkets, and rum. All the rum must be free. The Piegans called it white man's water, and they refused to buy water, any kind of water.

You had to give them what they wanted, Mad Jack told Dylan as they worked. If the Indians had lots to trade, like children they let it go freely and you did smashingly well. If they were poor, you still had to let them have something, or they would trade with the Lords and Ladies, or even start shooting you in the back in the wilds. "Lords and Ladies" was Jack's mocking appellation for what he also called the "DisHonourable Company."

First the gift of rum. One rule Jack stuck to, though

overfond of a tot himself, was that they had to leave the fort before they started drinking. Otherwise it was too dangerous. Dylan would see.

Dylan felt little sympathy for Jack when he complained about not being able to get all he wanted for his trade goods. One of Dylan's jobs as clerk was to keep track of what was traded and at what price. Jack was trying to get ten times the cost, at least. He bragged that when these Indians came in last autumn, he traded a keg of rum for peltries worth twenty-five or thirty pounds. It had cost the company one.

Jack grinned big when he told this story, like being a real white man was knowing how to get the best of people.

Jack was earning, or gouging, a handsome profit for the company. Dylan was writing it down. Sometimes the figures started to squiggle, as at the bank. He'd come all the way to the Rocky Goddamn Mountains to juggle figures again.

Well, at least figures weren't debauchery.

Out of the darkness of early evening, up from the mists along the river, in tempo with the ancient rhythms of the swirling water, through the incandescence of the last light of day, she undulated toward him, naked. Tendrils of mist brushed the rosy nipples of her breasts and slipped between her legs and around her arms, which were held up to him. Her hair gleamed, her eyes shone, and her body was luminous—it seemed in the early starlight to glow with welcoming.

A fantasy, of course, Bleu's fantasy, the picture he kept drawing in an inimitable mix of English, French, and unknown languages this afternoon during a lull in trading.

A powerful fantasy. Powerful enough to bring Dylan down here to the village at nearly dark, a matter not entirely safe. He told himself he wanted to see for himself— see the drunkenness, the debauchery, the licentiousness. He told himself he wanted to know, bottom-know, gut-know, and understand. So he told himself. He admitted in his heart, also, that he could not resist the allure Bleu had spun in words, pictures of Indian girls "in their season," as he put it, sexually feverish from rum, and preferring white men because of the baubles they got.

Dylan intended to act like a civilized man and a Christian in the wilderness. He had decided that did not mean he was not a man. He thought of Fore and acknowledged what he could not resist. This weakness he would simply admit and give in to without undue self-censure. He could not help it. He had no choice.

But he did mean to act like a civilized man. He had no intention of becoming like Mr. Stewart. Well, like the Stewart of Bleu's stories, if they were to be believed.

Bleu immediately had recognized Stewart's knives, now Dylan's knives. They launched him into Monsieur Stewart stories. They were just stories, and not flattering to Stewart. Stories of stupidity and clumsiness, stories of obtuseness, scatological stories, stories of sin, most of all stories of a man whose imagination was haunted by the barbarism of the Indians.

These last stories worried Dylan.

"When Monsieur Stewart was *bourgeois* here," said Bleu, "like Jack be now, and Jack clerk like Dylan, when Monsieur Stewart be *bourgeois* here, *oui,* his mind is *comme* on fire, *pris en feu,* with the violence. Crazy Frenchy, Monsieur Stewart. No, only Englishman be so *fou,* so . . . mad. At first he is, how you say, like virgin, among us but not one of us, not be touched by all such blood as peoples live with, like walk without touching ze ground.

"*Mais,* this one, he, how you say, fascinate, with ze blood, he especial want know about the scalping. I tell him what he asks, is simple tell. How cut, why cut, what mean. He fascinate. Delicious to him that some peoples take all scalp, not just topknot but all, down to . . ." Bleu pointed to his eyebrows, his ears, the nape of his neck.

"He ask me bring scalps, he put them on wall in bedroom, he trade for scalps wiz anyone who bring them. He say he want whole scalp"—again Bleu ran his finger from brow to ear to nape—"and he want whole head. I tell him scalp the part for the whole, peoples used take whole head, very medicine, now take topknot, is more easy. He offer me twenty dollar whole head. I . . ." Bleu made a motion of brushing something away. Maybe a shudder was beneath the gesture. "Very medicine," repeated Bleu.

"One day Monsieur Stewart drunk. He get habit go village at night, frig women, no? Is good, frig, *mais* Monsieur he make it bad. Feel bad medicine in himself, bad to do, act bad, and he no like ze women after such.

"This day village from far south, other fork Saskatchewan River, it come in. Assiniboines, never be here before. Monsieur he not know these Indians, he go anyway at night, frig. Women he get, *très belle*, no remember name, this man Hawk Cries want her bad. Bleu remembers his name, Hawk Cries, Monsieur Stewart never forget it.

"This woman *belle*, no? Though a man who is, *vraiment*, a man knows they are all alike, yes?" Bleu shot a lecherous grin at Dylan.

"Hawk Cries, he hide bushes, attack Monsieur Stewart after frig. Indun drunk, maybe mean to kill, maybe not, who know? Monsieur Stewart he have big anger spirit, he big with savage, throw knife." Bleu mimed the motion. Dylan was uncomfortably conscious of the pair of knives strapped onto his back.

Bleu thumped his chest in a stabbing motion, lurched, and gagged his apparent last breath. Gave Dylan a serious look.

"Monsieur all . . ." Bleu circled his hands in a frenzy, "agitate. Never kill man before. At first leave knife in chest, come back to fort, drink. Later go back, body still near bushes, maybe no one notice. Maybe take knife and no one know who kill. He take knife. Then use hatchet and knife, cut off head." Bleu drew a line across his neck.

"Now mad. Under *charme*, spell, in sway of own medicine. Take head, come back fort, get ladder. With guards watching, stick head onto picket by gate so all see. All peoples see, know who kill Hawk Cries, and who proud kill. Bleu when he sees, he take head down.

"Next day Assiniboines big council, much talk kill Monsieur Stewart. Some say he drunk, rum kill, not Monsieur. Some say he not drunk until after, come back for head. Woman say he not drunk, he big in the cod. Altogezer, maybe Assiniboines kill him, maybe kill all Frenchmen, burn fort.

"Bleu, I say, Monsieur is stupid, know nothing, probably drunk. I not think drunk but say to Indun drunk. Let him pay, says Bleu. So Monsieur pay. Good Northwest gun, tobacco, six horses. Dream of Monsieur *cher, très* expensive.

"After zat Monsieur look at knife like big medicine, bad medicine, very good, very dangerous, he not know. Look at himself very bad. Man have bad-medicine dream, not make good medicine, mind gets sick, he act sick, that's all. Stupid. Monsieur Stewart, life taste bad to him now. Stupid."

Out of the darkness of early evening, up from the mists along the river, in tempo with the ancient rhythms of the swirling water, through the incandescence of the last light of day, she undulated toward him, naked, tendrils of mist brushing the rosy nipples of her breasts, and slipping between her legs, and around her arms, which were held up to him. Her hair gleamed, her eyes shone, and her body was luminous, seemed in the early starlight to glow with welcoming.

The fantasy had Dylan in its thrall. He could find nothing like that. He wandered aimlessly through the village, searching to fulfill his dream. What he saw was drunk Indians, men and women. Many were lying on the ground, passed out. Dylan wondered why they drank more than was fun, drank until they got stuporous and sick. Your cod wouldn't even rise when you were that drunk.

In two different places men and women were sitting, kneeling, and standing around a robe playing a gambling game. He watched a few minutes. A fellow with a carved piece of wood or bone would hide it in one fist or the other and shuffle it invisibly back and forth. The drum would start thumping, and the man would begin to dance, twisting, contorting, wrenching his body, and all the while passing the bone back and forth, or pretending to. The drum would rise to a huge, throbbing crescendo, and stop. The dancer froze.

Bettors put valuables on their choice, right hand or left. The men risked knives, animal paws, pouches, even blankets. The women risked beads, moccasins, awls, hatchets, bells. Dylan wondered if anyone would get drunk enough tonight to risk a gun. He was sure someone would.

The bets were placed quickly, the tension feverish and rising. Still frozen, the dancer then opened a full hand, or an empty one and then the full one, and the crowd would cheer or moan. The game began again.

At the second game Dylan saw a young woman, really just a girl, take off the cotton blouse she wore and risk it. The Indians wore little cotton, for it was expensive. Bare-breasted, she knelt and bounced on her heels until the first hand opened. Dylan knew which hand she had bet on from her downcast face. She sat crestfallen for a few moments, stood, slipped out of her deerskin skirt, sat naked, and folded it in front of her. A man put a blanket next to it and looked at her with veiled eyes. She nodded.

As the drum rose and rose, the girl seemed almost to dance on her knees, her eyes enthralled with the dancer. The music stopped. The dancer opened one hand dramatically. The man and girl looked at each other. He took the dress and blanket. He spoke something to her. They went off into the darkness together hurriedly.

Dylan watched the game, inflamed. He must find a woman. In ten minutes the girl and man came back, she wearing the blanket, naked beneath. They sat far apart from each other, eyes indifferent to all but the game. He bet the skirt on the next round. She took off the blanket, folded it, and bet it.

He found a woman, but not his fantasy. She was a woman in her thirties, perhaps forty, worn and thick-bodied but at least not fat. As she first walked drunkenly toward him, she pointed to her crotch. When she got close, she brushed her hand on his cod. He held up a string of small bells. She grinned and took them.

In the darkness, on the ground, she put the bells near her shoulder. As they frigged with all their clothes on, they shifted until she bumped the bells on every thrust and they jingled forlornly.

*   *   *

The next morning Mad Jack introduced him to another of his white-man tools, the set of surveying instruments. Dylan immediately felt they might cleanse him. Thermometers, bulbs full of quicksilver, a sextant, a measuring wheel, a compass, and it got more wonderful yet—an artificial horizon, parallel glasses, a pocket watch, and best of all, the yearly *Nautical Almanac* and its accompanying handbook, *Requisite Tables*. All these were what the Indian world lacked.

They spent all that day and the next on techniques of surveying, which as a white-man leader Dylan needed. They took double meridian altitudes of the sun, which gave latitude, which was easier to get than longitude. But Dylan was keen, and learned quickly to calculate longitude by the method based on lunar distances. Jack showed him how the instruments could get into rough shape and throw the calculations off. Extreme cold affected them, he said, and liquids might make the bulbs and tubes burst. Dylan liked it all. He even liked the words—degrees, minutes, seconds, calibration, calculation, angle, azimuth, zenith. They made a clean world.

Jack let Dylan go out with Bleu to survey a creek thoroughly to learn the technique. After several days of field work, Dylan lost himself in the tools of mapmaking—a set of drafting instruments, ruler, pens and pencils, camel hair brushes, sticks of India ink, watercolors, Whatman's paper, and tracing paper. He loved making the map. It was scientific, it ordered jumbled actuality into comprehensible latitude and longitude, it let you understand, it created an abstract beauty for the mind. And you didn't have to remember how corporeal your actual experience there was, how grossly . . . Indian it all felt.

He made his first big purchase on credit from the company, a pocket watch. He would carry it always, a gleaming symbol of the difference between the white man and the Indian.

Chapter
Fourteen

October stretched toward November without Dru. Trading and hunting were over, so Dylan had time on his hands. He spent it wandering with his sextant. He spent it jesting with that wise fool of a jester Bleu. He spent it yearning for Dru.

He felt something happening in his soul this plains autumn, what the Indians called the moon after the leaves fall off, also called the moon when the geese fly south. It was an odd month in this vast country, as the season slid from summer to winter. Mornings were cold, evenings nippy. The wind and weather were still. In the pagan manner Bleu rose each morning with the dawn and, standing there by the bedroll in his underwear, said good morning ceremonially to the sun. Father Sun, he called it. Sometimes he seemed to make a genuine little ceremony of his greeting, and sometimes he seemed to toss it off as a burlesque. Yet even then Dylan could hear a genuineness in the salutation. The rest of the day the Frenchy was a regular sort of white man, helping Dylan willingly enough in the surveying he didn't believe in, and complaining mostly for fun. But Dylan had heard his dawn prayer, and knew that Bleu was a barbarian in his heart.

As a purely secular matter, Dylan admired the sunshine himself. Not only did it make getting out of that bedroll tolerable, it did something . . . almost spiritual. It gave the days a kind of grace. It turned the grasses a wondrous color, a tawny green that glowed from the inside out. And other grasses wine-colored, and the willow bushes orange-red. It made the very air . . . intoxicating. It shone so strong, even this late in the season, that the profane earth at times seemed to become luminous.

Bleu was a barbarian because he did not understand that the sun did not, could not, fill the world with spirit, or put a creature with a soul thereon to apprehend it.

It was November first exactly, according to Dylan's journal, that they saw far-off figures making their way toward the post. "Dru!" Dylan exclaimed.

"Zis be no Druid and Saga," said Bleu. "Monsieur Troyes, the Lemieux brothers, and a woman."

Dylan focused the telescope on the riders. How Bleu could see details across the plains at these distances, Dylan didn't know. Even with the Dolland telescope, Dylan couldn't be sure it wasn't Dru. But he could see long skirts on one of the riders.

"Word de Montreal," said Bleu.

"What word?"

Bleu shrugged.

"But where's Dru?"

Bleu shrugged again. "Tallyho."

It was word from Montreal, and from Mad Jack's expression, a very strange word. The Nor'West Company was to buy no more pemmican than it needed to feed its own men for next spring only. No expeditions were to be sent into remote country, no men sent out to bring the wandering tribes in to the trading posts, no expenses not strictly necessary incurred. On the other hand, all trade goods were to be exchanged for peltries of any kind, price no object. Only enough was to be kept for bare subsistence. In short, nothing was to be spent and all assets turned into the equivalent of cash, immediately.

"*Bleedin'* partners," cursed Mad Jack. Field partners, who saw the value long-term of establishing relationships with the Indians, were always complaining about the Montreal partners, who demanded more immediate profits.

The messenger was a Métis of great self-possession. The look on his face suggested Indian impatience with the quarrels of white men. "I know no more," he said in French.

"So what ze bludy hell goes on?" asked Bleu calculatingly.

"Capital," said Mad Jack disgustedly. According to him, the Nor'West Company had always outdone the HBC in enterprise, daring, and every sort of competence, especially understanding of the Indians. But the price wars verged on ruinous. The NWC partners spent fortunes on wine, women, and song when they had them, compiled no reserves, and sometimes could not compete with the vast resources of the landed and titled men who backed the Hudson's Bay Company. This was another episode of lack of capital, said Jack. The Nor'West men, good *voyageurs* and splendid *hommes du nord,* could have won this war hands down, Jack said, except for the foolishness of the Montreal partners.

Dylan wondered if Jack really knew what was going on. He wished Dru were here to help think things out. Where the hell were Dru and Saga anyway? It was November, and the weather was already risky for traveling.

At dinner Dylan covertly studied the messenger, one Yves Troyes. He was smashingly handsome, with a finely sculpted face, yet was darker even than most Indians, and thoroughly Indian in his mannerisms. The French he spoke was more city-refined than country-crude. Dylan wondered who his father had been. Troyes was not the descendant of longtime *habitants,* Dylan was sure of that. He had a certain elegance, an aloofness, and a certain nonchalance, that lent him the style of an aristocrat. Dylan wondered where he got his sense of . . . sovereignty.

Perhaps it was partly his daughter, Caroline. At least her father introduced her as Caroline. Curtseying, she corrected it to "Caro."

Caro Troyes was as handsome as her father, statuesque, with a thick braid of glowing russet hair that hung below her waist, skin of soft beige, and delicate features. She was a tall, slender girl, and had a way of carrying her body as though it was delicate and precious. She seemed

as aloof as her father, in an opposite way. Her eyes burned
at people. If Dylan could read body language, she was neither modest nor deferential toward men, but defiantly
proud. Yet she contributed nothing to the dinner conversation. Dylan guessed she was there on paternal orders, but
supremely uninterested. After dinner, while the men
talked, she sat on a chair in a corner and read a book.
Dylan couldn't see what it was.

He wondered about Caro. Who was her mother?
Where? Why was she traveling alone with her father, with
winter approaching, through a cold and vast Canadian wilderness? If she spoke her mind, what would she say? How
did a woman of French and Cree ancestry get a name such
as the English "Caroline"? Throughout the evening he
watched her, fascinated by her scorn for the society of
traders, men of commerce. He felt drawn to her, a little
foolish about her, and oddly protective of her.

Perhaps that's why he was not listening when Yves
Troyes suddenly mentioned his name. Dylan thought he'd
said, "I'd like Monsieur Davies to go with us."

Dylan looked up at the dark Métis. "Monsieur Davies," he said in French, "you have not met the Lemieux
brothers, our traveling companions. They're busy enjoying
their wives tonight, whom they haven't seen in many
months." This was said without a hint of impropriety, but
Bleu gave Dylan a licentious look.

"Interesting men, the Lemieux," said Mad Jack cryp-
tically.

"They wish to stay here with their families now, as
they should. My daughter and I require two more men for
our journey on to Captain Chick at Rocky Mountain
House. Bleu has agreed to come. And that unusual chap
who calls himself the Druid suggested you. By the way, he
sends his greetings."

"The Druid?" Dylan repeated stupidly.

"Yes, we saw him at Fort William."

Why was Dru all the way back at Fort William instead of Athabasca? Or here?

"He sends you a message. He regrets to say that he
will not arrive until spring. Urgent affairs. And suggests

that you make the journey to Rocky Mountain House with
myself and my daughter."

Yes, the trip on to the next fort to spread the word
from Montreal. The very strange word, and the strange urgency to get it to every factor.

"That would be good for you, lad," put in Mad Jack.
"Spend the winter there with Captain Chick. See another
outfit. Learn."

Dylan looked at Yves Troyes, who seemed aloof, un-
appealing. He looked at Caroline, who was aloof and very
appealing. He eyed Bleu and got an unreadable glance. He
thought of the cold, arduous trip through to the mountains.
He felt a nameless dread of this wilderness.

He looked again at Caroline. Her eyes were, well, he
hoped they were challenging. Foolishly, he stammered,
"When do we start?"

"What's the book you're reading?" Dylan finally
asked. It was after dinner, and nearly dark. In two days of
traveling, Caro had scarcely spoken to anyone, but spent
all her time in camp reading and all her time riding silent.
She rode willingly but wordlessly. She took their simple
meal of pemmican in silence, her eyes on her book. With
her eyes she declined to help with the simple camp chores,
fixing the squaw fire, putting up and taking down the tent.
Her father did her part without comment, much to Bleu's
amusement. Every night she volunteered to share the
men's duty of standing guard, and every night he refused.
These were almost her only words. She read, or looked
around with a transported expression on her face, or occasionally walked a little, as though enchanted, murmuring
to herself.

When they stopped at noon, and while the men set up
camp in the evening, she sketched in watercolors. Not on
a small, lap-held pad, but on big sheets of paper on an easel, as Dylan imagined a real artist would do. He was surprised at first to see a European spirit, especially a
feminine one, attracted to painting these vast scenes. Yet
he himself was learning to see a kind of magic in them,
especially now that they were rising off the infinite plains

into the foothills of the great mountain range. Dylan himself sensed magic in this landscape—a barbaric magic, perhaps, even the devil's magic, but still magic.

She showed no one the sketches. But Dylan saw the expression on her face when she brought the easel back to camp, rapt, even transported.

He was becoming fascinated with her. Yes, she was silent. Perhaps it was refusal to stoop to participate in low society. But it seemed otherwise, it seemed elevated, spiritual. In the evening she would read by the fire with a combination of intensity and rapture, like a monk seeking God and occasionally glimpsing His face.

Dylan watched her surreptitiously as she finished reading and turned toward the tent she shared with her father. That's when, miserable, ashamed of himself, Dylan blurted out, "What's the book you're reading?" He had a fleeting impression that Troyes gave him a look of alarm.

She turned, a finger in her slender book, and regarded him. Skeptically, perhaps? He could not say how. "I'm sorry I've not been sociable. I have not intended to be rude. I just don't know if . . ." She said in the tone of a quotation,

> I stood
> Among them, but not of them; in a shroud
> Of thoughts which were not their thoughts.

She let that sit for a moment. Then: "Have you heard of George Gordon, Lord Byron?" It was not a question of a lady to a commoner. It was appraising, but open to possibility.

"No," he said regretfully.

"Spend an hour with this," she said. "Then tell me what you see." She handed him her book with a friendly glance. *Childe Harold's Pilgrimage,* the title said, by this Lord Byron.

The hour was remarkable. Dylan huddled by the flickering light and meager warmth of the fire throughout the first watch, which Troyes took. Occasionally Dylan would stand up and pace, his mind on Childe Harold and on himself, trying on the mantle of the gloomy, tormented hero. He thought of his father, who didn't love him. Of his outcast state, driven from his own home, forced even to change his name. He thought of the sins of the flesh he had committed, which were his doom. The mantle fit.

He turned back to the enchanted world of the story. And there in the night, under Troyes's sardonic eye during the first watch, Dylan sailed into a new and better world.

Troyes finally went to bed, with a threat. "If I catch you with your nose in that book on watch," he said, "I'll fine you a month's pay." Dylan put the book down, amused that Troyes thought such a worldly threat would intimidate him.

Dylan didn't read, but his mind was still nowhere near his watch. He paced, picturing Childe Harold and seeing himself. Like Harold, he was neglected, ignored, and shunned, mysterious to others and even to himself, uncared for, melancholy even in moments of happiness, above all lonely. Here especially he was like Childe Harold:

Yet oft-times in his maddest mirthful mood
Strange pangs would flash along Childe Harold's brow
As if the memory of some dreadful feud
Or disappointed passion lurk'd below:
But this none knew, nor haply cared to know.

He learned something else about his life. His heart had thawed about wild nature. Something in the forests and the plains and the mountains which the party could now see, something about this wildness, this untamèdness, reverberated in him, touched his soul. Something reminded him of that grand day with Dru ringing the bells. You could not say what was so sublime—you had to feel it, to put your head on the bell and let the reverberations resonate through you, to sail through the air on the ropes with the world-shattering clang in your ears. So it was with nature.

He could not have told Father Quesnel—and certainly not his mother's husband—what was mesmerizing in nature. Yet if you let yourself, if you listened to it, smelled it, breathed it in, looked at it with the mystic eye . . . He was not a poet, he had no words for the grandeur, the lift of soul.

With a dark look at the tent, he picked up the book and thumbed through pages until he found the passage he wanted to read again. He whispered, but the words resounded in his head.

There is a pleasure in the pathless woods,
There is a rapture on the lonely shore,
There is society, where none intrudes,
By the deep sea and music in its roar:
I love not man the less, but Nature more,
From these our interviews, in which I steal
From all I may be, or have been before,
To mingle with the Universe, and feel
What I can ne'er express, yet cannot all conceal.

Bleu rolled out of his blankets and spotted the book in Dylan's hand. Dylan was sure he saw the Frenchy's eyes roll with disgust. Why? Dylan wondered. Surely this was the reason Caro kept this passion to herself.

"I don't feel like sleeping," he said to Bleu.

"We need a decent watch anyway," the man answered pointedly.

The words brought Dylan crashing back into the world of the mundane. Yes, this was why Caro kept her silence.

In fact, Dylan didn't feel a whit tired. His spirit was animated, tingling, pulsing with aliveness. He wrapped up in his blankets, propped against a tree, and watched the stars. He had never felt so excited to be alive.

Soon he saw from the Big Dipper that dawn was coming, that the darkness would begin to pale faintly now along the eastern horizon. In half an hour first light would rise into the world, and then would emerge a miracle, the majesty of the sun. He felt he had to watch it, to let the sun's beams flood into him, to drink them in like a rare liquor and let them warm him from within. He decided to get high, to find some pinnacle, some magical place to stand and be flooded with light.

"I'm going for a walk," he said to Bleu.

"Don't let your arse get cold." Bleu snorted out a half chuckle.

Vulgar assumption. Dylan felt no inclination to tell Bleu, or anyone of ordinary consciousness, what he would do. I understand, Caro. "I'll take a while," he added.

He found an outcropping of stone that jutted from the top of a hill. It felt like an altar. As the sky lightened, he could see to the east the great, rolling, rocky plain that two or three months ago struck him as so desolate. Now he saw that it was beautiful. It was painted this late autumn in every shade of brown—sere grasses that were dun, amber, and ginger, jutting rocks that were mahogany and sienna, bushes and willows that were cinnamon and gold. The few leaves left on the cottonwoods below him on the plain sprinkled the washes the color of lemon rind.

He turned and looked away from the sun, toward the high mountains rising from the night mists into the morning light. Here the aspens splotched the hillside with color of fluttering canaries, and bushes ran riot in magenta. These wild colors were unified there by the pure, white, glistening snow that lay like grace on the land and all the rocks. Far, far to the west, on the highest ridges and summits, the snow caught the first rays of the rising sun, and turned a molten rose-gold.

He sat very still and watched and felt. Light emanated from the sky, or generated from within the shining streams, or rose from the earth itself; he could not have said which. It felt like benediction.

He watched, and for once in his life did not form his experience into words. He let it remain, as it was, inside him and outside him, elemental as earth, fire, water, air. It felt like food of the spirit, ambrosial nourishment, life-giving sustenance, even breath itself. He felt it come into his eyes and so into his brain and heart and lungs and so into his blood, and by his blood be carried to every particle of his being, even his skin, his fingernails, his hair, and back to the liquid surface of his eyes. It permeated him, it suffused his being. It was like hearing ethereal music, the music of spheres, yet the music was utterly soundless.

Stirred by some powerful impulse, he slid forward onto his knees, face to the sun. He bowed his head, touched it to the naked rock of the altar. Suddenly, vibrantly, he felt the reverberation of the energy of the earth within his head, within all his bones. It was the dance of the planet itself—the intricate motions of the air, the subtle undulations of water, the green force that squeezed through grass and flowers and made them surge toward the sun, that sucked up through the great roots of trees and through the thick trunks and out into the delicate leaves, which danced in the fluxing air. He felt this force rise through him vigorously, ringingly, resoundingly, and his entire body pirouetted to it. To the outward eye he was still. Yet dervishlike, he whirled on the single place where he knelt, not worshiping the divine energies, but becoming them.

He felt the paradox: while he knelt utterly still, he danced.

Chapter

Fifteen

When he came back to camp, Dylan saw Caro for the first time.

She was simply tending the fire. She turned and looked at him and saw. And took an extra moment to see. He knew what she saw—that he had been up all night, racked by the pain of existence, transported by the vision of nobility, that he was haggard and exhausted yet uplifted by the very air he breathed.

She broke into a radiant smile. Amazing how the world could be transformed—you could be transformed—by what was in your mind.

He handed her the book. For both of them it was a moment of reverence. "Thank you. Thank you beyond thanks."

They looked each other in the eyes, hesitated, smiled foolishly.

Dylan stammered out, "I went up there"—he pointed—"to watch the sun rise. It was . . ." He shrugged helplessly. ". . . grand."

He squatted by the fire. This morning even the pemmican would taste like manna. "God, I'm starved," he said. Then foolishly, "I haven't slept at all."

They rode close together and talked all day. Troyes didn't like their incessant jabber, as he called it, but they didn't care. Like Bleu, he rode ahead and to the sides, scouting. And they were alone to show each other their souls.

Caro told him how she had been introduced to the works of Lord Byron. She'd spent the last three years in England, going to school. She liked learning but disliked school. It was fussily proper old ladies of all ages, concerned about carriage, manners, deportment, and decorum. Among the first of the accomplishments young ladies were to attain was music, which she'd adored. Her favorite instrument was the pianoforte. Though she'd not become accomplished at the instrument—that required years—she'd loved it, and the new pieces being written for it. The clavichord and harpsichord expressed only daintiness and prettiness, she said, while the pianoforte sang the soul. Some day Dylan must hear this new music in Montreal.

"I also learned to paint," she said. "That is my own window on the ultimate." She thought a long moment. He sensed that she was committing herself to self-revelation, struggling beyond her fear of sounding foolish, daring a new intimacy. "I do my best work in pencil," she said. "When I sketch heads." She gave him a special smile. "I would like to draw your head." She mused for a moment. "For me drawing is a way of looking beyond time at the infinite. I see past what's ephemeral to the essence of a person." She paused. "I hope I can show you."

On with her life's story: The best of her learning came not through the school curriculum, but through a friendship. Her favorite teacher lent her a copy of *The Sorrows of Young Werther,* a wonderfully romantic tale of the trials of soul of a young man. She looked at Dylan sidelong and added, "A young man not unlike you." That book opened up the inner world for Caro, the world of feelings neglected and even scorned by society. Then she read Goethe's *Faust,* which was monumental, God and the devil struggling for the soul of one man—she would tell him the whole story one day, Caro said. And then, from her dearest friend, *Childe Harold* came into her hands.

She considered her words. "It was as though the sky burst open," she said, "rent by lightning and shattered by a clap of thunder. Beyond the sky were revealed, on a cosmic scale, my own feelings, my own sense of being outcast, alone, and madly in love with a world equally cruel and beautiful."

After her cataclysmic experience of reading *Childe Harold,* "an experience of being awake all night, like you," she wanted more than anything in the world to meet the poet who set down human life so truly in rhymes.

Her best friend at school, Elaine, who preferred to be called Hélène, knew a lot about Byron. So did the other girls—the man's life was a delicious scandal. They told tales of how the poet, despite being born an aristocrat, was unconventional and cared nothing for society and its manners. He traveled to Italy and to Greece. He did as he pleased, and according to gossip, had many lovers.

To Caro it simply meant what she hoped—that the young lord lived with the glory that sang in his verses. He sought experience, life itself, scorching and searing as that might be. He held back from nothing, made himself vulnerable to existence in every way, lived like Icarus, flying boldly and dangerously near the sun. Of course he would have many lovers. Byron was gobbling life whole, in both its glory and its monstrosity.

The best part of the gossip was about the life he carried on with Lady Caroline Lamb. Here was a woman Caro admired by reputation and longed to know more about. Though Caroline Lamb was married to another man, she and Byron immediately recognized themselves as kindred spirits. In a gesture from their very souls, they began a love affair openly, as such affairs should be conducted, drinking both the ambrosia of soaring emotions and the castigation of society. Though report had it that they later fell out, Caroline Lamb was transforming the experience marvelously—she was writing a novel about her years with Byron.

Wonderful—that a woman would write a novel. That was the new way, the way of the liberated, the way Caro lived for. That was why she had taken Caroline's name as her own. Her name was now Caroline Corsair, she said— Corsair after the hero of Byron's poem of that name. Her father hated it, she said with a smile. Now he avoided calling her by any name at all, using the full "Caroline" only in formal situations to avoid embarrassment, and the familiar "Caro" never. She wouldn't answer to the name he and her mother had chosen. That was her baby name, she said, an appellation the world gave her before she started to forge her own soul.

At the Easter holiday in England, Caro hatched a daring plan to live as she dreamed of living. "That was when I learned that some are not willing . . ." She hesitated, evidently uncertain how to finish the sentence.

Caro broached her plan to Hélène. Well, she thought Byron was charming and singular, a wonderful emblem, even something of a cause, but . . .

"She didn't see." Something to raise an eyebrow, something to twitter about, maybe even to inspire an impudent or scandalous deed, like letting a boy go too far. Caro shrugged. "I looked at her as she spoke, her eyes full of mischief, and I knew that's all she saw. Nothing truly to inspire, nothing to make *the* difference, nothing to use to live a great life."

Caro looked off toward the western horizon for a long moment. She took a deep breath or two and plunged on.

"I wanted more—I wanted everything. I wanted to meet Byron." She looked at Dylan with defiant pride.

Hélène and she planned things boldly. Hélène forged a letter over her mother's signature informing school authorities that Caro was invited to the family estate for the holidays. Then Hélène's brother, Lord Peter, took Caro up to London to seek out the poet. Caro knew Lord Peter well. He had been her escort on several occasions. "He was fair-skinned and fair-haired and rather beautiful," Caro said. "I was a little enamored of him."

Dylan was surprised that Caro would praise a man as fair. What could be more beautiful, he thought, than the dark rose of her own complexion, or her own auburn hair?

She turned her large eyes toward him, and they seemed to see all of him.

"I gave myself to him," she said.

Dylan felt her inspect him for censure. He let her see none. In this new world, there could be none. "We put up in a hotel in Mayfair, not a truly respectable one. I gave myself to him freely, willingly. It was no seduction.

"It was the second day before I found out. Byron had

exiled himself to the Continent. A couple of years before, apparently. English society had been far too narrow for him, of course.

"Lord Peter had known all along. Provincial school-girls like Hélène and I, we were ignorant, but Lord Peter was worldly." Caro's eyes sparked with anger. "When I called him a deceiver, he laughed at me. Laughed. Then he teased me about being his 'dusky maiden,' and I under-stood." She hesitated. "The *bastard* thought because I am dark-skinned, I am merely to be used. Bloody English and their wogs." She looked hard at Dylan. "He was the *last* man in my life who will treat me that way." She thought a moment and smiled. "Even he regrets it. I made him take me home to his family, and denounced him in front of his mother and sister.

"So I gave up on meeting Lord Byron, but I did not give up on living a life writ in large, bold strokes."

Dylan had no idea what to say. He murmured, "I ad-mire you."

She beamed at him. "May I draw you over the noon hour?"

They always took their time at nooning. They let the horses rest. Bleu built a fire and cooked a big dinner. Troyes napped. This time Caro drew busts of Dylan, her easel propped high in the cool wind, the pages fluttering occasionally. She posed him just as she wanted him, chin tucked down, eyes peering out from deep beneath his brows. He held the pose carefully and listened to the rest of her story in silence.

She had come back from England last winter, a cold crossing of the North Atlantic, her time in finishing school at an end. She had no means to stay in England, and she wanted to travel in North America. She wanted to see the interior, the men of her own people, whom she'd never known. She wanted to draw them. When she'd mastered that . . . Well, she didn't know what she wanted to do next.

Of course, in her father's eyes she came back to marry the man he'd chosen for her, one of the partners of the Nor'West Company. She'd refused that marriage with a laugh—had declined even to hear the fellow's proposal, or to get to know him. The world could not choose her soul mates for her. Venturing forth, she would find her own.

Her eyes told Dylan what he wanted to hear. When she made her choice, it would be for a young man willing to live bravely, daringly, a man open to the fullness of life itself. He wondered if the words beneath her words were, "perhaps a man like Dylan Davies."

Caro finished the sketch after supper, in the last light of day, after the sun had gone behind the mountain, and they sat, artist and subject, in the lilac shadow of twilight. This time they adopted a silence and held it, a matter of respect for her work. He found himself pulled into something. With a light touch or with a word she would change the angle of his head, the attitude of an eyebrow, even the aspect of his thought. It made him feel different, an unfamiliar Dylan Davies, perhaps a new Dylan Davies, one growing in the strong light of Lord Byron's vision. He felt uncomfortable yet excited.

At last she took the drawing off the easel and brought it forward to him, smiling, pleased, holding it proudly yet carefully, as one bears a chalice.

Dylan was flabbergasted. He had no idea what to say.

It was stylized in a way he would have described as feminine, the lines graceful and arcing, lines more fluid and lilting than powerful. Likewise his appearance was made more artful than it was, the arc of his neck seen as slender and graceful, the curls of his hair arranged attractively, his eyelashes long, his mouth given a hint of cupid pucker—his whole face idealized.

But this was not what rendered him speechless. It was the violence of the red welts of scar tissue, the marks of the beast upon him. The brooding power of the expression on his face, the glow of . . . Authority? Command? Confidence, certainly, and something more. The eyes, looking boldly out from under dark brows, had an air of assurance, of dynamism, of passion, and, yes, of domination. As he looked, stunned, the words swam beneath the surface of his mind, words to name truly the spirit that infused the drawing, words that were shapes in the waters of his consciousness, as yet indistinct.

He was taking too long to respond—he could feel Caro's nervousness rising—but he felt struck dumb. The words rose through the dark waters of his mind.

Darkness. Yes. He felt a wash of relief, and then of alarm. She had drawn his darkness. She had seen him not as angel, but devil. No, he told himself, neither angel nor devil but . . .

A tide of feelings gushed through him, sweeping the pieces of his old personality away.

That was what he had seen in Byron, he thought, a new kind of man, not an angel, which meant a castrato the way the Church taught it, not a devil with cleft hoofs and a forked tail, but some new creature empowered with the forces of light *and* dark, some new intermingling, some new union, some alloy of . . . fire in the soul, strength, vitality, male vigor. It was emerging within him, like a great wave from the depth of the sea, and to be himself, he must sail on its crest.

Dylan looked into Caro's eyes. "I think," he said in unsparing honesty, "you have seen me so deeply as to show me my true self."

She took the drawing, signed her name to it, and wrote in a large, handsome script across the top, *Dylan Davies*. "It's yours," she said, and handed it to him. He accepted it.

Mesmerized, under the sway of newly acknowledged forces, Dylan took her arm. He led her away, he knew not where. He felt as though some superior power—God or Satan, he thought teasingly, or simply his new self?—guided him, lifted his feet, moved his hands, directed his eyes. He led her beyond a little ridge, away from camp, where two ordinary mortals sat, talked, cooked, ate, existed but did not live—give no thought to camp, laddo. He looked from the drawing in his left hand to Caro in his right. He saw high expectation in her face.

On the far side of the ridge, on a spot of mere dirt, he helped her sit. Then he helped her lie back. Without a word, under the sway, he began to unbutton her dress. Her face grew somber and her eyes large. There, under God's sky, within sight of the whole world, within hearing of the bloody camp, he slowly unbuttoned her dress entirely, gently slipped all her clothes off, and eased her on top of them. Still fully dressed, he rose over her, came between her legs, kissed and caressed her everywhere he'd ever imagined kissing and caressing a woman, and at last came into her and loved her gladly.

A question lanced at him. Here he was, lying beside Caro, his new lover, both of them naked, spent with love, growing chill in the dark and chuckling at even that, and a question was pricking at him and wouldn't go away.

It was: What's different? What's different about this act of sex?

He thought of Fore, and that didn't help. *He* was different. Like a reflected glint of sunlight it hit him, and he knew absolutely. He was happy. Now, he was happy. Then, even satiated, he was miserable.

Before, he felt wrong, grievously wrong. This, with Caro, was right, unmistakably right, overwhelmingly right. He knew it deeply. He was happy. It was his new, more powerful self. Which she had brought forth. He looked into her eyes with gratitude, and smiled his buoyant gladness.

She nicked her head forward, avoided his lips, and teased his ear with her tongue.

He chuckled.

He rolled over her for another moment of rightness.

Chapter
Sixteen

The days of the journey to Rocky Mountain House were their honeymoon. Dylan and Caro were playful, daring, outrageous. They rutted. They were more intimate spiritually even than physically—they shared far-ranging talk, sang, told every sort of joke, ribald and otherwise, talked about their childhoods, reminisced about the painful awkwardness of adolescence, spoke their hearts about the awfulness of their home life.

The talk was Dylan's father, Caro's mother. Dylan confessed his fear of the remote, domineering Ian Campbell. Caro spoke of the loneliness of being an only child, her refusal to learn her place, as her mother expected, her rebellion against the role the world set down for a half-breed girl. And of her mother's premature death, and of the months spent weeping. And of her vision—that she could go to England to be educated. Her maternal grandfather had left a small legacy. She begged her father for the use of it. Yves Troyes, preoccupied with rising in his business, let her go willingly enough, and off Caro went to England.

Yes, they were outrageous. They nearly pretended her father and Bleu did not exist. They rode and walked and sat at dinner with their eyes linked, intimate, exploring. Dylan began to believe the old love poems that said the eye is the window of the soul. When they looked into each other's eyes, it was intimacy, seduction, mating of the spirit.

The most evident outrage was that Caro asked her father to leave the tent and let Dylan take his place. She asked graciously, Troyes stammered out yes, and Bleu guffawed. It was a fine moment.

Dylan loved her. He had never imagined love could feel like this. He never even asked himself whether what they were doing was sinful. It was so clearly grand, lovely, the way people were meant to live.

He did wonder sometimes how she could feel so sure, always, of what her higher self was. She was so young, nineteen. Yet she seemed more experienced, more mature, more fully fledged with her new self than he was with his own. It's all right, he told himself. Dylan Davies, you're still feeling your way. He watched her. Always she simply looked inside herself and saw truth. Wonderfully, she always heeded.

Dylan cherished her. While he was learning to listen, his Caro was going off like one of those Chinese rockets he'd read about. She would make a brilliant streak against the sky of life, this woman. She lived from her depths. He admired her as much as he loved her. He would streak the same sky, parallel to her, or intertwined.

He was learning. Every noon, while she sketched, he wrote in his journal. He wrote an odd kind of journal, not what was happening today, but the story of his years at home, his family life, his time at school, his job, his relationships with people. He would show her his pages at night, by the fire, and she would ask questions. Luminous questions. It was wonderful what she could ask that would open the windows of his soul. Her questions helped him begin to see himself. His father lived in dread of everyone—fear ran his life. Philomene, the housekeeper, had loved Dylan and helped him grow. Mr. Johnson, the teacher who acted so helpful, was in fact very manipulative. Dylan had always resented the subtle, almost invisible superiority of Claude MacDonald.

Caro would ask him questions about what he wrote, and suddenly he saw into it, as though murky water turned clear, and knew the truth. And then he could write the truth. She thought he was meant to be a writer, like Byron. Writing was a way of stripping the soul naked, she said, before the world.

He thought that, empowered by her, he could be a writer.

He remembered Dru's story about the truth stone. There was a magic stone in Wales, the tale went, that gave any man who touched it the truth about himself. When you laid your hand on that stone, your heart was revealed to you. Dru said it was like hearing the music of your own soul, always there, but until now inaudible.

Caro was his truth stone. When he looked into her eyes, he knew his own heart.

Though he often felt tentative in his new power, it was already transforming his life. He was courteous to Yves Troyes without deference, and found he enjoyed the man's company more. He asked questions of Bleu and learned the ways of the mountains without feeling like an oaf, and he noticed that Bleu now treated him like a man. He did not ask Caro for conversation, for time, for love. He joined with her spontaneously, easily, in these fruits of their two beings. It was natural and appropriate. He was claiming his own manhood.

He thought of Dru a lot. He'd love to see Dru now, and have him meet Caro. Dru would love the way he was coming into his own, the way he was learning to see with his dreaming eye.

One night he worried about the teachings of the Church. He reflected on how it had nurtured his decency, his consideration, his awareness of others, his compassion, his idealism, his desire to be fully a *human* being, not a beast. It made him fretful. He lay awake next to Caro. The Church condemned what he was doing—there was no way around that.

As soon as they got moving the next morning, he took the risk and asked Caro what she thought. Wonderfully, she offered some good advice from one of her teachers. The Old Testament, said this teacher, was essentially made void by the New Testament. The Old Testament taught a list of prohibitions. Thou shalt not this, thou shalt not that. It wasn't wrong, but was a small view for those who really want to *live*.

"I'm no scholar," she said, "but I believe what Miss Youngman taught me. The message of Jesus of Nazareth in the New Testament throws the Old Testament over. You are the son of God, and He is within you. The guiding force of your life should not be a set of rules, but the inner sense, the voice of the God within you. And you hear that voice as love. Follow the voice of love."

The two of them agreed to reread the Gospels when they had the chance. "I think we'll find," she said, "that Jesus Christ is the greatest of revolutionaries."

Every day Dylan talked to Caro for hours in a state of high excitement. Every day he wrote in his journal. Every night he lay with her and explored new worlds of emotions.

On the next to last day he wrote,

I know now there is a larger platform to play upon, manhood. And here a man needs to step beyond the boundaries that children required for their growing up, the mere codes of society. Here he must both look into himself and out at this grand theater, this human society upon the earth, and decide what he could be on this most fascinating and infinitely complicated stage.

No, not decide. Discover. I must look within to see the truth. I have no idea what this truth is, but I know where to find it.

The last night before they got to the fort, Dylan and Caro wrapped up in blankets away from camp. They wanted to see the stars without interference from the fire. Dylan could never get over how many stars jammed the sky, here far from cities, in the great western wilderness.

They made love first, and then nestled and nuzzled and looked at the sky and talked for hours. The Big Dipper said half the night was gone before Dylan got the courage to speak what was on his mind.

He took the chain of German silver from around his neck. He looked at the fire opal in the dark. Strangely, in the dark the stone looked like a dark spot in the ring, a kind of hole, utterly without light, much less fire. For a moment he felt something being sucked out of his heart.

He risked it. He took the ring off the chain and

handed it to Caro. She was solemnly quiet as he got tinder from his pocket, made a tiny blaze, and held the ring over it. Now the fire opal glowed—will-o'-the-wisp light shone within it.

Caro's eyes glowed too.

She kissed him. She moved her body against his.

"It was my mother's," Dylan said, beginning to feel aroused.

"I know," she said, smiling. "You told me."

She was making damned sure he got aroused.

"It's all I have from her." Caro rolled him on top of her. "The only thing."

She held the ring with both hands in front of his face.

"Yes," she said. She pulled him into her body.

"Will you accept it?"

"Yes," she whispered. She was making him feel incredible.

"Will you wear it on your fourth finger?" he asked.

"Yes," she breathed, and slipped it onto the ring finger of her left hand.

"Will you marry me?" he asked.

She pulled his face down and kissed him hungrily.

"Yes," she said.

She thrust several times, and Dylan cried out.

They arrived at Rocky Mountain House just before dark on an evening that was deeply and peacefully cold. Arrangements were made hurriedly, and Dylan was pleased when Caro told Captain Chick gently, "I prefer not to share lodgings with my father but to room alone." He smiled at her with his eyes, but she made no response.

Captain Chick made a show of being accommodating. Of course, arrangements would be exactly as his guests liked, there was plenty of room, the Indian women would help them get settled, and dinner would be laid out in two hours. They must allow him to show them the hospitality of Rocky Mountain House.

Dylan was slightly disconcerted to find that he was on the gallery in a room with Bleu, next to all the rough trappers, while Caro was all the way across the quadrangle beside the main apartments, and her father next to her. Like segregation. But he was an agile fellow, Dylan thought, and would overcome small obstacles.

He was feeling uncertain of himself tonight. He didn't know why.

At dinner Captain Chick was expansive and entertaining. A big mulatto, a mixture of white, red, and black races according to the tale, well over six feet and surely fifteen stone, he seemed huge and dominating at the table. He wore a smart scarlet military coat with gold braid, stovepipe hat, and black breechcloth. As they came in to dinner, he took off the hat and revealed a gleaming head, shaved except for a topknot and braid. On his wrists dangled showy bracelets of gold engraved with intricate patterns Dylan couldn't see clearly. Around his neck hung a *gâge d'amour,* from one of what must be a legion of lovers. A necklace of huge claws of the grizzly bear lay atop the *gâge,* a boast of his courage. Under the stiff coat, which did not meet in the middle, he wore no shirt, and his broad chest gleamed—Dylan wondered if he oiled it. Since the breechcloth exposed a lot of dark leg and bottom, the overall effect was vulgarly carnal, Dylan thought—it reeked of the rutting bull.

He was cordial. Caro laughed gaily at his witticisms, and Troyes seemed eager to be ingratiating. Yet it seemed to Dylan the impersonal cordiality of the man who holds power over you, the teacher who graciously tells you that you failed, the executioner who offers you a last cup of tea, even the owner who plays with the monkey in its cage. Captain Chick did not so much entertain people as capture them, charm them into his sway.

Caro was on the left of the swarthy half-breed, her father to her left. To the Captain's immediate right sat a tall, handsome Indian woman, very dark-skinned, who seldom opened her mouth but wore a fashionable gown that showed her bosom enticingly. Though Captain Chick ignored her, surely she was his mistress. Dylan sat beside this woman, at the end of the large table.

The Captain commanded up a feast—hot, buttered

bread, boiled squash, roasted pumpkin, baked lake trout, and boudins, whatever they were. Captain Chick told stories and jokes about the English, who seemed a convenient butt for everyone.

There were no Englishmen at hand. The Captain's clerk was a thin Scot named MacDougal who seemed to have little to say but "Sod the English." MacDougal was small and dark and had a strange smile, as if he shared guilty knowledge with everyone. Next to MacDougal sat his wife, a tiny woman approaching middle age, probably older than her husband. She wore a dry expression and did not participate in the revelry. Directly across from her sat the smith, whose name Dylan never heard, and a woman fairer than he, though surely of mixed blood. When she did not have silverware in her hands, she did her knitting, and paid no attention whatever to the proceedings.

Captain Chick leaned close to Dylan's ear to explain the subtlety of the boudins to him before they tried them. They were something like the English or Scottish black pudding, the Captain said, but Dylan wasn't familiar with those either. The cook took the part of the buffalo entrails that had this nice, fleecy fat—Captain Chick pointed—cut it into portion-sized lengths, turned it inside out so the fat would be inside, and stuffed it with chopped tenderloin and certain secret seasonings. Then she tied it off on both ends like a sausage and roasted it a long time.

"A specialty of our hosts the Bloods," he said. The Blood Indians were cousins of the Piegans. Biting into a sausage, he winked at Dylan, as in complicity. Captain Chick was a man who celebrated his own huge appetites, and expected you to enjoy watching.

Dylan tried the sausage cautiously. He didn't know why it required such a sale. It was the best meat he'd ever tasted.

After dinner Captain Chick served some whiskey, rougher, rawer than Dylan was used to, clearly the stuff they traded to the Indians. He gave a one-man entertainment for his guests, with stories that showed himself, the big, swaggering half-breed, as the comic hero. Dylan was irritated to see Caro look enamored of this figure the Captain was presenting her, this mesmerizing illusion.

One story thrilled and frightened Dylan. To the north, beyond Lake Sophia, according to Captain Chick, lay great reaches of glacier. Once he'd taken a party of two onto the glacier, for no reason at all, except to let him brag he knew every inch of his territory, and for the general hell of it. Captain Chick was a man who swore in front of women and managed to seem charming while he did it.

The three spent the day winding their way among the great crevasses. When you looked down into them, said the Captain, they grew bluer and bluer with every few feet, until they finally became so enticing a deep aquamarine, they became seductive—you wanted to feel their cold embrace. The men peered at the strange *seracs,* sculptures shaped by the wind from snow-ice, and walked around cubes of ice as big as palaces.

On the way back they came to a place on a crevasse that was too wide to step across but not wide enough to require a bridge—an easy jump. Captain Chick himself didn't even take time to look at it carefully—he trotted the last two or three steps and bounded over it. The next fellow, the Frenchy, walked up to the crevasse, glanced down, backed up, took a run, and leapt over easily. The last man, the Englishman, walked up and looked down for a long moment. Backed up. Ran. Stopped at the edge of the crevasse. Looked down for a longer moment. Backed up. Ran harder. Stopped at the edge of the crevasse. Looked down, looked down, and looked down. Stepped into the hole and disappeared forever.

Captain Chick laughed hugely at his own story. Caro seemed enthralled by it. Dylan felt, unaccountably, that he was being diminished by this tale. Why? Captain Chick looked into his eyes intimately, roared anew with laughter, touched Caro's shoulder with his left hand while holding Dylan's eyes. Why did Dylan think he was being told, It's all right, little boy, don't worry?

He looked into Caro's room through the poor glass of the tiny window. She was in bed, reading by candlelight. Through the wavy glass he couldn't see the book, but it was surely Byron. They had no agreement that he was to come. They never did. He felt a little uncertain this time. He pressed his face against the glass, thinking ambivalently what it would look like to Caro. He tapped the glass with a fingernail. She looked up and smiled.

Caro bounded to the door, whisked him into her room and welcomed him with a fine kiss. She took him instantly to bed and teased him and brought desire high in him and then made it ebb—their lovemaking was fine. Dylan was a little surprised that she shushed him several times— evidently she wanted to flaunt her emancipated carnality in front of her father but not before the world. When they'd finished just once, Caro took him to the door and said good night. He felt a pang. She looked very beautiful there in the candlelight, smiling generously, her body perfectly nude and glowing with lovemaking. She embraced him. "Don't worry," she said in his ear, "everything's fine." And he was out the door.

He awoke full of knowledge. It was so sure, this knowledge, that he got up, pulled on his pants and a capote, and went barefooted and shirtless onto the gallery.

It was empty. He looked at his pocket watch. Five o'clock, not yet dawn. The knowledge felt so sure that he waited in a shadow, his feet freezing. After perhaps five minutes the knowledge confirmed itself: Captain Chick came out of his apartment. He looked fully dressed, in the clothes he wore to dinner, complete with stovepipe hat— had the man been to bed? Without even looking around, he took the few steps to Caro's door.

The man paused. Without knocking, he opened the door halfway. Was he going to burst in and rape her? But no, he waited. He seemed to tap lightly on the half-open door, perhaps with his fingernails. He waited, unmoving. At last he entered and closed the door behind him.

Without a second thought Dylan walked silently along the gallery toward Caro's room. The knowledge led him.

He leaned against a post—it might disguise his shape—and looked in through the wavy glass of the small window.

The two of them looked like figures in a strange, disturbing dream, seen perhaps underwater. Captain Chick stood to Dylan's right, perhaps waiting. Caro set the candle back on the bedside table, burning. She stood up from the bed in her long nightshirt, pulling her long hair back from her face with one hand. She cocked her head—perhaps Captain Chick had spoken, but Dylan couldn't hear through the wall—and she half smiled. Captain Chick stood motionless, but cast a spell, or emanated a force like a magnet. Dylan could sense it from here. It drew Caro toward him.

Dreamlike, less than real and more than real, she walked slowly toward Captain Chick, an appraising look on her face. She stopped inside an arm's length from him. She touched his bare breastbone between the lapels of his military coat with a forefinger. Then she slid forward against him and raised her lips to his. As they kissed, he lifted her nightshirt and held her buttocks tight against his groin. Meanwhile he kissed her hungrily—Dylan could feel him sucking the life out of her.

Caro pushed him away and stepped back, but not far, resisting Captain Chick's magnetism. She drew her nightshirt slowly over her head. She hesitated several times, posing with first her hips and pudenda revealed, then her belly, then her breasts, her head covered all the while. When she stood fully naked, she had the strangest smile Dylan had ever seen.

Captain Chick stood motionless.

Caro reached out and eased the lapels of his coat apart, a finger on each side. She bent her head to his chest and kissed his right nipple. Then she sucked gently, teasingly on the left. With one hand she undid the thong that held up Captain Chick's breechcloth. It fell to the floor. She did not look at his nakedness. Dylan felt sure the man's cod was as big as his forearm. She pressed herself against him and bit his chest.

Captain Chick took his hat off and tossed it toward the room's only chair. He lifted Caro's legs so that they were wrapped around his waist. Dylan could not tell if he entered her at this moment. Then, holding her, he stepped easily to the bed, flung both of them down, himself on top, and began to frig her vigorously.

Dylan watched it all. He wanted to leave but couldn't. He ordered himself to leave but couldn't. He felt the pull of the man's magnetism.

It did not take long. It was an act of ravishing, not love, of claiming ownership. The Captain frigged her savagely, brutishly. His little coat jigged up and down in back with his motion—didn't its buttons hurt her breasts? Legs splayed, she frigged back in a frenzy. Twice Dylan thought he could hear Caro's sharp little cries, even through the log walls. Before long the man's body stiffened, lengthened, shuddered.

For a moment of stillness the Captain held Caro's eye.

Then, still atop Caro, he turned his head, looked directly at the window, at Dylan.

Dylan could never be sure, through the distorting glass, but he fancied Captain Chick winked.

Chapter
Seventeen

D ylan wandered. He fled from that cursed window on that cursed gallery, got a horse, and set out westward in the predawn light. He had no idea where he was going, what he was doing, what he was thinking, what he was feeling. He didn't see the Rocky Mountain front rising huge in front of him, or the river, or the canyon it ran through, or the sky growing brighter, or the sun rising behind him. He was lucky—the sky was clear, his blindness would not run him into tempestuous weather.

Occasionally he had a mental image, a picture of Capture Chick ravishing Caro. Some images were memories. Others, equally vivid and indistinguishable, were imagination. He knew that because they were even more lascivious, more horrible, more demeaning to Caro and to him than what he had seen. And though he had watched in silence, cut off from the actual sounds by the window, the door, and walls, these images were accompanied by strange rhythms and music, the heavy clank of metal being flung against walls, the crunch of glass breaking under boots, perhaps a hint of a bell tinkling in the wind, and the thud of ceremonial drums under all.

Except for mental images, his eyes were blind, his mind was blank, numb, cold, stiff, in rigor mortis. He could not begin to process thought or feeling.

About mid-morning his belly spoke to him. He was hungry. Bloody hell, he'd brought no food. He didn't give a damn.

Once his eyes tried to speak to him—a movement, a straight line against the sky, something? He looked momentarily, saw nothing, and returned to blindness.

He lay on his back and soaked it in the hot water. It was unbelievable how much it hurt, and he had no idea why. He'd been lucky to find this small, sulfurous spring dribbling hot water into the river. Since it was only an inch or two deep, he had to soak the parts of his body in it separately. It was amazing how much he ached, all over. Not like he'd been beaten. More like he'd been trying to hold still against the pitching of a stagecoach ride, and his muscles were screaming, No more, let us rest. He'd soaked his arse and the backs of his legs. Next he would soak his arms and shoulders, one at a time.

He looked at the wavy grass in the hot stream. It was deeper than the water itself if you held the blades up, and it made the stream half solid. A curious grass, stiffish, with white-gray edges, like dried salt. Downstream a bit the rocks on the bottom were covered thick with creamy green algae. He got out of the hot water naked and walked along the stream to look carefully at its oddities. Farther downstream the algae, or whatever the vegetation was, turned rust-colored, purple, gold, ruby-red, gray, russet, and chartreuse. He squatted and looked minutely. There is lovely they are, as the Druid would say.

He had a pang of missing Dru.

He squatted in the water, aching feet and sore bottom in the hot wetness. He dabbled his fingers in it.

Feeling better, aren't you, laddo?

He started. Dru's voice, almost like it was real, almost like it spoke to the real ear, not the dreaming ear.

Aye, Druid.

What is it makes you feel better?

Dylan laughed. A fine, hot bath, civilizedlike, he said in his mind, a teasing falsehood.

Aye, laddo, she's *Mother* Nature, and she'll suckle ye.

He supposed he did feel better. His brain worked. He had words working now, and not just those *sodding* mental images. Maybe he was just a suckling babe on Mother's teat.

A shadow fell on him.

Captain Chick blocked the sun.

Behind him stood Saga.

Dylan grabbed for clothing, he didn't even know which piece, and stuffed it on his crotch.

"Feel small in the cod, eh, my boy?" Captain Chick grinned down at him, huge and triumphant. He let loose a big, warm chuckle.

Dylan thought now, too late, of his knives. He'd taken off his knives to soak his back, and then walked naked away from them.

He stared at Saga. Saga smirked back. Dylan looked at the Captain and jerked his head at Saga. "He's been here for weeks." Then where the hell was Dru? Dylan had no intention of asking. "He was out hunting yesterday."

Saga stepped forward, reached out with his quirt and touched the pink scar on one side of Dylan's face, then the other side, the scars of their battle over Fornicating Woman. He was still smirking. A new scar twisted the eyebrow Dylan ruined with the hilt of his knife. Saga's beauty was no longer pristine.

Captain Chick studied Dylan with amusement on his face. "Saga, we will meet you back at the fort." The Métis moved off.

Dylan roared in his mind, Where in hell did you come from?

"Saga told me he gave you your rather dramatic scars," said Captain Chick.

"How did you find me?" Dylan rasped. His voice was rough with anger at Saga. He was glad it didn't sound whiny.

"Zere are not so many alone horses wearing shoes in the country. Why don't you get your arse up and out, yes, up and out, and we'll talk?"

His expression changed suddenly, grew sympathetic, friendly, fatherly. "My boy, zere's nothing to be hithery-dithery about."

*   *   *

Walking toward Caro's room, the Captain had been aware of Dylan standing on the balcony. "Yes. Not many men can skulk about"—he moved his arm and hand like a gliding snake—"and escape the notice of Captain Chick," he said softly.

"Why didn't you do something about it?" demanded Dylan.

The Captain shrugged. "It was a mere distraction."

Dylan thought what it was a distraction from, and his guts churned. "So you knew."

Captain Chick hesitated. "When I thought about zat later, I thought, I don' know what it mean to him. Probably he brush it off. What is a woman, after all? Maybe he just come back from village looking for *la chatte*." The Captain chuckled. "Although, permit me to advise you, dawn would not be the time. Even Blood women do not spread their legs at dawn." He cackled. "Never mind, I thought I'd better follow along and make sure you were all right. You are my guest."

Dylan reached for his pants and started pulling them on. He eyed the knives in their holsters on the ground. He would be damned glad to get his knives back in position.

The Captain looked at him fixedly. "Dylan, heed me." He waited for Dylan to meet his gaze. Dylan could feel the spell in his eyes. "It is not important, me with Caro."

Dylan deliberately looked away, slipped his shirt on, sat down to put on his moccasins. She's not wearing your ring, he was raging in his head.

Captain Chick watched him all the while, perhaps appraising something. "We men understan' zese zings, no? A woman." He spread his arms. "We like zem, yes. Special one like Caro, much like, very fine. Beautiful, and very willing." He paused. "I promise you she was willing, plenty willing."

Dylan looked him in the eye. He was sure the Captain knew he had watched through the window, sure the Captain had even winked at him at the end. Or the end of the first round. So why was he pretending?

"A man knows zese things before he goes to her. I

knew, she knew. Very exciting for me to know is coming, very exciting for her too.

"But a woman. Like a fine dinner, a man sees, he tastes, he goes on. Tomorrow another dinner, maybe the same, maybe something new better, no? Sometimes a woman is even like handkerchief. You use, throw with the dirty linens, that's all." Perhaps the Captain saw the anger in Dylan's face. "Of course, Caro is too fine for that.

"But a man he not get jealous. I know you. You want live large, not live oh so cramped, no? Not cramped by usual way, not cramped by jealous, not envious. No such silly zing."

As Captain Chick talked, he watched Dylan curiously, fixedly. Dylan felt like prey. The Captain's restless intelligence came prowling, slinking, testing his reaction. He would change his words according to what worked. The trouble was, it all worked. Dylan felt held in thrall, and mesmerized but in danger. He was remembering Mr. Pico, the headmaster of his school. Dylan stalled, getting his coat on, strapping his knives on, arranging the straps just so, remembering.

Funny how Mr. Pico stayed in his mind after . . . it must be ten years. One day after school Dylan threw a ball and broke a window. He was sent to Mr. Pico for discipline.

Mr. Pico questioned him quietly, in a way that was soft yet insinuating. The affair for Mr. Pico was no accident, nor even a matter of boys will be boys. It was a symptom of something larger in Dylan, some innate irresponsibility, some lack of seriousness, some fundamental flaw that merely chanced to show itself through this event, some equivalent of original sin. Mr. Pico saw this stain in him, and of course he could not deny it. Mr. Pico knew— there was no fooling him.

Mr. Pico bore the authority, so his gentleness was fake. The man might do anything to him. Might make him go without dinner. Have him caned. Write his father. Might even kick him out of school. He was the master.

He let Dylan go back to class with only a reprimand, and a warning that this event would be mentioned in the school's periodic report to Ian Campbell.

Dylan was not deceived. The penalty was modest only because he was afraid, because he saw Mr. Pico's power and, knowing domination for what it was, bent his knee before it. What Mr. Pico exacted was this obeisance. If he exacted it wordlessly, without explicit threat, that only made it more terrible.

Dylan had tasted shame in his mouth like coppery, salty blood. He was ashamed of himself for acting submissive in front of Mr. Pico, for quailing, for being desperate to please. The headmaster knew anyone as scared as he was would toe the line from then on.

Dylan was not fool enough to accept such men as counselors and friends—men like Mr. Pico, Captain Chick, his father Ian Campbell, others with the mantle of authority, superior, imperious, manipulative men. These men could not be understanding and sympathetic, could not make gestures of generosity. For the relationship was one of power, and depended absolutely on his own submission. From your knees, you saw their magnanimity for the dominion it was. When you were before him on your knees, the king stepped forward and raised his sword high. Now with one motion he might knight you or decapitate you. You never knew. One stroke for either purpose, dependent on his whim. One stroke, and then a chuckle of pleasure.

Dylan stood, dressed, his knives in place, unable to stall any longer. As he stood, he was overcome by a great helplessness, a falling, an endless tumbling through space. He swayed.

I am jealous, Father, and I am terrified, so I am doomed. I am unworthy. I grovel.

But he would never, ever say these words to Captain Chick. Or anyone else.

A picture slapped his face. Captain Chick standing, holding Caro, her legs around his waist, she entirely naked, he from the waist down. He spun, whirling her round and round like a child. Caro laughed a belllike laugh of innocence, let her head fall back, let her hair swing. The Captain showed his teeth and leered.

It was not a memory—they had done no such thing.

He took one faltering step forward. Now, regardless of all else, regardless of the Captain, regardless of Saga, he must see Caro. Captain Chick took Dylan's elbow with a steadying hand.

"Now we go back to fort, eh? Everybody wants you zere. I want you, Caro wants you, everybody wants you. Sure to goodness." The Captain made the chuck-chucking sound he would make to a horse. "Is good."

He smiled broadly and put one arm around Dylan's shoulder.

Dylan shrugged the arm off petulantly. But he walked toward his horse.

"I want you," he said.

He paused in the open door and gazed at her, standing in the middle of the room. She looked grand, in a gray wool floor-length dress that seemed to make her green eyes, copper skin, and auburn hair even richer in color. Her hair hung to her waist in a single braid, as he liked it best. She looked graceful, dignified, ladylike. He felt choked with love, desire, yearning, all these mixed up, and more. He still hadn't stepped inside.

"I want you," said Caro. Her eyes were luminous, and perhaps sympathetic. She took several steps away, holding his eyes, and sat. "But I don't want what you are now. I want the large you."

Dylan walked toward her, but she shook her head very slightly, still looking at him with huge eyes. He stopped.

He didn't know what to do. Captain Chick had loaned them this room, the Captain's office, next to his bedroom, a so-called neutral site for their meeting. To Dylan it was charged with his presence, his ownership.

"Let's go for a walk," he said.

She shook her head. "It's dark anyway," she said. "Perhaps tomorrow, after luncheon."

"I want you," he said.

"Later," she said. "Not tonight."

The images of what she might do tonight jangled in his mind.

"I promise you," she told him evenly, graciously,

looking gorgeous, "if you spy on me one more time, I will
never speak to you again."

It was awkward. It was painful. Dylan and Caro sat
down by the river in the weak autumn sun and had a kind
of picnic, pemmican and apples. They pretended to ignore
the pain, the pain of the moment, the pain of the two
nights past, the pain of the future.

They talked of small things. She took his hand for a
few minutes, and that made him feel better. He looked often at the fourth finger of her left hand, at his mother's
ring. He told himself forlornly that it was still the symbol
of their future. Together.

He restrained himself. Not only did he not mention
Captain Chick, he did not allude in any way, even by tic
of mouth or eyebrow, to their difficulties. He told stories
of his boyhood. Funny stories, mostly. About the way their
parrot would fish brooches out from the cleavages of vis-
iting women. About the play he and Amalie wrote and performed for the neighborhood youngsters, the one that
ended with Amalie showing her bloomers. About the way
their housekeeper would always forget and say to the
Campbells, "Well, when I was a little boy . . ." And other
stories. Too many of them reminded him of sadnesses in
his life. Philomene had been sleeping with his father, and
he never knew it.

Once, when Caro caught him looking at the ring, she
said quietly and with a smile, "Yes, I'm still wearing it,"
and no more.

He quoted for her one of his favorite bits of verse
when he was a kid, long before he read Byron:

> Under the greenwood tree
> Who loves to lie with me,
> And turn his merry note
> Unto the sweet bird's throat,
> Come hither, come hither, come hither:
>> Here shall he see
>> No enemy
> But winter and rough weather.

They sang together, foolishly and happily, the old
French song,

> *Allouette, gentille allouette*
> *Allouette, je te plumerai*
> *Je te plumerai la tête*
> *Je te plumerai la tête*
> *et la tête*
> *et la tête*
> *Oh! allouette, gentille allouette*
> *Allouette, je te plumerai.*

They plunged through many verses, and at the end
they laughed and nearly cried and clasped each other's
hands and looked long into each other's eyes.

Caro put her hand on Dylan's knee. "I need something," she said gently, and put her head in his lap and
closed her eyes. They were still for a while, and he
thought maybe Caro was asleep. Then she said, "It's a
strange time." Her voice seemed a little quavery. "I want
to ask you for something." He couldn't see her face as
well as he wanted—it was turned away. "If I get too crazy
here, will you save me?" She seemed to contemplate.
They both knew the difficulty was that he already thought
she was acting too crazy. "If I try to give you this ring
back, will you just put me on a horse and take me away?"

Dylan smiled gravely. "I will." He put his hand on
her head and rubbed it. She smiled and sighed deeply.
They stayed like that for a long time.

Walking back to the fort, Dylan told himself it had
been a good time, a healing time. Their closeness was real,
palpable.

Then he told himself that tonight Caro would be close
to Captain Chick, underneath him, and he would be frigging
her wet *chatte*.

He felt his body stiffen with rage.

Calm, he told himself. Be calm and wait and all you
ever wanted is yours.

He swallowed and rolled his shoulders and glanced
sideways at Caro.

She looked lost in reverie.

*   *   *

That night at dinner the seating struck Dylan as symbolic. Captain Chick put Caro at his left and his Blood mistress at his right. Next to the mistress sat Monsieur Troyes. Next to Caro, Saga. Dylan was banished to the far end of the table.

The meal was gay, and Dylan got the impression that Monsieur Troyes was delighted that his daughter had made a liaison with so powerful a man as Captain Chick. But maybe he was imagining things, Dylan thought. He intended to keep to himself, not even to ask Saga where Dru was. All was frivolity and laughter, as far as an outsider would have been able to tell, right through dessert, and right on through the drink that followed.

Too much drink. Finally Dylan got up, made his excuses, and took his leave. The Captain bid him good night lightly. Caro stared at him warningly. He remembered her words: "If you spy on me one more time, I will never speak to you again."

He looked to see if she was wearing his ring. She was, but now on a chain around her neck.

Surprisingly, he slept, heavily, stuporously, like an animal without the gift or curse of imagination. He did not want to imagine what Caro was doing, and did not want to dream. He simply wanted to be alive, and sane, when this nightmare ended.

This time it was Caro who suggested the picnic.

He felt strange with her. It was awkward, painful, to be in her presence, yet it was also rich, still, deep, in a way right. Once Claude had invited him home to a concert given by his two sisters on duo harpsichords. They had played a funeral march from a symphony by Beethoven, a German they said was famous but whom Dylan had never heard of. The funeral march was somber, slow, with a kind of magisterial gravity. It seemed to move only in a small circle around a center point, and that point was infinitely painful, yet the experience of the pain was right, healing, human. Dylan found the family's applause at the end of the march jarring, embarrassing, making his experience silly. Sitting with Caro was like that performance, a heal-ing pain.

He never escaped from the agony of thinking what the two of them were like only a few days ago, when they would have been embracing each other, kissing, hurrying off to make love before soaring to the stars with incredible talk. Now they were wary of touching, feeling each other out delicately, concerned about sticking to safe subjects. Their best moments were childlike, lightly playful.

But Dylan needed this time. He needed it as the promise of a future. Even more, he needed to come gravely to his touchstone and see the truth within himself. This was deep, somber grief, but it was not the shattering anguish of his other waking hours.

She told him what an interesting man Captain Chick was, what an intriguing mind he had. She admired his boldness and dash. Other men sat back and longed, she said. The Captain seized what he wanted, and chuckled at those too frightened to take it back. He was a man, and unafraid to seize dominion over other men. She was ex-cited by Captain Chick all the more because he was a half-breed like herself, and brazen enough to take what he wanted from the ruling white men.

This talk made Dylan woebegone. Not so much be-cause Caro was infatuated with Captain Chick, or because she seemed well matched with another half-breed, but be-cause she was enamored of a kind of man Dylan could never be. Dominion, and all that it seemed to mean, was alien to him.

He considered telling her that the Captain would only use her until she ceased to amuse him, or until he could no longer flaunt his piracy in his, Dylan's, eyes, and discard her. He thought of telling her that Captain Chick compared women to handkerchiefs, to be used and thrown aside. But he didn't. It didn't feel right. Besides, he was sure it would backfire and Caro would think him a liar or hurl contempt at the tattletale. Then, too, he half feared Caro would se-cretly admire a man daring enough to use women as he wanted, defying the conventions.

She was also full of talk of Saga, in a way that made Dylan nervous. He was gorgeous, she said, and his beauty was dramatic, startling, the sort that unsettles conventional people. "A *dangerous* beauty," she emphasized, almost to herself. She wanted to know more about his background. Dylan didn't know why Saga didn't live with his Métis people. He knew Saga hated the English with the passion of most Métis. And he slipped in the fact that Saga was married.

"Is it true you gave him that scar?" Caro asked.

Dylan nodded.

"In a fight?"

Nodded.

"With a knife?" Her glance took in the weapons strapped on his back.

"Yes," Dylan muttered.

"It's a perfect scar," she said. "Without it he would look . . . innocent, above morality, devoid of humanity, like a statue. But the scar brings out his dark side."

Dylan was surprised Caro didn't think Saga's dark skin, almost black, did that well enough. But she was a dark-skinned person herself.

"He gave you your scars." Dylan nodded. He told her the story of the fight, and his bad throw that injured Saga with the knife handle. She said he should not worry. Saga was his brother—the half-breed had told her so. Yes, brothers quarrel, but if one tries to raise his hand against the other, the better self will intervene.

Dylan accepted being called the brother of a dark-skinned man. He knew Dru would want him to.

"Why does Saga live in the village?" she asked. Her glance indicated the Indian village up the river from the fort in the cottonwood grove.

Dylan said he didn't know. Actually, he hadn't realized Saga was not staying in the fort, sleeping in the big room with the other French Canadians.

"He's mentioned his mother. Is he living with her? Have you met her?"

Dylan certain had not met any mother of Saga's. He was sure his mother was back with the Métis, on the Red

River of the north. He wondered what trick Saga was pulling on Caro, and why.

"I hear she's in the village," Caro said, eyeing Dylan. He shrugged and shook his head.

Caro went on lightheartedly. Would Dylan like to hear a new theory she was developing? All men had their dark side, she said. Literature confirmed that—it was full of Mephistopheles, demons, vampires, trolls, monsters, evil gods, and the Satan of the Bible. The Church even created exorcists to cast these demons out. "Ill-favored human behavior," she said, "comes from the unnatural suppression of the dark side." The sins of greed and miserliness, for instance, came from the unhealthy suppression of acquisitiveness, a natural drive. The sin of debauchery and all perverted expressions of sexuality came from the suppression of the natural sex drive. To claim his full humanity, she argued, a man must become at home with his dark side, let his actions express his entire nature.

"Of course society will not tolerate that," she said. "They drove Byron into exile for it."

Dylan kept his mouth shut, but thought, That's rationalization.

"It's time to go back," she said at last. He offered her a hand up. She took it with her left hand but didn't rise. Instead she touched his mother's ring with her other hand. "I'm still wearing your ring," she said gravely. She studied his face. "I still need you in my life. I have no idea when I may want to be married. I'm flying. Don't try to pull me down."

Dylan inclined his head in acceptance.

She got up and dropped his hand. They rode to the fort in silence. When they dismounted in the corral, she touched his elbow and said, "I want to tell you something."

He waited.

"The Word"—they had all begun calling the message from Montreal the Word—"must go on to Chapelle's post. My father doesn't want to go. Saga has asked me to go with him, just the two of us. I've accepted."

Dylan looked into her eyes, hearing the funeral march.

"It's an easy trip, very safe, just a couple of days. On the way back Saga and I may take a few extra days to see a lake he says is beautiful."

She touched his cheek gently with one hand, looked at him with what seemed a kind of love, and walked away.

Chapter
Eighteen

No one could have been better company for Dylan than Bleu. Bleu was profane, blasphemous, coarse, lewd, obscene, vulgar, cynical, acrid, sardonic, misanthropic, and more in the same spirit. He was a good companion and a quick wit, indulging in few of his evasions, like "Just as you say" or "Chin up, there's a good fellow." He tolerated none of Dylan's self-pitying moods at all. When Dylan spoke of Caro and Saga together, Bleu brought him up short. The Frenchy rolled his eyes, gave a huge, ominous grin and proclaimed, *"Oui certainement,* and when zey finish zat, zey head for the blankets"—here he would give a nastily vigorous thumpety-thump of his fat hips—"and go tallyho!"

They were surveying. That's what Dylan told Bleu, and his companion had the grace not to laugh.

The hours on the trail passed slowly. Dylan tried to learn Bleu's habit of watching the country closely, noticing what animals grazed where, where beaver sign was, how wind and water shaped the land, even how the wind blew through certain areas and bent the trees. Instead he wondered whether Saga and Caro were back at the fort yet.

The instruments felt good in his hands, his measurements at sunrise, noon, and sunset, his calculations at night that kept him from having to think, the *Requisite Tables* that theoretically could show you how far into the pagan west you were from Greenwich.

In the middle a mental picture of Caro making tallyho with someone—anyone—would rise up and drive him crazy. Then he would pound his head and ask himself whether he was deluding himself about the glory of what he was doing with Caro.

What if the inner sense of profound rightness meant nothing?

What if Satan presented his temptations in the most scintillatingly alluring form?

What if the true cunning of evil was that it *seemed* so right?

Maybe their difficulties—her mad infidelities—were punishment for their transgressions. Maybe they were a sign, at least, of having strayed from the true path.

He brooded about asking Bleu's opinion. True, Bleu was a rustic. But when Dylan asked him his religion, the interpreter said firmly, *"Catholique."* Dylan pressed him about having drifted into pagan beliefs, like many of the half-breeds in the interior for generations. Bleu shook his head firmly. *"Catholique,"* he repeated. "Baptize. Twice go St. Boniface, confess." Dylan saw something stalwart in Bleu's faith, more stalwart than in his own. Maybe such loyalty brought a gift.

"Bleu," he said at last, "do you think the Church teaches right morality?"

Bleu gave the impression he always did, of being drawn away from a deep concentration to the world of human intercourse, not entirely willingly. "Is sure. What Caro do not right. What you do with her not right."

"Don't you think, sometimes, that such rules are for children? When we grow up, we're meant to see there's more to life than that? Meant to throw off the crutches and *live*?"

"Not right," Bleu repeated. "You not right, she not right, I not right, we all not right. We flesh, yes, we commit ze sin. Then we confess. I confess."

They rode in silence a small while.

"You, boy, you think you big, make new rules like God to yourself, you crazy. Not right. You go boom." He clapped his hands theatrically.

Dylan had a jolt of fear that this simple man was telling the truth. He quelled his heart.

*   *   *

Dylan wrote in his journal one day in mid-December.

It is so difficult. I sometimes think I am required by a perverse world to endure this greatest pain to get the greatest of prizes. I am not such a fool as to give up, to sink in my sea of woes, to fail to reach port. For Caro is the richest and finest of ports.

Yesterday we made love for the first time since she strayed . . .

Here he hesitated and dipped his pen unnecessarily, wrote,

into Captain Chick's sticky embrace. It was not spontaneous at all, but seemed closely planned in her mind. She asked me to her room after luncheon and directly, without hesitation, kissed me, opened my shirt, went to the bed and took off her clothes. It was tender, gentle, wonderful. It lacked the robustness, the vigor, the freedom of the old days, but surely that's understandable. We are trying to find our way back to each other across a gulf of pain. I confess I wept a little afterward. She said to me at the end, again, "Please be here for me. I need you. You are my Gibraltar."

I will be here for her. I do not understand what she has done, what she continues to do. Is it some rebellion, some great defiance of her upbringing, some declaration flung in the face of her father? What was her mother really like? Sometimes I want to tuck tail and flee from the pain she causes me. She has asked me, however, and I continue to offer her the haven she wants. I shall offer her love while the world offers lust, confident that she will know the difference. I shall not let pain drive me away from what I want most on this earth.

Though it is difficult, I do not offer Caro this treasure of my heart for her sake. I do it for

mine. I do it out of love. I do it, in fact, because
my very nature is to love Caro. As a flower's nature is to blossom, mine is to love Caro. Only in
that love can I live as myself.

He pondered for a moment. For some reason he felt
sure—almost sure—that Caro would belong to him in the
end. He thought he should write down why.

I know enough of human nature to know
that the joy Caro and I give each other, an ecstasy of body, mind, and spirit in one, is very
rare. No one will willingly give up that rapture.
Not I, and not Caro.

The band played on.

Everyone was drinking, dancing, telling jokes, shout-
ing out in exultation, and the band played on. That was the
rallying cry of Captain Chick's party to ring in the new
year of 1821. Rallying cry in this case meant revelrous
clamor. Less politely put, drunken shouts.

Doing a reel, some couple would tangle legs and fall,
sometimes taking another frolicker or two to the floor—
why not? The remaining dancers would do their tipsy best
not to miss a step. Around the fallen they would prance,
roaring, "The band played on." Even the Frenchies joined
in the roar, though Dylan was never sure they knew what
the words meant.

The band was hale and hearty, three fiddles, two fifes,
one tin pipe, one loud Indian drum, and one bagpipe. It
was a multiracial band if ever there was one, five
Frenchies—all half-breeds—one Irishman, one Scot, and
the mulatto Captain Chick on the drum.

As he danced, Dylan felt pulled up and down by the
music. Literally pulled up and down, as by an elemental
force. Down by Captain Chick's ominous drum. It throbbed
carnally, driving the dancers like blood coursing swift and
dark through the body, the beat of the heart, the rhythm of
mad, unrestrained sex. Dylan tried to keep his mind on the

bagpipe, which he loved, and the fiddles and fifes and pipe. They were spirit to the drum's carnality, melody, lilt, emotion, raising him up, inspiring his feet to lift into the air, and his spirits with them.

Yes, he was a little drunk.

The bagpipe was his favorite. He'd never danced to one before. Why or how MacDougal had gotten one into the remote Canadian wilderness he had no idea. The man was no artist on the instrument. In his hands it bawled, brayed, and blustered, wailed, shrieked, mewled, bellowed, and caterwauled. But his enthusiasm was somehow enough to overcome all the little blunders, the infelicities of sound, the homeliness. To Dylan's ears MacDougal's musical brazenness was manly, his coarseness martial, his raucousness vigorous. Even his squawks were the anguished cries of a noble heart.

Dylan was a little drunk because, as Captain Chick warned merrily, the wine was laced with laudanum. Also because he had to dance mostly with other men.

Everyone had to dance mostly with other men. There were a score of male cavorters and only four women—Caro, MacDougal's wife, the Captain's presumed mistress, and her Indian sister. Captain Chick set out a rule at the beginning: No one could dance with a female two dances in a row. Everyone would have to trip the light fantastic with stand-ins.

It could have been worse. Troyes and two other men were sick with influenza.

At first the Captain had no volunteers to be stand-ins. Then he waved bright, scarlet bandannas for the men to wear on their heads as a sign of femininity for the evening, and declared that dancers could keep the bandannas. He immediately had more takers than bandannas.

Everyone danced. From what Dylan could see, Caro had a grand time. In his first dance with her, well into the evening, she seemed very gay, in highest spirits made higher by spirituous liquors. She danced with him happily but he thought impersonally, like any other suitor. She seemed a little remote, a blithe dancer not quite in this world. Maybe it was the laudanum.

Saga tapped Dylan on the shoulder, smiled, and made

a courtly bow. Cutting in was not accepted. You got a full dance with your real woman. Dylan turned his back to Saga and whirled Caro away. He saw her look at Saga over his shoulder, with what feeling he couldn't tell.

He also danced with the Indian mistress, a woman whose name he never heard. He called her Mistress in his mind. She made him strut a little, conscious that he looked his best. He'd spent a month's pay in the trading room to cut a fine figure tonight, even buying a fine necklace of *cornaline d'Aleppo* beads, and had polished his knives carefully. He noticed Mistress looking at his knives at every chance. She looked fascinated. He liked dancing with her. Even the touch of a woman's hand felt good. He wanted to dance with her sister, who was more beautiful.

The band played on.

Everyone drank. Captain Chick broke open kegs of high wine and proclaimed this night a night to hold nothing back. Dylan had the impression everyone drank to excess. Including himself.

He sought out Sister for a dance. He eyed her seductively. She was more striking than beautiful, he supposed, but wonderfully desirable. Her slow, sensual smile said she was available. Sauce for the gander, Dylan thought vengefully.

The band played on.

What Dylan noticed was that the drum stopped. The band went on, but the drum stopped.

It seemed a most propitious moment. Caro was his partner for the second time—they were doing a gigue. When the drum stopped, Dylan felt liberated, set free from the downward pull of the carnal, and the song of the fiddles and pipe lifted him. Wonderful that he should be dancing with Caro at this moment.

He looked into her face. It was bright, even radiant, full of the music and the movement and, he had to admit, the wine and laudanum. He was glad to see it happy.

Her face, head, body—all blackened into shadow.

Captain Chick stood beside them. They stopped dancing, paralyzed by his presence. He bowed deeply, letting

Caro glow in the candlelight and then obscuring her again as he rose. In defiance of his own rule, he held out his hands for hers.

Dylan felt struck down. He gave the Captain Caro's fingers and turned away, unexplainably desolate. Stupid, he accused himself. This is mere dancing. You accept the frigging—why feel desolate now?

He turned back to them and refused to let himself scream.

They were not dancing. To Dylan, Caro looked entranced, mesmerized, held in the sway of psychic power. Captain Chick led her across the room. To the door of his apartment. He opened the door and Caro went through. The Captain gave the room a last look, the glance of the master, the conqueror. His eyes flicked across Dylan's face and went on, flicked back, lingered, and perhaps a faint smile curled the corners of his mouth.

When they came back, Caro was flushed—satiated, surely, with sex, with liquor, with laudanum, and with the dance.

At first the two did not dance. Captain Chick held Caro's hand high and perfectly still, displaying his trophy. Suddenly they whirled into motion. It was jarring, like a wax effigy jumping out at you.

Dylan sought out Sister. She was dancing with Bleu. Dylan decided not to await opportunity politely. "May I?" he said to his friend.

The interpreter looked at him most peculiarly. "Excuse me," answered Bleu, and gave Dylan the lady's hand.

Dylan did not commence the dance. With his free hand he stripped off the *cornaline d'Aleppo* necklace and held it out to Sister.

She took it, contemplated it, rubbed the beads between her fingers. Then she turned decisively and pulled him toward the door.

He put an arm around her waist and led her to the room he shared with Bleu. Next to it was the room where a half-dozen Frenchies slept. From there came the sound of a bed slapping against a wall, rhythmically, like a man

cutting wood. Who was it? he wondered. Not a Frenchy
and Mistress, he'd just seen Mistress dancing. Possibly
Mrs. MacDougal, he didn't know where she was, but
surely she was a sedate married woman. Maybe two
Frenchies together, sinning abominably. The night was
madness.

What Dylan wanted was to see Sister naked, to touch
her with his hands all over, and use her in ways he'd never
done a woman.

She let him do all of that. She invited, encouraged,
and inspired him, and he drank his fill.

As they went back toward the music, he felt prickly,
irritable, vexed, dissatisfied. He wondered if he'd done it
all too fast. Far from satiated, he felt ragingly empty.

The band played on.

In the room they separated immediately, Sister melting into some man's arms, Dylan didn't even see whose.

He couldn't see Caro.

Captain Chick was throbbing out the drumbeat.

Dylan found a chair in a corner, stood on it.

Caro was nowhere to be seen.

He looked, looked again, studied the room a third
time.

Caro was not here.

Knowledge came to him.

Saga was nowhere to be seen.

Dylan knew.

He forced himself out of the room, onto the gallery,
into the cold night, away from the pulsing music. He
looked at the pitiless stars. And looked and looked.

He did not know how long he stood there. Once he
glanced at the window of the Captain's room, where an in-
flaming sight awaited him, but it held no fascination for
him, only disgust.

At last he went into the ballroom where the music
could inundate him. He found another glass of wine and
downed it. He thought of the opiate in the wine, gave
thanks for it, and drank a second glass. Saga and Caro
came hand in hand out of the Captain's room.

He went to her. It was as though no one else was in the room. He saw only her, not even Saga. He felt the music. He felt whatever was rising within him, a desire to master, to overpower, to humiliate.

Something in him writhed. Yes, he wanted to humiliate Caro, and the feeling was exultant and hideous.

He held her eyes. She looked back, a bird fascinated by a snake. A thought flicked briefly across his mind: This is how it feels to be Captain Chick. Ugly.

He gave her his arm, and her hand came to it, iron to a magnet. He looked once at Saga, and saw the Métis could not stand in his way. He led her simply toward the door, aware in the universe only of her touch, the music, and his potency.

Outside he immediately pushed her against a gallery post, raised her skirt, and leaned against her. That was when he felt her fumbling at his cod. He glared at her with contempt, and lust.

He lifted her against the post. She wrapped her legs around him, held to the handles of the knives on his back, and cocked her hips toward him. He jammed himself into her roughly and frigged her furiously, driving her hard against the post.

"Yes, yes," she mewled.

He looked into space beyond the gallery rail, above the empty courtyard, and with each thrust threw himself vertiginously toward the fateful air, held away from death only by Caro's body.

As his excitement mounted, in his fantasy he and Caro lifted off the gallery into the black night and tumbled endlessly through time. They flew from this gallery, they flew from high cliffs, they flew from the distant stars of black, cold, infinite space. They spun slowly through the air, linked obscenely at the groin. Joined also by their intertwined hands, and their tongues, and their hair, which was nastily entangled. They thrashed against each other in grotesque passion. They began to fall, slowly but fatefully. He knew that if he could get free of Caro, he could fly and be safe. But he was bound to her everywhere, writhe as he might, bound by his cod, his fingers, his tongue, even the hair of his head. Bound by his hideous desire.

They plummeted.

As he ejaculated, they crashed to earth with a whump, and all went black.

For a moment he was lost between time and eternity.

In the real world he lurched sideways to the rail, still joined to Caro, leaned over it and puked over her shoulder.

In his mind he saw black vultures fly out from his mouth and flap away.

She was not repelled by him. She stayed, held in sway. He had drunk too much? Was he all right now?

Dylan could not force the words out: Get away from me. He wanted to say it, yes, to his once-beloved Caro. Get away from me.

She held his face, looked into his eyes, brought him close. Making a declaration, she kissed with ardor the mouth that had puked.

She drew back, looked at him challengingly in the eyes, and said, "You're splendid." She ran her tongue along his twin scars, licking the beast within him. Then she whirled away and went back to the dance.

The band played on.

Dylan knew what he had to do.

He walked as though pulled by a hidden force. It was like a dream he had when he was canoeing every day, alone in a quickening current. He could hear the waterfall ahead, and told himself he should get to the shore and portage, but he was curiously, inexplicably, unable to paddle to shore. He put his paddle away and floated passively. The last thing he saw in the dream was the spray. He felt the stomach-lurching tilt of the canoe.

Now he walked toward the drum, drawn inexorably forward.

Dancers didn't seem to notice him. He glided among them as though they were physical and he an airy spirit. He saw them, but they had no meaning for him, not even Saga, looking at him with hooded eyes. Saga didn't matter. Without knowing quite how he got there, Dylan stood in front of the band. No one noticed him but Captain Chick. The band played on, and the Captain made the drumbeat throb relentlessly.

Dylan glared at Captain Chick.

Also entranced, the Captain stopped thumping the drum.

Dylan felt his liberation from the inexorable beat. The dancers stopped dancing, the band stopped. Dylan felt all eyes upon him. He supposed they included Caro's, and he didn't care.

Into this moment of perfect silence Dylan spoke. "You are evil."

The Captain stood, his chest naked, a huge target.

The words came again louder. "You are evil."

Captain Chick looked calmly at him. "You cannot do it," he said simply. MacDougal, next to him with the bagpipe, inched away.

Now in a shout. "You are evil."

Captain Chick shook his head slowly with a small smile. "You cannot do it." He spread his military coat open with his hands to show his chest, broad and inviting.

Oh my father, cried Dylan inside himself. From this distance he could choose which rib, which access to the lifeblood.

He felt the tilt of the canoe, and reached for the right knife first.

He saw and felt it all as in a slow fall. Arm cocked, gripped, shooting forward, releasing, the arc of the knife past Captain Chick's ear, and thunking into the wall, vibrating. The left arm in motion half a beat behind, flinging, the arc of the knife perfectly into the bag of the pipe, the whoosh of air, the look of shock on the face of MacDougal.

Captain Chick's superior smile.

Dylan's wail, which burst forth and died slowly, as though from a falling body.

His flight, wailing and wailing.

Chapter
Nineteen

The guards found Dylan leaning idly against the wall in front of his room. They took him by the arms and escorted him to the front gate. He did not resist. The true life was already snuffed out in him, and he didn't care whether he lived or died.

He was thinking about nothing, nothing at all, certainly not why he chose, when faced with the broad target of Captain Chick's chest, to use his knife to pop a wheezing bag.

Bleu met them at the gate. "Captain Chick says tell you, Dylan Davies is banished from zis fort. As he is, wiz nothing. He hopes your death is comfortable, and reminds you that man say freezing to death is pleasant."

Bleu reached forward and embraced Dylan formally, without affection. The big interpreter whispered into his ear, "Peecneec, tomorrow noon." Stepping back, he left a blanket around Dylan's shoulders.

Dylan looked at Bleu emptily. Then he gave a stupid titter. Picnic tomorrow, the first day of the new year, on the frozen wasteland of the Canadian interior? Another titter.

Bleu clapped his shoulders.

"Good-bye," Dylan muttered.

"Just as you say," Bleu chipped in. "Chin up, there's a good fellow." Bleu nodded vigorously, stepped back, smiled in encouragement.

The guards swung the gate open. Heedless hands pushed Dylan into the night. The gate creaked back away.

Bleu waved.

Dylan heard the great bolt bang into place.

He didn't decide to live, or die, or do anything. He didn't decide. He didn't care. He sat against the gate of the fort, in the snow, leaning on it. After a while he realized he was sinking into the snow. His body heat was melting the snow underneath him, and he was sinking into its cold depths. That seemed as apropos as anything. Sink into the snow. Disappear until the spring thaw and return in ignoble form.

But not against the gate. They'd see you when they opened up. The guard might spot you from the blockhouse at first light. Your body would be in the way. They'd think you'd been trying to get back into the fort, which wasn't true. There was nothing in the fort Dylan Davies wanted. No, not even Caro. Nothing in the fort he gave a damn about either way. No, bloody well not Captain Chick.

He'd started calling Captain Chick "the Chickadee" in his mind. For some reason he thought it was funny. Or it was stupid, and stupid was fine.

He sniggered softly. No, she didn't want his sodding knives either, one stuck in a wall, the other buried in a bagpipe.

Besides, he was getting cold. The whiskey and opiate are wearing off, you idiot, and you can feel a little. Not with your heart, just your corpus. Corpse. He sniggered. He liked that. My corpse. Betrayed, it was now a corpse, even if it could move, more or less.

He decided to get up and move away from the gate, away from the fort. He didn't know where. The only warmth, as far as he could think, was in the Indian village, and that was the last place he would go. He was a white man, not a sodding Indian. He wouldn't go down there and—what abomination was left?—become a buggerer. He wouldn't even go down there and frig their wives and worship false gods. Existing in a godless universe was not as bad as that. He wouldn't go. He was a white man.

Lost. Lost beyond finding, beyond hope, like he'd slipped into another world, an upside-down fairy tale of a world, lightless, loveless, godless. But a white man in whatever world.

He staggered off. He would go down by the river. It was as good as anywhere, and there was a rocky place the sun would warm when it came up. He wanted to die in comfort. He sniffed out a laugh. He wanted to freeze to death in the warm sun, and other nonsense. He held the blanket tight at his neck.

He looked at the Big Dipper. The sun would rise soon. His debauchery had taken most of the night. He sniggered at himself. It had taken him all night to get lost. One night and lost forever.

My God, my God, why hast thou forsaken me?

Fool, he accused himself. Fool. He tramped on toward the river. No one ever worked harder to escape God than you did. Tramp. You came to the wilds. Tramp. You put yourself among benighted men. Tramp. You associated with savages. Tramp. You ignored the warnings of Mr. Stewart. Tramp. You let lust overcome you. Tramp. In your pride you tried to rise above God's ways for man.

I love you, Childe Harold, his heart twanged. The joke was, he meant it.

Tramp-tramp. Stomp Byron out. Tramp-tramp. Stomp Caro out. Tramp-tramp. Stomp yourself out. Tramp-tramp.

Dylan took his fingers alternately away from the blanket and shook them. He was getting cold, damnably cold. It was a mild night, for winter, but he was in danger of getting frosted.

Freeze like an icicle, laddo, and crack yourself into pieces. That's one way to disappear. One way to get rid of this nuisance, life.

Tramp, tramp.

Laddo. The word made him think of Dru. He wouldn't ever see Dru again. He had failed Dru.

Tramp, tramp.

That made him mad. He was willing to die—glad to die—but not to fail Dru. He tried to think what he could do to show that he was a man who had learned his wood-craft from the druid master.

He knew. He would build a fire by the river. He would survive until dawn, until noon, until tomorrow or the day after. Just to show he could do it. Maybe, if he was willing to eat, he would even make a snare like Fore showed him and set it and catch one of winter's small animals. Then, his belly defiantly full, he would go to the fort and let the frigging Chickadee shoot him.

"Almost I think you are not here," said Bleu.

Dylan started. He'd been asleep.

He heard the interpreter scrambling down.

Dylan was stretched out under an overhang in the rimrock above the river, invisible from above. "How'd you find me?"

Bleu pointed to the fire, then to his nose.

He swung a possibles sack down beside Dylan. "Good *idée* the fire like this," Bleu said.

Dylan had finally gotten cold enough to do something to get warm. He crawled into this overhang, some would have called it a cave, where there was no wind, got into a low place against the back wall, and built a fire of sagebrush and buffalo chips lengthwise, parallel to the rock and to his blanket. It served well. Since he had to keep feeding it, he could only sleep in patches.

Bleu pointed to the possibles sack, and Dylan opened it. His blanket coat, mukluks, his other shirt, his extra moccasins, his journal, his other small belongings, and a hunk of pemmican the size of his thumb. He held it up to Bleu, this deliberate mockery. The interpreter gave one of his Gallic shrugs.

"Is zis where you had Caro?" Bleu asked in a matter-of-fact tone.

Dylan looked at him, mystified.

"Peecneec," said Bleu.

So that's what Bleu meant last night. Meet me where you picnicked with Caro. Dylan was lucky they met up. "We picnicked just above," he said.

He sorted through the items. "This is not all," Dylan said.

"All you get," Bleu answered easily. "Almost." He

reached inside his capote and handed over Dylan's knives. "Captain Chick agree to this—you are harmless wiz knives, he say. He not give you back rifle. Maybe you shoot him coward from far, Captain say." Bleu shrugged.

So the Captain was having fun, handing out an insult and at the same time confiscating his fine Henry. Dylan didn't give a damn about the rifle—he cared nothing for himself—but he wished the Chickadee hadn't gotten it.

"What about my horse?"

"No good anyhow. He say, you want go Fort Augustus now, must snowshoe. If by horse, man and beast die." Confiscating the horse too, then.

Dylan didn't mention that he had no snowshoes and no way to make any. Bleu knew that—maybe that was why he was smiling wickedly.

"Captain Chick give Bleu the *permis* help you, ask only Bleu keep quiet. He ask me say one zing more." Bleu gave one of his eloquent looks of helplessness, a sort of this-is-the-way-it-is Gallic fatalism. "The Captain say, if you go"—Bleu made a broad gesture including the whole world—"go. If you come back to fort, he blow your brains out." With a wide-eyed smile, the interpreter put a finger to his temple, cocked his thumb, and clicked the hammer down.

Dylan nodded and smiled. Yes, the Chickadee would. Offer the means of survival, barely, and as an alternative, execution. Survival if Dylan was expert enough. And if he gave a bloody farthing about surviving. Which he didn't.

"You young bull," said Bleu. "Captain Chick he not old bull yet. Very strong."

Yes, the time-honored struggle, the interpreter was hinting. Was Dylan supposed to give way gently because of that? If he got a chance, he'd quench the thirst of his daggers in the Captain's blood.

Dylan sniffed out a laugh at his own expense. Dip your dagger deep this time, would you, laddo? Then why didn't you when you had the chance?

He offered Bleu his hand.

The interpreter touched it briefly, looked at Dylan curiously. With a *humph* of lifting his bulk, he got up to go.

Then he turned back. Hesitated. Finally spoke. "She-Wolf be at the village. She help."

She-Wolf? Who in hell was She-Wolf?

"She-Wolf, she help. Glad. You live. Why not go to her? Her tipi off to side. She live alone." He seemed to know that Dylan wouldn't go to the village, wouldn't accept any Indian's help. The interpreter really seemed to want to know why.

How do you tell a man whose life is purely of the body and not the spirit that you care not for such a life?

Dylan stuck out his hand again. Bleu touched it passingly, half willingly, still studying Dylan.

"Good-bye, my friend," said Dylan.

"*Au revoir,*" said the interpreter. He fished in his mind for the right English words. "Excuse me, there's a good lad."

On the sixth day the dilemma was becoming clear to Dylan. He could go back to the fort, where the Chickadee would shoot him. Probably the guards would shoot him on sight, or the Captain might hang him. He could go to the village and ask She-Wolf, whoever she might be, for help. Or he could starve to death.

Starving to death was becoming unacceptable. Dylan hated it. He ate the thumb's worth of pemmican on the night of the first day all at once, with water from the river. Since pemmican swells in your belly, it gave him some feeling of satiation. He hadn't had the feeling since.

Not that he'd starved absolutely. He'd walked out and found rose hips and eaten them, pulpy things, tasteless, a tease to his stomach. He wished he'd learned more about wild plants to feed on.

Setting snares wasn't going to work. The last two days he tried over and over to braid twine from strings he stripped from the runners of potentilla, strawberry plants. His hands were willing, but his mind wasn't. He would do a few braids, and then he would get savagely irritable and tear at the work and throw it away.

The problem wasn't dying, it was starving. His innards gnawed at him all the time. Yesterday his body began to feel achy. He was constantly peevish. Though once in a while he would drift into a pleasant, half-awake, dreamlike state, he was mostly damned uncomfortable.

Even at night he was miserable. His six-foot-long fire kept him warm, and the rock of the low cave warm. Feeding it a half-dozen times a night wasn't too bad. But he couldn't sleep without dreaming, and he could only dream of food. He wanted to envision his family, Montreal, the parish he grew up in, his friends, Dru, the trip out here—but all he could see was food, huge quantities of food, turning past him on a round table that rotated endlessly, a never-ending parade of viands, sauces, fruits, vegetables, breads, butter . . .

Sometimes he dreamed of the great feast he'd shared with Mr. Stewart, and beneath the procession of dishes, which in dream he only watched and never partook of, he would hear Mr. Stewart's voice, remembering the wilds, and warning him that to go among the Indians was to lose your soul.

Which was true enough. And in the dream he would accept losing his soul if he could get something to eat.

The waking Dylan was willing to die, but not to surrender his soul among the Indians.

It was curious. He knew that he had forfeited both this life and everlasting life at the throne of God. But he would not go further than he had gone. He had traveled here, and now he saw that he had gone deeper into corruption with every step, fornication, violence, loss of self in his infatuation with Caro, knives thrown at Captain Chick with murderous intent. Yet fate had refused him. Whether in divine or demonic guidance, he knew not.

Maybe something in his soul was still uncorrupted. Not pure enough, surely—he chuckled sardonically at that idea. But enough to keep him from going to the Indians merely to save his physical life. He would not surrender the rest of his soul to benightedness. He knew how terrible the darkness was.

Caro, he said to himself, I'm sorry.

In horror, he suppressed memories of trying to rape her.

If she had encouraged him and delighted in his perversion, did that not merely indicate how depraved each of them was, and how they defiled each other?

Now he was at last willing to die.

This morning he had made up his mind to go back to the fort and put an end to it. A good, quick end.

The Chickadee would not give him a chance, not again. The men in the blockhouse would have orders to shoot Dylan Davies on sight, no questions asked, no quarter given. If he did get to see the Captain, it would be with hands bound, and the audience would be brief. The Chickadee would not give Dylan another opportunity with his knives. The bastard better not.

Maybe the Chickadee would hang him. That prospect bothered Dylan. He didn't want to wait and have the fear mount him, shake him, jam him up his arse like an icicle, turn him finally into a sniveler, make him cry out for mercy. Especially in front of the Chickadee and Saga and Caro. Then take the long drop and have your head bent fatally and your tongue out like a purple eel and your pants full of shit, and finally your body hanging there for days before the Chickadee cut you down, hanging there long enough to let everybody know that there was nothing to you but what rots and stinks.

Surely the Chickadee would have him shot.

Nevertheless, every time he decided to head for the fort, his feet pointed another way. Usually he ended up walking up the stream toward the Blood village. He kept his distance. He stayed in the rocks on the side away from the river and watched one solitary tipi there. He wondered why it was apart from the others. Only one person seemed to live there, an elderly woman.

He imagined that this was She-Wolf. In his heart he knew she was a witch, and felt a terrible fascination observing her. She committed only mundane acts, picking up firewood for her tipi, getting water from the river, and once cooking something in a pot in front of the lodge, but that only made her seductive pull more awful. Too, something was familiar about the way she moved her body, and he was sure he'd been seeing her in his dreams. Yes, a witch.

To go to this She-Wolf would be the only real death.

He got tired and cold—he got cold easily these days—and went back to his cave and fed the fire and lay down again and napped in its warmth. That day, like the other days, he eventually realized that it was twilight and too late to go to the fort, because the guards wouldn't see him in the fading light and wouldn't be able to shoot.

But he was far too wise to go to She-Wolf. How could he let the body die without killing the spirit?

Dylan looked at Spider Woman. Sensations ran through him—feelings of warmth, pictures of other people, the sense of companionship, and most of all a sense of satiation, a wonderful fullness of belly. He could get rid of these feelings simply by turning his back on Spider Woman in her web. But then he got more and more miserable, his hunger ravening his spirit, loneliness forming on him like frost and crusting to ice.

When he could stand it no longer, he turned back to Spider Woman, and she spoke to him of food cooking over a fire shared with other people. Yes, she spoke to him without words, with only pictures and feelings. But that was subtle, for pictures and feelings were stronger, more enticing. Her web for him was food, warmth, human companionship. He would watch her and let her talk of such things without words, and finally he would turn his back and make them go away. She was a temptress, Spider Woman. She helped him get through the night, but she was a temptress.

He wondered if she was sent by the witch.

Dylan knew some Spider Woman stories from Dru, and some from Bleu. Such tales, Dru claimed, were borrowed from every band of pagans on the continent, for she was a heroine to all. She was a great helper—among her boons to the people were teaching them to weave. But Dylan was not fooled. Behind whatever temptations she might offer lay her trap, the web.

The other great hero of Dru and Bleu's stories was

Coyote. But this evil spirit had made no appearance yet. Dylan chuckled to himself. Apparently a fire could keep away even a spirit.

Sometimes he talked to Spider Woman out loud. "What I want," he would say, "is Yorkshire pudding. Not to mention the rib roast, plenty fat. Then for dessert, cherries. Nothing else for right now—I shouldn't overeat. Cherries . . ."

Then he would drift back into semidelirium. He knew he was half mad these days, along the processional of his starvation. " 'I am but mad north-north-west,' " he would rant suddenly, quoting. " 'When the wind is southerly, I know a hawk from a handsaw.' " He would be talking to Spider Woman or peering into the darkness for the eyes of Coyote or telling Mr. Stewart just how right he bloody well was or even playing an imaginary game of cards with Dru, and he would suddenly know he was mad, a bedlam, Hamlet north-north-west, or a small, pathetic Lear upon the heath.

Then he would turn his back to Spider Woman. He knew she wasn't real anyway. Spiders didn't live through the winter—or did they? He wasn't sure. Dru said there were two kinds of spiders, those that made webs and waited, and those that crawled and pounced on their prey. He didn't say whether they lived through the winter. This Spider Woman was a weaver of webs, but Dylan could turn his back and not get caught in her trap.

Which was going to the witch. Oh yes, that was the bait in her trap. But Dylan could ignore it. He needed to have no truck with pagan superstitions and creatures that weren't even real.

The river fog hovered among the tipis. Or was that the smoke that rose from between their ears and softly glided back down through the bare limbs of the cotton-woods and swirled a man's height above the ground? Was this the breath of the river? Or the breath of the people? Or both? It drifted, it shifted and changed shapes, now re-vealing, now hiding. It made the village eerie, mysterious, something from a dream, or from one of the Druid's tales.

Dylan did not know how he'd gotten here. He didn't remember walking, certainly didn't remember deciding to leave the cave and come here. He'd simply come to full wakefulness standing on the edge of the village in the predawn light, peering in. Or was he? Perhaps these tipis shrouded in fog were an illusion. The fog took them away and gave them back at its will. Sometimes Dylan no longer knew whether he was awake or asleep, in a world of reality or fantasy. Maybe he was actually back in his cave, and dying, and this village was his last dream.

He had lost track of the days since he had eaten. Only intermittently did he have the presence of mind to do much for himself. Occasionally he went to the river and stooped for water and picked up wood for his fire. He never gathered rose hips anymore, or tried to make snares.

He did dream. Waking and sleeping, he saw a procession of wonders, of splendors of imagination—castles, enchanted forests, strange and wonderful people, animals that were shape shifters, like kit foxes that became ravens that became mice that became trolls that became vultures. His way to death was a parade of phantasmagoria.

Sometimes he talked to the shape-shifting animals, and they revealed to him astonishing secrets, the keys to the universe men had sought for centuries. Yet he could not remember them later.

Dylan remembered now. This morning he had followed Wolf to this village. Wolf appeared to him near the river, while he was gathering fuel. The creature looked at him, trotted a few steps, looked at him again, trotted. He understood that Wolf wanted him to follow, and Dylan did. Then Wolf pranced up and down, nodding its head yes, moved off again, and waited once more for Dylan to come.

Dylan followed for a while, he thought. He wasn't sure, because he could no longer be sure what was real and what was not. He kept expecting Wolf to change shape into another animal or into a spirit. In Bleu's tales Coyote was the shape shifter, the creature that moved from identity to identity and was fixedly none. Coyote was also the trickster. Maybe Coyote this time appeared as Wolf.

Maybe this creature was an emissary from the spirit world, come to take him unto death. And that was well enough.

Maybe this village was not real. Maybe it was like Dru's stories seen with the dreaming eye, blindingly true but not actual, true not in the limited world of the senses but in the larger world of the spirit, which is the real world.

You can't eat it, laddo. It's the stuff dreams are made of.

In this shifting fog Dylan believed the village's unreality and stepped forth into its mystery. He wondered, though, why Wolf had not led him to the village in his usual way, away from the river and circling back to the solitary tipi of She-Wolf. Instead they'd come from the river end of the village and were passing all the way through it toward the lodge of the witch.

At first he wondered why he wasn't being intercepted. Where were the dogs? Mysteriously absent. Where were the warriors, alert to defend their families? Where were the monsters, guardians of this region of the supernatural, of conundrums, enigmas, riddles, secrets?

Then he understood. They were far subtler than he had imagined. In front of every lodge, hanging from a tripod, was a medicine bag, a skin pouch with the owner's conjuring items. According to report, every bag held something different, unique to the owner, revealed to him in a dream and powerful for him only, ways of communicating with dark gods. Dylan suddenly understood that these were the true guardians of this nether-world. He was passing from a world made bright by a benevolent Father-God into a realm of strange and alien magic. Yet he could not stop. As his legs had brought him to the edge of the village without his awareness, they drew him on. He watched Wolf in the mists, and followed.

She was the only person invisible this predawn light, the old woman. Dylan had a spasm of fear. She would see him and cast a spell over him, take him to her lodge and feed him witch's brew and make him her familiar. But all he did was watch Wolf and follow.

She was splitting wood with a tomahawk. Dylan noticed that her blows were almost soundless in the fog.

Near her, Wolf disappeared, perhaps around a tipi or into a patch of fog. Dylan walked toward her. For a moment the mists closed in on him and he couldn't see. He walked forward anyway.

Now, suddenly, he was beside the old woman, and she was picking up her firewood. Satisfyingly, Wolf re-emerged within the fog, part of it, a twisting shape, a breath of mist, a nothing.

Dylan noticed that the old woman wore something he'd never seen an Indian wear—socks. The incongruity of this imaginary touch reminded him that he was walking into a fantasy, the village was a mere dream, and he chuckled softly.

As though hearing him, Wolf played with the edges of the old woman's skirt to alert her. When she picked up a stick, it nosed her hand and posed, abruptly still, looking at Dylan.

Dylan laughed again. His mind was wonderful. He stepped forward to reach out to Wolf and play with it, if it didn't change back into mist.

Perhaps the old woman heard his soft laugh. She turned to Dylan and smiled.

Suddenly the world changed shape, shifted into a fog and crystallized in new form, a real form, not phantasmagoria but reality you can touch and hold against your bosom and it will keep you warm. Another world.

The old woman was the Druid himself, and she was smiling in welcome.

Dylan fainted.

Part Four

THE ROAD OF TRIALS

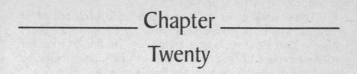

"It took ye long enough, laddo," said Dru as Dylan woke up.

He was holding a cup to Dylan's lips, feeding him warm liquid. Dylan lay full length on a buffalo robe in the tipi.

Where was Wolf? The Druid's last name meant *wolf*. Everything in this Indian world was a shape shifter. Dylan wondered whether Dru would shape-shift into Wolf. Or into the Chickadee.

Dylan raised a hand, took the cup from Dru, sipped broth. He wasn't particularly hungry. He felt very sleepy, infinitely sleepy. He would drift off a little more. Why not? Who could tell what universe he might wake up in?

When he woke, Dru was trying to feed him with a spoon. Dylan slurped. He was beginning to feel hungry. He slurped again.

"Why didn't you come get me?" he asked irritably.

"Oh, we checked on you every day, usually twice. You had to make up your own mind to come."

"Who's 'we'?"

"Me and Saga."

"You running some kind of test? I could have died before you decided I passed?"

"You had to make up your own mind to come," Dru repeated simply.

"I didn't," said Dylan, embarrassed. "Wolf came and got me."

Dru looked at Dylan in a lively way. After a moment he smiled. "Exactly," he said.

Dylan looked for no reason toward a back corner of the tipi, where the lodge skin came to the ground. There stood a slender, translucent spiderweb. He had to look for a long moment to find Spider Woman in it. But there she was, near the earth, where she had waited for him.

Immediately Dylan felt her pull, the drag of sleep taking him back under, like sinking into warm water. He felt panicky for a moment, and told himself he had to wake up. It was urgent that he ask Dru why he was tricked out as a woman. If Dylan didn't ask, he knew he'd gone mad. Or he was delirious, and all this was his dream, and he was dying? Still, he couldn't bring himself to the surface and speak the words of the question.

Sinking, he felt panic suck him into the depths. He had not come to safety, nor was he living in the imaginings of a madman. He had crossed over into some strange world, which was still more dangerous. Changed in spirit, humbled by circumstance, he had come here and crossed over, he knew not how. He wondered where on earth or under heaven he was. His last thought, passing into deep sleep, was that here the dogs would be parrots, and squawk.

His last picture, sinking into the darkness, was of Dru, stirring his witch's caldron with one hand, then stepping aside and squatting to pee.

He woke with a clear thought. He had come to a mad world, and he would accept it. For he wanted to live. Yes, he wanted to live.

Dru brought him some thin soup. It occurred to Dylan that this was one of the magic brews this witch would concoct. He accepted the bowl. Before he ate, he started to ask, "Why are you dressed up like a woman?" But he couldn't bring himself to do it. He was afraid the Druid would answer, "I am a woman."

He watched Dru walk to the fire, dip out some stew

for himself—or herself—and sit cross-legged to eat. As
Dru sat, Dylan studied his hips. Was this the pelvic structure of a man or a woman? He looked at the bosom of the
dress—did Dru have breasts? The chest was flat, but old
women often had scrawny dugs. Dylan tried to recall
Dru's voice. It might sound manlike, but elderly women
sometimes had low, gravelly voices.

Somehow, he should not ask. That would be violating
the new world he lived in. He felt it in a dizzying rush—
bloody hell, but he wanted to live, yes, live at any cost in
any circumstance, but live! To ask would be questioning
his new existence, and he would not do that. He could
only embrace it. He hugged the bowl and ate a little of the
thin soup, and went back to sleep.

A faint sound woke him up.

"You're sleeping a lot," said Dru, "like the prince of
the Lonesome Isle."

"Whoozat?" Dylan asked sleepily.

"A great Celtic hero," said Dru. "He undertook a
quest—to save the life of the queen of Erin by bringing
her water from the flaming fairy well known as Tubber
Tintye. On the advice of an old woman and with the help
of spirit guides, he journeyed toward Tubber Tintye, en-
countering many obstacles and having many adventures.

"Like you, laddo. You have made a long journey and
passed through many hazards. You had the help of an old
woman, me"—Dru cackled at this—"and you say the spirit
guide Wolf led you here. By report, along the way you
even survived the embrace of the succubus."

Dru was smiling broadly. So he knew about Caro. Or
did he mean Fore?

"You have come at last to this lodge, as the prince of
the Lonesome Isle came to the castle of Tubber Tintye.
Can you see this humble lodge as a great castle, laddo?
Things are not always as they seem to be."

For sure he could imagine this lodge as a castle. Not
one sodding thing about this place was what it seemed to
be, especially Dru.

"In the castle resided every manner of giant and beast

and monster, even the great whale. In this humble abode I will have to pass as a wizard, and Spider Woman, she you were looking at earlier, as a dragon. The modern age is not as heroic as the mythical past.

"In the castle, the prince found a succession of twelve maidens sleeping, each in her own chamber, and each more beautiful than the last. In the thirteenth chamber he found the queen of Tubber Tintye, and she was by far the most enchanting of all. The gold around her dazzled the prince's eyes. At her feet burned the fairy well. When he saw the queen, like you, he was overcome by the need to sleep. He lay beside her and slept for six days and nights."

Dru got up, went to the center fire, dipped stew out of the pot. "Wanna eat?" he asked.

Dylan took the bowl. "But what does this story represent?" he asked irritably. "Did he get the water and save the queen of Erin?"

"Later," said Dru.

Dylan was irked. Why start a story and not finish it? Was stopping a way of teaching? Or was Dru just moody? Again, he didn't have the nerve to ask.

Dylan woke up in the middle of the night. Dru was stirring.

Dylan started to turn over and go back to sleep. Then he realized that Dru was going outside. Yes, Dylan needed to go to the bathroom too. He slid out from between the blankets and slipped outside. Considering how weak he'd felt all day, his legs seemed steady. He stood in the clear, cold night—stunningly cold—and looked at the stars and squirted onto the ground. A sideways glance told him that Dru was squatting to pee. He stopped his own stream and listened. Yes, to pee.

Panic moved its fingers in Dylan's guts.

He looked up at the stars and sought out a couple of constellations. If earth was changed, at least the heavens were the same.

Dru touched him on the shoulder and pointed back into the lodge. A lodge, a fire, food, companionship, and mortal peril. His new life. He went.

*   *   *

In the dawn light Dru arose. "Stay in bed," he told Dylan. "Sleep some more. You need to get your strength back. I'll heat up some food." With that he stripped off his dress and changed into another.

It was relief for Dylan to know that, in anatomy, Dru was still male.

Then it seemed doubly chilling. A man who acted like a woman? A man-woman?

Now Dylan couldn't sleep. He brooded.

After his bowl of stew Dylan could wait no longer. "Why are you dressed up as a woman?"

"It's a long story," said Dru, and went back to doing whatever he was doing. It looked like quillwork.

Dylan tried to let it sit. Questions kept coming up his gullet. Pictures of Dru and some man in the buffalo robes kept forming. He tried to squelch all this, but it tasted like bile. Finally he blurted out, "Are you a man or a woman?"

Dru laughed. He beamed a smile at Dylan, a really lovely smile. Dylan felt a wash of relief.

"I'm not a buggerer," Dru said easily. "I have no husband. Or lover. When I want sex, my choice is Anastasie." He studied Dylan.

Did it matter? Dylan wondered. He'd crossed over. He was an Indian now.

"I live as a woman here." He waited a little. "They call me 'she' and 'her' in their language. They treat me as a woman. I may own a tipi, put it up and take it down, cook, and do other women's work. I do not have to go to the women's lodge, because I don't have the moon-bleeding. They expect fine craft work from me, and I do it." He held up his quillwork.

"I'm here winters. They don't use me for any ceremonies. They have a true man-woman for that. I couldn't let them depend on me for ceremonies, because my time living as a woman won't be much longer."

Dylan asked tremulously, "Why are you doing it?" He did not add the words "at all."

"You may interpret that as you will," Dru said. "You

may say that seven years ago I began to think a lot about being a woman. Began to feel I was missing half of life by living it as a man alone. Began to want to know how it would feel to be treated as a woman, and to look at the world as such a person. That would be true, as far as it went."

Dru waited for a response. Dylan was not about to give one.

"You may say that I wanted to get the knowledge of healing herbs, and could get it only as a woman. My teacher is dead now, died just this fall. This knowledge was handed down to her from her mother, who got it from her mother, and many mothers before. The woman had no daughter. Except for me." He looked up into Dylan's eyes. "It's a grand knowledge, and I wouldn't want to be without it."

Dru worked at his quills for a moment.

"Or you could say that I began to see myself as a woman in my dreams." He regarded Dylan levelly. "I did. In my dreams there was no transformation from manhood to womanhood. I simply was a woman, and had always been. A wise man of this tribe helped me understand my dreams. He helped me make my decision. He prepared the people to accept my decision. For four of the last six years, among these people, during the winter, I have been a woman.

"They are a people to honor dreams. Among them, whatever you dream, you are free to be." He hesitated. "No, it's stronger. What you dream you must seek to become, or go against your nature. However peculiar your dream may seem, they encourage you to seek it. In that way they are much more understanding than white people of individuality."

Dru smiled warmly at Dylan. "If that makes you uneasy, you'll be pleased to know that my life as a woman is at an end. It was always temporary. I've learned what I came to learn. And I'm more comfortable as a man."

Feeling Dru's eyes on him, waiting, Dylan nodded. Nodded again, and turned over in his blankets and closed his eyes.

Bloody hell, a shape-shifting world.

*   *   *

His decision was, this is your life now. You've earned it, live it.

He wondered what in hell that meant. Except for living in hell.

Today hell took the form of Saga. He showed up about lunchtime, ate with them, said almost nothing, and watched Dylan with nettling curiosity. When Saga asked why he had at last come to the lodge, Dylan held his tongue. Dru covered the moment with idle words.

Dylan's curiosity was why Saga was living in the fort right now. To frig Caro every night?

He bit back his anger. He spoke not a word to Saga during lunch. He felt desperate to hear something of Caro, but refused to ask, and Saga volunteered nothing. When Saga left, Dylan breathed again.

The most puzzling thing about Dru, a very puzzling man, was that he treated Saga like a son, somehow like a child Dru had once suckled. Which was both false and impossible.

Dylan was getting well. He was surprised that it took several days. His body was remarkably stiff, sore, and weak. He was constantly drowsy. He wondered if he was avoiding waking up to his new world.

He was ill in another way. It hurt to pee. His cod was dribbling pus.

When he told Dru, the Druid laughed and said he had a dose of the clap.

Caro, Dylan thought. He couldn't prove it, but he was sure he got it from Caro. It just fit.

Using his old woman's knowledge, Dru made a poultice that helped.

Dru helped pass the time telling stories, mostly short ones, like parables, told in the small intervals when Dylan was fully awake. Several were about the quest for the Holy Grail by the knights of King Arthur's Round Table. Dru explained that although the English had taken over the Arthur stories and claimed them as their own, Arthur was a Welshman, and the great grail stories were first Celtic.

The one that stuck in Dylan's mind was about the very beginning of the quest. When the knights had seen a vision of the grail and knew that their great goal must be to see it in actuality, they decided to go forth into the world separately, seeking, ever seeking. To go together, they considered, would be a disgrace.

Dylan thought that notion, of the individuality and the loneliness of the seeking, was marvelous.

Then the knights set out and entered the forest, in Dru's story, each in a place of his own choosing, a place where there was no path and where the forest was darkest.

That seemed to Dylan noble and inspiring.

Dylan told Dru about his infatuation with Lord Byron. The Druid had never heard of the poet. Byron seemed like the knights of the round table on their quest, Dylan said—unwilling merely to exist, willing to risk any effort and any unconventionality to go beyond ordinariness toward a nobility of spirit. Yet in this quest Byron often felt lonely, unloved, discouraged, cut off from mankind. Why?

Dru answered that what he knew of life came from the great stories of the Celts. In these stories, he said, the hero's adventure was utterly solitary, and that to complete it, all customary ways of living had to be discarded. Chuckling self-deprecatingly, he said, "A man on a quest might even have to appear as a woman, and learn the secrets of women." The farther the hero ventured, said Dru, the lonelier he always felt. But in the great stories, achievement of the solitary quest brought the adventurer back to the community he started from, and with a greater sense of community.

"I'm not so taken with Lord Byron anyway," said Dylan, "not anymore." He told the Druid how Caro had encouraged him to liberate himself, and then used her freedom promiscuously, and hurt him.

Telling the story, he remembered for the first time since he violated Caro on the gallery his mother's opal ring. He had assumed their engagement was off, but what about the ring? Not wanting Dru to know the extent of his foolishness, he said nothing about the memento.

"One person falling into difficulty does not discredit the quest," said Dru. "Even for her."

Dylan told Dru about Caro's praise of the dark side of man, and of men unafraid to indulge it.

Dru shrugged and said, "The gods have many energies, yes, some of them wildly carnal, like Dionysus, others contemplative, exalted in spirit, like Apollo. All these energies run deep and strong in human beings."

But, Dylan wanted to ask, what about sin? What is sin, and how does it get its hold on us?

He was tired, though, and sleepy. Besides, he feared he wouldn't like the answer.

Dylan brooded. At bedtime he finally spoke up.

"I have to get out of here."

Dru grinned at him. "You don't mean to go back to living in a cave?"

"No, back to Augustus. Or on to the High Missouri, to become a pagan Piegan."

"It's not time," Dru said seriously. Dru slipped between his robes and thought. At last he said, "Well, we could get to Augustus. Bit risky in midwinter."

Dru seemed to wait for Dylan to comment or explain. Dylan just let it go.

"I'll tell Saga tomorrow, then. Maybe Bleu will want to come too. There's nothing to keep us. It's time, actually." He looked at Dylan in the firelight. "It's my last winter here." Now Dylan could hear the smile in his voice. "I'll be confined to one gender from now on."

Dylan took the first deep breath he'd had since Wolf led him here. He rolled over. He breathed deep again and again. He refused to think of traveling with Saga.

Well, at least that was one bastard who wouldn't be plugging Caro.

Not that he gave the slightest damn who did plug her, he told himself.

He thought of Dru's Piegans and Bloods, who were always having revelations in dreams. Dylan didn't want to be someone who guided his life by dreams. He himself had a big dream. He remembered that dawn on the hill af-

ter he read Byron for the first time, and his great mystical
experience. He remembered the extraordinary feeling of
his bond with Caro.

Such were his dreams. Where had they got him?

Dreams were the unpredictable, the ungovernable.
They were the wild hairs of life. If you lived by them, you
were out of control. Indulging the energies of the gods of
both good and evil, whatever that meant.

Hell, he thought, grinning to himself and glancing
over at Dru in his buffalo robes, you might even end up in
a skirt.

He would get the hell out of here, Dylan decided. No,
he would not see Caro before he left, Caro the minion of
Captain Chick. No, he wouldn't be able to stand that.

He would go back to Augustus. He would work for
Mad Jack and learn the fur trade. Sometime, he would get
to go to Dru's mythical High Missouri. Insanity enough in
that, surely. And after a while, after Mr. Stewart's four
years, he would consider whether he wanted to stay in this
country and become a barbarian or go back to Montreal—
where a fellow could buy Byron's books—and face his father and act like a civilized man. Whatever that was.

The knights of the round table entered the forest each
at a place of his own choosing, Dylan remembered, the
darkest place of the woods, where there was no path.

Good way to get lost, he thought. Smiling, he closed
his eyes.

The trip might have been a terror,

Dylan wrote in his journal on February 8,

> I know that now. We came down from the moun-
> tains fast, covering at least twice the distance ev-
> ery day that we made with M. Troyes on the
> way up, arriving on February 6. If a big storm
> had come along, we'd have to had hole up,
> maybe for days. Dru is a splendid woodsman (all
> right, Saga and Bleu are too) or such a winter
> journey might be worth your life.

Mad Jack seemed glad to see me, I think because he intends to pile all his clerical work onto me and make me get his annual report ready for rendezvous. He said he was glad to have Bleu back to annoy him.

Dru and Saga stayed a few days and headed for Fort William. Dru said he wants to spend the time with Anastasie. (One advantage of being a man again.) He bore messages from Mad Jack to the powers at Fort William. Messages from Captain Chick too, he admitted.

I am lonely. I pore over figures, and the Druid flits over the plains and mountains as he pleases, like a water bug. (He says like an eagle. I tease, like a vulture.) I labor, he adventures.

I will not ask Caro for Mother's opal ring back. In truth, I don't want to see Caro at all. I regret the loss of the only memento I had from Mother. I often reach to my neck to touch it, and am always surprised to find it gone.

There is some justice in all this, surely. I gave Caro my heart, my soul, and Mother's ring. She gave me the clap.

He had a thought and smiled wryly to himself. Should he add to his journal that he now knew, truly, what his father had warned him about? In the first place the fur trade was mostly boredom. In the second place it was dangerous. And in the last place, if you didn't lose your life, you lost your soul.

Or at least your cod fell off.

Chapter

Twenty-One

The Lords and Ladies struck on a Sunday morning. Dylan kept track of the days of the week and the dates and the months. He wrote every day in his journal, a ledger book Mad Jack gave him. Jack said it would do him good to write down what he learned. Dylan did, but not exactly what Jack meant. He recorded his astronomical observations, as Jack insisted. He wrote down Piegan words frequently, their customs constantly, but never details or techniques of trading. Occasionally he wrote prayers or meditations, thoughts he believed Father Quesnel would want him to have in such a place. Mostly he wrote verses, very crabbed and awkward compared to Byron's, but songful with his loneliness.

He tried to finish a poem every Sunday. It was the civilized way to have days mean something, to lead toward or away from the Sabbath, not merely to be a seamless drift of sunrises and sunsets. As the Indians experienced days. As the beasts did. As even the plants did.

Besides, maybe if you acted honorably, your cod wouldn't fall off.

So he knew it was a Sunday morning. Dylan's custom was to walk down by the river, to sit, to stroll, to work on his poem. It did not matter how cold it was, or that he felt his rhymes forced and his meter thumping childishly. On Sundays he wrote his song of loneliness, unheard.

Courtney found him down on the riverbank, dangling his feet over the edge, staring at the ever-moving water.

Ice hung along the edges of the river. It was March, the moon of sore eyes, and cold.

Dylan knew Courtney, the factor of the HBC post, from one call he and Mad Jack had paid, a visit to introduce Dylan properly. Courtney had laid out for them an exterior of welcome and an interior Dylan didn't trust for a moment. He thought Courtney's heart was cold as a hailstone.

Their host served them rum and some kind of cakes made from ground seeds. He told them how successful his autumn had been, how many plews he'd traded for, mentioning particular bands and their leaders with apparent affection. Later Jack said it was all lies, a way to make them think he'd won the loyalty of Indians he'd barely even met. The Indians would never go over to the Lords and Ladies, said Jack, because the Lords and Ladies knew them not and cared nothing for them.

Now Courtney sat horseback above Dylan, not bothering to dismount. He looked down with a bitter smile. "I've taken Jack," he said. "He shouldn't have gone to the same lodge every Saturday night for the same woman. Made it easy."

"Taken him?" snapped Dylan. He stood up and faced Courtney.

"Arrested him. You don't know it, Mr. Davies, but you've thrown your lot in with a bunch of murderers. Jack O'Malley killed one of our men last August, and I mean to see him dragged to Montreal in chains and made to pay for it."

Dylan's mind was bursting with questions. Who got killed? How? Did Jack really do it? Was he drunk? Why didn't Courtney act until now? How serious was he? Dylan supposed he meant to gain advantage by acting just before the spring trading season. Dylan would be in charge, with no hope of replacement until summer. Mr. Courtney means to steal my trade, Dylan told himself. That's what it's all about, trade, and men's lives to the devil. The bastard actually feels proud of himself.

He said to Courtney, "I'm confident Jack is no murderer. But I see I'm standing in front of a kidnapper."

He wheeled and stalked off toward the fort. He felt

cold trickles run down each side of his spine. Courtney had made him sweat on a freezing day. He listened for the clops of hooves. Maybe Courtney would try to grab him now. He wondered whether he should turn around and try to take Courtney hostage. He had his knives, as always, and Courtney was no Captain Chick—Dylan could take this arse. He paused. Looked back. Courtney was simply sitting his mount, watching him. What was on the bastard's mind?

No, Dylan decided, he didn't want a confrontation that would lead to killing. He wasn't Mr. Stewart.

He would hold a war council with Bleu. Dylan strode on toward the fort. Feeling Courtney's eyes on him, he hoped his gait looked like a swagger.

Dylan felt Bleu's eyes on him like leeches, sucking at his confidence.

"*Oui,*" said Bleu, "Jack, he kill Aubrey Morris. Kill him with fists. Very angry."

"Why?"

A Gallic raising of eyebrows. "Just as you say." A smug look of eye.

Dylan was frustrated with the interpreter, but he supposed it meant, Some things you can't explain. "Was he drunk?"

"*Oui,* sure, drunk. Both drunk."

Bleu regarded Dylan. The man's mind was not on answering questions, it was on him, on the character of his new boss. Dylan wondered what the old interpreter was thinking.

"A woman."

Bleu shrugged as if to say, Naturally a woman.

"Was it murder?"

Another shrug, a purse of mouth and a lift of eyebrow. "Who knows? Jack hate him. Aubrey handsome, ze women like him, Jack mad for zis woman ... Everybody drunk." He paused, studying Dylan. "Jack say he hit, Aubrey go over backward, head on stone." Bleu tapped the back of his own head with his hand.

He regarded Dylan. "Wish the Druid was here," Bleu said. "Help."

"Was it murder?" Dylan insisted. He wondered all the while why he cared. This game was power, not morality.

"Tallyho," said Bleu.

The Balmat, Dylan decided, he would make the Balmat his second-in-command. That was what everyone called him, the Balmat. Dylan thought Yves Balmat a bright and likable fellow, not at all a typical smith—young, quick-minded, fair-haired and fair-skinned, his head always covered with a gay bandanna, amiable, full of fun, self-assured. Only the size of his arms told his trade.

Yet Dylan had a need to feel Balmat out. He wasn't sure of . . . something.

At the smithy Balmat was hammering on some piece of iron, as always. He stuck it in a barrel of water and steam hissed up. Dylan had heard Balmat beat an animated marching rhythm on his anvil, just for fun.

He watched without speaking while Balmat inspected his work. Balmat looked at him curiously and stuck another piece of iron in the fire.

What's holding me back? Why don't I speak?

"Monsieur Davies?"

He couldn't tell where the call was coming from.

"Monsieur Davies?"

The gallery, up by the pickets that faced the river. One of the Lemieux brothers was pointing at something between the fort and the river. Now the Balmat was looking at him very curiously. "Let's go!" Dylan yipped at him, and jerked his head at the wall facing the river. They ran toward Lemieux.

"Where is Bleu going, Mr. Davies?" whined Lemieux.

Up the ladder to the gallery.

First Dylan saw Bleu's wives with the family belongings. They led two horses, heavily laden. Who would have thought Bleu owned so much? He rode magisterially in front. About a mile in that direction stood the Lords and Ladies' post. Courtney.

Dylan squeezed down to keep his stomach from roiling. He spoke calmly. "Are those kegs of rum his?"

"Certainement non," said Lemieux. "No, he is not rich."

Dylan looked hard at the Balmat. "Come on," he snapped.

Bleu was nearly in the shadow of the HBC fort before they caught him. He didn't bestir himself to get there first. Dylan imagined that he rode with a taunting deliberation.

Dylan and the Balmat galloped around in front of Bleu and reined up. The Balmat was nearly close enough to bump him, and the smith's horse was antsy. The Balmat looked avid, ready to do something, anything. While they threw the saddles on, Dylan had told him about the kidnapping of Mad Jack.

"Where are you going?" Dylan demanded.

Bleu moved his hands expressively. "Many times Monsieur Courtney offer me job. I take." He looked mockingly at Dylan. "No man can say me no."

"You don't think I can run the fort," Dylan challenged him.

A shrug. "Excuse me."

Dylan looked at the packhorses. Both of them wore company brands. "How much of our goods are you trying to steal?"

"Thank you," said Bleu.

"How much?" demanded Dylan.

"Is not steal. Company owe me wage."

It was more or less true. Dylan kept the books. The company owed Bleu wages for several months. But Dylan couldn't remember how many goods Bleu had charged against those wages. More than Bleu had earned, he would bet.

The squaws led the packhorses up and sat their horses quietly, watching. Dylan guided his mount to where he could see the goods. The keg on one horse had NWC stamped on it. He would bet the other one did too. Dylan met Bleu's eyes.

Then it rose in him.

He lifted his hand to his right-hand knife and glared at Bleu. The interpreter's hand twitched toward his belt pistol and stopped. He had no chance to be quicker, and he'd watched Dylan practice. "Keep an eye on the bastard," Dylan said to the Balmat.

Dylan rode forward, leaned out, and cut the squaw hitch that held the load on one horse. All the goods crashed to the ground. Then he did the same to the other horse.

He faced Bleu. "Get the kegs off the ground," he said to Balmat without taking his eyes off Bleu. Balmat did. Dylan kept his right hand on the knife.

"Good-bye," he said to Bleu. "If I find you owe more, I will take it in pelt—Bleu hide." He could see Bleu wanted to grab his pistol and didn't dare.

"Tallyho," said Bleu. His wives got off their horses to pick their belongings up off the prairie and repack.

Dylan backed his mount away.

Like a king Bleu walked his horse away, leaving his wives to pack up.

Dylan kept his mount turned toward the HBC post. There, on the gallery, he could see someone watching. The man waved jauntily. Dylan would bet it was Courtney.

Dylan and the Balmat held war council in the office. Balmat immediately agreed that they would handle things themselves. No need for Captain Chick, the Balmat said nonchalantly. Dylan looked at his face hard. It was carefully composed innocence. So the Balmat had heard about the disaster with the Chickadee, and knew that Dylan would never ask him for help.

Well, hell, as long as the Balmat wanted to go it alone, Dylan didn't care what else he thought. They would show sodding Courtney.

So Dylan and the Balmat got out the sketch of the plan of the HBC fort and studied it. They would bloody well rescue Mad Jack. Dylan felt elated, full of boyish enthusiasm. He was hardly bothered by not having any ideas yet.

*   *   *

Rap-rap.

The young men looked at each other across the sketch, skittish.

Rap-rap on the door.

"Who's there?"

"Lemieux," said a quaking voice. "Please, Monsieur Davies, may I . . . may I come in?"

Dylan opened the door uncertainly. Lemieux slouched there in front of him. He was an odd duck, always hunched, seeming to look at the world out of the corners of his eyes, somehow aslant and obliquely, with an obsequious smile that looked fearful and insincere. In all this he was the same as his brother, an identical twin. No one ever knew which was which, so everyone just called them Lemieux and didn't worry about it. Dylan wondered if their wives cared which was which.

This was Ceran, though. Easy to tell. His twin Charles spoke no English.

Ceran Lemieux had three wives, Charles two, and Dylan wondered how such timorous men ever got any wives, much less took care of them. Dylan's fantasy was that the women took the Lemieuxes' larder and gave them back other men's children.

"Please, monsieur, are you . . . ?" He annoyed Dylan by peering around him into the room. When he saw the Balmat and the desk, he gave a reassured smile. "Oh, monsieur, I believe I can help. You have ze problem wiz Mad Jack . . . he is kidnapped, no? Bleu, he is gone over to the other side, no? Crazy problems, big . . . nuisance, no?" He squiggled his knees irksomely, and nodded in a way that looked like bowing.

"Pardon, monsieur," he said, and slick as an eel slipped by. Before Dylan could move, the man had the sketch in his hands. "This plan, I draw it. You see—C.L., *c'est moi*, Ceran Lemieux, it is me." He pointed to initials in the bottom right-hand corner.

True enough, saw Dylan, the drawing was signed C.L.

"I have the remember for the buildings, windows, doors, ways between, all such." He tapped his head with a forefinger. "Monsieur Stewart, he ask me draw, give two Witney blankets."

It looked like a good sketch. If two blankets was all the payment, Lemieux had been taken advantage of. He looked like a man who lived to be taken advantage of.

Dylan looked at the Balmat questioningly. "Let him help," said the Balmat. "He's a shrewd fellow." Which only made Dylan wonder what he was not mentioning.

Dylan looked at Lemieux. When you had a man like this for a partner, you never knew what you had. "All right," he said, "where will they keep Jack?"

Well, Lemieux asserted in his sidewise manner, the Lords and Ladies had Jack in one of two places. In the stink hole, or in the building *rouge,* where they lodged gentleman visitors. It was called *rouge* because the pickets along the adjoining palisade were painted red, before they ran out of paint.

Lemieux had gone over the other structures with them one by one with elaborate explanations of what was there and why there was no place for Jack, or it would be an insult to a man such as Jack or . . . In Gallic fashion he ran out of words and used his shoulders and eyebrows. He didn't explain why certain rooms would be an insult to Jack and the stink hole would not. It was the fort privy. In a small partition against a side wall, they shackled men who misbehaved. They used a padlocked door to give them food and water. Most days.

Before Dylan could ask why Courtney wouldn't want to insult Jack, Lemieux said in a definitive way, "I send my wife find out."

Dylan looked at the Balmat. He was wondering, So why doesn't the fellow say "one of my three wives"?

"He always says wife, like there was one," Balmat put in, speaking normally.

Pretending Balmat spoke in a whisper he didn't hear, Lemieux gave a triumphant smile. "My wife, the gentlemen of Hudson's Bay not know her from more Indun, think she come trade. I ask her buy . . . *needle,*" he said, as though the thought of a needle was a major breakthrough.

"Then," he announced, "Lemieux have the clever, the

quick, the crafty idea. Listen now most careful, and you agree with Lemieux."

Dylan insisted on committing the crucial act himself, and it was damned awkward.

He sent Lemieux to see the Lords and Ladies that day. The fellow used the pretext of maybe wanting a job. The Nor'West Company fort was going to fold up, he claimed to Courtney, because the young Monsieur Davies didn't know how to run things. Lemieux needed a job—he had his wife to support, *non*? To show his heart was in the right place, he even did a little trading with the Lords and Ladies. He gave two good winter plews for some lead and powder, permitting himself to be exploited. During the interview with Courtney he exaggerated his tics and mannerisms to a parody of himself. And he deliberately filled the room with flatulence. When Courtney rolled his eyes and even opened the window and door, Lemieux found it convenient to overcome the fresh air with more gas.

Courtney said he didn't really have an opening now, but yes, surely, a man like Lemieux was truly valuable, so he'd see if he could create a position and would let Lemieux know tomorrow. He waved his hands in front of his nose and struggled to keep a polite face.

Yes, Lemieux was easily granted permission to visit Jack in the stink hole. Yes, he told Dylan, Jack was truly there. Oh, what a sad sight, he wailed, our leader in the sheet house. Jack was shackled to the wall, hands and feet. His hair was wild, his face gaunt, his demeanor crazy. Lemieux thought he was becoming truly Mad Jack. Which was, after all, perhaps his destiny. *L'avenir le dira*— whatever will be, will be.

Of course, as Dylan ordered, Lemieux had not told him of tonight's rescue. Jack was to be as surprised as the Lords and Ladies. So Lemieux merely comforted the fellow a little, and gave him some pemmican with berries to keep off scurvy. Jack seemed so pathetic that Lemieux embraced him, even stroked his poor head, and told him falsely that Captain Chick was sending help.

Dylan was not to worry. When they went into the

privy in the dark, Jack wouldn't even respond, but would just think someone else was coming in to give offense with his bowels.

When Lemieux left Jack, of course, he remembered to leave the new powder, plus his own powder horn, and Dylan's. They were hanging from one of the roof joists in the left-hand corner highest away from Jack.

Dylan looked at himself in the full-length mirror in the trade room. He was surprised how much he liked the cut of his own jib in breechcloth and leggings. And the feel of the leather shirt on his skin was good. The whole thing was damn good. It wasn't even the look or the feel of Piegan dress he liked—it was the element of shape-shifting. You had to get used to that in this lunatic wilderness, he told himself. He changed stances in the mirror. He smiled at himself. He wiggled. He and the Balmat gave each other conspiratorial grins.

Now Dylan stripped off the clothes and went to work on his face, hands, and forearms. This was even more fun. Lemieux had brought some of the brown dye Indians used for face paint, for the two whites to disguise their skin. Dylan worked it well into his face and all the way up to his elbows. They needed to darken themselves thorough-ly—they'd be walking into the fort in broad daylight. Dark skins for dark deeds.

Dylan studied his face in a hand mirror. Nut brown looked good on him, but it made conspicuous lines on his eye-to-ear scars. He would convert those giveaways into . . . double lines with slashes of lightning in between.

Yes, it looked grand. Liking it so much made him nervous. Maybe he missed his calling—everyone else around here was a half-breed.

When he was finished dyeing his skin, Dylan put bear grease thick on his hair, to darken it. Then he donned the wolf-skin cap Lemieux had brought for him. It fit down snugly, the wolf's head atop a white lining of strouding, the entire beast hanging down Dylan's back and the tail dangling to the knees. Wonderful. Marvelous.

Beneath the wolf skin he strapped his knives. He

would now feel naked without them. And over everything he wrapped a *gangaro,* a white Witney blanket with red stripes. It covered him entirely, chin to toes. He could let go of the blanket at his throat and have a quick reach to a knife handle. He stood in front of the full-length mirror and preened.

The Balmat stepped into the image next to him. The Balmat's fair hair was hidden beneath a buffalo hat elaborately feathered, his whole body draped in a solid red blanket. His face was dark, his eyes glinting with humor. They made a perfect pair of savages. Shape changers. Devil magicians.

Now they would turn demons loose.

Dylan just walked into the Hudson Bay fort and went to the privy. Natural enough. Indians didn't use privies, and were closely watched in the fort anyway. But by his clothes he was a breed. Inside he used the privy—his fear helped him with that. And he called softly, "Jack. Mad Jack."

A whining moan came from the other side. Lemieux said Jack was in bad shape. Dylan had to prepare him, and keep him from crying out. The biggest risk in this whole enterprise was Mad Jack.

The Balmat went to the trade room. Little enough danger there. Neither the factor nor the clerk had ever seen him, or certainly hadn't taken notice of a mere smith. Low status in the world made a fine mask. He traded for gunpowder. Plus lead, just to make it look good.

Then he walked quickly around through the compound. Though he'd been told to waste no time, he wanted to see the layout for himself. It's my arse, he told himself. Then he headed for the privy. So far fine and dandy.

Mad Jack was whimpering on the other side of the partition. "You tell him?" asked the Balmat. Dylan nodded. Jack sounded like a whipped cur. Was the man scared half to death?

The Balmat hung the new gunpowder high on a nail

in the joist. The old powder was still there. Then he got a crowbar from under his blanket and removed two boards from behind the sitting shelf. He and Dylan slipped through into the gaol room. Jack crawled around on the floor, circled on his spot in the straw, curled up with his chains like a cur. Jack would be no good for anything anymore, which was fine with the Balmat.

He pulled the boards into place behind him. Dylan patted Jack's shoulder. The Balmat got the nails right back into their old holes. The job would stand a glance, but not a tug.

Then he showed Jack the files and pointed to the chains. The noise of the files was a risk. The Balmat mouthed to Dylan to wail and moan, and the new leader did a fine job. In the Balmat's opinion, Dylan was just daft enough to be a good fellow.

Jack started in wailing too, and Dylan stopped. The Balmat kept working on the rivets of Jack's chains with the files. He didn't know if Jack understood. I'm going to set you free with these tools, old boy.

Someone came in the other side to use the privy. Jack whimpered and the Balmat stopped filing. Dylan and the Balmat looked at each other silently. Instead of the sounds of bowels they heard the scraping of powder horns. Lemieux.

"The bastards, they give me a job," Lemieux said softly from the other side. "I am in my new quarters. Midnight. The start, it is mine. You won't have to listen so careful." He laughed at his own joke.

It was weird to talk to Lemieux when you couldn't see him. You couldn't hear him without imagining his crabbed posture, his wheedling face, his sly eyes.

"All right," said Dylan. Dylan and Balmat nodded at each other. "Get gone."

The stage was set.

About dark, Mad Jack started babbling again. Some of it was gibberish, as far as Dylan could tell. Some was childhood imaginings. Some was dire vision of Judgment Day, and of hell. That was worthy of Dylan's nightmare of

Hieronymus Bosch, and made him lust once more for Fornicating Woman. Some of Jack's babbling, unfortunately, was about the escape.

He was inconsolable. They were all going to be killed. Their heads were going to be crushed by great mills, their brains ground into mush for the Lords and Ladies' breakfast. They were going to be shattered, their bones cracked open for stew. After that, they were going to be lashed to horses that ran to the four winds, dragging and dribbling pieces of Nor'West men behind.

He could be neither gentled nor quieted. Occasionally someone would come in to use the privy. The variety of noises was remarkably and alarmingly varied on its own terms, but Jack added a wonderful music. Dylan almost put his hands on Jack's throat to silence him, but that might have led to a half-coherent protest. He thought of putting his hands to his own throat to choke back his insane desire to scream. Dylan was sure Jack had given them away. Once he even cried out Dylan's name, and Dylan raged to reach for a knife. Under his blanket he could feel his twin blades tingle.

The privy users seemed to take little notice of Jack, though. Only one acknowledged his rantings at all, and he howled at the moon like a prairie wolf, competing with the gaolbird, and then cackled nastily.

Dylan hated crouching here in the dark, silent. He couldn't see more of Jack and the Balmat than their shapes, couldn't see their eyes, didn't know what they were thinking, didn't dare speak. If someone caught on, the Lords and Ladies would catch them in the gaol like beaver with one foot trapped, then drowned.

As he waited for the signal to start the explosion, Dylan imagined that immense sound over and over. He thought of how much powder Lemieux had. He whispered to the Balmat, "We'll make the crack of doom sound like a tinkle."

Lemieux was mesmerized. As he sat doing his work, he was transfixed by his own mind, his picture of what would happen. He was stunned, dazed, stupefied by this event. Which had not happened.

His three wives and the two children still at home watched him. The wives were miffed at being moved about—today from Augustus into these new rooms, tonight back to Augustus in flight. They were sure they were going to end up without some of their belongings. They'd long since lost respect for their husband, and patience with him, so they paid no attention while he worked. The children had learned to live in mystification.

Lemieux was making a bomb. He meant it to be nasty. He started with a three-legged trade kettle. It was badly cracked, but he'd bound it together with shrinking rawhide. He coiled a fuse on the bottom and ran an end out a crack. He poured half of a small keg of gunpowder on top of the fuse. But that didn't fill the kettle. On a whim he went to the corral, got a handful of dry manure, and stuffed that on top of the loose powder. Still didn't fill. He went to the courtyard and gathered a double handful of small rocks. Now the kettle was full, but there were little spaces everywhere. He poured powder onto the lot until everything was snug.

Now he liked his bomb. Since the kettle was twice the size of a man's head, it ought to knock some things down. Oh, *quelle* bomb.

He gazed at the explosion in his mind. In his imagination the bomb was like a cannon. He set it by the main gate, and the cannon shot the pickets of the gate into the air like arrows. He pictured them arcing gracefully away, trailing fire, like Chinese fireworks.

Ah, Ceran, he said to himself—only he used his Christian name—ah, Ceran, you devil.

He went to the one of the pair of blockhouses that was occupied, leaving the bomb in a dark corner outside. It was only a matter of saying he couldn't sleep, sitting with the guard overlooking the main gate, and then slyly revealing that he had two gills of rum to help pass the night. Before long he left, with the guard slumped against one wall, rum in hand, singing bawdy songs incoherently.

The improvised bomb of Ceran Lemieux was even more grandly destructive than his childish imagination hoped. It did blow up the main gate. It also blew down most of the front palisade, and the blockhouses atop it. A splinter of wood the size of a man's forearm ran through the drunken guard. The blockhouses rolled across the ground like giant dice, broke, and fell apart in huge shards.

Ceran Lemieux was standing a hundred feet away. The blast picked him up like flotsam on the crest of a tidal wave and flung him against the nearest wall. He fell to the earth, crumpled and broken. He saw nothing and heard nothing—the blast blew his eardrums out. In his mind exploded the Chinese fireworks he'd always heard about and yearned to watch. The show in his head was almost as good as the one in real life, until it faded, dimmed, and went out.

Dylan's mind was still in the roar. The Balmat acted fast. He jerked the two boards off the partition, picked up Mad Jack like a child, and pushed him roughly through the hole. Dylan followed Balmat's behind. Then they were outside and running for the corral. Even carrying Mad Jack, the Balmat almost kept up.

Where was Lemieux?

Dylan looked around the corral in the light of the half-moon. Pandemonium among the horses—they were milling, tossing their heads and manes and hooves and tails, crying out like men drowning in a storm of high seas. Where was the guard? Dylan saw no guard. Where was Lemieux?

Looking back, Dylan saw the fellow sitting against a wall. Cursing, he ran back. He shouted, "Lemieux! Lemieux!"

He shook Lemieux by the head, and when he did, he felt it. The back part of the skull was mush.

Dylan looked for a long moment into the lifeless eyes, then ran.

He saw movement at the far end of the corral—the guard. No, one of Lemieux's wives. She had the gate open.

The guard surely went to see about the blast. "Where's Lemieux?" shouted the Balmat.

Dylan waved him forward. No matter, no matter anything. Get the devil out of here.

The horses broke for the open gate. As the lead horses escaped, others clogged the narrow way, bumping, falling, trampling each other.

The Balmat set Jack on the ground and threw his rope over a horse—wonderfully active man, the Balmat. Dylan heaved Jack up behind him and screamed at him to hold on.

In an instant Dylan roped his own horse, looped the rope into a primitive bridle, and jumped on. It was wonderful. In a crisis he could do anything.

He turned the horse toward the gate. The beasts were galloping out now, onto the prairie, bursting free, Dylan and his mount in the midst of them. But there were too many. They were choking the exit.

The Balmat's horse reared, and Dylan saw Mad Jack tumble off backward.

Dylan jumped off his mount, gripped the reins desperately, and made two strides, feeling shoulders and legs and hooves buffet him. He grabbed Jack and hoisted him over one shoulder. By a miracle, he flung Jack over the withers. Using the mane, he catapulted himself astride. The horse went out the gate with the others, in a stampede.

Dylan had no control of the horse. It ran with the others, a mile, two miles, he didn't know. The Balmat seemed to have some control but followed alongside. Finally the herd tired and slowed. The men got their horses to a trot, then to a stop.

They pitched off onto the ground. They huffed and puffed. They laughed. "We did it!" they yelled, and pounded each other's back.

Except for killing Lemieux, thought Dylan.

"We did it! Jack, we did it!" Dylan took Jack's limp arm. Shook it a little. Anxiously took his pulse.

He looked into the Balmat's puzzled eyes, and gave him the dead hand.

Chapter
Twenty-Two

D ylan lived in anxiety. It bubbled up his gullet like relentless heartburn. From minute to minute he wondered what the Lords and Ladies would do, how they might strike back. He felt like the fox while the hunters arc getting mounted. There was nothing he could do but wait.

He acknowledged to the Balmat that the rescue of Mad Jack had been a disaster. Two men dead, including the one they intended to rescue, the NWC post left leaderless, except for himself, and his leadership proven worthless.

To the men of the fort he acknowledged nothing. The clerk had now become the factor, and he had a trading post to run.

Courtney showed up before noon the second day after the rescue, in front of the main gate, with every man and gun he could muster. Dylan and the Balmat went to the blockhouse to hear him out. The man simply raved. On and on about how Dylan had left the HBC post vulnerable to Indian attack by blowing up the main gate, about how there were certain things white men just didn't do, and so on, and such balderdash. He shook his rifle and promised terrible revenge after his men had the palisade back up.

Knowing the history of the HBC men and the Nor'Westers, Dylan paid no attention to talk about how white men should behave. He knew that those civilized fellows at HBC would do worse than he'd done, given an excuse.

While the Lords and Ladies' factor shouted his threats, Dylan watched Bleu. The interpreter just sat his horse impassively. When Courtney finished, Bleu seemed to give an ironic shrug and rode off. Someone dumped the body of Lemieux in the snow.

The Lemieux families didn't want Ceran held for burial after the thaw. They took the body away somewhere and didn't come back with it. Probably built a burial scaffold and left it, said the Balmat.

After a couple of weeks, Dylan realized that Charles Lemieux had taken his brother's widows as his own wives, and adopted the children. Dylan wondered, with sick humor, whether the wives and children noticed the difference between the twins, or gave a damn.

Dylan hired a fellow from the Cree camp as interpreter, one Marcel Henry. A half-breed, of course. One curse of the country, it seemed, were these half-breeds in infinite supply, the sign of the white man's carnality. Dylan would have been quicker to find fault had he not lain with Fore and Caro and other women. Caro was different, he told himself, a special case.

Henry made secret contact with Bleu, who was his friend. What revenge did Courtney mean to take?

Bleu said he couldn't give such confidential information away.

Dylan gave Henry a pistol to salve Bleu's conscience.

No revenge yet, said Bleu. It will come through the Sarcees, who will be bribed to cause whatever trouble they can. He didn't even say thanks for the pistol.

But the Sarcees didn't trade with Dylan during the spring. Henry said they always came in the fall, when they came at all, after the buffalo hunt.

In the fall Dylan didn't expect to be the acting factor of Fort Augustus. Thank God. He knew the routine. Captain Chick would send men to the great rendezvous at Fort William. They would stop at Augustus to pick up the furs and the year's reports. Desperate reports, thought Dylan. And from Fort William, NWC would send a new factor, surely.

He was glad, and he wasn't. He liked being the boss. He liked trading—he was scrupulously fair and profitable

enough. He liked the feel of running the enterprise, and
nothing escaped his attention. But he was damned tired of
being afraid for his life every day.

Where in the hell was Dru?

So Dylan lived in a simmer for more than a month.

In May, the moon when the buffalo calves are yellow,
men did arrive from Rocky Mountain House. They bore
no message for him from Captain Chick. Dylan had been
imagining wonderfully sarcastic communications, complete with elaborate assurances of how well Caro was being taken care of.

Instead there was Monsieur Troyes, imperturbable as
ever. He bore a letter from Caro, in her spidery, feminine
hand:

> We have pitched our tent a mile up the
> river, at the top of the cottonwood grove. I can-
> not bring myself simply to come to the fort un-
> invited. Please come to me at once. I need you.
> Love,
> Caro

She was pregnant. Not huge yet, but unmistakably
pregnant.

He stood there, holding the reins of the winded horse,
feeling like an absolute arse.

She stood in front of the tent, her eyes world-weary,
her smile warm, altogether gorgeous. His mother's ring
was dangling from the slender gold chain around her neck.
Dylan could have melted into the warm spring afternoon.

"I'm sorry I hurt you." These were the first words she
said.

He felt it again. His body softened. He felt like the
earth broke open within him and the sweetest water welled
from the crusty ground of his innards and an elixir gushed
forth.

You are my touchstone, he thought. Truly.

He took her hand. They sat on a rock. She brought it

up immediately. "I'm six months along," she said, "almost seven. The child is yours." She touched his cheek and looked into his eyes. "I know without doubt," she said. She held his eyes. "The child is yours." She hesitated. "I'm so glad."

He found himself unable to say anything. He remembered a moment in one of Dru's Celtic stories, of two young lovers. The Irish girl is promised to the Welsh king. A young knight has been sent to escort her from her home to his liege's castle. There is a magic potion brewed by the bride's mother, a potion that will make the bride and groom love each other deeply. Mistaking it for wine, the bride and young knight drink it, and are thunderstruck by love for each other.

According to Dru, their servant said, "You have drunk your death."

The young man answered, "If you mean the love I feel, that is my life."

So it was for Dylan.

They talked of other things. Dylan told her about the verse he'd been writing. She said she'd been learning to paint on hides with dyes made from local plants. She modeled a painted elk hide for him. It was tanned very soft and white, the hair removed, and a great sunburst pattern painted on it. It was in the tradition of the ones he had seen the Piegans paint, yet very different—the big geometrical pattern of diamond shapes had been transformed into a giant ornament like a brooch made by a master jeweler, many diamond shapes of gems of many colors, some large and some small, each beautifully cut, polished, and faceted. The colors were vibrant, brilliant, dazzling as a sunrise. She wore it as a cloak, and it looked wonderful.

They talked of commonplace things, like brother and sister, as though they had known each other all their lives. It struck Dylan forcibly, as he sat beside Caro on that boulder in the sun of that balmy May afternoon, how strange it was to feel that someone you'd known only for a month or so was your oldest and truest friend, your sister, lover, wife, mother, and mother to your children, all at once. All of woman. Impossible but true.

She did say, sweetly and truly and without pretense, some things of consequence:

She regarded that time, well, about last Christmastide, as an episode of madness. Some day she might have more to say about it, but not yet.

She was uncomfortable being with child, uncomfortable physically. As a result she could not sleep next to Dylan, or anyone, and could not make love. He felt two stabs, of longing and of relief.

She detailed her physical complaints—she could not lie on her back to sleep, had lots of pain in her lower back, woke up with headaches, suffered from heartburn—all aches of the body that seemed so out of place for the flaming spirit that was Caro.

He said that to her.

"No," she answered, with her sad, world-embracing smile. She took his hand and put it on her belly. "This anchors me to the earth. I need an anchor."

She tired in the middle of their talk. He put a blanket over her and she napped on her side in the sunshine, Dylan sitting quietly beside her. He watched her tenderly as she dozed.

Her face had changed, subtly but unmistakably. It was less vibrant but more understanding, her eyes less sparkling but more compassionate, her demeanor less scintillating but softer and more sympathetic. There was nothing he would not have done for her—nothing, great God in heaven, nothing.

What he did that afternoon was to pack up the camp and move her and her father to the fort. He installed the two of them in his own quarters, which used to be Mad Jack's, the best-furnished rooms the fort offered. He himself moved in with the Balmat.

The next day Monsieur Troyes went downstream with the canoes toward Fort William. Dylan wondered that the man would leave Caro when her time was approaching. To him Monsieur Troyes was an enigma, and an uninteresting one.

Dylan sat with Caro all afternoon the day her father left. He read *Childe Harold* to her. They recited nursery rhymes. They laughed a lot. They settled on names for the child—Harold if a boy, Lara if a girl, both in honor of Byron. Caro was sure their child was a girl, and she loved the name Lara.

Dylan noticed that she said nothing of marrying, now or later. He didn't know what she intended. To be a mother without a husband was difficult anywhere, impossible in the wilds. But he knew: Now she was his—she would bring the child to its father.

Dylan would wait, as he had been unable to wait the first time. He would be present for her, available, willing, nurturing. Being near her would be more than comfort, more than gratification, more than fulfillment and fruition. It was life. His head had been underwater for months, his life the nasty dream of a drowning man, and Caro was sweet air itself, sucked hugely in.

Oddly, it would seem to him later, he thought only of the woman he loved, and little of the child growing in her belly.

Friendly Crees brought Dylan word of the canoes— more than a dozen of them, painted on the prows in the bright NorthWest Company fashion. So Dylan was ready when they came around the last bend and within sight of the fort—he fired the six-pounders as a greeting. He meant this gesture as a salute to the newly arriving factor of Fort Augustus, whoever he might be. And to the Druid, master woodsman. And a perhaps farewell salute to Dylan Elfed Davies, factor pro tempore, who had tillered the post through a difficult spring and summer for the bloody NorthWest Company and against the sodding Hudson's Bay Company.

The blast of the two cannons sounded thrilling to Dylan. He opened the big gate and walked out to meet his mentor and his new boss. He wanted Caro by his side at this moment, and sent word to her room, but she didn't appear.

Then, for once, he forgot about her. Courtney was coming out of Edmonton House with his clerk and riding toward the canoes. They appeared to be unarmed, but Dylan took no chances. He went back inside, got the

Balmat and Henry and two others with rifles, and headed again for the river.

Immediately he saw that there was no man who could be the new factor. Only Dru, Anastasie, Saga, Lady Sarah, and a lot of *voyageurs*. Dylan's stomach knotted.

Dru came up to Dylan with a grave face and embraced him solemnly.

"I quit," said Dru. These were his first words. Dylan felt unshed tears blister his eyeballs, he didn't know whether from hurt or anger. Dru turned and spoke clearly to Courtney: "I quit the goddamn NorthWest Company. I quit the goddamn fur trade." He looked older than Dylan had ever seen him. Anastasie and Saga watched Dylan's face for his reaction.

Mr. Courtney sat his mount, sneering down with a look of triumph. The Druid took an envelope in one hand and sailed it at the factor. It hit him in the chest and fell into the mud. "It's yours, Courtney, the whole sodding lot."

"Thank you, Mr. Bleddyn," Courtney said with sarcastic courtesy.

Dru looked Dylan in the eyes. "They've bought us out. The whole NorthWest Company, sold out."

Courtney spoke imperiously. "My men and I will take possession today, Mr. Davies. This afternoon. Starting now."

He turned his horse toward Fort Augustus. Dylan saw HBC men trooping toward his post already. Courtney reined in and turned back to Dylan. "Is that rifle you're carrying your own, Mr. Davies? Or the company's—*my* company's? I shall require you not to take company property. You may demonstrate what is yours personally through your books—in one hour."

Courtney kicked his horse, which cantered a dozen steps, wheeled and reared. "You will be out of the fort by nightfall. On foot. The horses are not yours. Nor are these canoes. It would be a shame to see you naked on the prairie." He laughed sardonically.

"Bastard," said Dru. "We ought to kill him."

"No," said Anastasie, "send him a woman with syphilis." They all cackled.

*   *   *

Dru told Dylan the story on the way to the fort. At Fort William the partisans out from Montreal told them that the Nor'West Company and the Hudson's Bay Company had merged. But everyone soon saw that the merger was phony. The owners of NWC got a lot of money and were out of the fur trade. HBC owned every post, every plew and otter and muskrat and wolf skin, every parfleche of pemmican, and every blanket, bead, and pound of powder.

Worse, it owned the employees. The Nor'West men were to work for the Lords and Ladies. They were probably the key to the purchase, said Dru, for they knew how to trade, how to deal with Indians, how to live in the country, all that the sodding HBCers had never learned. Hudson's Bay needed the *voyageurs*, *hivernants*, and *hommes du nord* of NWC. And had them by the short hairs. Most Nor'Westers owed the company money, advanced in trade goods against next year's wages. If they quit, they'd be thieves, liable to arrest, trial, and punishment.

They stood in the open gate of the fort, the two couples and Dylan, and looked around. The HBC clerk was standing in the courtyard taking inventory on ledger sheets. "Bastards," said Anastasie. Dylan looked at her agape. He'd never heard a woman cuss before.

"Sold us out," said Dru. He sighed. "This boyo will never work for the Lords and Ladies. How about you, lad?"

Dylan felt his friends—his family—looking at him for a response. He opened his mouth to say he would bloody well stick with them, but he didn't get it out. Madame Lemieux came up running. "Mademoiselle Caro asks for you, monsieur," she blurted out.

Dylan flinched. What was wrong with Caro? Why didn't this woman speak up?

"It is her time."

"I won't live," she said simply.

Her face glistened with perspiration. She was wan,

pale, suffering. She took Dylan's hand and looked at him
with supplicating eyes.

Then her body wrenched with pain.

The violence of the pain alarmed Dylan, and frightened him. How could people think suffering was enno-
bling? It was ugly.

"Of course you'll be fine," he stammered.

In her next calm moment she grasped his hands with
both of hers. "Take care of the child," she begged. "You,
not my father." The enigmatic Monsieur Troyes who was
always gone anyway. "Take care of her."

"*We'll* take care of her," he said gently.

She started to speak, but the next pain took her breath
away.

"Get gone," Dru said. He touched Dylan gently on
the arm. "We have work to do."

Dylan felt a rush of irritation at being kicked out. He
looked at Anastasie questioningly.

She shrugged. "Dru knows what to do, not me." At
that moment Dylan was grateful Dru had learned to be a
healing woman. He kissed Caro on the forehead and left.

"You are trespassing upon my quarters," said
Courtney, squeezing the words out one at a time and un-
derlining each one. "I require you to be gone."

Dylan didn't explain. Courtney knew that Caro was
delivering in there. You don't explain things to arses. You
just coerce them. Dylan stood in front of the door. The
Balmat was gone to the kitchen for hot water, lots of it.
Dylan could protect Caro against this one or any number
of arses.

"If you persist," Dylan said evenly, "I'll kill you." As
he said the words, he raised both hands to his knives. He
had a remarkable realization then. He meant his threat. Not
in anger or ferocity or bluster. Partly in justice. Mostly in
defense of what he loved.

Courtney must have seen something in Dylan's eyes.
He pivoted and stalked off.

Dylan took his hands off his knives. Something
moved in him, like some music finding a new key, closer

to the home key. He was a killer, potentially, a killer out of love.

Fine. That's the way it was.

He thought fleetingly of Mr. Stewart, and felt sorry for the man.

Before long Dylan wished Mr. Courtney would come back. Just to have something to do, Dylan would kill someone. Just to get his mind off the bloody silence from inside that room.

Since the Balmat passed the water and rags through that door, no word came from inside the room. Even standing close, Dylan could hear nothing.

He paced the gallery. The Balmat leaned against the rail and watched his friend with a look of suppressed amusement. Whenever the Balmat said anything, Dylan silenced him with a murderous glare. How could this idiot make noise, Dylan asked himself, and risk covering sounds that would be precious? *Idiot!*

He heard nothing, actually, until the door scraped. Anastasie stood there beaming. A tiny, naked infant rested in each of her arms. A boy and a girl. Twins.

Dylan staggered. His head whirled.

Twins. A boy and a girl. Harold and Lara.

"You may see her for just a moment," Anastasie said gently.

At first he couldn't see her. Dru was in the way, attending to something, and blood was shrieking at Dylan from everywhere in the room, on the bedclothes, on other sheets thrown off the bed, on rags heaped up, on Caro. He forced himself not to look at it, not to allow it into existence.

Dru stepped back, gestured Dylan forward. The sight of Caro sleeping scared him. She was wan, waxen. She looked relieved, but far from peaceful. Drained, and worse than drained. Desperate, half dead, withered, like fruit with the juice sucked out. What shocked him was that she looked ugly. Yes, his Caro. Limbs akimbo, body twisted, head thrown to the side too hard, face contorted. He wanted to straighten her up and then stroke her nurturingly, but he didn't dare.

Anastasie reached around him, untied Caro's night-gown at the bosom, reached to the end of the bed, picked up the two tiny people, Harold and Lara, and set them at Caro's breasts. They nuzzled and nursed.

A chill flickered through him. The children were dark-complexioned, darker far than Caro. Perhaps they looked dark because they lay on Caro's fair breasts.

Dylan wanted to jerk them away. He wasn't glad to see his children nursing from their mother. He had a wild and irrational conviction that they were sucking her life out. He wanted to grab them and hurl them away.

He noticed that Caro's eyelids were slightly open. He took her hand. Perhaps her face changed toward a smile, or at least softened. She gave his fingers the slightest squeeze.

Perhaps she drifted off to sleep again, perhaps not. After a few moments he felt her fingers tighten again, not affectionately this time. She looked into his eyes, and he saw awful, awful pain. "I won't live," she said.

"You must, you must," he answered pathetically.

"It's time to go," Dru said firmly.

Caro wrapped her arms around the children where they suckled. "Take care of them," she whispered. "Remember that they're truly yours."

"You'll be fine," Dylan urged.

Dru pushed him out the door.

Caro spoke very little during the next three days. With a kind of grace she permitted Dru and Anastasie to care for her, more for their sake than hers. Twice she told Dylan, "Lara looks so much like you." He had no idea whether it was true, especially since the child was so dark-complexioned. Often Caro slept with her hand in Dylan's. He sat beside her for hours on end, looking at her supplicatingly.

Harold and Lara nursed often, and that worried Dylan. He suggested that Anastasie get milk from one of the fort's fresh cows. Anastasie did. Dylan sat holding the children, dipped a handkerchief in the warm milk, and squeezed it drop by drop into their mouths. Whenever Caro saw him doing that, she glared at Dylan and demanded to nurse them. He gave in because he didn't want to spend her energy arguing.

Lots of the time she slept, sometimes in half delirium. She had a fever, which rose often and didn't fall often enough. Dru did his best to keep her cool with river water, sometimes wrapping her in wet sheets. Caro didn't seem to care what they did for her, as long as she could hold the children when she was conscious.

On the morning of the fourth day, Dylan was sitting with her in the predawn light. He got up to stretch, and stepped outside into the dawn air. In the glass of the window to her room he watched the sun come over the eastern horizon, a reflection smeared across each pane. He went back in, opened the curtains to let the sun in, and sat beside her. She seemed to be sleeping peacefully enough now. She'd had a hard night, turning and tossing and half crazy with fever.

The sun struck the wall above her bed. Dylan saw that in a few minutes it would slant down onto her form. He held her hand and waited for that moment, a beatification.

The sunlight came onto her body fully, and onto the tossed bedclothes. But it missed her face. He wanted to see her face shining in that golden dawn light. He waited, holding her hand, to see if the sunlight would shift slightly, or she might move down in bed.

He held her hand and waited. Held her hand and waited.

Reached out and put his hand below her nose. Felt nothing.

Touched her neck to feel her heartbeat. Felt nothing.
Understood.

Gently, tentatively, he slipped the necklace with his mother's opal ring from around Caro's neck. The slender gold chain was warm from the touch of her body. Suddenly, like life to death, it changed—it felt like a thread of icicle on his fingers. One lightninglike shiver jolted him.

With difficulty, in fear of its cold, he put the icy necklace around his own neck. With his own body he would keep it warm forever.

Then, like cold rain, the tears came.

They buried Caro Troyes on a mount above the river, north of the fort. Dylan refused to let her lie in the ground either post used as a cemetery. No, she lay in death as she had lived, alone. No one attended the little ceremony but Dylan, Dru, Anastasie, Saga, Lady Sarah, and the two children in Anastasie's arms. Dylan resented Saga's presence, but there was nothing he could do about it.

He read lines from Byron, slightly adapted:

I have not loved the world, nor the world me.

And:

                                    She stood
Among them, but not of them; in a shroud
Of thoughts which were not their thoughts.

And his favorite:

There is a pleasure in the pathless woods,
There is a rapture on the lonely shore,
There is society, where none intrudes,
By the deep sea and music in its roar:
I love not man the less, but Nature more,
From these our interviews, in which I steal
From all I may be, or have been before,
To mingle with the Universe, and feel
What I can ne'er express, yet cannot all conceal.

Chapter
Twenty-Three

At Dru's insistence they set out downstream in canoes immediately after the funeral. Dylan didn't know where he was going, but he was getting out of here, pressed no more by the obnoxious Courtney than his own wants. He didn't want to see Fort Augustus or Edmonton ever again. Ever. They would always be for him the place where Caro's spirit left her body.

He hardly knew what he wanted, about anything. He was numb and beyond numb. But he wanted out of here.

As they pushed away from shore, they saw smoke from the direction of Fort Augustus. Where the bank dropped low, they could see what was happening—the trading post was on fire in three or four places. Dylan and Dru looked at each other. Courtney was burning the NWC fort to the ground.

Frightened somehow, one of the children let out a cry. Anastasie cuddled him—it was Harold—and cooed at him.

The goat grunted. They'd bought a fresh nanny from Courtney to provide milk until they got back to the tribe. Every time Dylan thought of the goat, he felt disgusted. He seldom fed the children himself. Right now he could hardly bear to look at them.

What on God's earth was he going to do?

It became the winter of his despair.

For the children's sake, they spent the winter near

Fort William, with Anastasie's people. Dylan didn't know
what he wanted to do anyway, or where he wanted to go.
Everywhere was the same to him, as long as Caro was nowhere.

The children fared dubiously on goat's milk. On the
trip east neither child seemed to gain weight properly, especially Harold, who was constantly sick, unable to keep
milk down. Dru came up with a feeder that helped—he
sewed a buffalo teat onto a buffalo bladder. The nursing
bottle looked strangely primitive, but the children loved it.
Dru made a couple more on the way to Fort William.

Once the group got to Anastasie's Crees, they found
a wet nurse, and both children improved.

Dylan was moody, lackadaisical, lost in depression.
He seldom slept well and barely ate. The children lived
with their nurse, a plump, jolly young woman, and he
didn't even go to see them every day. He lay around the
lodge, near the fire, and stared through the smoke hole at
the empty, empty sky. Empty because Caro was nowhere
on the earth. He couldn't explain it, even to himself. She
had caused him the greatest pain he had known. And she
had shown him himself. Not only in Byron's verse—much
more in the way she was with him. He thought about it
and could find no better words than that. She saw his spirit
as clearly and simply as others see a flowing spring or a
gray stone or a piece of bark. The way she acted acknowledged it unmistakably, as people's behavior shows they see
a curve in the trail. No one else acknowledged it.

Dylan owed her all the joy and all the grief of his life.
He needed her.
She was gone, gone, gone.

He didn't go on the fall hunts. He quit practicing with
his knives. He quit keeping his journal. He nearly quit eating.

Dru tried to snap him out of it. The Druid said pointedly that without himself and Anastasie, the children's
godfather and godmother, Harold and Lara wouldn't even
be alive. Dylan just nodded. Anastasie blistered him for

his seeming indifference to his children. He didn't give a damn what she said.

Dylan never told them he wasn't sure Harold and Lara were his children. For one thing, Anastasie kept on with Caro's line, saying how much Lara looked like him. He couldn't see it. He saw mostly how dark she was, darker even than Harold.

One evening in the lodge he spoke of going out into the great woods and not coming back. Said he'd heard freezing to death was pleasant, even euphoric.

Dru slapped him. No words at all, just a slap, neither hard nor soft.

A moment later Dylan apologized. After he spoke the words, he felt real to himself, a peculiar feeling, like his body really belonged to him and he could feel his fingers and toes and be alert or torpid all on his own. He apologized to Dru for his uselessness.

Feeling hungry for a change, he ate a little.

When Dylan finished, Dru asked him bluntly, "What are you going to do with your children?" Dru and Anastasie had asked, or hinted, a score of times over the winter. Dylan always just shrugged. He didn't know.

He still didn't know. He couldn't bring himself to think. He depended on Dru and Anastasie for answers, mutely and helplessly, and for doing whatever needed to be done. Dylan was useless and willing to be useless.

It was Saga who came up with the idea that snapped Dylan back to reality. He suggested they fight.

Saga had learned to fight, to brawl, from a Métis whose name Dylan could never get. Saga had discovered that there were real techniques. You needed to know when to kick, how to kick, and when to keep your feet. Certain situations called for butting, others for throws. You hit with your elbows a lot and with your knuckles never. Frenchmen gouged and bit, but Saga wouldn't.

The two young men practiced fighting in the snow. Dylan liked it, found something akin to his soul in its ugliness. He even liked the pain of getting bitterly cold hands and feet. He fantasized a lot about hurting Saga, but he held back.

Many techniques were purely defensive, Saga showed him. These are the moves against a man who charges you with his head. This is how you counter the kick with both feet. If someone gets hold of your arm for a body throw, this is how you go with the throw and end up on your feet. It was intriguing. It was fun. It was nasty.

One day when they came into the lodge from their practice bout, Dylan suddenly knew what to do with the children. He looked Dru in the eye. "We're going to take them to Montreal," he said. "Put them in school. Raise them civilized."

Which meant, among other things, confront Ian Campbell, the children's grandfather. Confront and somehow come to terms with the old man. In his mind's eye Dylan could see only that trickle of blood, running down the side of his father's nose, from where Dylan struck him.

That night, before supper, Harold started coughing. Dru touched him, felt his fever, and immediately knew it for what it was, the coughing sickness the white people gave the red people, now common in every village.

Dru had seen the change in Dylan. The lad let his children into his imagination—he envisioned life bringing up two children—and immediately he let them into his heart. It was a grand thing. Dru feared it was too late for Harold. Yes, they recovered sometimes. Sometimes they were sick for a couple of years and died. Dru had seen them get sick one evening and be gone the next morning.

The child coughed all through the first night, a soft, gentle, half-audible whimper, like seeping blood. Dylan held Harold in his arms—his *son*—and rocked him and cooed at him and patted him gently when the coughs came. Dylan wiped the child constantly with a damp cloth to keep the fever down. He murmured that he would take care of Harold all through the winter, the spring, however many seasons or years were necessary. Dru hoped they would be necessary.

He went outside and raised his arms to the night sky and spoke silently to the powers of life, the power that makes clouds blow and rain fall and resides in all creatures and makes them grow. He didn't know what to say, because he hurt so terribly. He asked that the power living in Harold rise up and fight. He thanked the power for being in himself, and in those he loved, and simply for being.

Harold coughed all night and all day, and grew paler and weaker. Dylan held him and rocked him. Dru could see him reach for the hope that had been inborn and he'd let get away, but he found only blackness. Dru went outside several more times, yes, to speak to the powers, but also to remove himself just a little from the pain.

The second night, Dylan never did put Harold down. He held both of the children a lot, talking to them and for them, making up the conversation they couldn't have yet with each other. The lad knew what was important now. It was a terrible way to learn.

Harold coughed very little that night, only little whimpers, really, but his fever raged. When he was hot, he was squirmy, uncomfortable. Twice he cooled off and got peaceful.

The wet nurse came to feed the children, and Dylan gave up Harold very reluctantly. Harold would eat almost nothing. Finally Dylan took the child back greedily. Harold fell asleep immediately, comfortable in his father's arms. Twice he whimpered, but he stayed asleep.

About mid-morning he took a deep breath and suddenly opened his eyes. Dylan saw how bright his eyes were, and saw—or imagined—a hint of a smile in them. Harold waved his arms, almost like he was clapping his hands. He wiggled. He made a speechlike sound, followed by what sounded like a chuckle.

Then his body arced and twisted, like he was having a spasm. For a long moment he was rigid. Then, abruptly, Harold went soft against Dylan's chest.

Dylan put a palm on the child's chest. It didn't rise or fall. He put a finger beneath Harold's nose. Harold Yves Davies was dead.

*   *   *

Dylan nodded and followed Dru outside. Anastasie and Lady Sarah were wailing. Dylan didn't care what he did right now. It was all the same, and always would be the same.

Dru was carrying the pipe bag that always hung in an honored place in his lodge, the one he smoked ceremonially when they met Indians, and sometimes by himself. He was going to pray, or perform a ceremony, whatever. Dylan didn't care. It was all the same.

He followed Dru to a little rise and stood there stupidly while Dru lit the pipe and sent the smoke to the four winds, the earth, and the sky. Dylan could hardly see Dru for the awful pictures in his mind. Since it was the dead of winter, Harold would have to be put high on a scaffold, wrapped in blankets and hides and left there alone in the cold of the weather and the cold of infinity.

Words from Dru's ceremony or prayer or whatever it was came to Dylan's ears. He heard thanks. Then his mind would bolt away to Harold, being picked at by birds, his skin being dried by the sun and the winds, his skull showing through.

Words of thanks. Thanks to the earth. Thanks to the sun. Thanks to the very winds that would desiccate . . .

The man was mad. Not a word of grief or loss or pain.

Thanks to the powers of life, he heard Dru say. Thanks to the powers of growth. Thanks to the forked, the four-legged, the winged, the crawling and burrowing things, the creatures that swim, to the rooted, to all living creatures. To water. To Mother Earth and Father Sky.

It was all thanks. In his anguish, in this havoc and devastation, thanks seemed infinitely peculiar to Dylan.

Thanks again—Dylan heard his own name mentioned, and Lara's and Anastasie's, and others', but he was shivering, shivering in the aloneness that his son now felt. He heard Harold's name, and heard Dru say thank you for the gift of his life, and of their time with him.

Thanks for warmth, for sound, for taste, for color, for

the sight of the eyes. For the sight of the dreaming eye. For imagination. For feeling. For the gift of being alive.

Thank you, said Dru, the four winds, Mother Earth, Father Sky, all living creatures, and all the things that are.

Peculiar, yes, very peculiar, but Dylan did feel, in the wasteland of his soul, a small, warm, healing trickle.

Chapter
Twenty-Four

The house was time out of joint for Dylan. It was newly trimmed in white and robin's-egg blue. Flowers were planted. More than that, it felt different. No longer heavy and oppressive, but light and buoyant.

Regardless of what Amalie had persuaded him to do to the house, Ian Campbell would be neither light nor buoyant. Dylan knocked with trepidation.

Amalie opened the door, and Dylan saw a sliver of alarm, then a shaft of surprise, and at last a burst of delight. Dylan's little sister jumped into his arms. "I'm so *thrilled*!" Amalie cried. She held him at arm's length and looked into his face, her eyes alight, and then hugged him again. He could feel her, over his shoulder, looking at Dru and Anastasie and Lara. He felt her stiffen.

He drew back. "Amalie," he began, "this is Lara." He looked into her eyes as he pointed to his daughter in Anastasie's arms. "My daughter." A cloud crossed Amalie's face. Then Dylan saw her decide to muddle bravely on. "Morgan Griffiths Morgan Bleddyn is her godfather, and Anastasie Bleddyn her godmother."

Amalie did not step forward to take the child or coo over her. Even to Dylan, Lara looked very dark in her new white dress.

It was all right. He was prepared for strangeness. He had to admit that Dru and Anastasie, in buckskin clothes and with a cradle board, looked out of place in Montreal. He himself had donned cloth only to visit Amalie, and his outfit was still *voyageur*-style. He waited for her to look up at the friends he was introducing her to.

"Dru, Anastasie, this is my sister Amalie. Who's very beautiful, isn't she?"

Dru gave a simple and elegant formal bow. Dylan wouldn't have thought him capable of it. Amalie seemed embarrassed. "Miss Campbell," he said gently. Anastasie inclined her head slightly to the young woman.

All three of them smiled at Amalie. She was beautiful today, fair of hair and complexion. But Dylan was surprised that her yellow curls were pinned on top of her head. After only two years she looked older, much older than her twenty-one years. Yet she had not grown an inch, and still didn't come quite to five feet. His dear, tiny sister.

A little late, she said, "I'm pleased to meet you. Won't you come in?"

Not only had the house been painted outside, inside the hallway was transformed. No more the dark, musty feeling, the air of illness or decline. And the library—where he and Ian Campbell had come to blows—was brought back to life. Though the large pieces of furniture were the same, the rugs and draperies were new, and the place felt colorful, even resplendent. Amalie's touch was evident everywhere. Which meant their father was letting her have room to live.

"Where's Daddy Ni?" asked Dylan. For Dylan, Daddy Ni would always be right here in this room, raising that table overhead and smashing it toward Dylan's head.

Amalie hesitated, toed the rug nervously. "Dylan, there's a lot you don't know. Dada's fine, and he's gone." Dylan Davies, born Campbell, felt suddenly empty, hollowed out.

Amalie added briskly, "I mean, Dada's, he's much better—I'll tell you all about it." She thought for a moment. "Why don't I have Nicolette get luncheon ready and I'll . . . Oh, it's hard." Why was his sister so flustered? Where was his father? "Just wait patiently, sit, please, everyone, and I'll be right with you."

She fled to the kitchen. Dylan saw a woman servant,

presumably this Nicolette, hurry off down the street. He heard Amalie helping to make luncheon in the kitchen. He glanced nervously at Dru, and then looked away irritably. He hated it when Dru knew everything.

He took Lara from Anastasie, sat in his father's Queen Anne chair, and cradled her fondly. Since that night in the lodge when he'd decided to bring the two children to Montreal and make a life for them, his attitude toward Lara and Harold had changed completely. Actually, he felt like he did not make such a decision. He had looked at the twins, held them, cooed at them, rocked them, sang softly to them, nuzzled them. Then, in touch with reality rather than the contortions of his deciding mind, he knew what he wanted to do, how he wanted to live.

Now, his heart did not permit him even to picture Harold's face.

He shook Lara gently in his arms, and she burbled. She was a curious, bright-eyed, cheerful infant. It amazed Dylan how complete she was, a wholly formed, pint-sized human being with a grown-up strength of will. And full-blown personality, in fact, even at ten months. She was about to start talking.

Dylan saw that she was going to sleep now, put her in the cradle board and hung it from a chair.

He loved Lara. She had given him back his life.

It would be the devil's own job to make a life for her, but a joy.

Knock-knock!

The man in the doorway was . . . Claude MacDonald, Dylan's old roommate, smiling with all his charm. Which covered his wariness well enough.

Claude stepped into the library. Amalie came next to him and took his arm. "Dylan, I have a surprise for you too. Claude and I were married May the first.

"Mr. and Mrs. Bleddyn," she continued, "may I present my husband, Claude MacDonald? Claude, Morgan and Anastasie Bleddyn."

Dru repeated his bow, but less deep.

"Amalie—"

She interrupted him sweetly. "When we're seated, Dylan. This way."

It was a lovely meal—Amalie must have been planning for Claude to come home. They had hare soup, salmon croquettes, boiled vegetables, and strawberries with whipped cream. A sea change from pemmican and *sagamité*.

Dylan couldn't stop thinking about Claude and marriage. His old mate's idea of a beddable wife was someone else's wife, anyone else's. Well, maybe he'd changed his mind.

Amalie poured the coffee herself. As she sat down, she began. "Dylan, Claude has left the bank. He's investing in land, and he's partners with Daddy Ni." She smiled winningly, like that wasn't a bombshell. "Daddy Ni is marvelously recovered from his illness—he looks wonderful, so virile. He took, well, he took that Indian tar, you know, that medicine the Rat brought him from the interior. And he recovered. Truly, Dylan, his joints are all right, and he's his old self."

Dylan wasn't particularly pleased about that. The old Ian Campbell was the one who always left him and Amalie with their aunt and disappeared into the wilds, leaving his children alone, once for an entire year. But it was good news that Daddy Ni's health was better.

Amalie's story was not long. About the time Daddy Ni started improving, HBC bought out the Nor'West Company. Ian Campbell saw great opportunity in that—those Lords and Ladies didn't know, well, she wouldn't repeat his actual language, about running the trade profitably. As he regained his health, Daddy Ni had begun to dream again. He got a message to the Rat. His longtime partner materialized in Montreal bringing more Indian tar and evidently some critical information.

"I helped them find some financing," said Claude, "some of it in exchange for this house and a half share in the warehouse." That meant Dylan was now dining in Claude's house, not his family home.

"On May first, two months ago," Amalie said brightly, "Ian Campbell set off for what is reported to be great beaver country."

"Said he'll bring back a bloody fortune," added Claude, "twenty or thirty on the pound."

Dylan was struck with the reason for going into the wilderness, not pilgrimage, but money lust.

"Where'd they go?" put in Dru.

"Wouldn't say," answered Claude. "Military secret. Didn't even tell us. Mr. Campbell said with a big grin, 'This is war.' "

In the middle of luncheon Lara began to cry. Anastasie got up, brought her to the table, and fed her from one of the buffalo bladders she'd brought for the purpose.

"What the devil is that?" said Claude with a huge smile.

Amalie put a hand to her nose, apparently somewhere between fascinated and repelled.

Dru told them how he'd made them.

"Ingenious!" exclaimed Claude, forcing his smile even wider.

Common enough among the Indians, said Dru.

Anastasie went to the library, brought back another half-full bladder bottle, and handed it to Claude. Dylan's brother-in-law inspected it and offered it to Amalie, who flinched and shook her head no. Dylan supposed the ancient-looking buffalo dug was a little alarming.

Dru watched Lara in Anastasie's arms, nursing. The kid sucked like a greedy little creature, Dylan had to admit, all avidness and no table manners.

Looking at her made Dylan nervous. Lara was so dark, especially against Amalie's white linen tablecloth. He didn't know how his daughter turned out darker than either of her parents, and he didn't care.

Why the devil am I nervous in front of my own sister? he demanded of himself.

Lara belched loudly.

Amalie tittered.

"Not exactly the music of the spheres," said Dru with a smile.

*   *   *

When dessert came, fresh strawberries in cream, Amalie broached the subject. "Dylan, I hope you don't feel left out by Daddy Ni's business arrangements with Claude. I'm sure you would have been part of the business, but after two years of not knowing ... Well, we'd nearly given up hope."

Awkward pause.

"Right now we're all chiefs and no Indians, so to speak," put in Claude, with an eyebrow stressing this choice of words. "Of course your father would like you with him in the field, now that you're a blooded *coureur de bois*." Claude grinned, and his glance indicated Dylan's *gâge d'amour*. Dylan knew all this was intended as flattery. "But we don't know where the field is." He hesitated. "Do you want to stay in Montreal?"

Claude and Amalie tried not to look at each other.

"Yes, I'll need some sort of job," said Dylan.

"Ah, we'll come up with something at the warehouse." That was the hub of Campbell Trading Company, but the employment there was menial. "And you'll be wanting lodging of some sort."

Dylan marked that.

"Don't worry, if Mr. Campbell succeeds, we'll all be rolling in money." Claude stood and clapped Dylan on the shoulder. Everyone rose uncertainly.

"Would you like to see what I've done with the rest of the house?" asked Amalie.

"Yes, especially my room," said Dylan.

As they passed down the hall toward the stairs, Claude said softly in Dylan's ear, "I guess what we're actually wondering, old chap, is where the child's mother is."

Dylan looked him in the eye. "She's dead," he said. The picture of Harold in his arms at the last hit him so hard he swayed. He turned away so Claude couldn't see his face.

Dylan was startled. The room where he'd slept for twenty years, dreamed his boyhood dreams, and lusted his teenage lusts, was a nursery.

"I wanted the lightest room for the children," said Amalie, "and these windows are wonderful."

His bed was gone, and his desk. An open-sided crib instead, the latest thing.

"The children are only a hope now, of course," said Amalie shyly, one hand on her belly.

"Your books are stored in the attic," she said.

Dylan cared nothing for most of the books, which explained accounting procedures and the workings of business. He'd like to have the novels and the volumes of verse back.

"This room is just as Dada left it," Amalie said, gesturing across the hall. It was the room where Ian Campbell slept for years, when he was in town. "Dada may want a place of his own one day, but for now he'll stay with us."

"He's not planning to be here much," said Claude. "He's like you—favors the rough life."

Dru and Anastasie looked in too. Lara was asleep in the cradle board on her back. Dylan could see that Anastasie wanted to touch things and didn't dare.

"This room," Amalie said, opening another door, "I'm proud of."

It was the old guest bedroom, completely redone in the fashionable Queen Anne style. It was handsome, with its walnut, rosewood, and mahogany, and very alien. Dylan remembered Aunt Meredith spending all those years in that room. He didn't think she would like it now.

"I hope you'll use this room tonight, Dylan." She thought a moment and went on brightly. "The child and her godparents perhaps would be comfortable in the nursery?" She looked enthusiastically at Anastasie, who nodded. Dylan was sure Anastasie had never gotten to spend a night in a proper house.

"Tomorrow we'll have to switch things around. The McLeods will be staying with us. From Vermont? Quite wealthy. Claude is showing them some land."

"Fine opportunities," put in Claude. "Someone will do well in these lots."

Dylan had a strange imagining for a moment. In his mind's eye he saw the lodge pitched on the edge of the woods on the river above town, and himself, Lara, Dru, and Anastasie in it, plus Saga and Lady Sarah. In this waking dream Amalie and Claude came to visit with a prosperous-looking couple. He noticed particularly, for some reason, the trimmings of fur on the collars and cuffs of their elegant coats. Amalie was saying, "This is the center fire, which is proper to *these* people. This is the willow backrest, which is proper to people like Indians and Dylan . . . Davies. This is a cradle board, which proper Indians hang their children in. Of course, the children very indecorously make messes in the bottom."

In the real world Lara yawned audibly. He saw that she was waking up, and lifted her into his arms. Suddenly he wanted very much to hold her.

"Would you care to see the warehouse, which we now call the office?" said Claude eagerly. "I've made considerable changes. I'm quite proud of them, actually."

Dylan shrugged. Why not?

A shiny new vehicle stood in front of the house. "Did you notice my new carriage?" asked Claude. "I bought it to show people property. Must make a good impression. One day Amalie and I hope to have a carriage house. Well, off to the office?"

Dylan looked at Dru uncertainly. "I've never ridden in a carriage," said Anastasie with childish eagerness.

After they got out in front of the building that housed Campbell Trading, Claude stopped to talk to a frock-coated man on the street. The fellow glanced at Anastasie oddly, Dylan thought, probably put off by the presence of an Indian.

Claude gave Dylan a look that seemed to mean, Leave us, or even, Get them away from here. Moving off, Dylan heard Claude say something to the fellow about a "fine opportunity."

Dylan looked down the alley alongside the building. The old Campbell Trading Company sign had been moved into the alley, and apparently the new entrance for his father's business was the old freight door. In front the warehouse sign was gone, and Claude's new sign proclaimed, LAND OFFICE. Claude had said the business was trying to appeal to Yanks.

Dylan led Dru and Anastasie through his father's old office, now tripled in size and very much spruced up in appearance, into the huge storage space. He felt funny about it. This was the heart of the Campbell business, the end of the efforts of hundreds of very skilled men facing very real dangers in the wilds, sacrificing their blood, their sweat, their lives. Here the furs came from the interior and were shipped to London. Here the trade goods came from London and were shipped to the interior. With the Campbell family making a profit each direction.

As a boy Dylan had spent afternoons after school here with his father and liked the place, liked the pungent smells and the rough camaraderie of men. Now that he had been into the wilds, had seen what it took to get the hides to ship to England to provide fashionable hats for civilized people, he felt ambivalent about it.

It was a big, dark, low-ceilinged structure of logs. There were few windows and no candles. The chinking left holes, and on this summer day the doors were thrown open, creating slanting striations of bright light against blackness. Through this bleak pattern of black and white stripes moved a dozen or so men, working.

There were clerks checking shipping manifests, counting items and storing them on shelves, counting them and packing them into bundles for transport to Indian country. There were inspectors checking hides to make sure they were completely dry, other men grading the furs, others sorting them for shipment, others packing them into bales, or stenciling addresses onto the bales. Wrapped in oilcloth, the bales would cross the Atlantic in the hold of a ship. In London they would mark the difference between people of fashion and, well, the lower classes.

Dylan walked among stacks of beaver plews, kegs, tables loaded with trade goods. What he remembered best about the warehouse, and loved most, was its smells. There was the ripe smell of a dozen animals, not only beaver, but marten, fox, wolf, ermine, mink, and others. Making that pungent was the odor of decaying flesh, for not all the hides would be perfectly scraped and desiccated. There was the aroma of the alcohol they not only stored in kegs but sprinkled on the hides to keep vermin off. The oil-cloths wrapping the shipment bales smelled resinlike.

Mixed with these smells and confusing everything was the buzzing of thousands or millions of flies, drawn by the hides.

In the end of the building where goods were incoming instead of outgoing were his favorite smells, exotic fragrances from far away—Virginia tobacco in plugs, Mexican hemp, Louisiana sorghum, roasted coffee beans.

In a corner a man was mixing a batch of ink from powder. To Dylan fresh ink was one of the headiest of all smells.

And all of these brought back to him the presence of Ian Campbell, home in the evening after a long day in the warehouse trying to make a profit, bringing all these earthy aromas to the Campbell home. To Dylan it was the smell of his father, of attention, comfort, play, closeness.

He reminded himself forcibly that in those days his father was mostly gone into the wilds. As he was now.

"Suppose bringing back the skins of dead animals was the real reason we went to the wilderness?" asked Dru softly.

Before Dylan could respond, Claude said, "Oh yes, I'm always struck by that thought when I come back here, which is not often. Reality is rather always less than ideal, isn't it? That's why men must shield women and children from it." Dylan wondered if that was a veiled reference to Anastasie and Lara, who as Indians required no such protection in Claude's view. "But this bestial commerce does provide the comforts of living that separate us from the beasts." He smiled at his own play on words and added, "Ironic."

A swarthy man with a bandanna-wrapped head walked up to them. "Do you know Mr. Campbell?" Claude asked the man. "Dylan Campbell, Jacques-René, the warehouse manager." Now Dylan did remember—a longtime employee. They shook hands.

He corrected Claude. "My name is Dylan Davies now."

A queer look passed across Claude's face. "Yes, of

course, Davies." He looked back at Jacques-René. "Mr. Campbell's son." Then he introduced Dru and Anastasie, putting Dru first. He didn't mention Lara in her cradle board.

Dylan thought how strange white manners were—white women politely before white men, but Indians after everybody. His heart twisted. Such prejudice now included his child.

Jacques-René headed back to work, and Claude led them along the aisles. "I'm expanding the business considerably. It's not just the Indian trade anymore. Any kind of item that can be imported profitably for people in this city. To plug tobacco, for instance, we've added snuff. Sugar from the Caribbean. Silks from Canton. These goods are commonly shipped on the same vessels that bring our Indian goods, and they return money much more quickly. Instead of shipping them to the interior and waiting months for furs to come back, we sell them to local merchants for immediate payment, or within the month." His eyes gleamed at Dylan.

Dylan murmured the obligatory "Clever."

"Come, let me show you something." He led the way back to his well-appointed office. There on the wall was a map of Montreal. On the crooked streets some of the major buildings were labeled, and blue or red squares filled other small spaces. "This city is going to grow," he said. "It's suffering a little now because of the damned merger"—he looked wryly at Dylan and Dru "HBC mostly doesn't bring its business here. *But*. That has only permitted me to buy cheap. I've used my patrimony, not that it was great, to buy buildings and land. The red squares are lots for resale, and the blue ones are buildings we're renting out." There were half a dozen red squares and a dozen blue ones.

"Your father's enterprise is high risks for great rewards. Whether he succeeds or not, I think you can feel assured that I'm going to be able to take care of your sister and your future nephews and nieces quite well," he boasted, smiling.

"I'm glad," said Dylan sincerely. "What about that job?"

"It's a bit sticky," answered Claude. "I hate to let a man go when he's been loyal. I could work you in now as a shipping clerk. By winter we may require an additional bookkeeper."

Dylan looked sharply at his one-time lodging mate, now his brother-in-law. Sod that, he thought, a chance to work up to the job he'd thrown over at the bank. And not even that for sure. Claude knows I hate this, he thought. Not much for the only son of the founder and co-owner.

But now Dylan had his daughter to provide for. "Seems ..."

"I do quite understand," said Claude. "We'll do better as soon as we can. But I must say I'm a bit uncomfortable with all this. You know ..."

"We'll talk more later." Dylan regarded his one-time friend, apparently and unfortunately his superior in the family business. He stamped the face and the moment in his memory, accompanied by the music of loss.

Claude and Amalie took Dylan to Clamp's Coffee House for coffee and pastries. Sensitive to their apprehensions, Dru demurred, claiming that he and Anastasie wanted to settle into the nursery with Lara. Maybe they did. Dylan felt a little lost without Lara. The good black coffee gave him some comfort. He remembered when Ian Campbell used to take them out on saints' days, father, son, daughter, and Aunt Meredith standing in as mother, like a proper family. The memory warmed him.

Now the three talked of commonplace things, how Montreal was changing, the pushiness of the bloody Yanks in commerce, the merger, the fortunes the great Scots families had taken from beaver. Claude told a story of going to the Beaver Club with Ian Campbell. The dining and drinking were as hearty as ever, said Claude, but both he and his father-in-law were secretly glad to see that the attitudes of the Scots who had owned the Nor'West Company were not quite so grand. The edge was off their arrogance, truly.

Dylan thought that people seldom let go of their resentments. His father had never become one of the true fur barons.

At last Claude broached the subject. "What's this about changing your name?"

"When Daddy Ni and I had our . . . tiff, I dropped my last name in favor of the middle one. Right then I wanted to do what I wanted to do, and I didn't want him to be able to find me. Also, I was trying to emphasize my Welshness over my Scottishness. Dru, he was my mentor then, and he's Welsh." Dylan thought a moment. "I guess it was a brash thing to do."

"A hurtful thing to do," said Amalie with some color in her voice.

"Your father took some trouble to trace your movements," explained Claude. "When he found you'd gone to the *pays d'en haut*, it upset him very much. He raised you to do the opposite. He was even more upset that you'd changed your name. Rejected the family, it seemed, don't you know? Montreal Scots are a proud lot."

"Dylan," Amalie pitched in, "right now we're not sure what Dada would want. You're my brother, and you'll always be welcome in my home. I very much want the two of you to be reconciled. That's just my desire, though. The fact is . . ."

"The fact is," Claude continued her sentence, "Mr. Campbell has forbidden us even to speak your name in front of him. So I'm not sure how high a position he'd want me to give you. He is the senior partner."

Chapter
Twenty-Five

"Father, I've been turned out of my own home," said Dylan. "And the business." This time he used the word: "Disinherited."

Father Quesnel smiled across his desk in his kindly way. Dylan was surprised at how much the blackrobe had aged in just two years. His godfather looked frail now, the skin of his face translucent around his eyes, as though he were already becoming incorporeal on his way to heaven.

"Your father and sister didn't turn you out, Dylan," said his godfather benevolently. "You left."

"Daddy Ni clobbered me with a table," said Dylan. "I hit him back and shed his blood. That's the last that passed between us," Dylan said coldly.

"Dylan," murmured the priest chidingly.

"That's the last," repeated Dylan.

Father Quesnel spoke in a simple, declarative tone. "Your father used his resources to find out where you went. He knew within days, even though your Mr. Bleddyn is clever and covered your tracks well. Peche wanted to send men after you, but he came to his senses. You know he never wanted you near the fur trade. But he let you go.

"When Duncan Campbell Stewart came back from Fort William and said you'd declined to send a message, your father was deeply hurt. He wants to embrace you. He has a father's fear that he's alienated you forever. He also fears for your soul. He knows what *le pays d'en haut* does to men."

This was the pious story Dylan had grown up hearing from the Church. He was grown up now and knew it was ideal, not real. He didn't think his father was doing any bloody pining to get his only son back.

"Your father didn't run you off, Dylan. You left."

"Left, maybe," said Dylan irritably. "I didn't die."

"For all your family knew, you did," said his godfather. He let it sit a minute. "Two years and more."

Yes, all right, damn it, thought Dylan, I was blind to the pain I caused, and I do see it now. Do I have to be punished?

"Peche will be eager to take you into his business," Dylan's godfather went on. "When he knows you're back."

"A year from now," protested Dylan.

"Probably," said the priest. "And young Claude and Amalie will come through. Your father and I had dinner and a good talk the evening before he left. At Mansion House—Amalie and young Claude had the residence. He was in great spirits, best I've seen in . . . twenty years. He believes he has intelligence about a wonderful source of furs. He was looking forward to making a fortune, a real fortune this time, you know how he talks. He's always wanted to be grand as a McTavish."

Father Quesnel looked at Dylan with great gentleness and kindness. Dylan was touched.

"Will you bring your daughter to see me, Dylan?"

"Sure, Father, I wouldn't fail that. We're just taking today off carrying her around town." He hesitated.

"May we baptize her today?"

"Sure," said Dylan, sounding almost as certain as he wanted to sound.

"Half an hour before the angelus, then. I'll arrange it."

"Fine." Dylan changed the subject. "The looks we get on the street are something. Yesterday one woman pretended we didn't exist, even in our funny clothes, as they say, and with a way of walking they think is sneaky. I never realized I walk differently in moccasins until someone told me that. Well, this woman, dressed up like a swell, and with a servant to carry her packages, comes right up to us in the street to coo over Lara in her cradle board." Like a good storyteller, Dylan let it rest for a beat. " 'I'm utterly charmed,' the lady says to Anastasie. 'Your child is so darling.'

" 'His child,' says Anastasie, nodding at me, 'and don't she look just like him?'

"The lady turns her face into mine and gets one look at my white skin and near faints. Then she sets off like an army in hasty retreat. The servant had to scurry right along to keep up with her, escaping from us barbarians."

"God made us, Dylan. He didn't make us perfect or even good. Original sin, you know."

Dylan looked out of his hurt at the priest. "What would they say, Father, if the white-skinned one was the mother, and the father dark-skinned?"

Father Quesnel squirmed. "They wouldn't understand, Dylan. I'm not sure I would."

The words rang through Dylan's mind, and echoed: You too.

"You know, Dylan, considered alone, marriage between the races is understandable. We're all God's children, and the tie of love is one of God's mysteries. Thought of collectively, though, marriage between red and white represents a backward step. We're supposed to raise the Indians to our level, not join them on theirs."

Yes, thought Dylan, I know that's true. He felt deeply ashamed, and hated the feeling. A voice inside, the same voice that rang and echoed, was saying, Me too.

"Have you confessed, Dylan?"

"Not yet, Father."

"Do you want me to hear your confession now?"

"Later, Father."

"Promise me you'll confess this afternoon, Dylan. It's at one and at five."

This habit of going by timepieces again. Confession at five, baptism at five-thirty. Even though he always carried his pocket watch, it was hard for Dylan to get used to.

"Your spiritual welfare concerns me, Dylan. I know

that life in the *pays d'en haut* is not conducive to spiritual growth."

"Aye, Father." Bloody well right.

"I'm sure you discovered why your father didn't want you in the wilds."

"Aye, Father, I've much to confess." He felt ashamed. He touched the slash of scar on his right cheek. Every moment on the streets of Montreal and in the public places, he felt like his pair of scars was a confession, all too open, all too shameful. Thank heaven Father Quesnel would be too polite to ask about the scars, and that he knew without asking what Dylan had to confess.

Father Quesnel considered. "Dylan, do you know why your father was so adamant that you shouldn't follow him into the fur trade?"

"I guess I do," said Dylan uncomfortably. "There's not a temptation I didn't feel."

"It's more than that." Dylan could see his godfather's mind weighing matters. "Peche wanted to tell you, meant to tell you, and I think you need to know now. Dylan, he had a country wife."

"He *what*?" Dylan had the sensation of falling, a lurching, nauseating fall.

The phrase was a euphemism for a squaw taken as a more or less permanent woman, a man's wife in the wilds and mother to his wilderness children. Some of the men were loyal to their country wives and country families, cherishing them for all their lives. Others changed them like they changed handkerchiefs, or had a country wife in each of several tribes. Some also had city wives, two families entirely, one for the winter in Montreal, one for the summer among the Indians. Two groups of children, white and red, legal and natural, with the Church's sanction and without, one supposedly born of love and the other of appetite.

It was a scandal that all Montrealers knew of and no one talked about.

"Those months," said Dylan miserably, "once an entire year away from us."

"Yes," said Father Quesnel. "He went to the wilderness partly because he had the comforts of the flesh there, and none at home. I counseled him about it, I advised him to remarry, I urged him to stay in the city, away from the occasion of his sin." Father Quesnel waited, watching Dylan's face. "But he wouldn't, Dylan. You must understand his loneliness. It's hard for a man suited to marriage to live in chastity."

"Where? What tribe? Do I have half brothers and sisters?" He was not sitting in a chair in Father Quesnel's office. He was falling through the unreality of his life.

"I don't know many details, and they don't matter. There were children at one time. Whether any are still living, I don't know."

The priest read Dylan's mind. "He's not gone back there, Dylan. It's new country this time." The priest studied. "You should know," he said finally, "Peche said he loved her. When he got sick and couldn't go to this country wife, that was his terrible pain. He loved her."

Yes, thought Dylan, he was always thinking of them and not of us. Dylan was tumbling through space.

"Then, in the autumn after he hadn't gone, the first summer he'd missed in the wilderness in twenty years, I'd say, the Rat brought word that she died.

"It was awful. His sickness of spirit was worse than his sickness of body. I feared for his life."

Rage slowed Dylan's fall. *Bloody* hypocrite, he thought. *Sodding* bastard. But the fury was too deep, too mad for curses. It was wildfire raging up the dry gullies of his soul, and leaving desolation.

"My son, what are your thoughts?"

Dylan spoke slowly, dragging the words out, stressing each one. "I will never abandon my daughter.

"I will give her a father.

"I will never be like my father."

His godfather smiled gently. "I hope your thoughts, later, will be understanding, compassion, empathy. Your father loves you and Amalie, Dylan."

Dylan did not say it: Not as much as he loves *la chatte*. Not as much as he loves his other children. Not enough.

"Meanwhile, he is he and you are you. Do you feel certain of what you want to do for your child?"

Dylan admitted it. "No."

"What do you see in the future?"

"Father, I'm stuck. I need a job that pays enough to provide a house and a woman to watch Lara. I don't see that job in Daddy Ni's business." Dylan swallowed hard. "Even if he wanted to give it to me. Claude and Amalie are afraid he wouldn't want me to have any job."

"I'll have a word with them." Father Quesnel hesitated. "Dylan, tell me why you came back to Montreal."

In his anger and bitterness, it was hard to think straight. "I want Lara to grow up civilized. I want her to have every opportunity," he said finally. "To be an Indian, if she wants, or to go to Greenwich and study astronomy, to sing opera in Venice, or to sell flowers in a shop. Whatever she wants."

"You plan to send her to school here?"

"Yes, to church schools." Like he and Amalie themselves. "Then Mrs. Harcourt." A more fashionable school, where young ladies were tutored in art, music, dancing, and other accomplishments.

"Dylan, many Montreal fur traders have mixed-blood children. Do you recall any of them at Mrs. Harcourt's?"

Dylan thought, puzzled. "As a matter of fact, no."

"I think she discourages it. Perhaps more than discourages." The priest looked sympathetically at Dylan. "The wealthier traders, in fact have sent their mixed-blood children to England for their education, isn't that so?"

"I don't expect to be able to afford that."

"Ironic, isn't it, that England welcomes them and Montreal excludes them? In England, they're exotica. Here they're unacceptable." He shrugged. "Familiarity breeds contempt."

Dylan said pensively, "I hadn't thought of this."

"Remember, though, they're always welcome at the parish schools. And welcome in the house of God. We cherish their souls."

Dylan looked at the priest, half willing to acknowledge his unpleasant thought: You mean covet their souls.

"Those who are unequal in this world will be equal in God's love in the next," said Father Quesnel.

Dylan felt like he'd spent too much of his life pining for the next world.

His godfather stood and came around the desk. "I have an appointment," he said. He held his arms open and Dylan embraced him. "Five-thirty for the baptism," said the priest. "I look forward to seeing your daughter. My blessing will be heartfelt."

Dylan was preoccupied. He simmered and stewed. He paid almost no attention to his half sister, who was visibly nervous about some subject she wanted to broach.

At last Amalie leapt in. They were alone at the table, because Anastasie and Dru preferred to eat with Lara in the nursery. "Dylan, we want you to stay with us while you're in Montreal. You understand we're going to be crowded starting, well, late this afternoon when the McLeods arrive."

Claude spoke up. "They're crotchety and persnickety and won't stay in hotels. Very important prospects too. Old McLeod is apparently amused by the idea that an American should own half of Montreal. Word is, he intends to make substantial investments."

"Well, our point is," Amalie lurched on, "would you mind moving back to your old room?" The one that was now the nursery. Where Lara and Dru and Anastasie were all sleeping. Which meant . . . Amalie would never suggest . . .

"We can move a small bed in there. The house will be crowded, with the McLeods, but we want you."

"Of course," added Claude, "where you belong."

Dylan waited for the other shoe to drop. Amalie would never suggest that he sleep in the same room with Anastasie. Improper. It was almost cruel, the way he waited for her to blunder on.

"Lara needs Mrs. Bleddyn, of course, and the four of you . . . You see the problem."

The four of us can scarcely share sleeping quarters. It was bitterly funny. Dylan wondered where Amalie thought they usually slept. Apparently she didn't picture him and

Dru and Anastasie and Saga and Lady Sarah in the same lodge for two years. Certainly she didn't imagine the sounds he had often heard in the middle of the night, the groan and thump of human lovemaking.

Oh, Amalie, your civilization is a master without decency, much less love.

"So I've made arrangements at The Paddle and Pipe this morning," said Claude with false cheer. The Paddle and Pipe was an inn where *voyageurs* often drank and sometimes slept in upstairs rooms. "I wanted one of the best hotels, but . . . You understand."

Dylan did understand. His child was an *Indian*.

"The proprietor is a good fellow, and is making special efforts for the Bleddyns and Lara." Claude chuckled. "Everything is paid for, and he's promised to take very good care of them."

Care as good as could be taken in dirty, lousy rooms among rough, drunken men.

Dylan mustered all his self-control. "It's fine, I do understand. I don't think The Pipe and Paddle is a good idea, though. Dru and Anastasie were wanting to go back to the lodge anyway. They prefer it." Funny how a hide tipi could be cleaner than a fine home or hotel, morally cleaner. "I prefer it myself. It's difficult for me to adjust to . . . luxury so quickly."

He rose from the table, his feet wanting out of there. "What on my mind, actually," he said, "is to invite you to Lara's baptism." He smiled his best. "Half an hour before the evening angelus today."

Claude and Amalie got up too. Amalie looked so relieved it was comical. Claude hadn't quite recovered from his embarrassment. But they weren't going to urge him to change his mind and stay.

She said, "Thank you, we wouldn't miss it for anything."

Dylan wondered nastily, during the christening, what will you do with the very wealthy and important American McLeods?

Amalie pressed his hand fervently.

The cathedral once more. For Dylan it was always emotional. This was the home of his life of the spirit for twenty-two years.

From the rear of the nave he walked down the center aisle toward the crossing. There, where the transept intersected the nave, was the place of magic. There, coming to receive the host, laymen crossed from the world to the altar, from the mundane to the heavenly. Appropriately, the nave was half dark, the crossing flooded with brilliant light from the stained-glass windows, and the altar and the apse half visible beyond.

He stood at the edge of the crossing. He came here a pilgrim, as always. His goal was to confess his sins, and by confessing, set his heart right with God. But he was not the same pilgrim as before his venture into the wilderness. Now he was a man who knew something of life, and death. Of the greatest joy and the deepest sorrow. Of the earth, the sky, and of men.

He was not ready yet to go to the confessional box and speak the words of confession and hear the words of absolution, *"Ego te absolvo, in nomine patri, et filii, et spiritus sancti."* For once he felt the need to do what the priests and nuns had always advised him to do, prepare for his confession by reviewing his life since his last one. He knelt in front of the foremost pew, at the edge of the crossing.

He did not regret running away from home, but instead was proud of the spirit of sallying forth on a great adventure.

He regretted the spite that led him to strike back at his father, and the carelessness—literally *care*lessness— which permitted him to cause his father and sister worry.

He regretted the hardness of his heart, which had kept him from writing home for two years.

He regretted his liaison with Fore—not the fornication itself, which was merely a human act, so much as the fury, the hatred for Fore and self and for sex itself, in short, the spirit of the act. It was degrading.

He regretted his casual forkings, the ones he had bought from drunken Indian women. These acts now seemed to him pitiful for both partners.

He regretted drawing Saga's blood, and regretted more the ugly feelings that led him to throw that knife.

He did not regret making love with Caro, not a moment of it. It still seemed to him wondrous, if not quite complete, not quite transforming. In fact—he smiled in realization—it seemed to him *almost* redeeming. Yes, something had been wrong in it, thus the ugliness. But it was not the love he felt, he would not repent of that, nor the physical expression he gave it.

What he regretted most was his acts toward Caro and Captain Chick. Spying on them—not the deed itself, though it was low, but the abhorrence and self-loathing he felt during it. (They committed the acts—why loathe himself instead of them?) The panic and self-abasement of the next six weeks. The awful pretense of those weeks—the pretense that ugliness would somehow become beautiful, that these scenes out of Hieronymus Bosch could be redeemed. He did not understand, even now, how he got lost in these afflictions.

He regretted the feelings of misery and helplessness that made him raise his hands with knives against Captain Chick. He thanked God for the impulse of self-love that made him miss. He smiled at the thought that it was this impulse Captain Chick despised him for.

He regretted the foolishness, the lack of foresight, that led to the death of Lemieux, of the guard Lemieux killed, and of Mad Jack.

He regretted not that he fooled the Lords and Ladies, or knocked down their palisade, but his resort to deception and force.

He regretted his uncertainty, his quavering, his pitiful insecurity when Caro returned, and his self-deception.

He regretted his wallowing in self-pity after her death.

He thanked God for Lara, and for his brief time with Harold.

And for the grand earth, the forests, the rivers, the plains, the mountains, the world of creation he had discovered, ever regenerating itself, ever growing, ever living. While human beings walked in uncertainty and trepidation,

the earth showed the way, joyfully re-creating itself, showing the abundance, the creative vigor of life.

He regretted the moments—the eternities—he had
fallen into desolation of spirit. On an earth such as this,
desolation should be impossible.

He stood up. He looked around the cathedral. Yes, he
would speak these thoughts to the anonymous priest in the
confessional box—why not? And receive the priest's
blessing—why not? Speak thoughts of confession, which
were welcome here. Not speak thoughts of happiness, satisfaction, glorious discovery, which somehow were not.
These he would keep for himself, and for his journal.

The small group hovered around the baptismal font,
Dylan holding Lara, the priest setting out on his function.
Dru and Anastasie, Claude and Amalie, Father Quesnel
watching, joining in the celebration.

*"Ego te baptismo, in nomine patri, et filii, et spiritus
sancti."*

The priest sprinkled a drop or two of holy water onto
her forehead. Dylan remembered that holy water is God's
grace, given to Lara as a boon, a miracle.

"I christen thee Lara Caroline," said the priest.

Dylan recalled that *christen* meant to make Christian.
He smiled to himself. Lots of these Christians would never
accept his daughter as Christian.

Dylan looked happily across at Amalie. He was glad
surnames were not used at christenings, and she did not
have to hear Davies instead of Campbell.

Father Quesnel spoke briefly with the Druid and
Anastasie, and they answered—the baptismal promises,
Dylan knew. Amalie gave Lara a white baptismal gown.
The priest put a pinch of salt on the child's tongue for
health, first anointed her forehead with an oil he had
blessed, then a second oil of olive and balsam, which had
a lovely, sweet fragrance.

Dylan liked the ceremony. He liked the moment of
honoring formally. He liked the acknowledgment of something wondrous. He liked the accoutrements and gestures
that went with it—the black robes, white collars, cruci-

fixes, rosaries, the baptismal font holding the life energy of water, the white gown, and especially the sweet-smelling oils. He felt blessed by the ritual, and thanked the priest sincerely at its end. Father Quesnel embraced him by the shoulders and walked with him to the table where Dylan lighted a baptismal candle.

The family made its way through the shadows of the side aisle of the nave and through the great front doors to the outside world. As they came onto the church steps, the bells began to ring the angelus.

The great humped beasts of bells. Dylan and Dru looked at each other, remembering, smiling.

Suddenly, in the tolling of the bells, Dylan heard sounds, dozens of sounds. It was odd, bizarre, incredible. He was hearing without hearing, with the dreaming ear. It was bedlam and sense, a cacophony and a harmony at once, nonsense, yet he knew what it was about. Some of the sounds were voices, rough voices of men, in . . . snatches of bawdy *voyageur* songs. Some were shouts of men and women gambling the hand game, and the drum beneath. Some were the cries of loons on lonely, moon-shadowed lakes. Some were the thump of hoofbeats and the roars of men fighting, some the pulsing of rivers, some the squawking of crows, some the tenor ululating of Indian songs, the drum beating beneath. Some the moans of men and women in the act of love. Some of this bedlam fabric of sound was ancient, some recent, some his own future, some the future of his grandchildren. Beneath it all throbbed the drum.

Standing there on the cathedral steps in the opulent midsummer sunlight, he understood without understanding, and knew without knowing. He felt the blood and breath of his life.

He said softly and happily to Dru, "Let's go to the High Missouri."

Dru said, "It's time."

Chapter
Twenty-Six

"We'll figure it out when we get to Red River," said Dru over and over. "When we get to Red River."

That was his answer. The question was: When are we going to the High Missouri? To Dylan it was only a fairy-tale place, unreal, an adolescent dream. And yet this land of his imagination, remote, untouched, stirred him.

Not that he felt dissatisfied. He had company he liked, he had this seemingly endless string of days traveling through fine lake and river country, he had good physical exertion and plenty to eat, and he had a new volume of Byron bought in Montreal for the hour before sleep—he was reading "Lara."

During the day he thought constantly of his Lara. Amalie had insisted on keeping the girl until at least next summer, when she thought Dylan would come out of the wilderness with his furs. She seemed genuinely glad to have the child, talking about buying her one of the new open-sided cribs, and a standing stool to help her learn to walk. Dylan told himself it was the right thing. But he missed his daughter painfully, except when he read at night or slept. Two years, he supposed, until he would see her—he was a young man with places to go, challenges to face. But it was hard, and he wondered what their plans were, if Dru had plans. What about the High Missouri?

Now the outfit was beyond Lake Superior and Fort William, and Rainy Lake Fort and even Lake of the Woods, and yesterday they came to the Red River settlement. Or rather to their camp near the Métis settlements of Red River.

It turned out there was not one Red River settlement, but at least two, separate colonies of Métis and Scottish crofters, and neither one would have anything to do with the other. The Scots were centered around Fort Douglas, an HBC post down at the mouth of the Assiniboine River. The Métis were on the east side of Red River, around St. Boniface, a mission run by one Father Provencher. They rode down to see St. Boniface Mission and Fort Douglas and the surrounding farms. Dylan looked at the mission building, run by one lone priest in this vast wilderness, and thought, That could be me. When Dru suggested they stop in to pay their respects, he declined.

Dylan, Dru, and Saga had put up camp yesterday, and spent today riding borrowed mounts to Fort Douglas and back. But they didn't go in. The Métis, longtime Nor'Westers, refused to set foot in any establishment run by the Lords and Ladies. So did Dru and Saga. And Dylan.

Whatever his plans were, Dylan thought maybe the Druid intended to give these Métis some trade. If they could get rid of their trade goods, paying their obeisance to the god of commerce, maybe they could go a-wayfaring.

Dylan looked around camp contentedly. The crew was eating *sagamité* down by the canoes. Anastasie and Lady Sarah were making a stew of deer meat, wild onions, and wild rice in front of the bark wigwam that was their new home. It was good.

It was already the twelfth day of September, by Dylan's journal. Dru teased him about keeping the journal, saying it was his one ineradicable white-man habit, to try to control time by knowing the name of this day out of a billion seamless and indistinguishable turns of light and dark the earth made revolving around the sun, and perhaps trying to control the future by knowing the past.

Dylan answered that at least it allowed him to know when winter was coming.

Dru said it was easier to tell, and far more accurate, by the changes you saw around you every day—the grasses drying up, the mosquitoes disappearing, the leaf-bearing trees starting to change color, ice at the edges of the lakes and rivers at dawn, then ducks and geese migrating south in their big vees, honking out the news that the next snow would stay the winter. Also easy to tell time by looking at the sun, he said—Dylan should get rid of that pocket watch.

In any case it was well into September already, and they would have to choose a winter camp within a few weeks. Somewhere Dru was being secretive about. Here? You floated canoes, you didn't skid them on ice. They could trade everything they'd brought right here. Even if it was a thousand miles from where he wanted to be.

The *canots du nord*. Dylan looked down toward the bank of the creek at the canoes and men with satisfaction. It had all come together smoothly, and advantageously. Not one, but two canoes of the north, with five engagés, men hired to help. He chuckled, remembering. He supposed he had worked a sort of blackmail.

Once Dylan decided to go to the interior to trade, brother-in-law Claude had helped him all too willingly. They would go on shares, Claude said, Campbell Trading Company putting up the goods to trade to the Indians and a year's wages for the hired men. The Welsh Indian Company, which was the name Dylan and Dru and Saga gave themselves, would run the outfit in the field, make the decisions, and do the actual trading. The two companies would share the risks and the rewards equally. Dru said they were called the Welsh Indian Company not because two of them were Welsh and one Indian, but because one day they would find the lost tribe.

So they were partners with Saga now. Dylan guessed it no longer made him edgy. Every day Saga squinted through the sunlight reflected off the waters they paddled, regarding him from beneath that twisted eyebrow where the handle of the knife hit him, maybe thinking one day they would brawl with blood in their eyes. You never knew how long a man's memory was.

Yes, you never knew. Time was, he would have added the words: especially a half-breed's memory. Once he had indulged in such thoughts—half-breeds are sullen, half-

breeds are treacherous, half-breeds combine the worst features of both races. Now that he had Lara, he didn't permit
himself that kind of talk.

Dylan had smiled to Dru about Claude's eagerness to
help capitalize the Welsh Indian Company, claiming he
knew Ian Campbell would approve. Blankets, strouding,
trade axes, tobacco, whiskey, knives, kettles, beads, bells,
powder, lead—they asked for the usual. Claude marked it
down, keeping the quantities conservative, and ordered it
packed into *pièces* and hauled to the river.

Truth was, Dru said, the risk was negligible, for the
Welsh Indian Company was as small as Indian trading outfits got. Besides, it was a deal where Claude couldn't lose.
For less than a hundred Halifax pounds the bugger got his
embarrassing brother-in-law out of Montreal. He also
made things look good for Ian Campbell. If the investment
paid off, Claude and Mr. Campbell profited. If it didn't,
Claude would be one up on Dylan in Mr. Campbell's eyes.

Dru flicked an amused eyebrow upward. "Altogether
a charm." When Dru did that, it was the brow over his
bright eye that rose, exaggerating its gleam, an effect that
always nonplussed Dylan.

Yes, he thought, Claude got us out of Montreal,
where we were an embarrassment.

Of course, Claude thought they were heading out for
somewhere nearby, a close-to-the-vest trip for the first
venture, probably in his father's old country up toward
James Bay, with the thought of coming back in the spring
with a modest profit. Perhaps even the possibility of
meeting Ian Campbell and joining forces.

They did not disabuse him. For thirty years' work for
the Nor'Westers, Dru had a credit of almost sixty pounds.
They took the credit in merchandise, for a two-year trip
into remote country, not one year. They had no intention
of playing it cautious. If they did as well as report said
they could, they would make enough in the two years to
outfit themselves and go forward without partners. Dylan
did not want to walk in his father's steps, or somehow join
forces. Somewhere in that two-year circle would be the
High Missouri.

Ah, yes, his yearning for that place of his imagination was probably childish.

Before dinner Dru called a war council around the fire. Saga sat on the ground cross-legged, in his easy way. Dru held a book and rubbed it with his hands. Dylan thought how marked the three of them were on the face, Dru with a strange eye, Saga a scarred brow, himself the bright slashes of violence on his cheeks. Anastasie moved in and out, cooking, with an air that said it didn't matter what the men did, the women made life work.

Dru opened the book to a map. He pointed to Red River. Well off the route they'd taken before, to and from the North Saskatchewan River, which was far to the north.

"You need to get filled in," began Dru, looking at Dylan. "The Métis." Meaning these Cree who were partly French. "Ten years ago, Lord Selkirk's damn crofters came and started bloody farming. What you have to understand, what you've seen today, the Métis are not an Indian race." Yes, he'd seen they were unusual. They lived in permanent villages here, did not migrate, spoke their own variety of French. "Lots of them have some education. They're Catholics, yes, of their own sort. They even have a national flag, blue with a figure eight on its side." Dru snorted.

"Now ten years' bloody trouble. The sodding Lords and Ladies gave all the Métis country to Selkirk, a realm as big as England, twelve degrees of longitude and nigh as high.

"There is sure the Métis didn't accept the crofters or any other Scots colonizing their land. Red River valley may be fertile, but it's also the best buffalo country in the world. The Métis made a living getting pemmican for the Nor'Westers, late and lamented.

"Then the troubles. HBC burned down the Nor'Westers' Fort Gibraltar—this was six years ago. Some Métis cornered a big bunch of the bastards after that and killed them." He looked at Saga. "A bad business, that. Saga was there." Dru looked gravely at his friend, but Saga's face was expressionless. "Since that day, that lot of

Métis have had bad luck, men dropping dead in peculiar ways. That's part of the reason Saga has stayed away, been with me." He eyed Dylan soberly. "The rest is that some bloody-minded Highlanders might be looking for him. So keep your eyes open and speak up sharp."

Even now Saga kept his habitual look of impassivity.

"You may be sure of this: never will the Métis sit still for some Lords and Ladies in a boardroom in London giving their country to Scottish colonists. Never.

"So you see, here's the main chance. There's only Lords and Ladies at the Red River settlement now, no Nor'Westers under the sun, saving us, who are under a different name. The Métis won't take to trading with the Lords and Ladies. Better to do business with Nor'Westers calling themselves the Welsh Indian Company." Dru eyed Dylan sharply. "We'll build up near St. Boniface, laddo. Mission's half a day's ride east of the Lords and Ladies' fort, right where the Métis center. Saga will run things, and he's related to everyone. If he doesn't give too many presents to all his aunts and uncles, we'll eat the competition alive."

Saga didn't even smile. "What do you say?"

Dylan felt disappointed. "It sounds profitable," he made himself answer.

With a sidelong look and a quirky smile, Dru handed Dylan the book and showed him the cover. "The Red River trading post will be the sober part of our business. The business part. For you and me, laddo, I fancy a little more questing."

Dylan's heart rose into his throat.

It was called *History of the Expedition under the Command of Captains Lewis And Clark,* by Nicholas Biddle. Dylan had heard of the book, the tale of a military expedition mounted by the U.S. government to cross the continent to the Pacific. He hadn't been so enamored of the idea that they struck out across a virgin continent—his father said the Nor'Westers had already been across it years before, and knew most of the places the Americans traveled to. Like everyone, he'd been intrigued by the story of a young Snake woman named Sacajawea, who carried her newborn son across the continent and back. And he'd been taken with how receptive all the Indians were to the whites. At the time, he thought it showed how ready they were for civilization, for Christianity.

That thought embarrassed him now. St. Boniface Mission embarrassed him, though he couldn't have said why. The Métis reach for civilization embarrassed him.

Dru brought his attention back to the book, to the map, identified as the cartography of Captain William Clark, one of the two expedition leaders. It showed the Indian country as Clark knew it, mostly on the American side of the border, from St. Louis north to Lake Superior, west to the Pacific, and south to what Dylan supposed to be New Spain. Dylan threw some wood on the fire in front of the wigwam so they could see better.

The northern edges of this country the Nor'Westers had explored and knew it well enough. They had a post at the mouth of the Columbia River, taken from the Americans, and tribes from as far south as the Missouri River came into NWC posts to trade.

There was a fine stretch of buffalo and beaver country between the South Saskatchewan River and the Yellowstone, east of the mountains, and the High Missouri was its main artery. The Nor'Westers had avoided going into it. They had their own fur lands farther north, because of the long winters the best on the continent. Too, since the treaty of 1818, it was American territory, and they could be treated as smugglers. And the damned Piegans and Bloods and Blackfeet, kings of the whole region, refused to hunt beaver themselves, refused to let anyone else do it, and refused to let the fur men build a post in their country. Instead they brought their trade all the way to Rocky Mountain House or even to Augustus House, now late and lamented, on the Old North Trail.

Now that the Nor'Westers had become Lords and Ladies, it was even less likely that Canadian fur men would be going into these American lands. The American Manuel Lisa had made some attempts on the High Missouri, but he recently died. All of which opened the door to the Welsh Indian Company.

Dylan studied William Clark's meandering rivers and mountain barriers with a mapmaker's eye. It was a strange trick, always, to look at flat paper with latitudes and longitudes drawn on it, rivers and mountains sketched in, and translate that into a reality, something your foot would feel, your eyes would see, your nose would know. He had some novice skill at it.

Dru pointed to the labels Clark had written in, other than geographic labels. Indications of where tribes of Indians lived. "Ricaras." "Teton, band of Sioux 1500 souls." "A band of the Assiniboins 1000." Elsewhere bands of Assiniboines listed at twelve hundred and two thousand people.

Dru pointed carefully to the map, on the Missouri River, where Clark had labeled it "Mandans." Then he traced the river upstream to the west, past the mouth of the river marked "Yellowstone," which Dylan knew the Nor'West maps called the Roche Jaune, past the mouths of the "Muscle Shell" and the "Marias" to Clark's big label "FALLS," where the river came from the south, an area Clark had cluttered with big, clumpy lines that looked like caterpillars, his representation of mountains. This was what the *hivernants* called the High Missouri, the home of the tribes of the Blackfoot confederation, especially the Piegans, the biggest piece of country of the Rocky Mountains that white men didn't take beaver from. "BLACK FOOT INDIANS," said Clark's label.

Though the Piegans wouldn't permit any forts in their country, Dru said you could build one on the east edge of it, among the friendly Assiniboines, get the Piegan trade, and have easy access to Red River.

"This," said Dru, "may be El Dorado."

His plan was more subtle and more ambitious. He said the owners and *voyageurs* of the Welsh Indian Company should not depend on the Indians to get the beaver. The Indian way was slow, to break into the lodge during the winter and kill what you could find. Few Indians were dependable—they did not work steadily—and the Piegans would not do it at all. Traders looking to make their fortunes needed something more reliable. It was Dru's idea that they would run trap lines themselves, get their own beaver. Off and on fur men had done this, but only as a little something on the side, not a true commercial effort. The Welsh Indian Company, a fledgling outfit, would not just trade, it would trap.

Suddenly Dru stood up. "Welcome," he cried into the half darkness. An old man with a quizzical expression stepped from the shadows into camp. "It's just time to eat. Sit."

Dru gestured to his partners in introduction. "Dylan, Saga." Saga materialized from the shadows. "This is our sage of El Dorado, Toussaint Chabono." They offered their hands, and Chabono took them. "Chabono—Dylan Davies, a Welshman; and Saga, a Métis. Gentlemen, you've heard of Sacajawea, the Snake woman who interpreted for Lewis and Clark. This is the expedition's other interpreter, her husband."

Dylan was fascinated, but Chabono was vague. Yes, he knew the Mandans, he'd lived among them. Among the Minnetarees longer. *Bien sûr,* he knew the Piegans, and spoke somewhat their language. Hard people to deal with. Yes, you might do well trading among them, if you could keep your scalp. He said to Anastasie and Lady Sarah, deflecting the conversation, "Very good this dinner."

Yes, Chabono tell how to get to High Missouri. No, he not go there again, he have job Fort Minnetaree, interpret there for Père Noël. Dru gave Dylan a sideways glance. Who and what were Père Noël and Fort Minnetaree? Since Lisa died, Chabono went on, no Americans on Upper Missouri until this year, no job for Chabono. No, he concluded, Piegans too far, too much trouble.

Dylan wondered if the old man was drunk. After a while he decided Chabono was not exactly drunk. Maybe he drank a little all day, every day, so that a certain vagueness, uncertainty, and tremulousness were his constant companions. But he wasn't exactly drunk.

No, said Chabono, he would not travel with them to Mandan villages. Is easy—up the Assiniboine River and the Mouse River, then a short portage over to the Missouri, said Chabono, just a mile, then down to the Mandans. No, Chabono had business with the clerk of Fort Douglas, something to trade, *très* big business. He had to wait until the clerk came back from the big annual buffalo hunt—he had to. He showed a lascivious smile. "You go Piegans," he said, "get rich, ver' rich."

He gave Anastasie his dish of stew, barely touched. Dru handed him a cup of rum, which he slurped eagerly. Dylan wondered how old he was. From appearance, seventy and more, but part of that might be dissipation.

"Here's to El Dorado," said Dru, hoisting a cup.

Chabono raised his own cup in the toast and drank. He looked lewdly at Dylan. "Many plews among Piegans," he said unsteadily, "but Chabono got something especial." He leered. "Two women, yes, maybe too spirit' for slave. Not obey!" He snapped his fingers commandingly.

"Chabono maybe trade clerk woman. Today slave, tomorrow white-man wife." He grinned cunningly. "Got two sisters. Piegan, sure. You wan' buy woman?"

D ylan couldn't keep his mind on El Dorado. No, he
didn't want to buy a wife, even though he'd been
celibate for over a year. But he couldn't help
thinking about the women Chabono was offering. Slave
women? Stolen women? It aroused his disapproval. Against his will, it also aroused his lust.

Yes, said Dru. Stolen. Maybe by Chabono, more
likely by someone who traded them to him. The question,
Dru said, was what information about other traders hid
here? For instance, what traders had been among the Piegans? That was why they'd accepted the old man's invitation to dinner tonight, he said, to find out. Meanwhile
Dylan was to help Dru patch the canoes. That would help
him keep his mind off *la chatte* and on El Dorado.

Dru inspected the canoes and sewed tears with an awl
and slender, crooked spruce roots. Dylan smeared spruce
gum on as caulking.

Yes, El Dorado, he could manage to think about that.
It was good to live in Indian country, but damned if he
would live there poor.

He ventured, "Maybe the Piegans will drive us out."
He wondered, Why do I feel a need to say what can go
wrong?

Dru shrugged. He was like the *voyageurs* in many
ways, willing to wait and see what life brought, and to be
amused by whatever it was.

But Dru argued it this time. "We know their ways.

We know the Piegans. We speak the language. And
we're Britons, subjects of His Majesty George the
Fourth, or whichever bloody George it is, not sodding
Yanks." Dru looked at Dylan with a sideways smile.
"You know why they trade with us and kick the Amer-
icans in the arse?"

Dylan shook his head.

Dru looked Dylan in the eye. "We've told them
straight along that we want just to trade, and that the
Americans want to come and take their land." He laughed.
"The first commandment of commerce. Thou shalt tell lies
about thy rivals."

Dylan shook his head, half dizzy. He wondered what,
if anything, depended on old Chabono.

As a host, Chabono was a show-off. He gave commands to his main wife, called the sits-beside-him wife,
Turtle, with a imperious glance. This fat, middle-aged
woman ordered the two slave girls about like a squawking
jay. Dylan thought she was making a point of mastery to
the visitors.

Chabono, though, was making a point of their appeal. They were sisters, he said, from the Piegans, ver'
unusual, not many Piegan slaves. And sisters make the
best wives, *bien sûr*. Peace in the home.

"See how fine their shapes are," he said. He reached
out and held the arm of the one called Cree Medicine. She
stopped and allowed herself to be turned, even pirouetted
a little on her own. Dylan thought Chabono treated her
with affection. She was about twenty or twenty-one, appropriately modest, eyes cast down, and very comely, with
a soft, round body. Dylan flushed with the thought of the
fantasies she would inspire in him.

The other one, Red Sky at Morning, kept her distance
from Chabono without making it obvious. She was fifteen
or sixteen, Dylan guessed, and as much teenage angular as
Cree Medicine was womanly soft. Red Sky seemed to be
keeping some expression carefully off her face—no doubt
she feared a beating. Dylan thought the expression was

sullenness. Well, maybe it was fiery anger. He'd have to see it flare to know.

Chabono was showing them off to the three male guests, for sure. At first his salesmanship seemed mostly directed at Dru. After a while, rebuffed by Dru's disinterest, he turned it to Dylan. Dylan didn't want to buy a pair of sisters as wives. True, he had a yen to rent them. But he wouldn't permit himself that. He wouldn't rent any woman unless he lost his resolve, and not any slave woman under any circumstances.

He'd had a talk with Dru this afternoon about slave women, and no longer had any doubt what their relationship with Chabono was in the buffalo robes. He hated the idea of slavery, and he hated being around Chabono and his damned slaves. Especially because it made his cod ache.

Dru made a case that Indian slavery was not like black slavery. An Indian took a slave, Dru said, because he wanted to replace a loved one he'd lost. A wife, or just as likely a treasured small son or daughter. You didn't think of it as persecution, ultimately, but as a gift. After all, the slave once had to live among whatever tribe she was born to, and now got to live with your tribe, the Real People. Also the slave would want to submit as a woman to the more powerful man, the one with the courage to steal her from her weakling father or husband.

Of course, you made them earn their way a little. At first, especially, they would have to show obedience to the man and the sits-beside-him wife, a matter of respect. They would have to do some onerous jobs. They would have to show their willingness by being eager to please the mother and father, or the man and the sits-beside-him wife. Which would include pleasing the man in the robes. But he, being wise, would treat the slave wife with gentleness and tenderness. He wanted not unhappy acquiescence, but obedient love. He wanted not a slave, but a loving family member.

Dylan could imagine getting obedient love from Cree Medicine, but not from Red Sky at Morning.

After dinner the women retired to the tipi, the

buffalo-hide lodge of the plains, not the birchbark affair of
the woodlands. Dylan caught glimpses of them sewing or
beading or making small objects. He had the damnedest
impression about Red Sky—she seemed to be napping
flint, or maybe obsidian, the stone was so dark. But a
woman wouldn't do that. Well, maybe she was making a
knife for her husband-master. But a Plains Indian woman
wouldn't do that either.

Well, bloody hell, until today he hadn't known sod all
about Indian slavery.

Dru broached the delicate subject to Chabono. "How
did you come by *Piegan* slaves?" Of all the people of the
plains, the Piegans were probably the most arrogant, the
most chauvinistic, the least likely to tolerate someone taking their women as slaves, the most likely to avenge such
encroachment.

"Such is Père Noël," said Chabono, shaking his head
and smiling. "Père Noël thinks he conquer world. This
summer he make post at Minnetaree. Know Lisa dead,
know *Américains* not on upper river, want to make the
gran start. Trade Minnetaree, Mandan, Assiniboine."

Dylan could see Dru was irked. Someone else, evidently some other Frenchman, maybe some other
Nor'Wester, had the idea of stepping into the country of
the High Missouri since the Americans had fallen back.
Dylan wondered how much trouble it would cause. What
sort of man would give himself such an absurd name as
Saint Nicholas, Father Christmas, or the new American
name, Santa Claus? Well, at least the fellow wasn't going
to the Piegans. Now that he'd stolen their women, he
bloody well couldn't.

"Minnetarees long time go Lemhi Snakes, take
women slaves." He shrugged. His own wife, Sacajawea,
had been stolen by the Minnetarees, Dylan knew. "This
summer Père Noël want make some money, go to them
himself. Maybe want wife for himself." He made an expressive gesture with outstretched arms.

"But One Horn, leader, his medicine turn bad. Party
go back. Père Noël, him jump forward, say his medicine
good, say take women from Piegans." Chabono looked
most amused.

"All but two ignore Père Noël, come back to Minne-taree. Zem two, young, stay, go Piegans." Chabono made a dramatic pause. "Zey steal 'em." He shrugged as if to say, It makes no sense, but . . . "Four!" He shook his head in amazement.

"Two he take to Fort Snelling, trade. Two he give me, take to Red River, trade, cache half plews to him." He pursed his lips and cocked an eyebrow.

Dylan thought he was living in a twilight world, com-plete with demons run by Père Noël.

Many cups later, toward midnight, Chabono waxed enthusiastic. "*Bien sûr,* you shall grow rich. The Piegans won't have to walk and ride all the way to Fort Augustus just to trade." The old man wagged his head, whether from drunkenness or decrepitude, Dylan didn't know. "You smart, you go to Lemhi Snakes, bring some women back," he added.

Never this side of hell, thought Dylan.

More head-wagging. "Chabono, he has Snake woman wife once, bought her from Minnetaree, good wife." He eyed them, not with lust, as Dylan expected, but with what looked like greed in his eyes. "Slave," he said. "Cheap." He said it like they hadn't heard of Sacajawea, the slave and wife. Dylan thought he looked like he wanted to say more but he didn't.

Dru asked Chabono about the Mandans being the Welsh Indians. Dylan thought moodily that he himself wasn't inter-ested in the sodding Welsh Indians, he was interested in bea-ver plews. He hoped the Mandans had boatloads of them, if that's where they were going.

Chabono assured Dru the Mandans were not light-skinned and bearded, which he already knew. "Do they have a greatly advanced civilization?"

The old man shook his head no. Dylan thought he didn't understand the question.

Dru turned to Dylan. "The tribe most often reported to be the Welsh Indians," he said, "is the Mandans. Some say their name is a corruption of 'Madog.' " Dylan re-

membered the name of the legendary Welsh discoverer
and colonist of the Americas.

He turned back to Chabono. "Is it true that they bury
their dead in mounds?"

Chabono nodded somberly. Or perhaps it was just
head-wagging in the other direction.

"That's a Celtic practice, truly," said Dru. He grinned
broadly at Dylan. "We shall raise the ghost of Madog on
these shores."

"First," said Dylan, helping the old man up, "we'd
better get Chabono off to bed." Tomorrow or the next day
the canoes would be in good repair, and it was getting late
in the season.

Chabono refused help and trundled off toward his
lodge. The three partners of the Welsh Indian Company
started walking back to camp.

It was settled. Saga would stay among the Métis.
Dylan and Dru would go to the Mandans this winter and
build a post on the edge of Piegan country next summer.
Every summer thereafter they would bring the furs as far
as Red River. All was well. Maybe El Dorado was on the
horizon.

Dylan was leery of lusting for riches. He remembered
the legend of El Dorado, which meant in Spanish "the
golden man."

According to the tale, the Spanish had heard of a tribe
so rich in gold that the chief went about gilded, covered
with powdered gold. Dylan wondered if there might be
some truth to it—if you oiled a man at a special ceremony
once a year and sprinkled him with gold dust, would he
not in a sense be gilded? But the point was something
else: conquistador after conquistador had spent fortunes,
had broken horses and men, had stained the earth with the
blood of Spaniard and Indian, looking for El Dorado.
Meanwhile ignoring their true discovery, a new land, a
good place to live, to walk the earth, drink the water,
breathe the air, and raise children. The lust for El Dorado
blinded men.

Even trying to provide for your daughter could be
dangerous.

Dylan thought of Lara asleep in her new open-sided

crib in Montreal, and nodded to himself, and thought, I hope all is well.

But all was not well with Dylan Davies. His spirit was sour. Something was curdling his milk.

He thought of Chabono's lodge. He twisted his mouth. He felt a beginning of a rebellion in his belly.

Chapter
Twenty-Eight

It was Red Sky at Morning, the younger sister, who was the clever one. She saw that Dylan the idealist would help, she arranged the meeting at the creek while the women were supposed to be gathering wild rice, and she came up with the plan.

Dylan's plan would have been much more elaborate, or much more dramatic, or much more deceptive, or something. He wanted to cut his way into the lodge in the middle of the night, whack Chabono on the head, and make a dash for it. Unnecessary, Red Sky said.

Her plan was simple, with one or two fillips to make it elegant. This afternoon she would promise to make Chabono mukluks from moose hide. Tomorrow or the next day he and one or two of his cronies would go moose hunting. She would send along a quart of whiskey provided by Dylan to make sure they didn't come back before dark. And the two sisters and Dylan would move out just after dawn, when the hunters left. That would give them a full day's start.

Cree Medicine pitched in. The fillips, she said, were that they would not take the usual route, up the Assiniboine River to the west. Instead they would go south up Red River and up the Pembina River past Turtle Mountain, the road of the Turtle Mountain Indians.

"And we will not be a white man and two Piegan women," put in Red Sky. "No, a white man, a Métis man, and a Minnetaree woman." Cree Medicine showed him she had the moccasins to look Minnetaree, and would cover her dress with a blanket.

"You will get me some men's clothing," said Red Sky. "Yes, you will, and I am tall enough to wear it." Corduroy trousers, she wanted, hip-high leggings, a deerskin shirt, one of those blue wool coats with hoods and brass buttons, and even a bright red sash with tasseled ends for her waist.

Red Sky's eyes gleamed at the thought of this colorful disguise. Oh, *sacré,* she swore in her broken French, of course Dylan could come up with the whiskey and the clothes, and even some tobacco as gifts for her people. Was he not a rich trader?

Dylan looked at the two sisters. Yes, all right, he would deliver them out of slavery.

They were contrasting sisters, actually. Though Red Sky was younger, she was more assertive. Almost like a man, or so it seemed to Dylan, she knew her mind and spoke it. The spunky teenager precedes the compliant wife maybe, thought Dylan. He liked her fine as she was.

While Red Sky was the slender and firm-looking girl, Cree Medicine was round of body, with a languid and sensual way of moving. She said little, yet she seemed womanly. Her silence struck Dylan as maturity, not self-effacement. When Dylan looked into her eyes, he suspected depths in her, the blood wisdom of the feminine.

Yes, he would want them every night. His cod was hard and hungry all the time already. But he would stay away from them. And he knew they would help him in his propriety. The last thing Red Sky said as they left the talk by the creek was, with a hard, tight smile, *"Ça va dire, après ce soir Chabono pourrai plus nous tirez plus jamais."* Meaning, after tonight Chabono can't frig us anymore.

Dylan went off quietly to make the necessary preparations. Yes, damn, he was under the spell of Red Sky's crisp assurance and Cree's soft sensuality. And mad, as well, stealing the women of his fellow trader, stealing the canoe and equipment and trade goods of his own partners, his own trading company, his friend and mentor, and setting off on a risky trip across the Great Plains with winter coming on, going to the Piegans, who never welcomed whites.

He simply didn't care if he was under the influence of enchantresses, or taken with lunar madness, or drunk on chivalry, or what. He went steadily about the business of getting ready. He had no more communication from the two girls—maybe if he called them girls in his head, it would be easier for him to pretend they were only little sisters. He put pemmican and *sagamité* into a *pièce*, and blankets and extra clothes. He traded for some men's clothes for Red Sky. He made sure his shooting pouch had a bar of lead and a ball mold, and his horns were full of powder. Feeling an obscure need, he sharpened his knives. Just after dark he slipped out and moved one of the two *canots du nord* to the hiding place on the creek where he'd meet the sisters, loaded it, and hid it under some brush.

He took ten minutes and smoked a pipe and thought about Dru and Saga. He told himself he was skipping out on his friends. Worse, he was robbing his partners. He told himself other, similar stories. He tried to make them matter. He failed.

He argued the other side to himself. He was doing what was right. Dru's attitude toward Indian slavery was far too casual. The abominable American institution was simply wrong. He would make it up to his partners later. Maybe the Piegans would make him welcome and open the door to rich trading. Somehow he didn't believe that. Well, he didn't know how, but he would make it up to his partners.

He never mentioned to himself his almost mystical yearning for the High Missouri, where the sisters' people lived.

The first day they moved fast, all three of them paddling, working the eddies hard and forging their way upstream. Dylan figured this was their free day. They'd be missed about dark tonight. When the sun went down, they kept paddling by the light of the moon for an hour or two, slept briefly like *voyageurs* under the canoe, and hit the water before first light in the morning. During the day they saw one outfit of Métis coming downriver, and wondered if those fellows would give them away. Before nightfall they had made the turn into the Pembina River, named for the high cranberry bushes along its banks, more than fifty miles from the Red River settlements.

From now on they would see almost no one heading for the settlements. Dylan breathed easier.

For three days they kept moving fast. When no one caught up with them the fourth day, Dylan decided they'd gotten away clean. He realized with a start that he was surprised.

That night Cree unfolded the lodge covers she had brought, and Dylan got a laugh—it was Chabono's lodge. They'd stolen the roof over the old man's head. But Cree told Dylan that the lodge always belongs to the woman. Remember that, Red Sky said pointedly. Cree erected the short, light poles of the lodge for summer traveling by herself. Red Sky built a center fire. Her disguise as a man was so good it unsettled Dylan.

Cree told Dylan to sit behind the center fire, which he knew was the place of honor. He was supposed to sit still, he realized, and let his women take care of him. All right, he would smoke.

He noticed, as they got things ready, that Cree laid out the blankets in the lodge, Red Sky's on one side, his own and hers as one pallet at the back center, where the father and mother always slept. He wondered if she intended to service him in bed as automatically as she fixed his meal. He wouldn't accept, but he teased himself by imagining just what she had in mind. They ate. They said little or nothing. Dylan had the impression that Red Sky was out of sorts somehow. Too bad, he was enjoying himself hugely.

He stood up and went outside to pee. When he got back, he would tell Cree to move her blankets to one side. He knew she would obey.

Looking around as he peed, he saw a dark line against the night sky.

A person, stock-still. A person looking at him.
"There's trouble," said Saga's voice.

After Saga explained the trouble, and Dylan decided
how they'd deal with it, the Métis delivered a written message from Dru. It began,

The fact that you're reading this message means
you know about the enemies on your trail. I like
your attitude. You're easy to track, though, even
if Red Sky's disguise helps a little. Idealism will
get you killed unless you're bloody good. And
entirely merciless.

Dylan looked up at Saga, who was doing his impassive expression.

You didn't take enough pemmican, here's some
more. Also more trade goods for the Piegans.
We're partners, remember?
    Good luck and a warm cod. I'll see you at
the Mandan villages this winter if you make it,
or at Red River in the spring. Find the holy grail
and drink from it.

                                   The Druid

Postscript: You fooled me. I didn't know you
were leaving. Saga did. When he claims it was a
good way to get rid of you, you're supposed to
know it's a joke.

Dylan, Saga, and Red Sky waited, crouched in the
willows. It was past midnight. Soon the bastards would be
creeping in. The three watched the bottomland carefully.
They were waiting for human shadows to come, moving
silently among the dapplings of moon shadows. To come
menacingly, with malicious intent.
    Which was fine. Cree would take care of the canoe.

Dylan, Saga, and Red Sky had malicious intent of their own for this end.

Several hours ago, when Saga stepped into the lodge, Dylan had asked, "How'd you follow us?"

In a loquacious moment, for him, Saga had said, "Following you was easy. Not getting spotted by Chabono, also following you, that was the trick."

They didn't have time to talk about the whys and wherefores, Saga said. Chabono and four other Métis were a mile downstream, their canoe half hidden, the men waiting until Dylan and the women were asleep. When they left the settlements, they boasted they were going to take two slaves and one scalp.

Saga and Red Sky were both full of ideas. Dylan listened. Then, with an authority that surprised him, he said what they would do. That was why Cree was now down by the stalkers' canoe with an ax, ready to tear hell out of it when Chabono left to do the dirty deeds. And Saga, Red Sky, and Dylan were waiting here in the dark.

His eyes said movement but his ears said silence. A disharmony. He waited. He told himself to breathe again. Yes, the creepers. The Big Dipper said halfway between midnight and dawn. They were so silent Dylan could hardly believe they were coming. He saw only shadows, moon shadows, undulating with the shape of the ground and the brush.

Dylan motioned with a hand. Saga and Red Sky crawled off in opposite directions, to their posts.

Soon four shadows slithered to the tipi. They spread out, two disappearing behind the wedge of darkness where the lodge stood, then reappearing and approaching the door. Dylan could tell Chabono's silhouette by the shape of the two feathers stuck sideways into the soft toque on his head. The shadows massed for a moment. Dylan wondered whether they whispered, or communicated only with their eyes.

Dylan breathed shallowly. Only a dozen steps away, he was afraid of being heard.

One shadow shifted to the door. After a moment

Dylan saw a blacker blackness in the side of the lodge, another darkness next to it, waiting. Then three dark blobs slid one by one into the tipi. Chabono's silhouette stayed outside.

Dylan could not wait long. They would discover quickly that the forms sleeping inside were only clothes and trade goods wrapped in blankets.

He stood up and stepped toward old Chabono, tomahawk in hand. He would fell the old bastard with the blunt side.

Chabono bolted.

Dylan roared at Saga and Red Sky. He leapt after Chabono, swung the tomahawk. It glanced off the old man's back and sailed out of Dylan's hand. Chabono got his footing back and ran.

Automatically, Dylan grasped his right-hand knife and whicked it hard at the old man.

It stuck. Somewhere on the right side.

Yelling and bawling from the lodge.

A triumphant ululation from Red Sky.

Dylan looked back. Where the dark wedge had stood, there was nothing but the forms of Red Sky and Saga, beating the lumps under the lodge covers flat on the ground.

It had worked. It was a simple setup. They undid the top tie on the lodge poles and loosened the cover. When Saga and Red Sky heaved on their ropes, the lodge poles collapsed and the assassins were tangled up under the cover.

Saga and Red Sky were dealing out a beating with the flat sides of tomahawks.

Dylan lit the candle lantern he'd hung from a branch.

Chabono was moaning and groaning, making an awful racket. Dylan checked the knife. It was stuck in the flesh of the right armpit. Chabono would have a useless arm for a while.

Dylan put a foot on the old man's back and jerked the knife out fast. Chabono bellowed.

Dylan looked at the blade. His first honest human blood with it. Never you mind, Mr. Stewart. Dylan rolled

Chabono over briskly and tied his feet and hands with rawhide.

Saga was yelling at the assassins to come out crawling. In two minutes they had the whole crew bound tight. Saga took their moccasins.

Red Sky lit the cooking fire outside the tipi. Dylan noticed that she didn't put the lodge back up. She made a fine-looking warrior, and her face was full of combat exhilaration.

Dylan looked at his knife blade in the light of the fire, gleaming red. He wiped it clean on the grass. Yes, first blood, good.

"We did it," he said to both of them. Red Sky grinned big. Saga's smile started in his eyes but didn't get to his lips.

Dylan took the lead. "Saga wants to scalp you. He can get a price for the scalps over at Fort Snelling."

The three Métis said nothing. Their aloof faces spoke all. They would never talk.

"He didn't say kill you," Dylan went on. "He wouldn't do that to his countrymen. But you can cover your skulls with hats."

Chabono started talking. Ceaselessly. He apologized, begged, and wheedled. He said it was all a joke, just a little fun between friends. He rolled around on the ground. He whined pitifully about his wound. He tried demanding, simpering, and pleading. He said a lot of things Dylan paid no attention to.

Dylan did pay attention to Cree, who walked quietly into camp and said she'd destroyed the assassins' canoe. Then she set out quietly folding the lodge and lashing the poles together. They'd get no more sleep tonight.

Dylan laid down the law. He'd wrecked their canoe. He'd taken their footwear. He was also taking their guns, which were miserable *fusils* anyway. He was taking their pemmican, and everything else except the clothes on their backs and their knives.

Chabono fell into a song of lament. Dylan paid no attention to the words.

"I'm leaving you this wire," he said, throwing down a coil of it, "to make snares. Saga says you're good

enough not to starve. You have knives, so you can skin
what you snare."

He paused. "You may get sore feet. You may have a
bad time. You'll have to walk into your lodges humiliated."

He looked each of them in the eye. "If ever you raise
a hand against me or mine, my partners and I will kill you,
your wives, and all your children." It felt surprisingly good
to make this threat, like stating a law of nature.

Saga added, "I promise, and my brothers promise."

"Next time you think of making a human being into
a slave," Dylan finished, talking to Chabono, "think
again."

Chapter
Twenty-Nine

S aga came into camp about dusk. Red Sky acted like he should eat and get gone, which seemed rude to Dylan. For the first time since they'd known each other, over their simple dinner of soup made from pemmican, Dylan tried to draw Saga out. Worked hard at it. Saga was not only his partner, but maybe his friend. Hadn't he trailed Chabono to save their lives? Hadn't he helped defeat that miserable crew? Hadn't he followed them all day, watching to make sure that Chabono and the others headed home instead of coming after Dylan and his women?

Cree said, "Tomorrow, you will follow them toward Red River?"

Saga nodded and chewed. He'd already said they walked tenderly on their bare feet toward the settlements half the day. After noon Saga had left off watching them and come back upstream at a jog. He just wanted to let Dylan know everything was fine. The nod meant he would keep an eye on the ruffians for another day, after he jogged far enough to find them.

"Do you like running across the plains?" Dylan asked. He always felt childish and foolish around Saga. The Métis just looked at him, not in an unfriendly way, perhaps amused, and kept eating.

Dylan had a romantic picture of it in his mind, Saga a lone pacer on these vast inland steppes, able to run lithely for scores of miles in a day, his shadow dancing ahead and slanted to the right, his lean, swift body a dark line above the golden grasses of autumn, only his handsome face caught in the sun, and that just on one side. So half the face was gilt and the other in shadow. Half white man, half dark man with scarred brow.

Dylan thought that's how Caro would paint it. He felt a pang for Caro—he felt every day and every hour the emptiness where his passion for her once was. He looked at Saga's face, beautifully formed, and for once felt no jealousy. All feelings to do with Caro were in the past, all except emptiness.

Saga never did join in the conversation. When he'd eaten, he touched a hand to the bandanna that bound his hair, nodded slightly, and disappeared into the night.

Red Sky looked after him like it was about time and went back to napping her obsidian. Dylan had no idea where she'd gotten the volcanic glass, or why she was making heads for spears and blades for knives.

Again Cree made her robe and blankets into one pallet with Dylan's. He said nothing until they went to bed. Dylan let the women go in five minutes before he did. The center fire was out. Red Sky had melted into the shadows on her side. Dylan neither saw nor heard her, but he couldn't help thinking about her nakedness there in the darkness. He cleared his throat and said, "Cree, move your blankets to the north side." He said it in what he hoped was a tone of gentle command. He stuck out his right arm, pointing to the side of the tipi where he wanted her, a futile gesture, because he couldn't see in the darkness.

Cree took his right hand. Her eyes must be adjusted to the dark, he thought. She nuzzled the hand against her cheek, and then put it on her neck. She stepped close to him, touched him from knee to breast with her nude body, put her hands behind his head, held him.

Dylan pulled away, opening his mouth to protest. She put a hand over his mouth, didn't let him talk, brushed him lightly on the lips.

He said, "Cree, damn it . . ."

She pushed him and tripped him and he fell onto the blankets. He burbled something, but her laughter drowned it out. Then she was on top of him, her lips on his neck, one hand undoing the buttons of his shirt, the other on his cod through his pants, and she was playing and teasing and chuckling warmly, and murmuring, "Poor, sad French-man, poor, sad."

The only dumb thing he could do now, thought Dylan, would be to play the virgin.

Up the Pembina River they went, across to the Mouse River, always upstream. He was looking forward to the Missouri itself, his river of enchantment. Dylan wondered what the Blackfoot word for this river meant, but Cree and Red Sky couldn't say it in French. Soon the short portage to the Missouri. Soon his dreamed-of journey up Big Muddy.

The best thing happened on the trip—nothing. They were efficient but not hurried, up at first light, on the river steadily all day, in camp an hour before dark. In a week they would be onto the Missouri, and Red Sky said they'd get to her people's country in another week or ten days. Dylan figured that would be mid-October. Red Sky said that the moon of leaves falling was the big autumn buffalo hunt, and the people might be anywhere, but right after the hunt they would go into their longtime winter camp on the Musselshell.

They talked constantly in the Blackfoot language. Dylan's Blackfoot from his Fort Augustus days was rough, but he was smoothing it up now.

Every day Cree did a lot of work, cooking, taking the lodge down and putting it up, sometimes sewing. Every night she came joyfully to Dylan's blankets and wore him out. She had a grand attitude, willing to serve without ever being servile, confident, womanly and strong in her wom-anliness, never weak but always saucy and playful. Dylan couldn't help loving her body, full and plush. Not that he wouldn't have liked Red Sky's body. He didn't always cast his eyes down as she dressed in the mornings, but some-times teased himself with her youthful slenderness, her breasts small and light and perfectly shaped, like half lem-ons.

Red Sky participated in none of the domestic work. She snared small animals to supplement their diet. She asked for permission to practice with Dylan's knives, and got it. She flaked her flint. She asked to be taught to shoot his rifle, but he said they could afford neither to waste powder and lead nor to make unnecessary noise. Then she acted sulky as a teenage boy.

Dylan wondered what Red Sky thought about the bedroom sounds every night. He tried to be quiet, but Cree was uninhibited. He decided Red Sky must have heard such sounds all her life. First from her parents, and then, Dylan thought unhappily, from Chabono and Cree.

He could hardly imagine that it was also Chabono and Red Sky. But he knew Chabono, and knew it must be. He wondered, then, why Red Sky kept her distance from him, held herself a little haughtily, avoided not only touch, but all familiarity, like she wasn't family, wasn't Cree's sister but a guest.

Cree's sister. Among the Piegans younger sisters were often second wives, he knew that. A white man—Frenchman in the Piegan way of speaking—a white man would be especially likely to have a second wife, being rich.

Cree and Red Sky were not his slaves—he'd set them free, he claimed no rights of ownership. He wondered if Cree and Red Sky expected him to make advances toward the younger sister, and wondered why he didn't. He even wondered if they might be insulted that he didn't, or think him peculiar. He supposed, after thinking about it, that he was expected to take Red Sky to his bed, or go to hers.

He knew, from body language, from sideways looks, that they expected it. As slaves, they assumed he would make whatever use of them he pleased. He'd be damned if he'd act like that. He felt bad enough about allowing himself to cavort with Cree, but he was a man, after all, and she an eager woman. He hated the damnable Yank institution of slavery, and he had to demonstrate some standards.

Sometimes he wondered whether the sisters had husbands at home. Cree was of marriageable age, Red Sky near enough. He didn't permit himself to pursue that thought far. He was taking them home, and he would give them back. To whatever families they had. Period. Sod all.

*   *   *

They got into camp on the Missouri in the last light, and he could barely see the river of his dreams. Hurriedly he ate, lay down, made love with Cree, and had a dream. It seemed to last all night. He ached with it, he writhed with it, he was afraid he was keeping Cree awake with it.

In the dream, he and Red Sky were walking through the British Museum (he had never even seen an art museum), dressed like a well-to-do *bourgeois* couple and looking at the art on the walls. Which was not paintings or any other separate works of art, but the wall covering itself, silks with sylvan scenes depicted in silver and gold brocade. In these scenes he and Red Sky were represented making love in ways that were all various and looked elegant, esthetically beautiful. On the walls he was a Grecian hero and she Diana, goddess of the hunt.

Dylan and Red Sky walked slowly through the handsome rooms, in a stately fashion, looking at themselves in their mythological embraces, fully joined and enraptured. They strolled in complete silence, in a way that was curiously cool and impersonal. It seemed formal, a very proper dance with the steps set to grave and noble music. Dylan was drenched with erotic feeling.

They came to a room of frescoes showing their joinings, unions made in formal gardens, beside paradisiacal waterfalls, in lush forests of Rousseau, in refined gardens of Eden. The joined nudes were larger than life, still graceful, always of formal beauty, but sensuous and impassioned now—Red Sky's breasts small but exquisitely shaped, legs long and alluring, Dylan's muscles supple, strong, articulated in thrust, Red Sky's hair flowing backward like shining black water, her mouth opon in ardor, her eyes glazed with ecstasy.

Dylan woke up, trembling. Cree was shaking him very lightly. "Are you all right?" she asked.

The dream kept on, even now that he was awake. He was in the frescoes. He and Red Sky were making love with supreme passion. The music swelled and throbbed, still decorous but unbearably urgent.

He said softly and simply to Cree, "I am dreaming of making love with Red Sky. I can't stop."

"Go to her," said Cree matter-of-factly. "She's yours."

Mesmerized, he did.

As he crawled to Red Sky's pallet, he might have been dreaming still. He eased under the blankets next to her, their warm bodies in sensual contact. He caressed her. Red Sky seemed wide-awake and perhaps half compliant. Poor child, she was nervous. He kissed her gently.

Suddenly he felt her palm on his chest, pushing. "No," she whispered.

Confused, he touched her breast erotically.

"No," she said firmly, and loudly.

Dylan heard Cree sit up.

"I—" Dylan began.

"Please," said Red Sky, her voice raspy and harsh.

Dylan got up and went away. He stood in the middle of the lodge for a moment. He felt his foot in the edge of the ashes of the center fire.

Cree launched in and blistered Red Sky in Blackfoot. Dylan paid no mind. His mind was swaying in humiliation. Red Sky didn't want him. He heard Cree remind her younger sister that he saved her from a cruel master, that she was Monsieur Dylan's, that she must do as he wanted, certainly give him what her other masters took freely. . . .

Red Sky answered in a wan voice. Something about her nature. Something about Monsieur Dylan a good-enough man . . .

"No," said Dylan, loud enough that they both heard. Silence was in the lodge. His mind rang with humiliation, the reverberations going on and on, like a gong in a dream. Yes, she had let other men use her body, and yes, he was embarrassed. But certain things he would not do.

"Don't reprimand her," he said to Cree.

He got into his robes behind Cree. He could feel her body stiff with anger. Playfully, to ease her out of it, he stroked her ribs below her breasts. She relaxed. After a long time they both fell asleep.

*   *   *

The next evening, during dinner, Dylan watched Red Sky carefully. She'd been remote all day, scarcely taking notice of her companions, lost in thoughts or feelings, walling herself away from his gaze. He thought she wanted something and lacked the courage to speak. He wondered what. He felt benevolently ready, whatever it was.

After dinner she turned to them, took a deep breath, and said she wanted to say something. Dylan urged her on.

"If Cree sit by your side," she said, "I willing sit in my place for now," Red Sky began. It was her Indian way of saying she would be a second wife to her sister's husband, a usual arrangement. That was good, until Dylan got them home, which was all he wanted to do.

She looked inquiringly at Cree. Perhaps she wondered how long Cree wanted this arrangement to last. Not long, as far as Dylan was concerned. A country wife among the Blackfoot for a season, yes, that was a custom of the fur men and the Indians. Not a real family.

Now she looked nakedly at Dylan. "I will be a good wife." She hesitated. "I ask one permission, big one." She seemed to verge on trembling. "I ask be allowed be alone in my robes for . . . I don' know how long, weeks maybe. Entirely alone."

Cree looked harshly at her sister, but Dylan silenced her with a raised hand. Dimly he saw Red Sky take a deep breath.

The gong of humiliation was sounding again, as in a dream.

"I like you," Red Sky plunged. "I will be loyal. I may come to care for you. But . . ."

She could not bring herself to plunge on. Dylan waited, and asked Cree with a glance to wait.

"When we are at home," Red Sky murmured shakily. "I will seek the counsel of Owl Claw."

Cree gasped, then covered her mouth with a hand.

Red Sky looked frontally at Dylan, knowing he didn't understand the significance of this statement.

"My dreams tell me . . ." She hesitated. "I will seek Owl Claw's counsel to help me understand my dreams." She spoke with courage. "I will go where they call me."

He looked at Cree. She was more than angry, more

than taken aback—she was truly shocked and frightened.
She knew what Red Sky was hinting. He was sure she
wouldn't tell him.

Dylan sat on the bank in the early darkness, listening
to the swish of the river, making its way downstream to
the Gulf of Mexico. It said no words to him as it traveled,
but was mute, impartially mute, magisterially mute.
Doubtless, if the river thought, it would have thought
words irrelevant. If communication was needed, its flowing, spinning, braiding, rollicking, playing motion toward
the ocean was its song.

Dylan said no words to himself, not even that he
would naturally honor Red Sky's choice, whatever it was.
He knew he was flotsam. He could feel himself borne forward, always forward, on a river vaster and darker and
more powerful and stranger, far, far stranger, than he had
imagined. It would drag him through reeds and cattails. It
would slide him onto sandbars. It would jiggle and jar and
even jolt him at its will. It would suck him into the whirl-
pool of its depths. It would float him among odd creatures,
bizarre forms of life, fishes and crabs and turtles and
snakes and other scaly and slimy and shelled creatures. It
would even introduce him to monsters.

To him Red Sky was now an odd creature, but no
monster. He was fond of her. They had a connection of
tenderness.

He had a sudden fantasy. A whale rose out of his
river—illogically out of the *river*—and swallowed him. He
was living in its innards. It was doing with him as it liked,
gobbling up strange companions for him, lying on the bottom, making him live in the dark, among entrails, and
wait.

The sisters were talking animatedly. You'd never
have thought Red Sky had gone through an important confrontation two hours ago. But then, she was a teenager.

Cree started in merrily. "Since we're your wives, we

want you to give us something. Something nice, pretty, not practical."

Dylan gave a mock moan. In the Blackfoot language he said with phony disgust, "Wives!"

He got a candle lantern and led them behind the lodge to where he kept the trade goods stored at night, staked down under an oiled cloth. Cree pulled a couple of stakes. Red Sky held the lantern while Dylan made a show of looking through items without letting them see. The teenager was bouncing on her feet with anticipation.

He ran beads through his fingers. Good but not good enough. He considered vermilion. He wanted to give them one item, not a lot of this and that, so it needed to be something special. Some one thing . . .

He had it. Bells.

He held up strings of little hawk bells for each of them. The women each grabbed a string with a squeal of delight and started prancing, shaking the bells into a carillon peal. Indian women loved the hawk bells—sewed them onto the dresses they used for happy dances. The rows of brass looked smart, and they made a light, clear jingle that fit the occasion wonderfully.

Their faces said they were thrilled.

Dylan waited by the center fire while they danced around—it was cold outside. When they came in, Red Sky said she was going to sleep with her string around her neck. Cree had something more serious in mind. "Tell us a story about bells," she said. "There's a reason you chose bells."

How did his wife—temporary wife—know?

Dylan decided to tell them about his bells and make it more light than it was, more of a lark. He said nothing about the grave-digging, but put in the fat sexton. He did tell briefly about going up high into the bell tower to see the great humped bells and embrace them. He was getting more serious than he meant to.

So he switched to riding the ropes up and down. And with a thrill in his voice he went on to jumping from rope to rope, up this one, down another, and the tremendous sound.

Remembering the sound, he let his voice become

graver. He recalled how the clangor deafened him, how it was more than sound, it was a world, and he was inside. And at the end, when you couldn't hear the sound, you could still feel, ever so slightly, the air vibrating.

Their faces let him see he had moved them. He felt a little embarrassed. "So I'm glad to get to give you bells," he said clumsily. "They're special to me."

When they slipped into the robes, Cree spooned close behind him. This was the way she liked to start their love-making every night. She said softly, "I think you are a hero."

He waggled his bottom and made a pooh-poohing sound.

She made him turn and look at her. She had a grave and loving expression on her face. She made him see it, and then began to move against him.

That was when he realized he didn't think about Caro constantly anymore, maybe not even every day. He felt that was a betrayal. His body moved against Cree's.

What he was forgetting, really, was the dominion of death, its reign over all.

But Cree moved against him still, and without wanting to, he responded. He decided to keep forgetting for a few minutes.

_____ Chapter _____
Thirty

B efore noon Dylan saw two riders on the bluffs to the
north, silhouetted against the sky, motionless as sen-
tinel rocks.

He spoke softly to Cree Medicine. She chattered rap-
idly in the Blackfoot language at Red Sky, and Dylan
caught almost all her excited words. The teenager gave her
older sister a squeeze, pointed, giggled, and acted like a
kid. Cree Medicine gave Red Sky a long hug back. Dylan
got the feeling they were home now. They'd been camped
here for three days, at the usual winter camp of their people, but only now were they home.

The village arrived piece by piece. First the outriders
down the bluffs, then more young men of whatever warrior society they belonged to, the people's guards, riding
up and down the bottom and checking the far side of the
river and the tops of the bluff on both sides. A camp must
be a haven.

Then the line of travois after travois, all dragged by
horses, scores of women putting up lodges with hundreds
of children and dogs underfoot.

Last came the men and youths. The grown men set
about serious tasks, mounting the tripods that would hold
their medicine bundles in front of the lodges, staking their
best buffalo horses and war-horses near their tipis. The
teenage boys raced and cavorted on ponies until the men
got them to gather the mounts all together, put them on
good grass farther down the bottom, and set out guards.

As the women and travois began to file into camp,

Cree Medicine grasped Dylan by the arm and said, "You must never speak to my mother, or even look her in the eye. Especially not end up alone with her. Never." She pinched his arm to add to the urgency of her tone.

Dylan thought he might disregard this business of a husband and mother-in-law avoiding each other, though it was customary. For one thing, he was not Cree Medicine's husband, just her temporary protector. He would give her back, he had decided. For another, if he made contact with his so-called mother-in-law, they would just regard him as a foreigner who didn't know any better. Which was fine. In fact, it would give him latitude to do things his own way, and be regarded as following his own medicine. If you don't know enough to do something right, he said to himself with a chuckle, make a point of doing it your own way, like it came straight from God.

He noticed people being careful not to notice him. Lodges went up around him—they were making a great circle of tipis with an opening toward the east. The small travel lodge he shared with Cree Medicine and Red Sky was included roughly in the circle, a kind of outpost to the big lodge of their family.

So he smoked his pipe and pretended to take no notice of anyone as Cree Medicine and Red Sky greeted the women of the family. Hugs first, some tears, finally babble and laughter and a few shrieks of delight. He supposed he was to ignore these displays of emotion, but he didn't know. Dylan saw out of the corner of his eye that a man of perhaps fifty looked at him briefly and then averted his eyes. Dylan supposed that was the girls' father, White Raven.

He watched out of the corner of his eye as White Raven hung his medicine bundle from a tripod of sticks in front of the lodge. White Raven went about this business solemnly, with no indication a stranger was nearby and observing. Dylan wondered what was in the bundle. Personal totems, he knew—Bleu had showed him a bundle taken from a dead Piegan. It had several beaded bags, a bell, thong wristlets with beads, a hairpiece made of eagle feathers and tail feathers of a raven, a scalp, a badger skin, a twist of tobacco, bags of paint for the face, and other oddments he couldn't remember. Both Piegan men and women owned such bundles, which were never opened or looked upon except by the owner. They believed power—medicine—resided in these bits and pieces of animal and earth. Nothing else made Dylan so aware that they were pagans.

He still liked the pun, Piegan and pagan, pronounced the same way.

Then White Raven walked down several lodges toward the horns of the circle and assisted a man in hanging a lot of rawhide cases from a tripod. It must be a big and complicated medicine bundle—Dylan had never seen one that filled so many cases, small black square ones, two big multicolored parfleches shaped like satchels, and a cylindrical case. They covered the tripod as thick as a potentate showing off his finest silks.

"Beaver bundle," Cree Medicine said to him reverently.

He gave a little nod. That meant it would hold a lot of totem items, plus the gear for some of the principal Piegan ceremonies, especially pipes, drums, and rattles. He recalled with a shiver that Bleu said the hollow globes of the rattles were made of buffalo scrotums.

He shivered again. He realized his hands were cool even against the hot clay of the pipe, and he could feel his feet getting numb.

Somehow it came to him, not as thought of cold, or memory of cold, but as cold itself, seeping into him. He was in a Piegan camp, the only white man in five hundred miles, and he was officially uninvited. The Piegans were famous for their persistence and creativity in torturing outsiders. He was utterly at their mercy.

He had fantasized his adventure would bring him among alien and dangerous creatures. They were at hand.

He supposed the crown of his head should be prickling a little. It was more like tadpoles were slithering up and down his spine.

His first hurdle was White Raven. Cree Medicine brought Dylan to her father's lodge before the noon meal.

He was given the seat of a guest of honor, beside the head of the house. White Raven lit the pipe, and Dylan was able to remember his pipe etiquette and keep his hands steady as he smoked. The women, Cree Medicine, Red Sky, a woman who was probably their mother, Calf Robe, and a young teenager who must be their sister, stayed in the back of the lodge, pretending to mind their own business. Now that Dylan was close, he noticed that White Raven had amazingly long silver-black hair. Before, it had been fastened up somehow. Now it stretched elegantly behind him on the ground for two or three feet, surely arranged with care by his wives or daughters. Now that he was relaxed, White Raven also had a strikingly benevolent face, at once assured, kindly, and wise, like a seer.

White Raven asked no questions. He accepted Dylan's gift of tobacco, speaking and using sign language at once.

Dylan had prepared his speech carefully in the Blackfoot language. He thanked White Raven for his hospitality, spoke his admiration of the Piegan people, and offered to be of service. He intended the use of Blackfoot as a special compliment. The Blackfoot regarded other people with some contempt, and seldom troubled to learn their languages, but waited for them to learn the speech of the Real People.

The old man was silent awhile, as though contemplating Dylan's conventional utterances. Then he spoke slowly but without signs, which Dylan took as a compliment to his command of the language. The old warrior thanked Dylan in an Olympian way for bringing his daughters back to the people. Dylan thought maybe the old fellow was uncertain of his intentions toward his daughters. He could reassure him about that. Or would the old man feel mortified if he simply gave them back? Would the old man expect him to become a Piegan and take care of them forever? Would White Raven be insulted if he left to rejoin Dru and Saga? Murderously insulted? White Raven ended by inviting Dylan to ask for whatever he wanted.

Dylan let a few moments pass to show that he was considering what his host had said. Then he replied that he would like the opportunity to make some gifts to the chiefs, and waited for an answer.

White Raven nodded, thought for a few moments, and answered affirmatively. He turned his head and spoke softly to the women. In moments the noon meal was in wooden bowls with horn spoons. The two men ate heartily, and the women kept to themselves.

Dylan thought he had jumped the first hurdle.

Shaking Plume was built like a rake, all shoulder and a slat of a body, with an acne-ravaged face above. At first Dylan thought he was too ugly to be a leader. Then he noticed the flash of Shaking Plume's eyes, and saw authority there, and the will to command. The quality Dylan disliked in Captain Chick and his father and all men who saw themselves as rulers over others. He felt himself blocked, and tried to tell himself the feeling was reasonless.

A half-dozen men sat in the circle around the center fire in Shaking Plume's lodge. Dylan recognized only White Raven. The others would be counselors and members of the pipe society, Dylan supposed, the heads of warrior societies, or other leaders in war, perhaps healers, seers, wise men. Men whose collective wisdom and influence Shaking Plume used to rule the people of the village. *Rule* was the operable word.

Shaking Plume offered Dylan a brief and unceremonious welcome to his camp, without generous words or effusive body language. From Shaking Plume's rear Cree Medicine translated, for Shaking Plume refused to slow his speech down for a foreigner. And it was good for Dylan to have translation, to be sure what was being said, and to give him time to consider his replies. It was also good to have a friend in this council—two friends, Cree behind him and White Raven next to him. He decided to keep his mind on their benevolence, and not the authority of the man who would interrogate him.

Dylan offered Shaking Plume gifts of tobacco, plus blankets, strouding, and beads, including some large and beautiful chevrons. He was obliged to strike the right balance. Too few gifts would suggest a sour heart. Too many would suggest fear, and an attempt to bribe. Shaking Plume accepted in a detached way, neither encouraging nor discouraging.

Dylan explained that he was not an American, nor a Briton, but one of what the Piegans called Frenchmen, men from Canada, who were known to the Piegans since before the memories of the oldest men. He had come here to see and meet the Piegans of this country, who were known by report and honored by Frenchmen everywhere, especially those at Fort Augustus, on the far end of the Old North Trail, where he formerly lived. He hoped to make friends among a people of such wide repute. He thought perhaps the Piegans did not want to have to travel so many sleeps to Fort Augustus to get the things they wanted. If their hearts were open to him, he would trade them the few items he brought, and he would return next summer with Frenchmen friends to trade more.

Shaking Plume gave Dylan's words a polite space of time, and then asked, "Do you have the white man's water?" Meaning whiskey.

Dylan didn't know what to answer. He did, a modest amount. He and Dru and Saga had talked it over carefully before leaving Montreal. Liquor debauched the Indians, there was no question of that. When they drank, they fought, brawled, raped, and even killed each other and white men. But it helped the traders. Once the Indians developed a great thirst, they would hunt beaver and buffalo and other fur bearers to a fare-thee-well. Various traders had tried to do without whiskey, but they always were forced to come back to it.

Piegans were a little different, because their tolerance for their liquor was slight. The custom with the Piegans at Fort Augustus was to mix the pure alcohol with water one part to eight or nine, spiced with the usual tobacco, pepper, molasses, Jamaican ginger, and whatever else was handy. Then they'd give out cups of booze one morning—the Piegans refused to trade for white man's water, because all water should be free—and start trading the next day, after the riots.

This village probably knew little of whiskey. Dylan wanted to lie. Finally he said, "A little."

He meant to add that the stuff was poison and the people should stay away from it, but Shaking Plume preempted him. "You will not give whiskey to anyone in this village," the chief said in a tone of command.

Shaking Plume looked at Dylan, who answered, "That is good."

The chief regarded his counselors, and Dylan saw unspoken communication pass between them. At length Shaking Plume said in a closed way, "My friend Three Horns has some questions for you." As Cree translated these words, Dylan could hear the tension in her voice. He understood that he had to get around the obstacle of Three Horns to get to trade.

The man Shaking Plume indicated was squat, and his face looked pugnacious. He asked baldly, accusingly, "Why did you steal the wives of my son Ermine Head?"

Dylan kept his face from showing feeling. He wondered why Three Horns said "wives." He'd gathered that Cree had a husband, but not Red Sky. Was one of the other women, the ones Père Noël kept, married to this man's son, whoever that might be? Who was this man? Of what stature and influence? Who was his son Ermine Head?

It was a quagmire.

"Another man stole the Piegan women," said Dylan, "a man named Père Noël."

Three Horns bolted forward with lots of words at once. "The Frenchman says another Frenchman stole them. Perhaps it was his friend, perhaps his brother, perhaps he himself held the horses during the theft. I ask, what is the evidence of our eyes—who has our women? If a Crow stole our horses, and the thief's brother came back riding them, would we listen to his plea that he didn't steal them, his brother did? Or would we take our horses back, and dance over the Crow's scalp?"

The man stopped suddenly. Dylan wondered whether Three Horns saw what he suspected, the disapproval of the counselors for the rudeness of his rush of accusations.

Dylan waited to frame a measured response.

"Another man stole the Piegan women. I saw his partner with two of them only. I did not trade for them—I helped them escape. They are Piegan women, meant to be no man's slaves. Now I return them freely to their people. I thank them for bringing me here."

Everyone sat in silence. They didn't look at each other, or communicate in any way. Dylan could feel the universal amazement in the lodge, or stupefaction. They didn't know whether to believe his claim, or if it was true, what to think of it. This wasn't the way anyone treated women.

Dylan thought with satisfaction that there might be usefulness in being a foreigner who didn't know how to act.

Shaking Plume rattled something at Cree in the Blackfoot language. The sentences lashed fast and harsh as whips, and Dylan was sure of no word but her name, and the word *true*. He supposed Shaking Plume was asking her to confirm or deny Dylan's assertion, and asking in a way that bespoke disbelief.

"The first Frenchman stole us and made us slaves," said Cree, speaking in a measured way for Dylan's sake. "He was a man of perhaps fifty winters. He used us as slaves," she added with some resentment. "Then he gave us to another Frenchman to *sell*," she added, stressing the word. "We were homesick. Monsieur Dylan took pity on us and helped us get away, and brought us back here." She stopped. It would be one of her virtues to answer no more than she was asked.

Shaking Plume spoke softly and respectfully to a young man, who grunted assent and left the lodge. Hearing Red Sky's name, Dylan supposed the chief had asked for her to be brought here.

Shaking Plume asked Cree something more sharply—Dylan heard the word *slave*.

"Monsieur Dylan said he would help us return to our village and our families," Cree said. "He told us we were not slaves but free, and offered to help us get home."

Shaking Plume spoke fast again, his words like thrown stones.

Dylan couldn't follow the rapid Blackfoot. Suddenly he knew, and his heart spun and sank, and he felt himself sucked into mysterious and fatal depths. He was sure

Shaking Plume was asking Cree whether he had frigged them.

Lascivious pictures came raging into his mind, accompanied by the clangor of a death knell. His testicles squirmed.

"I think Monsieur Dylan brought us back," Cree Medicine answered with her eyes cast down humbly, "because he wanted to make friends with the Piegans, and because his heart was warm toward Red Sky and me."

She flicked her eyes fleetingly up at Dylan, and immediately back to the ground. He thought she was saying she'd done what she could. He knew that even so slight a gesture as a look in the eyes might be thought brazen by these counselors. It was a courageous act. He thought that perhaps this woman truly cared for him.

Red Sky came in behind the young man, her eyes properly on the ground. She knelt to the right of Cree.

Dylan forced his body to be still. His fate rested in the hands of a teenager, who spurned him. Humiliation puckered his spirit.

Shaking Plume's rapid Blackfoot shot at Red Sky, seeming to Dylan the same words asked of Cree Medicine.

"Four of us were digging prairie turnips near Willow Creek," she said, speaking slowly. "Père Noël, a big Frenchman, came with Minnetarees on horseback and pointed guns at us. We dared not scream, but I attacked him with my turnip digger. He threw me to the ground and laughed at me. The others gave in peacefully. They had big American horses and made us ride double day and night until we got to the Milk River.

"The big one, Noël, laughed a lot in a cruel way. He acted fond of me and ordered me around and said he would keep me for himself."

Shaking Plume coughed a little, sounding impatient. Dylan wondered whether these counselors cared nothing about the fact that their young women had been raped.

"At the Mandan villages he sold Cree Medicine and me to Chabono—like horses he sold us. That one took us to Red River to sell us again. He thought it was good to get as far as possible from the guns of the Piegan men."

Shaking Plume interrupted her. Dylan had the impression Red Sky would have kept going with the story at great length. He had no idea whether she would paint him as a rescuer or another tyrant. In his fear he missed Shaking Plume's words entirely.

He noticed that Red Sky hesitated. For a moment Dylan thought she was going to look up, but she didn't. She said tremulously but with emphasis, "*I* planned our escape, and Monsieur Dylan helped. I think he helped because he . . ." Was she groping for words? Did she not know what she wanted to say?

At last she took the plunge. She even had the boldness to look Shaking Plume in the eye. "Monsieur Dylan hated to see an old man own us and use us as he pleased. He wanted us to be able to live as human beings."

The counselors sat mute in the face of this claim. For Dylan the silence sang.

Then he thought, Maybe they're not silent in acceptance or admiration. Maybe they're aghast at her rudeness in meeting the chief's gaze.

The tadpoles kept slithering up and down his spine.

When Shaking Plume spoke, there was reproof in his voice, and he addressed himself to the sister who was properly demure. Dylan grasped the word *husband*.

Cree answered softly and with her eyes cast down, as a woman should. But she enunciated the words with great clarity. "I have set up my lodge. I have built a fire, and laid out the robes. I welcome my husband Monsieur Dylan to my lodge."

Only Shaking Plume's commanding eye kept the pugnacious Three Horns from bursting out.

Finally, Shaking Plume said simply, "What about your . . . Ermine Head?"

Dylan's testicles twisted. He would have given one to know anything at all about this Ermine Head.

"Monsieur Dylan is my husband," said Cree Medicine.

Emotions tossed Dylan like choppy waves.

Could she divorce Ermine Head so easily? Dylan had heard that Piegan women owned the lodge, and to divorce the man, needed only to set his belongings outside. He'd also heard Piegan men had the right to beat their women as much as they pleased, and even to cut off the nose of a faithless wife. He wondered which was true.

His skin trembled. Was he safe now? No torture, no scalping? But did he now have a wife? Did he want one? Was he trapped?

Three Horns finally burst into a torrent of angry words. Shaking Plume burst back. Dylan couldn't follow all the language, but he saw the naked emotions. Three Horns was furious at this humiliation of his son Ermine Head. Shaking Plume was upbraiding him harshly for his rude speech. Three Horns half rose and pointed at Cree and then jammed his finger emphatically at Red Sky. Finally the squat man jumped up and hurled himself out of the lodge.

Speaking calmly now, Shaking Plume told Dylan that he regretted the impoliteness of this man, and asked Dylan's forbearance.

In his best Blackfoot, Dylan spoke his understanding.

Shaking Plume turned to Red Sky, with some wariness, Dylan thought. He said, "Do you have anything more to say, my willful daughter?"

Dylan felt despair. Was Red Sky now to be offered as a sacrifice to the wrath of Three Horns and Ermine Head?

"I was promised to my sister's husband," she began, and to speak at all was brazen. Dylan was afraid she was going to anger Shaking Plume with another long speech. "Before we were stolen, I refused to go to Ermine Head because he beat her without reason. I refuse to go to him now."

She paused, and looked up first at Shaking Plume and then at Dylan. He saw that she was defying the male authority in this lodge, knowingly. The softness of her voice and the gentleness of her words could not undo the daring of her act: She was making a choice. "I wish to accept my sister's husband, Monsieur Dylan."

White Raven saw Shaking Plume look briefly at him. He kept his face impassive. He, White Raven, her father, did not know what to think of this remarkable gesture, this seizing of self-power by his daughter. So how was the leader to know? Perhaps Red Sky at Morning was a manly-hearted woman. The Piegans had a tradition of such women, and the people honored them, women who took upon themselves the air and authority of men. Even if jokes got told about their husbands, the people honored such women. Time would tell whether Red Sky at Morning was one of them, or merely displaying the bad manners of a teenager. Or maybe . . .

Shaking Plume passed it over, this extraordinary behavior. He was wise. Instead he spoke to the young Frenchman White Raven's daughters had attached themselves to.

"Tomorrow morning you may open your parfleches for trade."

The Frenchman did not show his relief in his face, which was good. Or his greed, or his triumph. He kept his face polite, as he should.

The silence was full of everyone's consent. After a few moments the counselors began to leave.

White Raven walked behind his daughters and their new husband. They weren't talking. He hoped that meant their minds were on the momentous events of the last hour.

He was concerned about Red Sky at Morning. Since she was a small child, she had been different, and he loved her difference. He loved Cree Medicine's womanliness, her pleasure in the tasks and roles of a woman, which seemed to White Raven to spring from a wisdom, an ability to see and savor. He loved Red Sky at Morning for her difference, her impatience with convention, with the very parts of life Cree Medicine liked. He felt, without thought, that in some distinct way that couldn't be spoken, this difference *was* Red Sky.

Maybe it was just immaturity and bad manners. Time would tell. But his mother had predicted that Red Sky at Morning would be a manly-hearted woman. White Raven hoped so. He smiled at himself. This was a kindlier explanation, he thought, than the alternative—that he didn't know how to raise a daughter properly.

He turned his mind away from Red Sky's future. It was useless to think about it. His daughter, like all people, was a living spirit. He wanted to watch her show the courage to live as that spirit directed her.

He sat on a rock and watched his daughters go to their lodge with their new husband. Amazing, he thought, the days of the earth. One day he had three daughters, one married—though in difficulties—and two at home. The next day he had one—two were simply gone, disappeared, evaporated. And on a day not long thereafter he had two daughters married to a foreigner. Life was itself the great Coyote, the trickster, the shape changer.

He looked after them fondly. The young man had behaved himself well, White Raven thought. He had been brave to venture to the people at all. He had chosen good circumstances to come, bringing Cree Medicine and Red Sky. He had evidently pleased them with his conduct on the way here. White Raven assumed that included pleasing them in the blankets, if Red Sky was not too sovereign to permit herself to be topped. White Raven smiled to himself. This was the sort of humor the people indulged in about manly-hearted women. If his daughters saw the matter truly, the young fellow cared for them, and honored them in his ways.

White Raven supposed this Monsieur Dylan would not be their husband for a lifetime, as White Raven had been Calf Robe's husband, and that saddened him. These Frenchmen came and went as they pleased, or so he heard, and left children like droppings. It was incomprehensible, except that the Frenchmen were foreigners and unenlightened, and you could expect no more from them than from teenage boys blinded by the lusts of the body. Still, a few

Frenchmen bound themselves to their women truly. Perhaps Monsieur Dylan would be one of these.

White Raven held no real hope of that. He thought his daughters' fate sad. True, it was no worse than their situation with that great oaf Ermine Head. And their marriage would bring them the Frenchman goods—pots, knives, awls, blankets, and the like—all the things women wanted, and would bring these things more cheaply and conveniently to all the people. It was good enough. And if their father raised no objection, as he deliberately had not, none of the leaders would interfere.

White Raven sniffed the air with pleasure. It was an autumn sunset, and the air was cooling and filled with wood smoke and the smells of cooking. This was a combination White Raven was fond of. He would eat now.

Then, he thought, he better have a talk with his daughters' new husband, and begin to make him aware of the dangers of having Ermine Head and Three Horns as enemies.

The three of them, man and two wives, walked through the cool air of the late autumn afternoon toward their lodge. Dylan wondered what was in the mind of White Raven, his new father-in-law, walking behind them. No one spoke.

Feelings thrilled through Dylan: passion for his new wives. For Cree especially, and lustful memories. Renewed desire for Red Sky too, who had made her choice. Also greed: now he could trade freely. Triumph: he was alive. Resentment: he was trapped by two wives. Confusion: he had a motherless child in Montreal, and childless wives among the Piegans.

He was all mixed up. And that was without admitting to himself one feeling, a cold, snaky fear. When he looked at his wives, he wondered if he had finally given up all hope and become a barbarian.

The three walked together to the lodge, and Dylan went with his wives into his home. *Wives, home*—difficult words for him.

Cree immediately began getting dinner ready, her eyes down, her face worried.

She had reason to worry. After only a moment's hesitation Red Sky looked Dylan in the eye and spoke boldly. "You are a good man," she said. "I am glad of your protection. Without it I would have to marry Ermine Head, or another."

She spoke smoothly, easily, as though her directness to her husband were not brazen. "You remember I am to consult with Owl Claw. The course of my life may change at that time. I ask you, humbly, until that time," she said, "please to let me be alone in the robes."

So. With effort, he controlled his feelings. "As you wish," he said.

Cree's hand was over her mouth, her eyes round. He didn't know whether her astonishment was at Red Sky's request or his response.

Desperate, he slipped outside. He looked at the sunset reddening the western sky and suddenly remembered—now for the first time—an old sailor's saying he'd heard. He was amazed he'd never thought of it in respect to Red Sky at Morning, his sort-of wife, until now.

> Red Sky at morning,
> Sailors take warning.
> Red Sky at night,
> Sailor's delight.

He laughed. Laughed sardonically, miserably. She was truly named, Red Sky at Morning, and no delight at night. He cackled.

He remembered that his father had disparaged business partnerships mockingly as the worst of all worlds, calling them "like marriage without sex." Now Dylan was snared in just such a partnership.

Cree sat on the blankets at the back of the lodge, her knees forward and legs tucked back, sewing her husband a pair of moccasins. Monsieur Dylan was outside, perhaps walking, perhaps living in his head, as he did too much.

For herself, she would not live in hers. She would not
wonder whether her sister would become a manly-hearted
woman, even a woman warrior, even ... She cut off her
thoughts. She would not wonder whether bad-heartedness
would arise between Monsieur Dylan and Red Sky, or
what that bad-heartedness might lead to. These matters
rode the winds, which blew from every direction and to
every direction, and only the foolish tried to predict them.

She would keep her mind on what mattered. This afternoon she had borrowed deer hide from her mother for
new moccasins, and moose hide for winter moccasins. Tomorrow she, Red Sky, and their mother would get to work
tanning skins fresh from the buffalo hunt for a lodge, a
full-sized lodge to replace this summer tipi, one suitable
for Monsieur Dylan and his two wives. At night she would
strip the bark off willow rods, straighten them, and make
them into a backrest for Monsieur Dylan, decorated nicely
with snippets of blue and red strouding her mother had left
over. With this wifeliness she would make a home.

She was aware, keenly aware, as she sat there poking
her awl through the deer hide, that she was taking the big
step toward making a home tonight. She had come into
camp with her new husband, pitched their lodge next to
her parents', and ignored utterly the man who once called
himself her husband. She did not even allow her eyes to
see Ermine Head, though he stood in front of the lodge of
Tail Feathers, glaring at her. Probably Ermine Head had
lived with Tail Feathers, his brother-friend, the five moons
she was gone. That did not concern her. Ermine Head
would never concern her again. Before the eyes of all the
people, she was making her choice.

Tonight she was sewing for her husband. In a few
minutes, or an hour, they would lie down in the blankets
together. She would make sure, on this night, that they
made love. When they woke up with the new dawn, they
would be a couple, a family, in the eyes of the people.
Even Ermine Head.

Chapter
Thirty-One

A scratch at the door flap. Cree sat up in the robes, alarmed. The light was only a hint at the smoke hole, and the lodge was dark. It was much too early for anyone to come calling. She looked at Dylan, hesitated, and then took matters into her own hands and spoke. "Who's there?"

Her father's voice called from outside, "Monsieur Dylan, there is trouble."

She whispered to her husband, and told her father full voice that they would be out in a minute. Red Sky was sitting up too. Monsieur Dylan would need them, all three of them. He was a man of ideas too high, and any trouble might be bad trouble.

They were dressed in a flash, Cree quickly lit the fire, and Red Sky opened the door flap for their father. "Monsieur Dylan," he said, "come outside."

White Raven led them all behind the lodge, and in the half-light they saw. They always stored the trade goods staked down under the oiled cloth, for the lodge was too small. In the night someone had pulled the stakes, opened the *pièces*, scattered things about, and probably done some stealing.

"Ermine Head," said White Raven and Cree at once.

Dylan said, "The whiskey."

The two kegs were gone.

What the bloody hell. He looked into Cree's eyes and

then into her father's. He didn't need to be told. Cree's ex-husband was getting drunk somewhere, and getting others drunk, and there would be trouble, and Shaking Plume would blame Dylan for it. After all, Dylan brought the whiskey into these people's world.

He turned to White Raven. "Will they mix it with water?" The Piegans to the north would know to dilute the pure alcohol, but these warriors might not. If they didn't, it would kill them.

White Raven nodded. "They will. It is probably Ermine Head and his friends." From the tone, not young men White Raven respected.

"We must stop them," said White Raven, his eyes meeting Dylan's.

Dylan nodded.

In the lodge he strapped on his knives, stuck a pistol in his sash, and primed his rifle.

He looked at his wives before he went out. On Cree's face was a look of sorrow. On Red Sky's, exultation.

The young men were gambling at the hoop-and-pole game. No one was watching for trouble. They could hardly play. If they'd started out to provoke a fight, ready and alert, they were now just drunk. White Raven felt disgusted.

Hoop and pole was a game of coordination of hand and eye—you rolled a hoop the size of the palm of your hand, with a target in the center the size of a thumb joint, and tried to jab your pole through it, like a spear. They were far too drunk to bring off such a trick. They just thrust and missed and fell and rolled in their dirt and laughed. No one was sober enough to score and actually win a bet.

To quell his disgust, White Raven reminded himself that these were young men, mostly still in their teens, and as yet had no sense of responsibility to the people. Young men never did.

Ermine Head in fact was old enough to move up to the next men's society, but he stayed back with his younger brother-friend, Tail Feathers. This was another sign of his immaturity. White Raven wondered why he had ever let his eldest daughter marry such a man, even if he himself had struck the match when they were still children.

He looked at his son-in-law's face and wondered if this one was more grown-up than Ermine Head and his friends. He thought probably so. If not, Monsieur Dylan could use this confrontation to grow up a little. Life was full of opportunities.

Dylan saw that one keg was empty—broken open, in fact, stomped on or slammed down somehow. This would be simple. He walked right among the young men sprawled out on the ground, and stood the other keg on its end. It was mostly full.

He looked at them one by one. He wished he knew which one was Ermine Head—he felt stupid not knowing. And which one was Tail Feathers.

"Are the Piegans cowards?" said Dylan, doing his best version of a snarl. "And thieves?"

He felt like working himself into a righteous fury. "Are you children that you come sneaking in the night?" He stomped. He glared. He wanted to erupt with angry accusations, but the Blackfoot words came slowly, and that made him angry. "Are you Dog Faces that you steal from your neighbors?" Nothing would make a Piegan madder than calling him a Dog Face.

"You are not my neighbor." The words were mild, lightly taunting. They came from a youth of striking, handsome dress, nearing twenty, probably, but boyish-looking. He was sitting up—now he stood up. The lad was smiling slightly, showing off in front of his comrades.

Dylan knew how to back him down. He handed White Raven his rifle. Holding the youth's eyes, he raised the keg over his head. Then he turned and slammed it down on a rock. The staves cracked, and the white man's water gushed out onto the ground.

At least no one could get drunk on it now.

Dylan saw too late that the whiskey splattered on the youth's long, quilled breechcloth. Water ruined quillwork.

He decided to brazen it out. "Do you want to complain now, like a girl, about your spoiled clothes?"

Another young man rose up beside the youth. Dylan raged on, "Do you want to fight? Or do you have to have your friend fight for you?"

The youth's kick came with the right leg, but Dylan was ready, grabbed the foot and heaved upward.

The youth went down face first.

Dylan looked at the feathers in the kid's hair. The tail feathers of a magpie, about half a dozen of them.

He stared into the face of the kid's friend, and saw for the first time that his braids were wrapped in ermine skins. Ermine skins arranged so that the small heads stuck out conspicuously, the teeth like thorns.

He had found Ermine Head and his brother-friend Tail Feathers. He felt a pang. Ermine Head was a handsome man with chiseled features. Why were enemies always the sort of men women found attractive?

It was an open-handed slap, and Dylan was not ready for that. It nicked his cheek.

As it came back the other way, Dylan stepped inside it and rammed his knee upward.

Ermine Head turned his hip into the knee. The fellow knew how to tussle.

He made a fancy swirl for another slap.

His feet squirted out from under him on the whiskey-slick earth.

He landed on his back in the booze.

Dylan didn't know what to do. He felt White Raven's hand pull him back. He went.

Ermine Head got up, almost slipped again, and shook his fist at Dylan. He bellowed some Blackfoot words Dylan was too agitated to understand.

Well, Dylan told himself, you've teased the bear, and now it's mad.

"My son," said White Raven, "you may have to kill him."

They were in the Frenchman's lodge. White Raven and his daughters had been out and about the camp, listening. Ermine Head was bragging that he would kill the Frenchman. The Frenchman was full of lies. The Frenchman had insulted him. So Ermine Head had sworn a blood oath.

Nothing would be said, of course, about Dylan taking Ermine Head's wife. It would be beneath a Piegan's dignity to fight for a woman.

"He is painting himself now," said White Raven.

White Raven wondered if Monsieur Dylan understood the gravity of Ermine Head's oath. He was afraid of offending Monsieur Dylan. You didn't tell a man what even a youth knew. Ermine Head could not back down. One of the two would probably be dead today. Perhaps Monsieur Dylan could beat Ermine Head within an inch of his life, but . . .

"He is painting himself," White Raven repeated, hoping that the Frenchman understood what was unspoken.

Dylan looked at his father-in-law. He did understand the painting, and appreciated the mute effort to warn him. The clown was getting his personal medicine in order. He would have seen some animal spirits in a dream, and would consider them his advisors, perhaps his protectors. He would dress himself and paint his face and body as they had shown him in the dream. Then, his world in order, he would face any danger.

"He said he doesn't need medicine to rid the people of a Frenchman." But not to paint would be a defiance of the powers. So that was an empty brag. "He says he doesn't need weapons to kill a Frenchman," added White Raven.

"Can I rely on that?" asked Dylan.

"He will carry a knife, probably two," White Raven said simply.

Dylan looked into Cree's eyes and saw her fear. Him too. The thought of a blade made his flesh crawl.

"Is Weasel Head a good fighter?"

Dylan had decided for his own amusement to call Ermine Head, Weasel Head. By converting the winter pelt to the summer one, he made Weasel ugly instead of beautiful. And danger was ugly.

White Raven's eyes registered the change of name, but he only shrugged. "He practices all the time with his friends, and has a great reputation among them. They are only boys. And he doesn't have the medicine for this."

Dylan just looked at the old man. In his experience, quickness and savvy and strength and steel won fights, not medicine.

"I will go with you," said White Raven. He let that sit a minute.

Dylan supposed the old man was simply showing support. He nodded his gratitude at White Raven.

"I will watch for Tail Feathers," said White Raven.

Dylan looked sharply at the old man. That particular treachery hadn't occurred to him. Again he nodded his gratitude.

"I think you will have to kill Ermine Head," White Raven said gently. Odd, that such information could be communicated gently. "He is a brutal man. His rages take him beyond fear." Dylan wondered what brutality and rage Cree had felt from the ugly Weasel Head. Maybe he could just cut the man's features so they looked brutal forever. "You might get away with beating him until he almost dies. Or crippling him. But then he would always be your enemy. Worse, his father and uncles and brothers and friends would be your enemies. Better to kill."

Dylan wondered whether it was true, he would have to kill or be killed. There was nothing he wanted less than killing. You didn't cement your relationship with a people with murder. By making the family carry a grudge against you. But that was just his excuse, he knew.

He looked at his hands. He couldn't imagine killing anyone. He couldn't imagine looking at his very hands, the hands that brought food to his lips, and touched Cree intimately, knowing that they had taken life. He was still a white man.

Uncertain, he said to everyone at large, White Raven and his wives, "I will prepare myself."

He took off his pants, to leave his feet and legs freer and faster.

He thought a moment and got out the military coat. He had brought it as a present for an important man. In this case a farewell gift to Shaking Plume. Indians loved showy coats like this—midnight-blue, with gold and silver trim. Dylan thought he would wear it. He liked the martial look it gave him. Unbuttoned, it would move freely, not hindering his arms. The thick-woven material would provide some protection against the slashes of a blade. Yes, it was a good idea.

First he would add something. He got a string of hawk bells and tied them to his sash, outside the hips. He would not sneak. He'd ding-a-ling while he walked and while he fought. Not timid music but an honest pealing and chiming. He would make a joyful sound under the sun.

He saw White Raven's puzzlement, and smiled at his friend. The bells were good.

When he was in the jacket, he asked Cree for use of a hand mirror he'd given her. She showed him his image. That was when he remembered Captain Chick in a similar scarlet jacket, also bare-breasted beneath, corrupt king of all he beheld.

Dylan also saw again the pink scars along his cheekbones, and they gave him an idea. He went to one of the *pièces,* found the right parfleche, and rummaged until he came up with the vermilion he'd brought to trade to Indian women. Using the mirror and a stick, he drew a thin line along the top of one scar, inspected himself, and drew another line on the bottom edge of the scar. He liked the effect. Not what he thought of when he first dreamed the slashes, or saw them painted on Fore's face, but related to that. A blood relative, he thought with ironic satisfaction. He repeated it on the other side. He liked the stripes. A soldier's stripes, in blood red.

He turned to White Raven and to his wives, and saw from their faces that he looked imposing. Then it occurred to him, for the first time, that like Weasel Head, he had painted his face as he saw it in a dream.

As Dylan finished painting his face, White Raven contemplated what his new son-in-law did not know, which could cost him his life. He pondered what he must tell Monsieur Dylan, and what he must hold back.

"I wish to speak with you a little, my son," said White Raven. The old man hoped Monsieur Dylan noticed that he was being treated as a true son-in-law.

Cree and Red Sky moved to the back of the lodge, giving an impression of privacy for the men. Then Red Sky circled behind everyone and slipped out of the door flap. White Raven wondered where his daughter was going. Why she couldn't stay with the family at a time like this? Why she couldn't act like a woman? But he had another task to accomplish right now.

"Killing a man is a hard thing," said White Raven.

He watched Monsieur Dylan's face for a reaction. He hoped that his son-in-law was not one of those sick in spirit who killed easily, casually. He saw that he had guessed the young man's feelings truly.

"Even an enemy has something of Napi in him." Napi, the Blackfoot Creator. "A fellow Piegan . . . a hard thing."

He waited again. "It feels wrong. It is wrong, always, when it is a personal act, an act of anger, an act of the unknown, even an act of self-defense."

He held Dylan's eyes. Probably Monsieur Dylan was wondering what this old man was trying to do to him.

"In this case the people of this village know it is right," said White Raven, looking fixedly at Dylan. The young foreigner would not have noticed that the people were taking no action to stop the childishness. They let Ermine Head make a fool of himself. None of his relatives interfered. None of the village elders put an end to Ermine Head's bragging and taunting. After long tolerance, they were letting Ermine Head suffer the consequences of his foul-spiritedness.

Of course, Ermine Head might kill Monsieur Dylan. In that case Monsieur Dylan was a man of foul spirit too, and the people would be well rid of him.

"Ermine Head has acted with ill spirit toward the people. Toward other young men and women. Toward my family. Toward my daughter."

White Raven saw receptivity in Dylan's eyes. He plunged forward now, seizing his opportunity. "It is not your will that Ermine Head should suffer for his actions, but ours. The will of the people and of the spirits. The will of life itself.

"When you raise your arm against him, it is not a personal act. It is not you who strikes down Ermine Head. It is us. It is spirit. It is life." After a moment White Raven added, "We will merely act with your hands."

When they stood up to go to the fray, Dylan jingled. His mind was far from the bells, and it brought him up short. He smiled to himself. If he was going to die, he wanted to go out ringing.

Dylan and White Raven stood in the middle of the great circle of tipis, with solemn bearing. Normally the circle would be full of children and dogs playing. Men would be crossing on their way here or there. Women would be sitting outside their lodges, watching the children while they worked on the hides from the recent hunt. The village would be a hubbub of shouts and laughter and complaints and yaps.

The circle was deserted as a graveyard.

Dylan had given White Raven his pistol, loaded and primed. He had his throwing knives strapped comfortably to the back of the brigade jacket. He had his belt knife on his hip. He had a trade knife tucked into his sash in back. He even had his patch knife in the little inside pocket of the jacket, a foolish thing to carry, but like the bells, it made him feel better. He didn't know how fair a fight this was going to be. He didn't even know where Weasel Head was. He looked at White Raven questioningly.

White Raven shrugged as though to say, Maybe he's gone hunting.

Maybe he's gone to steal some Crow women for Père Noël. Maybe the bastard is holding you in his sights from a tree.

Dylan would wait.

*   *   *

Weasel Head made them wait forever, probably over an hour. Then, suddenly, White Raven coughed softly and looked hard at the far end of the circle, opposite the horns. Weasel had simply materialized there. He was wrapped in a red blanket from eyebrow to toenail. Dylan couldn't see what weapons he had.

"Wait," White Raven said under his breath.

But that was not Dylan's way. That was the way of sneaks and thieves and men of New Spain who fought with knives, and maybe the way of Piegans, but it was not a white-man way, or of a man brave enough to wear bells when he fought. Dylan walked steadily, almost quickly toward his opponent.

Weasel disappeared.

Dylan marched after him relentlessly. He could only be behind a lodge, sneaking and hiding. White Raven followed at a respectful distance. Dylan didn't want to hear his warnings anyway. He wanted to meet this malevolence head-on and squash it.

A whirl of scarlet.

A blanket falling from a tree limb.

A scuffling sound from the other direction.

Dylan dodged sideways hard.

Weasel roared as he flew by, his knife hand arcing toward Dylan.

Dylan felt the pull on his shoulder and spun and ended on his feet, balanced, ready.

Weasel was grinning at him, also balanced and ready, knife held low. His face was painted in vertical halves, yellow on the left, red on the right. White dots the size of bird's eggs speckled it. In some eerie way it made him more handsome and more cruel, like this was the appearance he was meant to have, seductive and repellent at once.

Weasel said something low and taunting. He cackled, like this was play. Dylan had decided not to let himself understand any Blackfoot words. There was no need to know anything but what the man's hands and feet were doing.

Weasel backed away, then turned and walked away from the circle.

Dylan felt his shoulder, and his hand came away

bloody. The first charge of the fray had nearly been serious. The thick jacket had saved him from a disabled left
arm.

He watched Weasel a moment, and followed.

He supposed White Raven would keep him from getting shot. Or at least shoot the murderer. Dylan couldn't
afford to think about that. Or think at all. He needed his
mind for feint, parry, and thrust.

Weasel let himself be seen intermittently. And be
heard—he jabbered whatever it was he was jabbering,
pointlessly. It was like following a noisy crow that would
fly, land on a limb, and caw teasingly at you. But this
crow would finally turn and attack.

Dylan walked slowly and steadily after his foe, jingling. He wondered if the jingling unnerved Weasel Head.
Weasel led him west, upstream, along the bluffs that faced
the river. The bastard stayed close to the bluffs, Dylan well
away. He was wondering where Tail Feathers was.

Weasel climbed the rocks and showed himself about
twenty feet up. Dylan stood out among the cottonwoods,
waiting. He had no intention of giving Weasel an advantage with the high ground. To show his patience, he sat
down twenty paces from the rocks and lit his white clay
pipe. He got up and moved another twenty paces away and
sat. White Raven stood nearby, eyes and ears alert.

Weasel stood and watched and cawed at them. Dylan
could imagine the smirk on his face. It would do him no
good. Dylan meant to make sure they would fight on level
ground, and just the two of them. He was thinking that
with self-satisfaction when he heard shouts from the river
behind him, male and female cries.

White Raven ran toward the river. Dylan sat and kept
an appearance of calm and watched Weasel.

In two minutes White Raven was back with Red Sky
and Tail Feathers. The teenager who thought himself a
warrior had his arms pinned with a rawhide rope, and Red

Sky held the other end of it. Humiliation was splashed all over Tail Feathers' face.

White Raven said briefly that Tail Feathers had been hiding behind a cutbank with an arrow notched. Red Sky said she'd gotten close to him by walking in the river, and roped him. . . .

Dylan said he would hear the story later. He was watching Weasel fiercely now.

White Raven ordered Red Sky to take Tail Feathers to camp and tell everyone what he'd done. He said a woman would be plenty to march such a sneak and coward into camp, all trussed up.

"They would have shot you with an arrow and then stabbed through the wound to make it look like a knife thrust," said White Raven.

Dylan just nodded, and waited.

Finally, out of choices, Weasel came into the cottonwood bottom to have it out. Came in his style, braggadocio.

Dylan disregarded the boasts and the insults. He heard the Blackfoot words, but didn't connect them into sentences or meanings in his mind. It was easy. He was keeping his mind on that knife and Weasel's feet. Nothing else mattered.

Weasel sauntered toward him. Went to a tree. Stepped away from it. Until Weasel switched hands with his knife, Dylan didn't notice that the other hand now held a spear. Weasel grinned maliciously.

White Raven eased away from Dylan. Maybe if Weasel did something that was out of bounds, White Raven would protect Dylan with the pistol. The advantage of a spear to a knife evidently wasn't out of bounds.

Weasel dashed forward.

Dylan stepped behind a tree, and Weasel sent up a caterwaul of mockery.

Dylan didn't know if the bastard would throw the spear or try to get close enough to thrust it. The hoop-and-pole game stuck in his mind. They didn't throw the sticks—they thrust them.

Dylan didn't mean to give the bastard a throwing target anyway. But maybe if he did, he could get the spear.

He stepped into the open, his eyes on Weasel's feet. He would have to set his feet to throw hard. The feet didn't move.

In slow, drawn-out Blackfoot, Dylan insulted Weasel. He deliberately did it white-man style because the Piegans didn't use these sorts of insults. He said Weasel's mother was a dog. The best part of Weasel ran down his father's leg, Dylan said. This was a battle of wits, and Dylan claimed to be surprised Weasel came unarmed. Weasel didn't seem to react to any of these taunts. The bastard waited.

Dylan thought of one good Piegan insult. He shouted out that Weasel's real name was One-Unable-to-Marry. Weasel had no relatives, Dylan went on, or at least no Piegan would admit remembering he carried the same blood as Weasel.

Now the weaselly man came forward, sidewise, approaching his quarry obliquely.

Dylan's throat vised. When he told himself this was what he wanted, an end to the matter, the spasm eased a little.

Weasel slipped his knife into his belt and reached into a rotten place at the base of a cottonwood. His arm came back with a shield made of buffalo hide. Which would do damn well, Dylan admitted to himself, at deflecting thrown knives.

Now Weasel came on more confidently. Dylan stood his ground. He didn't think Weasel would throw the spear. Too much chance of losing it.

Dylan was going to have to get in close to cut his enemy. How would he get inside that spear point?

No, he realized. Not close. He stuck his belt knife into his sash, and put his right hand on the hilt of one of his throwing knives. He kept his left hand down. Didn't want to give away his plan.

He thought of White Raven's words: Not your hands, but ours.

That felt good. This man's life should be ended. Life itself would strike the blow, with Dylan's hands. Good.

Weasel circled. Dylan thought he was uncertain.
Good.

Weasel circled. Dylan faced him.

Weasel circled.

And charged.

Weasel thrust the spear, but Dylan was already in the
air, kicking the spear away, kicking the shield, kicking
Weasel.

But Weasel didn't go down.

Somehow Dylan was jabbed. When the spear jerked
out, he fell heavily on his back.

He tried to roll to get up, and felt the agony. His inside right thigh, next to his balls.

He slapped at the spear. It raked his side.

He was on his back, the pain roaring, and he couldn't
roll, couldn't get up, and now Weasel would come.

He sat up, both hands to his shoulder blades. Weasel
smiled the smile of triumph.

The right-hand knife whisked toward Weasel's groin.

The shield started down to block it.

The left-hand knife socketed in his throat.

It pierced to its handle, its point up.

Dylan vomited.

He looked at the wound on his inner thigh. It was
bad. The flint spearhead had gone in at least an inch and
been jerked out.

Then he saw the bright red blood pumping out.
Pumping, then dribbling, then pumping again.

He knew what that blood was.

He was going to die.

It was all right. He had let the force of the people, or
of life, flow through him. He rode that force to his death.

His eyesight glazed. He fell back toward the earth.
The last thing he heard was the tinkling of his bells.

Chapter
Thirty-Two

It was a thin and distant wail, a melodic arc singing no human scale, repeating and repeating, infinitely repeating.

He wondered if he was hearing the music of the spheres. On his way to hell.

But, no, he was being touched from time to time, touched in some sort of rhythm with the music, and he needed to pee.

It was clear, absolutely clear, that he couldn't move. Immobility was a new and permanent condition of his life, like sinfulness. He couldn't get up to pee. He let go where he lay. After a moment he heard a hollow sound that told him he was squirting into something.

He took a chance and let his eyes open.

Swirling impressions. Half darkness. Flickering shadows made by a fire. Hands. An ancient face. Thin and distant singing.

He passed out.

Hands on his leg. Something wet and cool on his inner thigh, like river mud.

A dry cloth wiping his wet forehead.

Oblivion.

The music again. Odd, illogical music, a soughing of the wind or voices, he couldn't tell. It came to him that he was hearing the music of the other side. In his case it must be devil music. He smiled.

The music stopped. A voice murmured. The devil welcoming him to hell. He tried to think of something witty to say, and felt his lips moving clumsily, and heard a bestial sound from himself.

Two or three voices making sounds that were not words. Speak English, you devils, he thought to himself.

A cool, damp skin wiped his forehead and his face, and he realized he was feverish.

It was the strangest human face he'd ever seen. Very old, with webs of cracks, like the old porcelain his father had. Wizened, shrunk, full of hollows. Toothless. Hair black and thick as a young person's. Eyes deeply recessed, black and fathomless.

It leaned forward, and he saw the foot of a big bird of some kind, perhaps an owl, thonged tight against the collarbone. If there was a person connected to the head, it was kneeling between his legs.

Then it opened its mouth, and he saw widely separated teeth, like splayed fingers, behind the lips. The maw opened, and the head bent toward his groin.

Panic fluttered him into unconsciousness.

Sharp pain brought him awake. The head was still between his thighs. Hands were holding his arms and legs down.

Pain again, and he bellowed.

Hands rose from between his thighs, and he saw a flake of obsidian with blood on the edge, and maybe pus mixed with the blood. His mind was better now—he knew pus and blood for what they were.

The ancient face was smiling. He knew now that it was the face of a woman, a very old woman.

Hands with skin thin as parchment brought a piece of bone, like a whistle, to the wrinkled lips. Her lips smiled at him, but her eyes were black and fathomless still. "I must suck the poison out," her lips said.

Her head bent to his groin, and he floated away in pain.

Soon he heard from between his legs the sounds of spitting.

It came to him that she spoke the words in the Blackfoot language. All the words he'd been hearing were in the Blackfoot language. He smiled at himself. Speak English, you devils, he'd ordered mockingly. Or French, the language of fashionable demons.

He turned a quarter of the way over. His groin screamed when he moved. Then it throbbed. The only escape was sleep.

It was raining hot water. Unbelievable—it was raining hot water. He felt it on his face, his chest, which must be bare, his arms, his naked belly and groin and legs.

The thin, distant wailing again.

Drops again, almost too hot to stand.

He didn't open his eyes—he was too scared. He was among devils. Or Piegans. He chuckled evilly. Piegans and devils, the same thing.

Her name was Owl Claw, she said. She wasn't kneeling between his thighs now, and that was a relief. Cree was sitting beside him. He felt very lucid now, even able to understand Owl Claw's Blackfoot words.

She had a friendly but businesslike manner. She had labored several days against the foulness in him, she said, and now he was stronger than it. The foulness had made him hot and sweaty and cold and clammy, it had taken over his mind and made him crazy, but she had purged it.

She was folding things into hide wraps and putting them into a parfleche. Dylan supposed this was her medical kit, and he was glad to see the instruments of torture go away. Actually, he knew it was her medicine bundle, a collection of sacred objects that should be looked upon only with profound reverence.

As she stood, he looked at the owl foot thonged against her ancient neck. Owl Claw, he thought. This must be the woman Red Sky—his wife Red Sky—said she must see to decide her future. He wondered what this medical doctor could tell Red Sky.

She said she'd come back to see him this evening and left. Red Sky left with her.

Dylan looked around. Cree was still sitting next to him, looking at him. Looking at him fondly, perhaps.

"You're going to get well," she said.

Dylan nodded. He said, "Tell me exactly what Owl Claw did to me."

Yes, she would tell him while she spooned broth into his mouth.

It was maddening. He was up against taboo again, against some Piegan custom where you weren't allowed to know what was happening, or to admit you knew what was happening. Like you were supposed to pretend your mother-in-law wasn't there, like you neither saw nor heard her, and certainly couldn't speak to her. Like you weren't allowed to know what was in a medicine bundle, and if you saw some item by accident, you were not supposed to look upon it or ever acknowledge you knew it existed.

The white people pretended ladies didn't have legs or wear undergarments and got with child by divine intervention. Indians thought all of these pretenses beyond belief. They only pretended they didn't have mothers-in-law, and made impenetrable secrets of healing methods, and diligently obscured the nature of their relationships with spirits that were only imaginings anyway.

Regardless, the story was that Owl Claw lanced his infected wound repeatedly with a piece of obsidian, used an eagle-wing bone to suck the pus out, spat out the poison, poulticed the wound with herbs and other substances known only to her, bathed him with cold water to keep his fever down, sprinkled hot water on him with a buffalo tail or by blowing through the hollow bone of an eagle wing. That was the practical part. The mystical part was that she blew the eagle-bone whistle over him, made the wing and head and body motions of her spiritual helper the owl, and sang magic songs to cast out the devils, songs given to her in visions.

Sorry, but Dylan was in an impatient, white-man mood. Now that he knew all was hidden behind veils of mystery, he didn't feel like contemplating the magic Owl Claw worked, or even hearing any more about it.

But he was grateful. He didn't doubt that the old woman saved his life. He felt most glad to have that life. He was not done adventuring.

It occurred to him that he didn't know what he wanted. The only answer he could think of, immediately, was that he wanted what he felt at that dawn on the hill above camp, when he'd read Byron all night for the first time, and he watched the sun rise, and he knew things in a way beyond what thinking could help you know. It was like hearing the music that was always playing but not always audible, and feeling the miracle within it.

Or he wanted to swing again on the bell ropes, and soar up and down, and be inside the peals.

He thought about Ermine Head being gone to the sand hills, as the Piegans put it. His body would be up on a scaffold somewhere, protected from the birds only by a blanket, drying in the sun and wind, sightless, unable to hear, powerless to feel the rising sun or hear birdsong, to taste meat or feel the touch of a woman, or even to feel the warm winds and cold winds that would sough and sigh and whip and bluster and blast and finally turn that body into desiccated scraps.

Dylan felt very good to be alive.

He said so to Cree.

She put the bowl and the spoon down and took one of his hands in both of hers. She leaned over and put her cheek against his forehead.

"Do you know what Cree Medicine means in our language?" she asked him.

Dylan shook his head no. He was getting tired, but it was good to feel her hand, to hear her voice.

"I am named after one of my grandmothers," Cree said. "This was a grandmother who had no children." Cree took a deep breath and let it out. "Her sister was Owl

Claw's mother. The way of this first Cree Medicine was to live without a man, as Owl Claw does. She had strong dreams, and many animal spirits came to her to offer their power. She was revered among the people, as Owl Claw is.

"One of her powers was to make the medicine of love. If a young man asked her, she gave him a song that would charm his beloved, persuade her to stand in his blanket with him, or go to the willows with him. Or she could carve a love flute that would make music to enchant the girl." Cree smiled mischievously.

Dylan was sleepy but attended carefully to Cree's words. He felt her touch and her care as a refuge.

"This kind of medicine, the power to make people love, we call Cree Medicine, because we used to get it from the Crees. It is a special feeling, this love, and sometimes a madness. Most of us bind ourselves to a man or a woman out of affection, but not this kind of love. It is power, brings either fortune or misfortune." She fumbled for words. "It is power, is grand but dangerous."

She bent over and kissed him lightly on the lips. "When I was born, Cree Medicine was a very old woman. My father asked her to choose my name. The honored people among us choose names for the newborn. She gave away her name to me. She told my parents the name would be fortunate for me, that I would feel this love and it would not make me mad. She also said I would be Cree Medicine in myself, that I would find a man who would be especially blessed and empowered, and I would love him. . . ." His wife paused thoughtfully. "She also said that something about me would enchant a man and make him want me."

He felt her hand get a little tense.

"I always knew that Ermine Head was not for me. Our fathers matched us when we were young, before I started the moon-bleeding. Often it turns out well to be matched with a man you respect and who treats you well but you feel only affection for. But I knew my medicine set me out to feel something grand. So I knew Ermine Head was not the one."

She sighed. "I defied him. I provoked him. I was insolent to him. He was right to beat me. I deserved it. But," she said, "I was trying to put an end to that marriage so I could go on to my calling.

"When we were kidnapped," she went on, "I was glad. I knew the right man was not in our tribe. When I first saw you, I did not know you are the man. But when you sat down to talk to Red Sky and me about escape, I began to understand your heart. The day you told us the story of the day you rang the bells, I knew completely, thrillingly.

"I also saw that you were small-hearted for the time being, made sad by something. I heard that you had a child and no woman, that your woman died, and another child. You never spoke of this, but others told me. I knew you thought you could not yet love me, or any woman. But I knew I possessed the gift that could heal you, that had the power to revive your spirit, the Cree Medicine. This is the gift I bring to our marriage.

"My Cree Medicine is my way, my power, and now our power. Others are different. Each person has his way, his power." She got an odd look in her eye. "The first woman of this name. Owl Claw. Red Sky. Each follows her own medicine—there is no choice.

"From the beginning I saw that you wanted me, and I saw that you fought against it. But I am Cree Medicine, and I felt the power of it. I knew you would take me for your woman, that you would love me. That is my power."

She kissed him dryly on the lips, as she knew he liked in his white-man way, with a hint of lingering.

"Perhaps you don't know even yet how much you love me, but I do," said Cree. "It is the gift I bring to you, this Cree Medicine. It is a dangerous thing, and an ecstasy."

When Dylan stopped sleeping most of the time, on the second evening, he realized he hadn't seen Red Sky. He asked Cree where she was. With Owl Claw, Cree said, and changed the subject.

When he asked again the next evening, Cree expanded her answer to, "With Owl Claw, mostly in the sweat lodge."

He wondered why the two women would sweat repeatedly. That normally meant getting purified for other ceremonies or deeds, but he knew of no ceremonies women would be purifying themselves for at the beginning of winter, not the beaver ceremonies, not the sun dance ceremonies, not any. He told himself that where Red Sky was concerned, there was no use asking because there was no understanding.

The next day, when Cree said Red Sky had gone to seek a vision in the traditional way, Dylan knew for sure there was no understanding. Women didn't go on vision quests. Even men did not go in the winter. Exasperated, he gave up struggling to understand. He had Cree in his robes, and despite his injury, she was beginning to feel good again, and that was enough.

In four days Dylan was up and walking around and feeling chipper. He tired easily, though, and joked to Cree that Owl Claw had sucked not only the pus, but the strength out of him. Cree's reaction told him he shouldn't make that sort of joke.

Instead she brought up the subject of gifts to be made to Owl Claw. Normally, three horses would be about right, she thought. But Dylan needed to be seen as a generous man in the tribe, as all leaders were generous men. So four horses.

Dylan pointed out a little testily that he didn't have any horses. Cree shrugged. He would, after he did some trading. And she would tell everyone that he would trade tomorrow morning. He started to protest. Rubbish, said Cree, you can trade sitting down.

She had another subject to bring up. Ermine Head's family was finished with grief for now. They accepted what had happened, or accepted as much as they ever would. Shaking Plume had forbidden them firmly to seek revenge, and Cree believed Dylan was safe. But he was never to mention the event to the people of this village, much less boast of it. If ever he counted coup's, he was not to mention his fight with Ermine Head. Her tone indicated that was all, and enough said.

He was finding out how a sits-beside-him wife, obliged to be outwardly submissive, could run her husband.

The trading was good. He got about the same prices as he would have at Fort Augustus. He thought about asking more—these people didn't have to go all the way to Augustus—but with nods and glances, Cree kept his prices moderate. He was obliged to trade for those four horses, and Cree made them not just any four specimens of horseflesh. They were first-class animals, young, not yet trained as war-horses or buffalo runners, but splendid beasts. They were inordinately expensive.

His take wasn't much. He hadn't brought many trading goods to start with—he and the sisters traveled light—and the fine ponies cut far into it. He only hoped that he'd accomplished something much more important, establishing a valuable trading connection.

He walked as far as Owl Claw's lodge with Cree to stake out the horses. A woman of middle age, whom Cree introduced as Elk-Crying-in-the-River, came out of the lodge, talked quietly with Cree, disappeared in the direction of the women's lodge, and brought Owl Claw back.

Dylan really saw Owl Claw now for the first time. Though her face was wizened, her body was still plump and ripe-looking. She was huge-breasted. Her eyes seemed mysterious, and she spoke as though coming back to earth from a distant realm.

She accepted the horses gracefully, though the gift did not seem important to her. She seemed eager to be on her way.

As they walked back to their lodge, Cree explained that Owl Claw and Red Sky were alternately in the women's lodge and the sweat lodge, purifying themselves and counseling.

"I have had a dream," said Red Sky. She smiled broadly. Her quest for a vision had been fulfilled, she was telling them. It gave her a new confidence. Yet as she spoke around the center fire, after dinner in the lodge, she also felt tremulous.

"I do not see everything yet, but I want to tell you what I do see." Bold words for a woman. Her message was as much her manner as her words.

"I will not be a mother," Red Sky went on. "I will follow the way of the warrior." Cree made a little closed-mouth cry and covered her face with both hands up to her eyes. "Understand, this is not the way of men. It is the way of the woman warrior, which is . . . its own. I will learn the arts of war and the hunt. As I do that, I will stop the every-month-bleeding. This much I know."

Red Sky let the words be, and waited to see if her sister and the man who was half her husband had anything to say.

Dylan was flabbergasted.

"When the bleeding stops, I hope to grow muscular like a man, and strong and fast like a man. If I am greatly blessed, the people will sing of my coups."

After a considerable wait, Red Sky at Morning went on. "I do not see all yet. Owl Claw and I have talked a lot, and I think I know the way, but she says to be patient and accept the guidance of my helping spirit, which is the calling eagle." Red Sky waited a little, and spoke the next words with quiet clarity, even luminosity. "If ever I marry, many years from now, I will marry women. And perhaps, after my years of hunting and war, like Owl Claw in old age I will learn the mysteries of healing for the benefit of the people."

She said all this with some of the eagerness of a teenager, yet with the serenity of someone much older and wiser.

"Owl Claw says all of this may yet change, that the ways of women like me are many. That my medicine may change. I don't think so. I respect her word, but I don't think so."

Cree went forward on her knees and embraced her sister. Red Sky wiped away tears. When they parted, Dylan said the words of a blessing White Raven had spoken: "Napi, Father the Sun, give Red Sky light, that her path may be free from danger."

Red Sky pressed his hand—it was good of the Frenchman to understand so well. She got up and said she wanted to tell her mother and father and would be back soon.

Dylan felt stupefied. Dru had hinted that on the Missouri he would see into the mysteries of life. What he seemed to see was only that life was a changeling, something unexpected, a shape shifter, the coyote-trickster of legend, always assuming mysterious forms in the blowing mists.

He asked Cree, "Owl Claw lives with a woman?"

Cree looked at him openly and nodded. "They live as man and woman." She pondered a moment and murmured, *"sakwo'mapi akikwan."* He supposed it meant something like "lesbians."

After taking this amazement in, he asked, "Did Owl Claw ever marry? A man?"

Cree nodded. "She has four children. When she came to the age of the end of every-moon-bleeding, she left her husband to live with an older woman who lived as a man." Cree let it sit for a moment. "Now she lives with a younger woman."

As long as he was dealing in amazement, Dylan thought, he might as well plunge on recklessly. "Why did Red Sky say her every-moon-bleeding would stop?"

Cree spoke solemnly, a little as though explaining great things to a child. "It is a strong medicine, the every-moon-bleeding. Any bleeding is strong medicine. No one can hunt, or fight enemies, with the spirits deafened by the clamor of blood medicine, which interferes with the other medicine."

Dylan pondered. In Red Sky he had lost a wife he had never had. More pertinently, he felt he'd lost a friend. Maybe one day he'd gain a hunting partner. He was nonplussed.

In perhaps half an hour Red Sky came back from her parents' lodge. She still looked radiant, and now her face

was gleaming with tears. In silence she picked up her
robes, rolled them, tied them, shouldered them and left the
lodge.

Dylan and Cree stepped outside and watched her
walk toward the lodge of Owl Claw and Elk Crying-in-
the-River. In the early winter night she seemed to Dylan
brave, lonely, and forlorn.

White Raven came later that evening and asked
Dylan to come to his lodge tomorrow when the sun was
high. He wanted to give Monsieur Dylan a name.

After White Raven left, before Dylan could ask why,
Cree said it was an honor to have a name among the Piegans. White Raven had asked someone, an older person,
someone of distinction, to choose a name. It would be be-
stowed with ritual and prayer.

Dylan looked askance at his wife. He wasn't a complete ignoramus. When he thought about it, though, he
wondered why he wasn't being adopted. Then he supposed
it was because he was her husband and already a member
of the tribe.

White Raven sat in the place of honor directly behind
the fire. Beside him, in the honored place to the host's left,
sat the old man who owned the beaver bundle. White
Raven told Dylan to sit beside this white-haired and kind-
faced man, Two Runners. Several other men sat to Dylan's
left, and he told himself to remember their names.

To White Raven's right in the circle, Dylan saw
women—Calf Robe first, Owl Claw next, White Raven's
three daughters, and others he didn't know.

White Raven began by tweezing an ember from the
fire and lighting the pipe. He blew smoke four times to the
sun, and one each to the four winds. The pipe was passed
clockwise, and each man smoked. As it passed, whether
away from or toward White Raven, the bowl always
pointed to him.

When all the men had smoked, White Raven set a
coal from the fire on the ground in front of himself and

burned sweetgrass on it. Dylan loved the sweet, incenselike smell it gave off. Then White Raven rubbed himself in the smoke rising from the grass, and chanted this prayer:

This morning Father Sun shines into the lodge.
His power is strong.
Last night Mother Moon shone into the lodge.
Her power is strong.
I pray that Morning Star, when he rises at dawn,
Will shine in and bless us and bring us long life.

Then all joined their voices in chorus:

Mother Earth, have pity on us
And give us food to eat.
Father Sun, bless all our children,
And may our paths be straight.

White Raven looked at Two Runners, and Dylan understood that it was time for the granting of a name. He swung between thrill and panic. What if he got a name that meant nothing to him, or was an embarrassment, like Dog Lifting His Hind Leg?

Cree had told him more of the basics of this name-choosing. Distinguished men were chosen to give names to infants. The men often chose names based on events out of their own lives, perhaps a time they counted coup, or something from a vision they had, perhaps paint they wore or something in their own medicine bundle. Girl children were likely to be named after war deeds of their fathers or other male ancestors, so many of their names mentioned blows—like Strikes Twice—or horses. Young men like Dylan often got new names based on their own exploits, their coups or their dreams. But Dylan had no coups or dreams.

Two Runners reached toward Cree. She took something concealed within her blanket. A string of hawk bells. Dylan hadn't heard them because she was wearing the bells he'd given her.

Then Two Runners began to dance, and to cry out a

song over the light tinkling of the bells. Though Dylan
couldn't understand all the words, stretched out over shifting notes, he soon understood that Two Runners was imitating what he saw the Frenchman do on the day of the
fight, and what White Raven must have told everyone.
Even though Dylan struck a Piegan, the old man was honoring his courage. Dylan watched more solemnly. Then, in
the dance, Two Runners began to mime movements that
had nothing to do with the fight. It took Dylan a while to
understand what Two Runners was imitating. Then he got
it: the old man was swinging on ropes. Dylan's mind
tilted. Time was suspended in dance, song, and the accompanying ting-a-ling of the bells.

When Two Runners stopped, he faced Dylan directly
and spoke oratorically. "These are bells made by the medicine of Frenchmen. In a great lodge one day at sunset, in
the village called Montreal, you rang the great bells there,
bells tall as men, other bells big as lodges. As the bells
rang, you had a vision that called you forth into the world,
seeking coups. You followed that vision, and at last it has
brought you to us. We welcome you, and offer you a
home, a haven from wandering. From this day we will call
you by the name His-Many-Bells-Ringing."

He set the string of bells at the initiate's feet.

Everyone got up and went outside. There the camp
crier waited. When he heard the new name, he walked ceremonially around the circle of lodges, crying it out to all
the people. Over and over he repeated the words His-
Many-Bells-Ringing.

Dylan watched, and tears ran down his face.

Part Five

AT ONE

Chapter
Thirty-Three

Red Sky said eagerly, cockily, "Bells, I want to go after Père Noël. The two of us. I want his scalp." She called him by the English word *Bells* for short. All the other Piegans called him by the one long Piegan word His-Many-Bells-Ringing.

Sometimes an adult, now she was a teenager again. She and Owl Claw came to the lodge after supper. Red Sky accepted Dylan's offer of the pipe like a man, and afterward spoke solemnly of her dreams. She was dreaming, repeatedly, of striking coups. She and Owl Claw saw that for now her medicine was calling her to make coups. They didn't see beyond that.

So now it was Père Noël she wanted. Dylan nodded. Yes, it was right. And it was like her. Too bold, too brazen, too . . .

He told her they didn't know who Père Noël was. It was a silly name, he explained, calling yourself after a saint, one of the Frenchman spirits. He started to say it was like a Piegan calling himself Napi or Natosi, Sun or Moon, or Kakatoo-se Poka, Star Boy, or Scarface. Foolishness, or a macabre joke. But Dylan stopped himself halfway through. Calling yourself Santa Claus was merely naughty. The Blackfoot equivalents were sacrilegious.

"I want him," said Red Sky, smiling.

He explained they didn't know where the fellow was.

He built a fort at the Minnetaree villages, she said. Someone there will know.

It's nearly winter, Dylan complained.

"Then the raid will bring us more honor," said Red Sky.

He was stumped.

"Père Noël treated me like a slave," Red Sky said. Dylan wondered if she meant especially a sexual slave. "I'm going to scalp his cod hairs." There was an edge in this.

There was nothing bloodier than a woman, thought Dylan.

Owl Claw said quietly, "It is her medicine."

Later Dylan talked with Cree about it. "She can only go with you," Cree said. "Or alone. Our men won't go with her. She might bleed."

"What about me? Why would I go with her?"

Cree grinned. "You're a Frenchman—you're crazy." She hesitated. "Really, your medicine is different. You're a Frenchman."

One day soon he would correct her to Welshman. She would explain to the others that it was a kind of Frenchman.

Yes, she wanted Dylan to help her sister. It was only the moon after the first snowfall, November. The river was icy, but the plains were open. The horses would go well now. The snows would come, true. She thought they should go to the Mandan villages first, then Dylan and Red Sky would go off and do their deeds, and all would spend the winter among the Mandans. With Dylan's friend the Druid. Maybe the Druid would want to strike coups with them.

He suspected the sisters had worked it out beforehand.

True, she went on, it was nearly one moon to the Mandans, the way a village traveled. But they would travel light, without the furs he traded for, and go as men at war went, very swiftly. They could be at the Mandans in a week, she claimed. There they could find out about Père Noël.

She fell silent. Yes, she had it all worked out. He wondered if she had even more worked out.

"I'd like to spend the winter with the Druid," admitted Dylan.

"Tomorrow morning," he said, "I will trade for good horses." First-class animals, two per rider. "Tell Red Sky we leave at dawn the next day."

Cree smiled. "You must keep Red Sky on a tight rein," she said. "She may not want to wait to go to the Mandans and back to the Minnetarees."

Dylan nodded. "Why does she talk about scalping his . . . ?"

"Because she's angry," said Cree, sounding irritated at Dylan for not understanding. "She's a woman not meant for men, and Père Noël frigged her." Piegans spoke words about sex without hesitation or embarrassment, both men and women. Cree let that sit until Dylan nodded.

"Also," Cree said wickedly, "she probably wants a pouch made of his scrotum."

Dylan blinked at her.

"I'm serious," said Cree, breaking into a grin now. "They make nice, soft pouches. But with human males you need three or four to get one big enough."

Dru heard a scratch at the lodge door, called out "Come in," and Dylan stepped through. It was emotional for Dru, but he restrained himself. They embraced, and then Dru pulled back, afraid he was embarrassing Dylan. Anastasie hugged him too, with less scruple. As they embraced, the two Piegan slave women came in behind. So.

Dylan introduced Cree Medicine as his wife. He seemed not to know how to speak of Red Sky, but Dru and Anastasie pretended not to notice his embarrassment, and made both women welcome as family.

If he hadn't taken the girl to wife, how did Dylan come to be traveling with her? Well, the laddo had an attraction to sticky candy.

Over dinner Dylan got down to business, which meant telling Dru he had some furs cached on the Musselshell and bragging that he had a good friendship with one village of Piegans. They'd be glad for the Welsh Indians to trap in their country, come spring, said Dylan.

The laddo was selling the notion of the friendship because he had but few furs, Dru guessed. Well, he didn't re-
alize how splendid the friendship would be, what a fine
deed he'd done, what a risk he'd taken, and how glad his
father in spirit was to see him hale and hearty.

Dylan also told about their trip here, from the village
on the Musselshell across the plains to the Yellowstone,
downstream, then across to the Little Missouri and down
the Knife River to this village. Only ten days, the laddo
said. Dru let his eyes acknowledge the difficulty to Dylan,
and added, "Well done."

After supper, when Dru got out the pipe, Cree spoke
up, in French. "Monsieur Dylan has a new name," she
said. "His-Many-Bells-Ringing." She gave it as she had
memorized it in English and repeated the name in the
Blackfoot language.

Dru took a long moment. It was fine to show gladness in your face, but not to become sentimental. He lit the
pipe and handed it to Dylan. "A grand name," he permitted himself to say. "A name you have earned. Anastasie
and I will introduce you here, and among all Indian peoples, as His-Many-Bells-Ringing."

He saw that Dylan was deeply pleased by this gesture. Yes, laddo, he thought, immerse yourself utterly.

To Dru's surprise, Red Sky spoke up. She was bold.
She wanted to know where Père Noël was.

Dru didn't know how to answer. He wondered why
she wanted to know about her captor, her slaver. He had
not met this fellow of the silly name, this St. Nicholas.
The man was out on the fall hunt now, imitating the new
American practice of trapping beaver in addition to trading
for them. He should be back soon—the season was late.
Might be back already, for word from the Minnetarees
wasn't always quick, close as they were, just a day's ride.

He told them this much. He didn't add that he had
told the men to make friends with the crew of this St.
Nicholas, a flamboyant and energetic fellow who was admired by the Indians and might have made a worthy ally
and friend.

"She wants to strike coup on him," explained Dylan.
"I will be going with her."

Dru looked at Red Sky as though for the first time. Now he noticed certain touches in her dress, masculine touches, signs he might have picked out before but didn't. Now Dru remembered her boldness in speaking out like a man, and looking him in the eye without deference. Now he understood why she was not Dylan's wife.

He loved Indians. They represented so many more possibilities of living than conventional white people. And life is such a coyote, he thought, its energy expressed through forms myriad, forms strange, forms wondrous.

He glanced at Anastasie and saw awareness in her eyes. This would be a hard thing, going against this man, who now could only make a formidable enemy.

Yet the river flowed into this obstacle, and not some other way.

He looked at Red Sky, at His-Many-Bells-Ringing, back at Red Sky in understanding.

"I will send to the Minnetarees tomorrow to find out about Père Noël," he said. He looked at Red Sky. "Would you accept another companion on this adventure?"

She smiled, and it was the wonderful smile of an innocent and exuberant child. "Gladly," she said.

Fort Minnetaree was a fine place for its size, with a stout palisade and buildings in two corners. It was built a couple of miles from the Minnetaree villages, in a good location above the river, which might eventually provide pasture and tillable fields. As if to declare the owner's style, the logs of the palisade were painted sky-blue, and the second stories of the buildings, where they stuck up like blockhouses, were edged in gold paint. A flamboyant style, Dylan judged. A tiny fort, but a declaration.

Then he saw the sign above the gate. FORT ST. NICHO- LAS, it proclaimed. Dylan almost laughed out loud. Well, everyone called it Fort Minnetaree, which was an improvement.

The owner was absent. Gone until spring, said one of the engagés. The clerk, Mr. Harris, could say more, if he would. *Sacré,* a man never knew about Mr. Harris, a tight *mongol,* an idiot. Not like Père Noël.

When she heard the name Harris, Red Sky refused to go on. They would have to come back in a few days, she said. She absolutely insisted. She offered no explanation, except that Harris was with Père Noël when he took her.

Dylan fumbled for words and found none.

She was their comrade-in-arms; Dru and Dylan yielded, and rode toward home.

Suddenly she said, "Three men have had me. He's one." Which was blunt.

Dylan felt his cod hairs tingle.

Red Sky smiled wickedly at him. "Don't worry," she said, "your scalps are safe. Both of them."

When they came in to see Mr. Harris four days later, Dru traded half their horses for traps. There was plenty of horseflesh among the Piegans, he said, but they couldn't have too many traps. Besides, he didn't want Mr. Harris to think they were spies. Which they were.

Red Sky stood silent, far back, obscure, while Dru traded. She was dressed completely as a man, and her face painted starkly, solid black on the left side and solid red on the right. Dylan was surprised at how much it altered her appearance. It was a face to frighten children.

Harris seemed not to notice. He was a middle-aged man with a thick thatch of sandy hair and a grizzled beard, a pipe always between his teeth, and a sour aspect. If he had a first name, no one seemed to know it, and he referred to himself as Mr. Harris. A Scot now bilious, now gloomy, Dylan decided. Though he seldom appeared to look at the three of them, and seemed not to give a damn about them, Dylan thought Harris was observing everything, and marking in his mind all they said. Competitors, that was what Harris seemed to see, not allies.

Yes, Père Noël was among the Assiniboines. It sounded like Harris told them this in the tone of, The Assiniboines are taken, keep off. Yes, Dylan thought, he would be back in the spring, but Mr. Harris didn't know for how long. Père Noël was the *bourgeois,* and Little Seven was his partisan. Harris was their clerk, not their confidant.

No, said the Druid, they couldn't tell Mr. Harris their business. It would have to wait for Monsieur . . . Noël personally.

Harris didn't offer the name Père Noël was born with.

During the interview, Dylan couldn't keep his eyes off Red Sky. She held her blanket half over her face and peered out from within the folds. She said nothing. Dylan thought her eyes glared at Harris with hatred. Or contempt. Or something.

"It will be a good winter," said Dru. "We'll make one trip to Red River. At a good spot in the weather. Not unreasonable, as you see, if you're careful." They were walking the horses back toward the Mandans, the river in sight. Dru was smiling, relaxed, expansive. "We'll both improve our Blackfoot. That's where the future lies, with those Piegans of Shaking Plume's. These women will teach us."

"And I'll read Byron," said Dylan.

"Aye, laddo." This appeared to amuse Dru. "You read your Byron. A Welshman reading a British bard." Dylan knew—sing your own songs, Dru would say.

Dru pondered a moment. "Know what I used to do? Funny, it is. When I wanted to really get a new language down? I made up verses in it."

He wheezed a laugh at himself. "Verses, really. I'd make nursery ditties. Play with the rhymes, even. Indian languages are easy to rhyme." He looked around at the fine winter day, enjoying himself. "When I worked on Cree, I put little troubadour stories into the Cree tongue for Anastasie and Saga." Dru snorted. "They thought I was utterly mad and rhymes were a form of torture.

"That's how far a Welshman falls, laddo. Instead of writing poesy, he copies off verses in barbarous tongues."

Red Sky. Dylan looked around for her. She was back on the rise, horse and rider dark against the sky.

Dru noticed Dylan's glance and looked tickled. He nodded at Dylan. They both looked back at Red Sky. She raised her hand. Dru raised his in salute. So did Dylan. She turned her pony and disappeared below the ridge line.

"A warrior," said Dru.

"Where's she going?" asked Dylan.

Dru shrugged. "Wherever her warrior spirit takes her," said Dru.

She came back empty-handed, and Dylan was embarrassed at how relieved he felt.

Whatever she'd done, Red Sky hadn't gained any patience. Dru gave her a throwing knife and she beat a tree trunk into a pulp with it. They let her shoot their rifles on occasion. She declared irritably that as soon as she could steal some ponies, she'd have her own gun powder and ball, and shooting pouch.

She sat to the side of the lodge a lot on sunny days and chipped away at the flint she'd brought——Dylan decided she must have pounds of it stashed away. You couldn't walk in the chipping area for coming away with little pieces in your moccasin soles.

She built a small sweat lodge from willows in the manner of her people, declining to use the Mandan lodges, and purified herself often. Cree helped her. It was probably a sign of her trust in Dylan that sometimes he brought the hot rocks into the sweat for her, and she walked around nude in front of him. Naturally, she never went into the lodge where the menstruating women secluded themselves.

She practiced hand-to-hand fighting with Dylan, and insisted that he go at her hard. She was lithe and remarkably quick, but her slightness was a disadvantage. Dylan wondered if she'd muscle up, as she swore she would. Or stop bleeding. Could a woman stop bleeding because she decided to? Or was it Red Sky's nature to become a man and not to bleed? Or would she pretend? What did she mean, being a woman warrior wasn't an imitation of the ways of men but somehow its own way?

She stayed with Anastasie when Dru and Dylan were gone to Red River three weeks, no explanation offered or needed.

It was a drizzling March afternoon, nearing sunset, when a young Minnetaree left his horse at the edge of the village, walked up to their lodge, saw Red Sky chipping at her flint, and spoke briefly to her. He was a round-faced youth, with what seemed to Dylan a sweetly friendly countenance, but he spoke only to Red Sky. He gave his message in signs, and Dylan politely averted his eyes. She went into the lodge, got a knife she'd made, gave it to him, and he left.

"Père Noël came back," she announced in the lodge. "He's already gone out again, hunting on Owl Creek." She was gathering her gear. She wouldn't even wait until morning. Dru and Dylan rode with her.

Chapter
Thirty-Four

The tale was, Père Noël came in from winter camp and went straight back out to hunt for a white buffalo. The Minnetarees had glimpsed it twice in the last moon, once a group of women out digging prairie turnips, and once an old man walking. The old man followed the white buffalo, but he was afoot, and the herd ran off. Now the men, young and old, were making their medicine, riding out to seek the elusive creature, failing, making medicine again, venturing out onto the infinite plains on their quest.

A white buffalo. Dylan could see the light in Red Sky's face. The holy grail of the Indians of the northern plains, the shimmering and elusive vision that lured warriors into great quests. Such buffalo were talked about constantly, seen at best infrequently, slain perhaps once in a generation. To take one would be a great coup, talked about by your grandchildren's grandchildren. The hide would be specially tanned and offered as a sacrifice to the sun, and all the people would be blessed through this offering.

For a man to slay a white buffalo—it would establish him among the people for life as a man blessed, a man of affinity with spirit. For a woman to do it—it would make her storied among the people, a great hero of the winter counts, a figure of legend and fable for generations to come. For a woman wanting to be accepted as a warrior . . . it was a coup hardly to be dreamed of.

Dylan was desperately curious to see what would

have a greater hold on Red Sky, the lure of the buffalo or revenge against the man who enslaved her.

They did not talk about that or anything else that night in camp, a miserable, wet bivouac with only blankets for warmth. Dylan and Dru slept dry under the oiled cloth they brought, but Red Sky declined to join them and got soaked. In the morning they ate pemmican silently and rode on.

Dylan thought of the *bourgeois* Père Noël. This hunting the white buffalo fit the nasty picture he was building of the man. To Père Noël the buffalo was not an object of religious veneration. Dylan outlined to himself carefully the reasons a white man would want to kill one. First, greed. He could trade the hide for a fortune in furs. Second, reputation. The Indians would revere him. Third and perhaps most important, power. No one would dare go against the medicine of a man who killed a white buffalo.

It was like a Muslim competing with the knights of the round table to find the original Holy Grail, the chalice of the Last Supper. The chalice would have no meaning in itself to him. He would want it only because of the sway it would give him over Christians and the Church.

What sort of man, then? A Captain Chick. A cynic, a master, a tyrant, a luster for power.

No, Dylan did not like this Père Noël.

It was a spring day that shone with sun and sprinkled gently and blustered raw, all by turns. Late that afternoon Dru was relieved when Red Sky said they'd stop early, on this rivulet flowing into Owl Creek. She said Père Noël was camped with about twenty Minnetarees nearly five miles downstream at the mouth of Broken Leg Creek. She wanted to bivouac here and scout things out tomorrow. He might have moved the camp. He might be bivouacked away from it. He might be anything. She wanted to be sure.

Dru had a lot of thoughts he didn't speak. He was impressed with this strange young woman's zeal for revenge. Not that he didn't understand why. From the look in Dylan's eye, he thought his son in spirit was nearly as bloody-minded, and wondered why. The way the young take the blind and indifferent assaults of life as personal insults? Or what, exactly?

He was tempted to explain something to Dylan. If he, a trader, attacked another rival trader, or backed up an Indian who did, the fur men would never forget it. They would ostracize him. They might try to take him to Montreal or St. Louis in chains for trial. They might even assassinate him. A breach in the common front against the so-called savages would not be tolerated. Particularly a blow against someone's manhood of such a personal sort as Red Sky planned.

But Dru was not a man to rail against the way things were, whether a bitter wind or raging waters or the anger of a person who could not be assuaged. He accepted.

After they ate their pemmican, he did address Red Sky. "We will help you hunt the white buffalo," he said simply.

She inclined her head in acknowledgment. "Thank you. I will be able to hunt the buffalo when I have set myself right. When I have fulfilled my oath to take Père Noël's scalp."

When they were ready to roll into the blankets, Red Sky laid out the plan.

That fact left Dylan feeling unsettled. Dru should have decided the strategy, or even he. They were warriors. They were men. They had experience.

Yet Dru did not seem unsettled. He listened to her idea, nodded, turned over to sleep.

It was a simple plan. Red Sky wanted to take no risk of being recognized. For some reason, she was sure Père Noël would guess how bloody-minded she was. So Dru and Dylan would get up in the middle of the night, ride quietly downstream, and locate the camp. If they saw Père Noël for sure, one would keep watch, the other come back for Red Sky. If not, Dru would go into camp and ask for the *bourgeois*. Dru was less associated with Red Sky than Dylan. They would take no action but would simply report back to her.

Lying awake in his blankets, Dylan tried to feel easy about taking marching orders from a woman. Maybe Dru accepted her as a warrior, and that made the difference. But of the three warriors, she was the green hand. Why didn't the older hands lead?

Yes, he remembered what he had learned at Fort Augustus, especially what Bleu had told him. A man had a dream or another medicine sign that he should venture forth. He told selected others about his sign and invited them to go along. The medicine led the party, and the one man had a bond with the medicine, so he made the decisions. Or rather, the medicine made them through him.

Maybe Dru saw it that way, and so accepted Red Sky's leadership.

But it didn't make sense to Dylan. Or at least he didn't like it.

He fretted and rolled over and fretted and thrashed and fretted almost until Dru shook him. The Big Dipper said past midnight—he seldom looked at his pocket watch anymore—and it was time to go.

The camp was in the cottonwoods just upstream of the mouth. Dru studied it with the naked eye through the first light seeping into the sky. The laddo was carrying the Dolland telescope. It was a large camp for a buffalo-hunting expedition. Père Noël had a military tent for travel on the plains, one big enough to sleep a dozen men, and in front of it a tightly stretched paulin for sitting and eating under. Dru had seen such tents occasionally for HBC mucky-mucks, but he never understood them. Stoves were a cumbersome thing to be packing around the wilderness. And what good was a tent you couldn't have a fire in? Père Noël even had a chair to take his leisure on. Funny fellow.

Actually, Dru did understand why white men insisted on such tents. They were making a show of being white men. It was a flag of pride, a declaration of superiority. He did not like such men. They were flaunting their ignorance. Until now he could mock them all as Lords and Ladies. He had no idea why an independent trader would set himself up to look as foolish as an HBC man, an alien.

Dylan looked sideways at Dru. Both of them were lying on rocks on a low bluff about a hundred yards from camp, in front of a rock shelf so they wouldn't be silhouetted. They had done well by the moon, getting into this position, and had a perfect view of the camp. He put his eye back to the Dolland.

No one was up and about yet. Père Noël must have taught them the regal habit of sleeping in.

Dylan couldn't see perfectly through the glass in the half-light, but he didn't like what he saw. A few ponies were staked beyond the cottonwoods, where the grass was thick, but not enough for the twenty men they'd heard about. Most of the men must be out hunting, riding one horse and leading a buffalo runner. Surely leading a buffalo runner for this great event. They were probably bivouacked somewhere. Maybe they thought they had scent or sign of the white buffalo. If so, they might not be back for days. He would have to take a frustrating message to Red Sky: the *bourgeois* was making a royal procession out on the plains, route and present location unknown.

Dylan could picture Père Noël playing king of this camp, though. Sitting on the camp chair while his *voyageur* cronies and Minnetaree sycophants looked up at him from the ground in admiration, sat awed by his stories, repeated his bits of wisdom to each other, and laughed at his jokes. Nearby two young slave women cooked. Dylan couldn't see their faces. The tale-telling group made an exclamatory sound, and over that Dylan could almost hear the high, hard, haughty laughter of Père Noël.

Why did the man take such a name? A *bourgeois* of arrogant bearing and hard demeanor, identified by Cree as an English Frenchman—this fellow could hardly be a French version of Father Christmas.

Dylan had a grand thought. In his imagination he saw himself and Dru creeping up on the camp, finding three men left behind, enslaving them, and forcing them to brew up Père Noël's coffee and pour whiskey and generally toady to their captors until their chief came back. The chief turned out to be Captain Chick, still naked of breast under his brigade jacket, but downcast of face. They paraded him in chains up the creek and delivered him to Red Sky, who accepted regally.

Click!

Dylan froze.

That was the click of a lock, a gun lock being cocked, wasn't it?

He turned his head slowly to the rear. He glimpsed Dru already facing him with a mortified expression.

On the rock shelf stood two Minnetarees. One held a flintlock on them, a good rifle, not a *fusil*. The other was making signs in a commanding way. He had a tickled expression on a face that still looked sweet. It was Red Sky's round-faced messenger.

Dylan looked at Dru. Well, the messenger had told them truly where Père Noël's camp was. And had known when and how they would approach. And had waited with exemplary patience. And closed the trap smoothly. A perfect setup.

Because he didn't want Red Sky to get hurt, Dylan told the truth.

It was the Indian of the round and sweet face who was sitting on Père Noël's canvas camp chair, which he and the other Minnetarees evidently thought funny. Now Dylan could see the cunning in the face, and his name turned out to be Blade.

In signs Blade asked where Red Sky was and what she wanted to do to Père Noël. From his expression, maybe Dru didn't like Dylan to tell. Dylan said she was at their camp five miles back, waiting. He thought Red Sky was less likely to get hurt being captured unawares in her camp than attempting a lone rescue of her partners. Which was bloody well what she would do. It would suit her fantasies dangerously well.

Blade spoke in tones of confident command to four

other Minnetarees, with jerks of the head toward Dylan and Dru. Two of them sat down near the prisoners, and the other two started to leave with Blade.

Dylan asked if he and Dru could have something to eat. Blade brought them pemmican. He cut it with the bone-handled knife Red Sky had bribed him with. Dylan asked if their hands could be untied so they could eat it. Blade said no. Maybe they could fill their bellies with their eyes. He seemed to think his joke was funny.

It was lucky Blade thought the next part was funny. When he got back, he said Red Sky was not at the biv-ouac. After midnight she had followed Dylan and Dru on foot away from the camp, leading her pony, the signs said. How curious that Dylan and Dru hadn't noticed. They might not see Minnetarees sneaking up on them, that was understandable, but a woman? That was funny.

Her tracks veered off and followed the trail of Père Noël and the hunters toward the white buffalo. Blade was tickled by that too. The tracks would lead in many circles, here and there, he said, for Red Sky didn't know where Père Noël was camped. Like a mole, she would root about, blind.

He looked at his chums as he said this next part. She was as likely to find a white buffalo as Père Noël. That got a good laugh. And a lot more likely to hurt the buffalo. A bigger laugh.

What did she want with Père Noël anyway? A child, really, not yet a woman, but not bad-looking. Père Noël had something for her, and it would keep her busy for a couple of years, giving suck. He gave it to her last sum-mer. She must be infatuated with it, and back for more.

The bastard had more to say of that sort, there is praise be. Dru kept giving Dylan quashing looks, and the lad didn't seem to be doing too badly. He felt for the boyo. If the lad didn't provoke this bugger Blade, but let things rest and let Blade go off to serve his master, then he might be able to do more than feel for Dylan. He already had a flint in his hand. He only needed some privacy, or darkness.

He wondered if Dylan had noticed the name of the trading company stenciled on the keg sitting by the door of the big tent. He doubted it.

A reasonable precaution, really. To cross the boundary and do business in the United States was illegal. If you affronted the authorities, smuggling could even be charged. To smuggle was easy, but to do it openly was taking unnecessary risks. So you changed your own name and the name of your company for your operations below the border. A fellow of fine fancy, like this one, would give his company a name with a flourish, like the St. Nicholas Trading Company. And himself a name like Father Christmas.

Dru looked sideways at Dylan. The lad wasn't suffering too much from Blade's teasing.

Dru smiled to himself, inside, without letting his face change. The irony was delectable, really, the sort of touch the master changeling Life liked to use playfully and bring his creation to a high luster.

If he could cut them loose, Dru thought, Dylan would find out soon enough who Père Noël was. A pungent surprise.

Dru squirmed. Yes, he could work the edge of the spare flint against the ropes. He only needed time. Meanwhile he could contemplate. He had savory thoughts. Life never let you run from your ogres. It always put the two of you in the coliseum and made you fight it out. Which, win or lose, was your salvation.

On a less exalted level, would Red Sky catch her quarry, the mythological Père Noël? And would he and Dylan catch up with them before she performed her symbolic act? And would they let her take the hairy token of revenge?

Love was the greatest changeling of all.

Chapter
Thirty-Five

Red Sky was frustrated. She wanted to know for sure what was going on, and by God, or whatever spirit the Frenchmen took their strange oaths by, she didn't.

She was pleased with herself in every respect but this frustration. She had observed how the land lay, she had seen the sources of water, she had noticed the lie of the great herd on the plains, she had asked herself where she would camp, and she had calculated very well. Here she was, within sight of Père Noël's tiny bivouac, by a rivulet in a fold on the plain, with willows but no wood and nothing to mark the spot but the lean-to facing a low boulder. This could only be his camp—and now it didn't make sense.

If she had been raised to be a warrior, as she asked her father to raise her, because he had fathered no sons, she would have learned to wait and watch patiently. But she had not. No one had paid any attention when she said she was born to be a warrior, a female warrior.

Now she was having to learn everything by herself, without instruction. Even Owl Claw could not help her. Owl Claw had married a man, raised children, taken fully the woman's role. Only after the end of her years of menstruation did she become as she was, and live with a woman. Nor did Owl Claw know a woman among the people whose medicine had called her to be a warrior. There were stories from the time before the memories of the oldest grandfathers, and Red Sky nurtured herself with these stories. But there was no teacher and no living exemplar. Had there been, Red Sky would have known sooner what her medicine was, and would not have waited until her seventeenth year to take the warrior's path. To learn to make weapons and to use them, to track animals and men patiently, to perform the act of blood power, taking the life of living creatures and bringing it to your lodge and to feed your family's life.

She supposed sixteen-year-old male warriors had as much trouble waiting as she did. And she supposed that she could move silently down to that camp and see who was there, if anyone. Not invisibly, not in broad daylight, but silently.

Maybe no one was there. That was what she was afraid of. This morning four Minnetarees had gotten up, made medicine, and ridden off in different directions. Curious, she thought, that they should go in different directions. Perhaps each hoped his medicine and his alone would find the white buffalo, and depended solely on that.

In the half day since, nothing had moved in the camp. There was no sign of Père Noël. But this was the place he would camp. And there was that lean-to pitched low to the ground, the way Frenchmen did when they didn't have their canoes to sleep under, and no Minnetaree had slept in that, or would sleep in it.

Maybe Père Noël was gone, and his Frenchman gear was stored under that piece of canvas. Maybe while she was stealing close, he would ride into camp and see her, and raise his rifle at her. Maybe he was asleep, drunk, under there. Or maybe he was taking his pleasure on the body of a weeping fifteen-year-old Minnetaree girl.

Red Sky snorted. Most likely the last.

She could not wait for dark. The four Minnetarees would come back. Now, as the sun rose to high noon, was the time.

The lean-to slanted toward the low boulder, as though in a salute. She would make the boulder memorable for Père Noël.

*   *   *

Dru smiled grimly at what he saw through the glass. In the spirit of every man, he believed, this story roamed. When it told itself in the night, you called it a nightmare. Which was a small word for a fear that earthquaked both mind and spirit. To be spread out on a rock, naked, at the mercy of a woman you'd stuck your own blade into, and she holding a knife with intent to cut your balls off.

Dru handed the glass to Dylan.

Dylan adjusted the focus of the telescope two or three times. His breathing was coming hard, his chest tight.

He saw Père Noël spread out on a boulder. Red Sky was standing over him, a knife in her hand.

Père Noël's face was . . .

Père Noël was his father, Ian Campbell.

Dylan looked sideways at Dru. His mind slipped and slid, panicking.

OhmyGod.

They had no horses. He looked around wildly, frustrated.

His father . . .

He started running.

OhmyGodbleedingJesus.

He ran faster.

Twenty minutes earlier Ian Campbell had smiled sardonically.

It was all turned to rot in his nostrils.

He did not look at it in his mind from every angle, as he was accustomed to do, mocking himself. He did not tell himself how many ways he had failed, and on what a grand scale. He did not dwell on the two women who died, whom he loved. Nor the two country wives he once had, natives of the interior, whom he had callously abandoned. Nor the Cree daughter he had doted on, and who died in his arms that terrible winter.

He snorted. That winter he had stayed in the interior because she was sick, stayed away from his true family in Montreal, worried them to death, that winter he got the illness, the rheumatism that felled him now. That winter cost him the love of his one son, Dylan Elfed Davis Campbell, who now so rejected his paternity that he had changed his very name.

He coughed, and his chest spoke of his mortality. He rolled over his blankets, onto his back. No position was comfortable for long, the way his joints hurt.

Isn't it fine, Ian Campbell? Isn't it fine?

He had thought himself a man of size and strength, ambition and vision, grand desires and grand fulfillments. That was why he had set out into the wilderness to begin with. The wilderness was unshaped, open, malleable, and a man could with force of will and energy seize what he wanted from it, even the foundations of empire itself.

He raised his hand and looked at it. Crabbed, distorted, the hand of a cripple. He worked the fingers toward a fist, ignoring the pain. This fist had seized nothing. It had hurt people, maybe—it was a fist. But it had reached for dominion, for riches, for power, for rule. It had reached to make by might what other Scots had made, even here in Canada, the foundations of a clan as great as the old clans, a resurrection of the House of Campbell.

Ah, illusion.

Now his fingers were drawn up permanently into a grotesque caricature of a hand. Joke.

Yes, a great and macabre joke on himself, now an old man while only fifty, sick unto dying, owner of a single, pathetic, small fort in a wasteland of savages and uselessness, partner of the fool who had married his daughter, emperor of emptiness.

This, he mocked himself, this is your son's patrimony. This is why you worked this too-short lifetime, this is what took too long to create. This is why you named your headquarters Fort St. Nicholas as a last, all-surpassing gift to your son. This is what you dreamed of placing into his hands with pomp and ceremony. This is your legacy, your final Christmas gift. He gave an evil chuckle.

Now he mocked himself openly. Your son left hearth and home, rejected you, rejected your advice to him. Well enough, you said, if he's to be a fur trader, let's make him

a prince of fur traders. I'll build something, shape something worth handing down. But my joints have betrayed
me. Not enough life left. Ian Campbell was able to leave
only a few hides, a few trade goods, one small fortification, that was all.

He wouldn't be able to hand over the white buffalo
either. He had hoped, but it was too late.

He did not cry out, My son, oh my son. No, he forbade himself that. That utterance would kill him, and he
wished to perpetuate this great madness, this insistence on
half living, sick and hobbled, yet still plodding forward, in
some direction, on the way to dusty death. At least it gave
him the satisfaction of despising himself.

A shadow.

He had heard nothing, which showed the diminution
of his powers, but the shadow fell on his face.

He looked sideways into the opening of the lean-to.

The young Piegan girl he had stolen.

She was looking at him, an obsidian knife in her
hand, and bloodlust in her eye.

What was her name? Red Sky at Morning. Take
warning, indeed. He had tried to tame her with his cod, to
no avail. Ah, futility.

He smiled at her, an acrid, fearless smile, monstrously
welcoming.

"Death, thou hast a comely face," he said in the English he knew she didn't understand. "A comely face, but
a dry twat."

Red Sky had prepared herself, and she was preparing
Père Noël.

She was staking the slaver on the low boulder in front
of the lean-to, hands and feet tied to stakes. He acted
damned uncomfortable and damned scared. That was the
way she wanted him. She was almost sorry he had not re-
sisted more, but the spirit was gone out of the man. He
had started to rise, slowly, feebly. She cracked him once

on the head with the side of her tomahawk, and the slaver collapsed. And why not, since he didn't revere spirit?

She tied a rawhide rope to his left hand and stretched it out diagonally away from his right foot. The man would be spread-eagled, utterly vulnerable.

He was stripped naked. That had been hard for Red Sky. She didn't even want to look upon his body. She hated the sight of his cod, as the Frenchmen called it, especially. His *oots-chee-naan*. But this was the sacrifice she had promised, and prayed for, and his physical nakedness seemed right, a sign of spiritual nakedness.

She tied the right hand and drove the stake deep.

She had prepared herself since those days in the sweat lodge with Owl Claw, way back in the moon when the geese fly south. She had opened herself to spirit in a thousand ways, and looked at her own heart, and had come to know a rightness there. She had prayed this morning, and every morning.

She had chipped dozens of obsidian blades for this moment. Now she lashed the sharpest and most beautifully formed to a piece of grizzly bear jaw Owl Claw gave her. It was ready.

It would be hard to take the scrotum of a man, and cast the testicles on the ground, and leave the body to bleed from the crotch until the spirit dribbled out with the blood and mingled with the wind. Owl Claw had emphasized that when a warrior let blood flow, she touched powerful medicine, powerful for good, powerful for ill. It was dangerous. It was also the path her medicine helpers asked her to walk.

She finished tying the left foot, pulled the entire body taut, and pounded the stake into the earth.

He was stirring, lolling his head back and forth, half conscious now. It made no difference.

She arranged the tinder and twigs she'd brought, struck her flint, blew on the sparks in the tinder, and got a small flame.

Now she must cleanse herself in the smoke of the cedar.

When she heard the pounding of feet, her spirit wrenched. How had she not followed spirit?

At this distance she could only see a figure running. Still kneeling in front of the fire, she washed her arms and breast and face once more in the smoke of the cedar.

She would not perform the bloody act quickly before the runner came. It was not an act to be hurried.

She stood and faced the runner and waited. As she began to make him out, she wondered.

Dylan slowed and walked toward Red Sky and his father. His mind could barely see what his eyes saw. The father, the ogre. The nakedness under the sky. The angry young woman. The black blade in her hand. He walked slowly.

Red Sky was careful not to move, except to turn her head to watch Dylan. She wondered, wondered at everything.

Dylan came close to look upon his father—it *was* his father—and then forced his eyes away from the naked loins. Progenitors of grief, those loins. And of pain, and of conflict, and of turmoil, and of . . . life.

He felt washed along, borne up and down and around, twirled and tumbled, swept and lifted and buffeted and . . . He was in the river of his emotions, at the mercy of their sweep and thrust.

Pain and conflict and turmoil and strife and riot and tumult—they were all there, and other things as well, majesty and passion and exhilaration and rapture, and he was of them, and this was the river, and the river was blood. The words *love* and *life* tossed into his mind like jetsam, but he pushed them away.

He turned to Red Sky because he knew what he had to do. "Put down the knife," he said calmly. "Père Noël is Ian Campbell, my father."

When Ian Campbell heard the voice, he managed to raise his head. His mind had crossed over Jordan in advance of his body—he didn't want to be around to feel his body suffer—and he had trouble coming back. Besides, his eyes were bleary with fever and from the pain shooting through his sodding head. Therefore he could not credit what he saw.

His son, who despised him for what he'd done with his cod. The Piegan girl, who despised him for what he'd done with his cod. Facing each other with battle alertness, their bodies tense, their eyes locked, their wills engaged.

His deliverer unto death, and his potential deliverer back to life. But they both wanted a piece of Ian Campbell, ah, yes.

He did not know what he wanted, or from whom, and he didn't care. They would fight over this weak, old, naked, trussed-up carcass, and take whatever they pleased.

He nodded and grinned and felt a mad laugh bubbling up from his gut, and let it burst out.

Dylan didn't know what she was going to do. He thought she might fight. They had practiced together, and he had shown her what he knew, and he did not underestimate her. She would be quick and dangerous. Especially because, as Dru often told them, it was the size of the spirit in the fighter that counted. In Red Sky spirit shone fierce.

He felt no anger toward Red Sky. He felt bound to her in comradeship, even kinship. But it was simple. He would protect his father against her or anyone.

He waited. He accepted. They would fight or they would not. They would live or die. Ian Campbell would live or die. Dylan did not know. But he would play the game as it came to him.

He watched her eyes, and saw it all in the balance.

Red Sky felt the force within her, raging, like a rushing river that slams into a rock wall and gushes up in roars of white water. She did not think, but only felt the violence.

After a long while she felt it roil back, felt the torrent swell sideways and coil itself and surge on downstream.

She took her hand off the hilt of the knife. She could

never have used this knife on His-Many-Bells-Ringing anyway.

"Don't let me see him in the country again," she said.

Bells nodded. She thought he understood.

"I'm going to hunt the white buffalo."

With that she simply walked away.

Chapter

Thirty-Six

Dylan looked into his father's eyes, wondering what in heaven or hell he would see there.

Somehow he had not expected to see pleading. It touched him.

He cut the ropes.

He got a blanket out of the lean-to and covered the old man. Ian Campbell curled up beneath it.

"You sick again?" Dylan asked.

The old man nodded.

Dylan got a cloth, wet it, and wiped his father's feverish brow. The old man seemed only half conscious.

"I'm going to move you," he told his father.

The old man started to mutter some sort of protest, but Dylan ignored it. He laid the rest of the blankets neatly between the lean-to and the sacrificial boulder.

He slipped his arms under his father at the shoulders and knees. Again he ignored a mutter of protest. When he lifted, he was surprised that his father was not especially heavy. He'd lost weight, a lot of weight.

Dylan went onto one knee to lay his father on the blankets. But he stopped there. Stopped and held the burden there for a moment, looked into the face.

The eyes opened.

Dylan saw pain there, and fear, and anguish, and the other lacerations of a lifetime.

Something in him altered, subtly but unmistakably. He set his father down, got the damp cloth, wiped the forehead again, and said with a small smile and a tone in which tenderness might have been heard, "Will you get well? For me?"

Ian Campbell seemed better tonight, Dru thought. They hadn't moved him yet, and getting him back to Fort Minnetaree would be chancy, but he seemed better, and Dru knew he had the skills to treat a fever. He thought emotional solace would help the man. Campbell and Dylan had reminisced a little. Campbell and Dru had told war stories. All of it seemed to lift the sick man's spirits.

Campbell had felt better a year ago, he said, and had wanted to risk the wilderness. Now he knew he might get better again, but he couldn't go adventuring. Dru hoped he knew.

Ian Campbell had been eager to babble out why he risked the wilderness once more. His grand plan, what he wanted to build for his son, the great opportunity in the American withdrawal from the upper Missouri. He'd built Fort St. Nicholas in a central location, with good access back to Red River, and . . .

Yes, Dylan said, he understood, sort of. Ian Campbell had done it all for his son. Sort of.

Why, the very names told the tale, said the sick man, not quite raving. Père Noël. Fort St. Nicholas. Didn't Dylan see that it was all for him? The restitution, at last, for a lifetime of not giving enough? Named for a Christmas Dylan had been cheated out of, a Christmas Ian Campbell had never been able to forgive himself for. . . . It was all Dylan's, the trading post, the goods, the furs, everything, he'd done it all for Dylan.

Dylan didn't say much. It was babbling, but it was manifestly true. Dru guessed the man now known as His-Many-Bells-Ringing was hearing some bells ringing clearly inside.

Now Ian Campbell was asleep, exhausted. After a while he would wake up and Dru would try to get some more broth down him.

Dru lit his pipe and handed Dylan some tobacco.

He saw Dylan smile to himself. Did he understand? Can you really repeat an entire childhood in your mind and see it as it seemed to your parent? Can you really look out through a father's eyes, and see wholly?

"What do you think?" asked Dylan softly.

Dru told him Campbell's grand plan was a good one. Not unlike his own. Might have been what the Welsh Indian Company did if it had any capital.

Dru watched Dylan to see if this was what he wanted to hear. He couldn't tell. Taking over the Campbell trading business would be fine, he said. Merge it with the Welsh Indian Company, that would be good. Ian Campbell himself could be a partner, or not. Dru didn't know if this was what Dylan was asking.

Campbell woke up. The man was half clear, and willing to try the broth. While Dru fed him, the fellow babbled at Dylan, justifying things that no longer mattered. Did Dylan understand? he wanted to know. He didn't come home that winter because he had a sick child, a little girl, he was crazy about that little girl. He knew he was hurting his children back in Montreal, but . . .

A long silence. Finally Dylan broke it. "You're going to be a grandfather," he said.

Dru hadn't known Cree was with child. He was glad.

Silence again. At last Ian Campbell said, "Tell me."

So Dylan said simply that his wife was pregnant, that the child would be born late in the summer, probably during the moon of the home days, before the first frost. He did not say his wife was Cree Medicine, whom Ian Campbell had enslaved and used in the robes. Dru was proud of him for restraining himself.

Campbell reached out and covered Dylan's hand with his own for a moment. "Thank you," he said. "Maybe I could live at Fort St. Nicholas and see my grandchildren a lot."

Dylan nodded thoughtfully.

Dru wondered why Dylan was withholding. What about Lara? And Harold?

Dylan watched his father's face struggle. The man felt he had a life to justify, a world to make up for.

"I had two country wives, do you know that? Many

men had more. When your mother died, I . . ." The son saw anguish on the father's face. "The solace of the flesh." Dylan half wished the old man wouldn't go on.

"I abandoned them both. Went home one fall and just never went back. The second time because I got sick, but the first time . . ." Ian Campbell's voice wavered. "You have a brother among the Crees on Camp River south of St. James Bay. Name Alexander. About five years younger. A good lad. Probably hates his white father now. With good reason. They all have good reason to hate us, the Indians, and one day they'll rise up and kill us all."

Not us, thought Dylan. The white men. I am His-Many-Bells-Ringing. My children will be Piegans.

Ian Campbell was quiet for a moment. "If I make another journey ever, if the damned Indian tar rescues me a little, it will be to see Alexander." He looked at Dylan. "Maybe we can give him a job as a fur trader."

Dru looked at his patient to see if Campbell had fallen asleep. But no, he seemed to be thinking. Dru offered the spoon, but Campbell shook his head no.

"The worst we brought them was disease," he said. "Cholera, smallpox, the coughing sickness.

"Look," he said, holding out his crippled hands. "These hands . . ." He hesitated, and choked back something. "That winter I was gone, it was because . . . Alexander's sister got sick. Snowbird." He got out the name with difficulty. "I doted on her. And felt guilty about it." He chuckled a nasty chuckle. "Only a white man can feel guilty and let it make him act worse.

"I doted on her and wanted to be with her and Alexander and her mother and I wanted to be away from that house . . ." Dru thought Ian Campbell strangled what he was about to say. "That sad house of ours." Where two wives died, thought Dru.

"Late that summer Snowbird came down with the coughing sickness." He shook his head bitterly. "Which we brought them. I stayed with her. The only time in those two decades I didn't go back to Montreal for the winter. I

wasn't sorry to stay with them, I was glad. I wanted to be
there with a woman beside me at night—do you know yet
what that means, lad?—and away from the place. . . .

"Yes, *yes,* it meant I was away from you and your
sister, and I missed Christmas, which you blamed me so
terribly for. Yes, yes, yes."

Campbell stared off into the twilight. The darkness
was almost full.

"And I wasn't sorry, that was the worst of it, I was
glad.

"So God punished me, if you can believe a God
would make a world like this. In February, Snowbird died
in my arms. Coughed twice, once hard and once like a
whimper, and died in my arms."

Ian Campbell fell silent, his eyes gently closed, tears
running down his face.

Dru saw the tears on the cheeks of Dylan's father, and
saw Harold's father see them.

Dylan reached over and put his hand on Ian
Campbell's. It was warm. Crippled, ugly, bony, but warm,
and human.

Campbell's eyes opened slowly. Dylan willed them to
look into his face. In grief they did, and saw the grief
there. Dylan felt the warm tears trickle down his own face.

Now he said the obligatory words.

"My son Harold, your grandson, died in my arms last
winter. Of the coughing sickness."

Dru had read of a poetic fancy, from the days of the
great Celtic bards, about lovers. When they looked into
each other's eyes, it went, sometimes there would be a true
meeting of minds and spirits, and it happened through the
beam of the gaze itself. It was as though lightning bolted
from eye to eye, brilliant but soundless, from one mind to
the other, and thoughts and feelings and intuitions and
even the most intimate experiences of life leapt electrically
from spirit to spirit. In that flicker of time, in that eternal

moment, there was true understanding, an intertwining of spirits, even an ultimate oneness.

Now Dru saw that oneness.

Feelings lighted and flew from the branches of Dylan's heart like sparrows. They hovered and fluttered.

He studied his father's prone figure and his wearied face. He realized now what was odd. His face was above his father's. All those years, even sick, Ian Campbell had risen to stand higher than his son. Now the man lay ill, his face no longer proud. Dylan saw all the struggle of humankind in it, all the reaching, all the grasping, all the hope, all the sorrow. He wanted to balm it.

"I bring you a gift," he said. The feelings fluttered still. "In Montreal with Amalie is Lara, your granddaughter." He saw his father's face still waiting. "I will bring her to see you next summer." Still waiting. "She is my gift of love to you."

Ian Campbell clasped Dylan's hand in both of his.

"I am proud to be your son, Ian Campbell," said Dylan.

He leaned over and kissed his father's forehead.

The sparrows lifted from Dylan's heart and flew away, taking something with them, perhaps his youth. The branches where they once sat quavered in the air, and then gentled.

Part Six

A BOON

Chapter
Thirty-Seven

They transported Ian Campbell across the plains toward the Minnetaree villages on a travois. The very next day he was much better, and even wanted to sit a horse. The day after that worse. Basically, though, he gained. Dru thought his patient was doing very well, thank you. That Indian tar did seem to help sometimes, and he could concoct more of it, but that was not the remedy. After half a century of struggling, Ian Campbell had earned some peace.

Dru was more concerned about Dylan Davies, once Dylan Campbell, now His-Many-Bells-Ringing.

Dylan seemed distracted. He talked about wanting to be with Cree. He spoke of the spring trapping season, which was already at hand. He spoke of the people's spring buffalo hunt, and he used poetic language—their acceptance of the gifts of a fecund earth after a barren winter, he called it. He praised the wisdom of White Raven, which he said he wanted to emulate.

He seemed glad to be with his father, when he was mentally with Ian Campbell. They talked lightly, and joked sometimes, and Campbell gave advice about trading that was unneeded and unheeded. When he was not talking, though, Dylan's mind seemed to be elsewhere. It was as if Dru thought, he was hearing some indistinct, far-off, wind-blown music that came to his ear intermittently, and no one else's at all.

Dru nodded to himself, and smiled to himself.

"So what's really on your mind?" he asked his spiritual son.

"The High Missouri," said Dylan. "It's calling."

At Fort Minnetaree they did get news of Red Sky. She'd gone back to Ian Campbell's camp that night and stolen the best buffalo-running horse of the lot. It had been staked right next to its sleeping owner, and he was furious.

Ian Campbell laughed as loud as anyone.

As they left, Dylan promised his father that he would see both his grandchildren next summer. One brought from a Piegan village, the other from Montreal, both would be right here at the fort.

They took their time getting home. Cree probably got a little impatient to see her family and tell them about the child on the way, but she said nothing. Instead of hurrying, they trapped the Milk River and its tributaries flowing from the west, out of the Bearpaw Mountains. Dru and Dylan got top-notch at making beaver come to medicine— finding the best sets, getting in and out of creeks without leaving scent, using the bait mixture just so, planting the stick so the beaver drowned instead of gnawing his way free. They would trap as well as any Americans.

No one complained. When Cree said she missed her sister, Dylan answered that he missed his father. Well, Cree commented, she didn't. Everyone laughed, and it was an easy laugh. Dylan thought his future probably would include putting his father and his wife together, sometime.

Dylan knew Dru was probably wondering what was on his mind, moving slowly like this, camping in sweet places and not moving on, trapping the creeks more thoroughly than they had to. They didn't need the beaver that much. Still, they were taking pelts, and Cree spent her days scraping them and stretching them on willow frames. And Dylan kept saying he wanted to take his time, to move gently, savoring all. He offered no explanation.

In fact, he didn't know why. But this was the country

of the High Missouri. He was looking for something. He
didn't know what, but he felt it around him everywhere,
vibrant. He thought one day his head might know what it
was.

They came into the village camp late in the moon
when the buffalo plant is in flower. Even as she was putting up the lodge, Cree touched her belly in a certain way
and smiled to let her mother know that a child grew within
her.

There would be time enough for words later tonight.
Cree was glad to be home. For now came the time of the
great ceremonies of renewal, first the sun dance, during
the first moon of the home days, and then the beaver ceremonies, in the moon of when the leaves are yellow. And
between those two her child would be born. A daughter.
She knew it would be a daughter. She felt, somehow, that
this child replaced the womb lost to the people when Red
Sky followed her medicine. Red Sky, whom they probably
wouldn't see until after the child was born.

You must always follow your medicine, yes, but the
loss of a womb, the loss of children of the people, was a
sadness. A daughter, Cree was sure.

Her husband His-Many-Bells-Ringing and the man
called the Druid, well, they might have some traveling in
mind, some exploits. Men always did. But they would go
alone. Cree would stay in her village until her child entered the circle of the people.

His-Many-Bells-Ringing went the first night to White
Raven. He felt like a different person now, a person living
in . . . He could not have said what, but it was blessed, and
he was grateful for it. In this state he wanted to listen to
White Raven show him the world as the Piegans saw it.
Though the Piegans did not even know the planets circled
the sun, and not vice versa, they knew something Dylan
wanted.

He had thought of a way to start. Cree had given him

a key to her father's life. As a pubescent boy, White Raven
had had a great dream, a vision that would help the people. Because of that dream he had devoted his life to learning the beaver ceremony, the most ancient and elaborate of
all Piegan ceremonies, involving hundreds of songs. He
would one day be the owner of Two Runners' beaver bundle, she said.

"Tell me about the beaver ceremony," said His-Many-
Bells-Ringing. They were having a pipe after supper in
front of the lodge.

White Raven considered. He was glad that his son-in-
law wanted to understand the medicine of his adopted people, but the young man was speaking before he thought.
He could say there was a tale of how the people got the
beaver bundle, which gave birth to the ceremonies in
honor of Tail Feathers Woman, Star Boy, and Scarface,
which in turn gave birth to the medicine lodge ceremony,
but he could not tell these stories now. When the snows
were deep against the back of the lodge, that would be the
time.

"I would be glad to speak to you about this," he said,
"but summer is not the time for stories."

Dylan no longer felt so young, so restless. He listened
to White Raven patiently, struck with what he was learning in being refused. He saw that for White Raven, as for
Dru, the meanings of things lay in stories and not in theories or explanations.

"In the moon of the first frost," White Raven said,
"we will dance the beaver ceremonies, and you will see
their holiness."

On other nights White Raven did talk at length to
His-Many-Bells-Ringing, and in this talk was a notion of
how the world works, and Dylan did begin to understand.
Actually, there wasn't much to understand, if by that you
meant analyze. In White Raven's view, you knew that life
was spirit, something everywhere abiding, making water
run and wind blow and leaves bud and grass grow, and animals make more generations of themselves. White Raven

didn't understand such things in the way scholars tried to, he simply honored them. Saluted their presence in everything. Their immanence, Father Quesnel would have said.

White Raven didn't ask him to learn about it. There was not so much to learn as much to honor. He suggested that His-Many-Bells-Ringing endure the sweat lodge, raise his voice in song, seek a vision, dance with the people in their dances, and pay silent, rapt attention to his dreams.

One night White Raven said that wisdom was not in thinking, any thinking at all. It was in hearing the pulse of the drum, feeling the thump of the foot on the earth, sensing the throb of your heart in tune with the drum, and in tune with the hearts of all the people. Then, for the fortunate, it was in dreaming.

His-Many-Bells-Ringing must dance in the sun dance, White Raven said. Must come to know not by thought, but by immersion, not with his head, but with his feet, his arms, his bottom, his balls, his heart.

Dylan pondered, and waited. It felt odd to him, the idea of participating in a dance. Two years ago, when he first heard them, the songs of the Piegans sounded profoundly alien to his ears, the drumbeats coarsely elemental, the dancing queer, base, alarming. Now he could at least imagine it seeming different. In his state of blessedness he was willing to wait, to inquire, to look, and perhaps find out how to be a human being.

He chuckled to himself. Yes, quite possibly a barbarian. Certainly not a civilized man. Pagan Piegan.

He reached into his pocket, got out his watch and handed it to White Raven. Though the old man had noticed it, he'd never had a chance to look at it. Dylan showed him the second, minute, and hour hands and said they measured time. He opened the back and showed White Raven the intricacies of the gears that ran the watch. White Raven was fascinated. He said he didn't see any need to measure time by hours and minutes and seconds, or whatever they were called—what was the point?—but he loved the clever movements of the mechanism, the luster of the gold plate, the shine of the glass. A perfectly wonderful bit of uselessness, he thought.

"I want you to have it," said Dylan. "A gift."

"You don't want to tell the time in the hours anymore?"

Dylan shook his head. "Maybe I need to get my mind away from the tick of the watch and in tune with the beat of the drum."

Chapter
Thirty-Eight

"Let's go," said Dru.

Dylan didn't know what the devil he was talking about.

It was dawn. They were just up, just outside for the first breath of sweet air and the first touch of the sun.

"Let's go," repeated the Druid, smiling enigmatically. He held up the book, Nicholas Biddle on the Lewis & Clark expedition. He tapped it. "The White Cliffs," he said. "The Falls. The Gates of the Mountains. The Three Forks of the Missouri."

The Druid had been reading Biddle every evening while Dylan sat at White Raven's feet, devouring the book, almost memorizing it, like a mystic cabala. He had birthed within himself the notion that the river itself held some secret, some great life-enhancement, and that only on the bosom of the river could it be tasted, drunk like the sweetest of waters.

They were free. The trading was done. The sun dance was a month away. They were free.

Dylan thought maybe this old man was as right as the other old men, Ian Campbell and White Raven. The young man wanted to drink those waters. He said, "Let's go."

They made a dugout from a cottonwood for a canoe. They wanted to travel on the river itself. The country was very broken and would be hard to cross. Lewis and Clark had gone straight up the river, and so had the traders who followed them. Dylan and Dru thought the river held the promise of a blessing.

"This is the moon of high water," White Raven reminded them quietly. They took that as a good omen.

Entering the Missouri at the mouth of Stonewall Creek, they were immediately in a land of enchantment. The river flowed between white cliffs, and the cliffs, as Lewis and Clark said, "exhibited a most extraordinary romantic appearance." They rose two or three hundred feet above the river, sank back to a grassy plain, and rose again. They were white sandstone, which eroded away, and a caprock of sterner stuff. So the wind and rain had played here like an artist mad with whimsy, creating phantasmagorical shapes. Huge toadstools, dark caprock supported by a slender, curving white stem. Gargoyles. Immense baubles of stone. Formal gardens with stone hedges. Oriental trees with dark crowns and shimmering white trunks. A showplace of stone.

Most of all, the cliffs reminded Dylan of buildings made by an architect with infinite materials, centuries to build, the very forces of nature for his workmen, and extravagant imagination. The style was Greek, but wildly ornamented. Stately columns ended in pyramidal roofs decorated with bas-reliefs. Galleries stretched hither and yon, illogically. Expansive stairs footed all. And gardens of statuary were flung to the sides. Sometimes the buildings were whole, perfect, untouched by time. Other times they were romantic ruins, half pulled down, in a sad and poignant deshabille.

They pushed the canoe through eddy after eddy, sometimes drifting back down a little to see a scene once more, or from a slightly different aspect. Sometimes they got out and walked up to structures and touched them, to know with their hands these works were nature and not art.

"You see," said Dru with a wistful smile, "the old stories are true. This is the heroic age upon the earth."

By unspoken consent they fell into silence. After two days they passed beyond the White Cliffs, into a stretch of river bounded by high dirt bluffs. Beyond the bluffs, from time to time, they could see the high mountain ranges of eternal snows. They were coming to the highest Rockies. They saw, and it suited them not to speak.

After several more days they came to the great Falls of the Missouri described by the captains. Dylan had stopped looking at the book to describe what he was seeing. He wanted no words between himself and his experience. He wanted to drink the waters purely, for himself and by himself.

The series of falls stirred awe in him. The two men portaged the dugout around them slowly, stopping often, hardly laboring. In the water Dylan felt power beyond power. Above and below this place the river often flowed slowly, sometimes undetectably. Here it sauntered majestically up to a fault in the rock and struck downward in hammer blows. This, thought Dylan, is the power that is in it always. This is a sign, lest we forget.

He thought it was the same power that inhabited the earth everywhere, dangerous, exhilarating, enhancing or destructive according to its own will, always immanent. The empty air could whip and howl. The clouds could bellow forth torrents. A clear sky could burst into lightning. The earth itself could shake, and ravage and ruin and wreck, and show a new face tomorrow. And all these things gave birth to each other, to infinite birthing.

Above the falls the country changed. They were approaching the high mountains now through a hilly grassland. Before long they could see the first of the great barriers of the mountains, what Dylan remembered the captains called the Gates of the Mountains. In silence they paddled the canoe through the valley toward the huge rock walls. At the last moment the river poured out of a desperately narrow canyon, notched into walls more than a thousand feet high. In silence they entered the canyon, fought the white water, occasionally portaged, fought the white water, and after miles and miles emerged into a huge valley, what the fur men called a hole.

It seemed to Dylan that they had not spoken for days,

perhaps a week. He did not want to speak. He felt their silence a bond, a link to each other, a link to the earth, a link to something within.

The big ranges humped up now in all directions, aloof, imperial. The river crashed in their faces, moon-of-high-water strong, and they worked against it. Dylan never thought anymore—he paddled hard, saw, heard, felt the icy water, and paddled hard. He did not tell himself he was hearing the rhythms of the earth, he simply was.

Time became infinite for him, an endless sequence of light and darkness, a time such as the primeval earth felt, with no measuring mind to gauge it. So he did not know, and did not wonder, whether it was still June or now July when they came to the Three Forks of the Missouri.

These were headwaters of the great river of the center of the continent, the fountainhead. It was a meeting of three rivers, which the captains had given names Dylan did not remember. The westernmost one had led the explorers over the continental divide and onto the waters of the Pacific, he knew that. It was a low place, a bottomland thick with willows and good grass, the rivers braided, meandering, a place of nearly as much water as land. And the banks ran full, swollen with snowmelt, big with the fecundity of the earth.

They camped. Dylan wanted to stay here a little.

That night Dru broke the silence.

"I want to go on by myself," he said.

Dylan accepted that Dru knew that His-Many-Bells-Ringing needed to be alone in this place.

"What will you do?" Dylan asked.

"Go to the Lemhi Snakes on the Jefferson Fork," said Dru. These were the people of Sacajawea, who lived near the pass over the Rockies used by the captains.

"Why?" Dylan knew it was not to make contact for trading, but something within Dru's personal world.

"I met a Snake at the Minnetarees'," Dru said with a shrug. "He told me about the old enemies of the Snakes, the ones who live to the west, in the great desert no water flows out of." Dru hesitated. "Their name was Ungapumbe Undavich. Since the Snakes moved across the mountains, they haven't seen these people, but they may still be there. They were tall," he said, "very tall, almost giants." He grinned. "Blue-eyed. Red-haired. Fair-skinned. And fighters most fierce."

Dylan laughed. Every man needed a myth to keep him going.

"Most surely my Welsh Indians," said Dru, his eyes merry. "I want to find out about them." He paused. "I will meet you here in a week or ten days." He looked at the man now known as His-Many-Bells-Ringing.

"Let's meet the Piegans in time for the sun dance," Dylan said seriously.

His-Many-Bells-Ringing was apprehensive about the week. He had come here to see—yes, surely, this was his first quest for a vision—and what if he saw nothing? What if the earth had no mysteries, but was just brutely physical? What if it had mysteries and disdained to show them profanely? What if the music he could not quite detect, the music hinted at but never heard, was his imagination?

He didn't know what to do. Surely there were rituals, gestures he needed to make to invite understanding. He didn't know them.

But he did what he could. He stripped naked. He gathered cedar, burned it on a small fire, and cleansed himself with the smoke. He gathered sweet sage and burned it to invite whatever spirits existed to come to him.

He sat by his fire and sang songs. Any songs at first, childhood ditties, street songs, songs of the *voyageurs,* songs of the Church. But the words didn't feel right to him, so he sang the melodies without words. He thought of translating the old words into the Blackfoot language, to see if they would metamorphose somehow, but he didn't. The melodies alone felt right, uncluttered by words.

When he slept, he remembered his dreams, but they didn't seem sacred to him. Mainly he dreamed, as always, of sequences of effort that never ended. Usually he was traveling on a great sailing ship across a boundless ocean. He was an officer. Every day he gave the orders and helped the men trim the sails and use the winds to make mile after mile after mile. And again the next day, and the next day, with never a landfall. Sometimes they had storms, terrible storms, and rode them out. Sometimes they fought high seas and vicious winds. Mostly they just sailed, and never a landfall.

He had other dreams. In one he was trying to get his father to say some words, magic words, perhaps, an incantation, a spell, words that would open a castle door, or the like. But his father wouldn't say them. However he asked, angled, begged, wheedled, Ian Campbell wouldn't say the words. If he did, Dylan knew, his father would become someone else, and so would he. Dylan wanted desperately to feel what that was like. But his father wouldn't say the words, never would.

Dylan was very aware that no spirit appeared to him.

A coyote did appear, but it was a real, ordinary, physical coyote. It stood off to the left of the fire and just looked at him. True, it did stay a long time, unnaturally long, almost supernaturally long. Then it was gone, and Dylan went to sleep. While he was sleeping, the coyote touched his bare hand with its damp, cool muzzle. Frightened, Dylan pretended to keep sleeping. Then, unable to bear the tension, he opened his eyes. The coyote was gone.

The next morning he tried to figure out what of that experience was real and what was dream. He couldn't. He thought it was all some mixture of sensation and dreamseeing and imagination, or a kind of waking dream. He didn't know what. But it wasn't a vision. Probably not.

On the fourth day he decided to walk up the mountain. When evening came he was in the timber but far short of the heights. Instead of sleeping, he kept walking. Maybe he would walk all night. Maybe he would get to the summit at dawn and have a great panoramic view.

At midsummer in the high country, days are long and the twilights seem to last forever. But this time it got dark early. The clouds closed in, ominous, suffocating. The sky got a dark gray, an ugly gray. It began to rain.

Foolishly, His-Many-Bells-Ringing kept walking toward the summit.

Rain poured down. Once sleet slashed at him. Water ran underfoot. Dirt and rock got slippery. He walked.

Lightning began to hammer the ridges, and thunder clapped him in the head. He knew it was dangerous. He didn't care.

He came to a ridge, and now, out of the trees, he could see the electrical storm. The lightning played on the ridges, but it was the rough play of gods huge and heedlessly destructive. They pounded the earth, buffeted boulders, smacked summits, pummeled, knocked, swatted, clubbed, bruised, and battered the earth.

Sometime Dylan had to cover his ears. His consciousness pitched and rolled and trembled and quaked.

Madly, utterly madly, he began to sing.

At that moment the brute force was transformed into something else, the thunder raised itself from a bewildering, overwhelming, killing cacophony into a kind of music, a kind of art, more than human, touched by the divine.

He sang louder. He had no idea what he was singing, but he bellowed. He did not know what he sang for, but he roared his soul into the sky.

The roar was a kind of incantatory wail, and he heard in it the song that once seemed so alien, the song of the beaver dance of the Piegans. And within the song, part of it, its heartbeat, was the throbbing of the drum, muted thunder.

He let his feet begin to move to the drum. His feet danced, his body danced, all of him danced, as it soon would dance in the people's homage to the sun.

Now, dancing and singing, he heard them roar. The bells.

The thunder and his body and his voice combined somehow, thunder the pedal tones, his body the sounding board, his song the melody, and there gushed forth a vast pealing of bells. Awesome bells, the most tremendous bells ever cast, resounding forth a music primeval, bonging out a knell such as the earth had never heard, or the one made at the moment of creation, or maybe a music it made every moment since and no one ever heard because it was too loud. Glorious music His-Many-Bells-Ringing heard at last, music he sang, music he was.

When the storm eased, after dawn, he was not only hoarse, his throat ached. He had rung his many bells until there was nothing more to ring. He was utterly, sublimely happy.

He sat on the ridge and watched the light seep back into the sky and bring the earth to his eyes. It emerged gradually, peacefully, beautifully from the mists.

As the sky cleared, he saw the rain everywhere. It dripped from the needles of the pine, fir, and spruce. It dropped from the leaves of the quaking aspens. It glistened on the feathers of the jays and the fur of the squirrels. It ran in tiny fingers down the mountain. It made rivulets which followed intimately, like lovers, the smallest undulations of the flesh of the entire mountainside. It formed into tiny streams—gullies that were dry yesterday and would be dry tomorrow bubbled wet today. It ran into the small flowing creeks and into the big jostling creeks and it bolted and charged down the mountain and onto the plain and into the three forks, and there, on the plain that lay open and gleaming before him, it braided itself into the great bands of silver water.

Yes, the High Missouri.

He laughed, and wept, and his tears ran down his face and onto the earth and mingled with the rain and trickled toward the river.

ABOUT THE AUTHOR

WIN BLEVINS is a former music, drama, and movie critic whose books include *Give Your Heart to the Hawks; Charbonneau: Man of Two Dreams; The Misadventures of Silk and Shakespeare;* and an ambitious lexicon of Western words, *Dictionary of the American West.* Blevins has written three previous novels in the Rivers West series, *The Yellowstone, The Powder River,* and *The Snake River.* He lives with his wife and the youngest of his three children in Jackson Hole, Wyoming.

If you enjoyed Win Blevins' epic tale, *The High Missouri,* be sure to look for the next installment of the Rivers West saga at your local bookstore. Each new volume takes you on a voyage of exploration along one of the great rivers of North America with the courageous pioneers who challenged the unknown.

Turn the page for an exciting preview of the next book in Bantam's unique historical series.

Rivers West
THE RIO GRANDE
by
Jory Sherman

(On sale in Winter 1994 wherever Bantam Books are sold.)

Chapter
One

Rosa Seguìn felt the cords in her throat tighten. Her stomach knotted into a fist and her palms and forehead broke out in a Gethsemanic sweat. She uttered a small cry and turned from the window of the little *jacàl* by the Rio Grande River. She waded through the thin bar of afternoon sunlight that slanted through the window and headed for the shadowy doorway, her heart throbbing in her throat like a wounded quail.

"Pedro, *se vienen*," she called. *"Soldados. Ay de mì."*

Pedro Seguìn rose from the cot where he had been taking his *siesta* and rubbed sleepy eyes.

"Soldiers?" he said stupidly. "Coming here? *Porqué?"*

Rosa entered the room—there were but two, constructed of wood, grass, and mud—and he saw the anguish on her face as if she had been stricken by a sudden blow.

"I do not know why," she said.

"Cuanto?"

"They are six," she said. "What could they want?"

"Do not be afraid," he said, rising from the mat that was nestled against the wall. He wore the summer clothes of the *peòn*. He slipped bare feet into woven sandals, reached for his straw *sombrero* on the barrel chair near the front door. Pedro summered his sheep above the big river, drove them back to Taos in the fall, there to market the fat ones. In the spring, he harvested the wool, let the sheep lamb among the deep grasses of the mountain valleys, along the clear sweet streams of the Rocky Mountains.

"But, why are they here?"

Pedro shrugged, but he knew. This morning, up in the shepherds' camp, they had found an elk hanging outside the *jacàl* where the men slept. They all knew who had left it there. They had seen the man more than once, knew he was friendly. Sometimes he was with a lone Indian, sometimes by himself, but he lived up there, somewhere high up where the big river sprang from the giant thighs of the mountains, where *El Rio Grande del Norte* was but a trickle, where the Utes stayed and the Arapahoes roamed.

"I will talk to them," he said. "Do not have fear."

"But I have fear. I do not like soldiers."

Rosa had Pueblo blood in her veins. Pedro was from the south, and his mother had been born a Yaqui. The soldiers did not like the Indians, even though some of them had such blood, the blood of Spaniards, pumping through their black hearts.

Pedro went to the window, donning his sombrero.

"Do you see them?" asked Rosa.

Pedro looked through the opening in the side of the *jacàl*, cursed under his breath.

"Spaniards," he said. He turned to Rosa. "Not just six. There are a dozen."

"Ai, Madre de Diós," she breathed. Flowers sprouted from little clay vases in the room. Now, they smelled like funeral bouquets, cloying, heavy in the lifeless, mudfloored room.

The soldiers were still some distance away, riding single file up the canyon. There were glints of light, silvery, as if one of the soldiers was holding a mirror to the sun, flashing signals to someone far away. There were no pack animals, so Pedro knew they were part of a larger force. They were cavalry, with lances, rifles, swords. One man carried a guidon, its pennant flapping in the light wind that blew down the canyon. Their brass buttons, the silver on their bridles and saddles, glistened in the sun. They rode with arrogance, bristled with a force that was like leashed lightning basking in the gentle glow of a thunderhead floating in the bright sea of sunlight.

"Hijos de mala leche," said Pedro. "Bastards."

"What will you do, my cherished one?" asked Rosa.

"I do not know. We must see what it is that they want."

"They will have many questions."

"Como siempre."

Pedro frowned. He looked at the machete that stood near the doorway. Its wooden handle was wrapped with string that had turned black with the grime of working hands, its blade sharp enough to slice a hair in twain. That was his only weapon. It was a tool he used to chop wood, cut brush. It was a weapon too, but it would do him little good against soldiers. He stepped through the doorway, pushing his straw hat back on his head. He looked like a man swathed for burial in his white peon shirt and trousers, his feet clad in woven sandals like a mendicant's, his toenails crammed with the dirt of mountains.

"Stay inside," he said to Rosa. It would do no good. He knew the soldiers would search the *jacàl,* like ferrets, blood drops in their glittering eyes, teeth sharp as razors, the meanness in them boiling just below the surface, visible as cactus spines on their dark faces. He could feel their evil from far away as if their breaths had made a hot wind that blew against his face, shut off his own breathing.

"What will you do?" she asked.

"I will talk to the soldiers," said Pedro, his voice steady despite the deep fear that was in him, that roiled his senses like sour wine in the stomach.

"Ten cuidado," said Rosa. "Be careful."

Pedro walked through the small doorway, stopped a dozen paces from the *jacàl* to wait for the soldiers. Rosa stayed well back from the doorway, in shadow, watching as the uniformed men made their way up the trail along the river, like a snake crawling toward the hens, unhurried, sure, deadly.

As they drew closer, Pedro saw the piping on their tunics. Their brass buttons shone in the sun. They wore the field sombreros, light summer trousers, sweated dark like the horses they rode. The leader held up his hand, shouted something to his troops. The platoon flared out, drew rifles from stiff scabbards attached to their saddles.

Pedro felt a sinking sensation as the soldiers placed their rifles across the pommels of their saddles. He wanted to cross himself, to pray. He wanted also to curse so that God would know his hatred, his fear.

He had seen soldiers in the territory before, of course, but they were always riding on the plain, far off in the distance. He had seen them in Taos and Santa Fe, and sometimes along the trail to the mountains from Taos. He had never encountered them like this, although he knew they sometimes chased bandits or hunted Indians. Perhaps these soldiers were looking for a bandit or an escaped prisoner. But, he knew who they were looking for. In Taos, that was all they talked about and they disgusted him with their lurid descriptions of what the soldiers would do to the man when they found him.

"I am Captain Escobar," said the leader when he approached Pedro. "What are you called? Where do you live?"

"I am called Pedro Sequín. I live in Taos."

"What are you doing here?"

"I have the sheep. I was taking the siesta."

The captain, a young man in his late twenties, was a Spaniard. Most of the other soldiers had the fair complexions of men born in the old country. The man carrying the guidon was a Mexican, like Pedro.

"Where are your sheep?"

Pedro cocked a thumb toward the mountains.

"In the high meadow, beyond that ridge," he said.

The captain frowned.

"We will go there, but first I want you to tell me about the big *gringo*."

Pedro swallowed a hard lump in his throat.

"The big *gringo*?"

"The one they call 'El Gigante.' "

"I do not know of such a *gringo*," said Pedro, his mouth dry as a withered corn husk.

"You are a lying little worm," said the captain. He gestured to his men and several dismounted, converged on Pedro.

Pedro started to back away. The captain pulled his pistol, aimed it at the shepherd's head. The pistol was large, with a big Spanish lock. Pedro could almost hear the powder sizzle in the pan. The captain had only to cock it and squeeze its trigger and he would be dead before he smelled the white smoke.

"Halt!" the captain ordered.

Pedro stopped in his tracks.

His hands trembled and he thought of Rosa inside the hut. The first soldier came up to him and raised his rifle. He struck Pedro in the chest with the brass-clad butt, knocking him to the ground. A sharp pain hammered Pedro's ribs and he felt the wind go out of him. He gasped as the second soldier swung his rifle, striking him in the jaw. He heard a crack and wondered if his jawbone was broken. He moved his jaw and the pain blinded him.

One of the soldiers kicked Pedro in the groin as the captain dismounted, pistol in hand.

Rosa screamed, startling the captain and his troops.

"*Adentro,*" ordered the captain. "Bring whoever's in there outside."

Then, Escobar turned to Pedro, put the pistol, a Spanish flintlock in .69 caliber, to the shepherd's temple.

"I want to know where El Gigante is," said the captain. "You talk or I will blow your brains to pulp."

Pedro tried to speak, but his mouth wouldn't work. The pain in his jaw made him wince, brought tears to his eyes.

One of the soldiers snatched Pedro's hat from his head, grabbed a clump of hair, pulled the shepherd's head back so that he stared into the gaping black eye of the flintlock pistol.

"I do not know this gigante," said Pedro, his pulse pounding in his temple, the pain throbbing through his face with the drum of a thousand hammers, the searing hurt of a thousand knives. "Truly, I do not."

"But you have seen him?" asked Captain Escobar. "Do you know where he has built his fort?"

"I do not know of any fort, *Capitan.* I am a herder of sheep."

"*Mentiroso,*" hissed Escobar.

Pedro heard Rosa scream. He heard the husky grunts of the soldiers inside the *jacàl*. He winced again, but not from pain.

"They will violate your woman," said Escobar. "All of them. I want the truth."

"I—I have seen him. Once." Pedro's voice trembled. "I do not know him. He is very big. He lives with the Indians."

"The Indians?"

"Yes. Many Indians. Shoshones. I think he traps in the mountains."

"Shoshones? Or Comanches?"

"The ones who catch the wild horses," said Pedro. "I think they trade with the Blackfoot and Crow. They hunt the buffalo."

"Shoshones," said Escobar. "This is very bad." He looked around him, nodded to one of the soldiers, held up his hand toward the sun, tilted it back and forth. The soldier took a polished metal mirror from his pocket. There was a cross cut in the center as a sight.

"I think this man, El Gigante," said Pedro, "is just a hunter. Maybe he is *Indio*."

"He is a spy," spat Escobar. "He is *Americano*. He may be with the Shoshones, but he has been seen with the southern Comanches also."

"I do not know," said Pedro honestly. It was true. He had seen the huge man only a few times. He had the Spanish tongue. He spoke Shoshone and he made the sign with his hands. He dressed in buckskins and beads and he wore a bright red bandanna around his head in summer. He was a fearsome sight. Pedro did not know where the man came from, but he saw him bringing packets of furs down from the mountains one spring and El Gigante waved to him, rode wide of the sea of sheep moving up the slopes to the grassy meadows. But, one of the shepherds told him the Indians were Wind River Shoshones, that they lived on the Arkansas River and hunted buffalo, traded with the *Indios* of the northern plains. They seemed as fearsome as their cousins, the Comanche, to Pedro.

"What should we do with this *mentiroso*?" asked the captain of no one. "This motherless liar."

"Cut his tongue out," said the soldier pulling on Pedro's hair. He gave his wrist a twist and Pedro cried out. Inside the *jacàl*, he heard the soldiers and the muffled sobs of Rosa. He shut his eyes, but he could not shut out the obscene pictures.

"Slit his throat," said another soldier, grinning widely. He looked at the *jacàl* and rubbed his crotch. There was a hard knot bulging inside his pants.

"Beat him," said Escobar, turning away. He walked over to the soldier with the mirror. "Call in the scouts," he said.

The soldier, a young Spaniard, flashed the mirror in his hand. He flashed in all directions of the compass. The captain spoke to the other men on horseback. They dismounted. Two men held Pedro while two others took turns beating and kicking him. Pedro lost consciousness within two minutes after the beatings started.

The captain walked inside the *jacàl*. He wrinkled his nose in disgust at the smells of sheep and cooked mutton, grease and smoke, the wildflowers reeking the scent of graveyards.

The woman was spread-eagled on the floor, her private parts exposed. One soldier was squatting in the corner, watching as another took his turn with the woman, his trousers around his knees.

"Hurry up," said Escobar. "There are others waiting."

"Send them in, *Capitán*," said the man in the corner. "She will be very juicy for them."

The captain went back outside, gulped in fresh air. He nodded to the other soldiers. Pedro lay on his side, barely breathing, his face distorted from the beating, blood trickling from both nostrils, his lips crushed, bruised like trampled fruit.

"Where are those scouts?" asked Escobar.

"Already, I see one," said a soldier, looking off to the north.

"And, there is Chato," said another, looking to the southwest.

The two Indians converged on the patrol from different directions. Their bandannas, tied around their heads, were dull with dust, their features dark, leathery.

Chato arrived first. Then, his *compañero,* Mosca, rode up, his face impassive, his dark eyes flashing with secrets.

"Where is Cholla?" asked Escobar.

"Muerto," said Chato.

"Dead? Where?"

Chato pointed back toward the mountains from whence he'd come.

"Who killed him?"

"No sabe," said Chato.

Mosca sat his horse, silent as stone. Cholla was his blood brother.

"How was he killed?" asked the captain, the anger in him burning his words like torches.

Chato held up a broken arrow.

"Shoshone," he said.

"Did you see anything, Chato? Mosca?"

Chato looked at Mosca, his eyes expressionless, like buttons in a doll's face.

"Many pony tracks. There, there." Mosca made a sweep with his arm covering a broad expanse to the north and west." Like Chato, he spoke simple Spanish.

"Many tracks also," said Chato.

"Indians?"

"Shoshone," Chato replied.

"Where are they now?" asked the captain.

"No sabe," Chato said again, but he looked to the mountains as if trying to see over the ridges and into the aspens, the spruce and pine.

"They watch us," said Mosca.

"Is this true, Chato?" asked Escobar.

"They are here," the Indian replied. "They know we are here."

"Hijo de puta," cursed the captain.

He gave rapid orders to his men. Three soldiers staggered from the *jacàl,* a fourth came out a moment later, tucking his shirt inside his trousers. Their rifles rattled as they mounted their horses. Leather creaked like greasy parchment.

Inside the *jacàl,* Rosa sobbed softly, holding her face in her hands, hiding from her deep shame, hiding from the stern gaze of God.

The soldiers reined their horses into formation, retreated from the shadows of the mountains, following the sheep paths down to the plain. They crossed between two bluffs that bracketed the Rio Grande River.

The two Pueblo scouts rode on through, into the open, then clapped heels to their horses' flanks. The captain yelled at them: "Bring Garza, quick!" The scouts gave no sign that they had heard Escobar. In moments, they had disappeared.

Escobar cursed them in a liquid stream of Castilian Spanish.

"Corporal Espinoza," the captain called.

"Yes, my captain."

"Go and find Lieutenant Garza. Tell him to bring his men up. *Andale.*"

That's when the Shoshones struck. Arrows flew through the air from hidden positions, striking several soldiers. Men tumbled from their mounts. Corporal Francisco Espinoza took an arrow in the throat, slid like an oiled slicker from his saddle. Others began shooting at shadows. A big-bore rifle boomed and Captain Enrico León de Escobar y Salazar grabbed his flaming chest as he fell backward over the high Spanish cantle. His horse kicked him as he fell over its backside, but he didn't feel the blow.

The Shoshones arose from their positions and screamed like devils from hell as they charged the remaining soldiers in the column. The faces of the warriors were painted hideously, strangely demonic as the sun lit the hues, made the colors move like something hideous crawling on their flesh. The soldiers screamed, too, in terror, and tried to reload rifles that had become useless. One swung his horse and pulled his lance free of its scabbard. A Shoshone arrow knifed into his belly and the skin parted easily and flowered crimson like some obscene red flower and he groaned in pain that was not mortal, but crude and animal, issued from a torn mouth that had already tasted hellfire. Another arrow sliced through the Spaniard's throat, cutting his vocal cords like twine under a butcher's knife.

It was over in seconds that seemed eternal in their agony. The last *soldado* saw a huge, terrifying man charging him, a big pistol in his hand. The pistol barked. A puff of smoke and orange flame billowed from the barrel.

"El Gigante," the soldier said just as the ball struck him in the center of his chest, smashing through bone and gristle like a deadly seed, flattening as it coursed through his lungs and broke out through his back through a hole as big as a saucer.

The Shoshones took the scalps of the soldiers, snatching them from live heads and dead, caught up the loose horses. The big American mounted his own horse, a fine black animal, nearly seventeen hands high, and rode toward the *jacàl,* an amulet bobbing against his massive bare chest.

A few seconds later, one of the Shoshones, riding a pinto, followed after him. He carried two fresh Spanish scalps, dripping blood and sweat, on his lance, and carried a rifle made in Mexico.

It was late April of 1805 and the Rio Grande River, like some amorphous lumbering beast, glistened in the sun, flowing quietly out of the mountains as it began its long winding journey to the south, to the Texas border, to the sun-splashed Gulf of Mexico.

Don Coldsmith's
THE SPANISH BIT SAGA
The acclaimed chronicle of the Great Plains' native people.

THUNDERSTICK
Singing Wolf has reached his seventeenth summer—
and manhood. But a stranger has come, bringing to the
People a weapon of extraordinary power, magic, and
danger: the thunderstick. Together, Wolf and the
stranger may save the Elk-dog People.

Also by Don Coldsmith

THE SPUR AWARD-WINNING NOVEL
▰▰▰ NICKAJACK ▰▰▰
Robert J. Conley

"A gripping, sensitive, and poignant book. I found myself asking not 'how much of this is true?' but 'how little of this is fiction?'"—Don Coldsmith, author of the Spanish Bit Saga

The man named Nickajack rides toward Tahlequah, capital of the new Cherokee Nation, to meet his fate. Behind him stretch years of violence and suffering that began when the white man forced the People to leave their land and homes for the uknown territory of the West. For most, this was a bitter defeat that culminated in the tragedy that would be forever known as the Trail of Tears. For Nickajack, it has been a journey down trails he never chose, to kill a man he never knew, and now it could end in a retribution he can never evade...even when he has the chance.

Robert J. Conley, the acclaimed chronicler of Cherokee history, tells the haunting, Spur Award-winning story of a nation uprooted from its past and of one man, brave and true, trapped in a cycle of increasing violence by a people looking for justice—and revenge.